PRAISE FOR *A SIN*

"[A] unique premise of ghostly rendez   ....med
with first loves for all three men . . . Clever uses of newspaper accounts,
military reports, and letters to loved ones advance the plot and
complement the dialogue effectively and interestingly . . . superb . . .
highly recommended."

—Historical Novel Society

"[Zhang] Ling deserves all the credit for communicating the universal
language of love and war, but credit is also due to Shelly Bryant, the
translator, based on how vividly and movingly the novel reads."

—*Enchanted Prose*

"Zhang Ling helps the reader see events through a distinctly Chinese
perspective in which characters speak from the afterlife and natural
objects have human agency. A thought-provoking work of fiction."

—KATU-TV (Portland, OR)

"As a writer of perception and sensitivity, Zhang teases out the many
layers of the devastating weight that the war had been putting on the
individual, especially women . . . creates gripping suspense . . . In a
unique narrative style, *A Single Swallow* compels readers to reflect on
innocence and humanity through the prism of war."

—*Chinese Literature Today*

"Themes of gender, memory, and trauma are woven throughout the
narrative . . . the story is not just about friendship; it is also about one
woman, a single swallow, who changes the lives of three men forever."

—*World Literature Today*

PRAISE FOR ZHANG LING

"I am in awe of Zhang Ling's literary talent. Truly extraordinary. In her stories, readers have the chance to explore and gain a great understanding of not only the Chinese mind-set but also the heart and soul."

—Anchee Min, bestselling author of *Red Azalea*

"Few writers could bring a story about China and other nations together as seamlessly as Zhang Ling. I would suggest it is her merit as an author, and it is the value of her novels."

—Mo Yan, winner of the Nobel Prize in Literature

"[Zhang Ling] tackles a work of fiction as if it were fact . . . with a profound respect for historical truth as it impacts the real world, she successfully creates characters and stories that are both vivid and moving."

—*Shenzhen and Hong Kong Book Review*

"Zhang Ling's concern for war and disaster has remained constant throughout the years as she delves deeply into human strength and tenacity in the face of extremely adverse situations."

—*Beijing News Book Review Weekly*

"[In this novel] we see not only the cruelty of war but also humans wrestling with fate . . . the novel blends the harsh reality of war seamlessly into the daily lives of the common people, weaving human destiny into the course of the war . . . *A Single Swallow* puts the novelist's ability and talent on full display."

—*Shanghai Wenhui Daily*

WHERE WATERS MEET

ALSO BY ZHANG LING

A Single Swallow

WHERE
WATERS
MEET

ZHANG LING

AMAZON **CROSSING**

We acknowledge the support of the Canada Council for the Arts.

Canada Council   Conseil des arts
for the Arts   du Canada

Creation of this work was funded in part by an Ontario Arts Council grant.

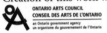

ONTARIO ARTS COUNCIL
CONSEIL DES ARTS DE L'ONTARIO
an Ontario government agency
un organisme du gouvernement de l'Ontario

Published by Amazon Crossing, Seattle

www.apub.com

Amazon, the Amazon logo, and Amazon Crossing are trademarks of Amazon.com, Inc., or its affiliates.

ISBN-13: 9781662510380 (hardcover)
ISBN-13: 9781662509001 (paperback)
ISBN-13: 9781662509018 (digital)

Cover design by David Drummond
Cover image: © suns07butterfly / Shutterstock; © Beliavskii Igor / Shutterstock; © white snow / Shutterstock

Printed in the United States of America
First edition

WHERE
WATERS
MEET

Chapter I

A Death, a Memory Box, and an Oyster with a Pearl

1.

George Whyller's mother-in-law, Rain Yuan, died ten days ago, unexpectedly.

Sure, she had been sick for a while: renal infection, diabetes, a stomach ulcer, rheumatoid arthritis, and the towering Alzheimer's. But none of these things could cause one to kick the bucket so suddenly. *A heart attack,* they said. But she had always had a perfect heart. *Well, when one gets to her age, the organs don't give you much of a warning.* Her age? For heaven's sake, she was only eighty-three. There are parts of the world where people live to be a hundred and twenty—she was a spring chicken.

Screw science.

Rain was not her real name. No one in their right mind would call herself Rain unless she was a rock star or the mother of Snow White (the real one, not the stepmother). Her legal name, as recorded in her passport, was Chunyu Yuan, *Chunyu* meaning "spring rain" in Chinese.

When a man marries a Chinese woman, he marries the whole family. Luckily for George, the family of his wife, Phoenix, had been trimmed, through death, disappearance, and estrangement, to only a mother and an aunt, with the aunt living thousands of miles away in Shanghai and thus hardly a bother.

What remained of that family, namely Phoenix and her widowed mother, had been close. *Close* was not even the word. For most of their lives, other than a few necessary periods, Phoenix and Rain had always lived together, prior to Rain's nursing-home days, of course. Phoenix brought her mother into her marriage, like an inseparable conjoined twin. Rain's passing unhinged Phoenix and the worst part of it was she didn't know she was a wretched mess.

George had left work a little early today. He and Phoenix planned to have an early dinner and then drive together to Pinewoods, the nursing home where Rain had died, to pick up Rain's stuff before the reception closed at eight.

It was 4:09 p.m., April 20, 2011.

Southbound along Birchmount Road, the traffic was quite smooth, something rarely seen in a city like Toronto at this hour of the day. George practically sailed through and got home sooner than expected.

Setting his briefcase on the hardwood floor, he sat down on the footstool by the door, starting, automatically, to remove his leather shoes, replacing them with slippers made of cheap plastic. It was a habit Rain had pushed upon him when he married Phoenix six years ago. A habit, among others, that he had protested against half-heartedly for a while before giving up. Rain was a tireless buffing machine, smoothing out all the bumps where she treaded, by patience, or by sheer maternal force.

Walking towards the living room, he suddenly halted, noticing Phoenix standing in front of the bay window. He hadn't expected to see her for another hour at least. Phoenix was an ESL teacher in an immigration settlement center. She had two afternoon classes on Wednesdays. By the time she finished teaching and hopped on the subway, then switched to a bus and walked a block to reach home, it was usually around 6:15 p.m.

She was peering through a gap in the lace curtains onto the street, her arms folded and her shoulders squeezing together as if cold. They lived in a quiet neighborhood of central Scarborough. There wasn't much going on all day, other than an occasional trickle of bikers, adults mostly, and some Jehovah's Witnesses walking around in pairs, selling God door-to-door.

How long had she been there? She must have watched him pull into the driveway, get out of his gray Altima, and fumble in his pocket— filled with a packet of cigarettes (he was a social smoker), a wadded handkerchief, and some crumpled gas receipts—for his house keys.

"You are early . . ." He paused as he noticed the suitcase beside the white leather sofa. It was an ancient piece of luggage, born before the age of rolling wheels, made of heavy fabric in a yellowish gray, the color of twenty-year-old dust. Strangely, this fossil held itself together despite a partially damaged lock socket and a few dents and scratches.

It was Rain's suitcase, one of the few things she had brought all the way from China. Once he had offered to replace it with a more modern version, but Rain had stoutly refused. "Let it be, it's her memory box," Phoenix told him later.

So Phoenix had been to Pinewoods without him, and without telling him.

Phoenix turned around, smiling vaguely, murmuring a faint yes to the question in his eyes.

"Did you get all her . . . ?" He carefully picked his words and tone, as though she were a piece of Ming porcelain, too fragile to withstand the brushing of air. Nobody likes to lose a mother, but Rain's death had hit Phoenix a few pounds harder than was usual.

"Yes," she cut in tersely, another monosyllabic roadblock to conversation.

"I'll do spaghetti today, the meat sauce is ready in the fridge." He switched subjects, finding himself again gauging the volume and tone of his voice for fear of overstepping.

He turned on the stove to boil water for spaghetti. It was Wednesday and his turn to cook, a rule they had set in the early days of their marriage. Before proposing to her, he had considered all kinds of stumbles in their life together, a mixed-race marriage with a mother-in-law stuck in the middle. Not exactly a fairy-tale situation. Yet he had never imagined that the choice of food would be their first major roadblock. He could tolerate well enough their Chinese cooking: the deep-frying, soy sauce, green onion, minced garlic. But his cream and cheese were Rain's poison.

Eventually they had worked out, after a few grudging meals, a little plan—a balance in power, as George would say. Every Tuesday, Thursday, and Saturday, the mother and daughter would cook up a Chinese storm, and on the rest of the weekdays he could have his say over the dinner menu. On Sunday, the three of them would go out to eat, taking turns in the choice of restaurants. Before long, he noticed, with wry amusement, that Rain had started to fry her veggies with butter, and sesame seeds made an exotic appearance on top of the salads he made.

Things have a strange way of working themselves out, he concluded. Force and reaction, pressure and endurance. In the sphere of marital science, one needs chemistry to kick open the door, but after that, it's physics that governs the running of it.

The water was soon boiling, the lid and the pot joining in an awful racket—click, click, click. It took him a while before he realized he hadn't thrown in the noodles.

"You better turn on the fan."

She was standing right behind him. He sensed her presence before he heard her voice.

"It'll be ready in a wink," he said, suddenly annoyed by the tiptoeing in his voice. Ever since he walked into the house, he hadn't been able to utter a simple, meaningful sentence.

He knew why.

It was the suitcase sitting in the living room, with all its guarded coolness. Maybe it was the fabric, smelling of mildew and history. Maybe it was the broken lock, revealing half a secret, inspiring exploration rather than closure.

It was the soul of Rain, lurking about the house, watching their every move, alive and alert even in death.

He switched off the stove, waited for the noise of the pot to die down, and then turned towards Phoenix, locking eyes.

"What do you plan to do with her ashes, Nix?"

His voice had started out tentative but slowly found its course. As soon as he heard the word *ashes*, he knew the hardest part was behind him.

She didn't answer. The corners of her mouth twitched, hinting at tears that didn't come. In complete stillness she stood, eyes desolate and unmoored, a lost cat. Her cheeks were fuller the night before.

He put his arms around her. The chill seeping through the fabric of her blouse made him aware, suddenly, of the tenebrous distance between them. Grief was messy, with its many folds, layers, and loose ends that were vaguely familiar to him from the days when he had lost Jane, his first wife. A void filled with amorphous grayness, as he came to remember it, a numbness to the evanescence of all things. He didn't want to go back there. Powerless then, and more so now that the pain was once removed.

No longer attempting a conversation, he let go of her and restarted the stove.

She wafted past the kitchen, sitting down at the dinner table and staring, through the bare window, into the backyard. The huge maple tree with its young leaves cast a dancing shadow on the lawn in the rustling evening breeze. Baby dandelions were popping up, here and there, amid the grass in its first growth spurt, unruly but full of life. This season's grass had never known Rain, her life, or her death—to it, her absence was a mere irrelevance.

"She was in a fetal position when she died," muttered Phoenix dryly. "She was tired of being a ma, she just wanted to be a child."

2.

George had met Phoenix seven years ago, in the winter of 2004, when she brought her mother in to see him. By then he had worked as an audiologist for nearly thirty years, first in Edmonton, then in Toronto. *A fossil,* he later told Phoenix, self-mockingly, referring to his long work experience relative to the brief history of his profession.

"She shouts on the phone, and the TV is loud," reported Phoenix, a complaint George had heard so often from a family member.

Rain understood little English. Other than a demure "Good morning," she remained silent for the most part. In the shadow of her daughter, she smiled a sheepish smile, a thin line appearing and disappearing, then appearing again, between her eyebrows, in anticipation of a change in facial expression. Despite the central heating, she left her coat on. It was a nondescript plaid coat, colors faded by years of diligent washing, but still clean and neat, every button gleaming. Obviously suffering from a cold, she sniffled and wheezed, unaware of the noise she was making.

The receptionist was off that day because of a family illness, so George had to run the front desk as well. He handed Phoenix the patient chart, which she began to fill out by writing down her mother's name, "Chunyu," followed by "Rain" in brackets.

An explanation, more elaborate than necessary, followed. The difference, and the connection, between the two versions of the name, linguistic, cultural, content aspects, et cetera. "Yuan is her family name, but in Chinese, family name is placed before the given name. Our friends here just call her Rain—so much easier."

"It makes sense, family first," he concurred affably, while conscious of the people waiting at the reception area.

"Sorry, I ramble." She apologized half-mindedly, sensing, with a little pleasure, that the voluble teacher in her had found a not-totally-unappreciative pair of ears.

She does not wear a wedding ring. He couldn't believe himself for noticing such a detail in a woman he knew practically nothing about, other than her name. Phoenix in English, Yuan Feng in Chinese.

Phoenix's English was nearly flawless, if one could ignore an occasional omission of the *s* at the end of a verb in third-person singular form, a subtle sign betraying the acquired nature of the language. Later, he would come to know that she had, by then, lived in Canada for seventeen years.

His clinic was located near the intersection of Birchmount and Finch, an area with a vibrant immigrant population. He had seen, over the years, quite a number of Chinese women walk through the door. She was a little different from them. While most of them avoided direct eye contact, and refrained, timidly, from talking unless spoken to, Phoenix looked straight into his eyes, attentive and communicative. When she talked, her lips, her lashes, the tip of her nose, her hair (a lustrous abundance tied up in a casual knot), and even the buttons of her magenta cardigan all bounced briskly, a vivid picture of life.

There was something else in her eyes when she smiled, which he would later come to understand as sadness. But then, when they stood face to face, in an office messy with patients' files and phones ringing off the hook, he didn't know what it was. He just felt her smile and voice had a texture and substance to them, wrapping him up in some sort of a glow, making breathing a task. It was a very strange feeling, reminding him of his gawky adolescent years in Cincinnati that he had thought long forgotten. In an inexplicable and fatalistic way, he knew at that moment he had fallen for this woman.

He showed them into the soundproof booth and explained the procedure of a hearing test. Closing the booth door behind him, he discovered, to his astonishment, that his mind went completely blank. This was a procedure he had performed thousands of times over the past thirty years, every step wired into him like a memory chip, which he could retrieve, at any given moment, even in sleep. But today, all of a sudden, it eluded him.

It was that magenta presence in the booth, serving as an interpreter, who had distracted him.

He finally finished the test, with no memory of how. It was the muscles that had executed the movements, the old, reliable, mechanical backup system when the brain bailed out on him.

"There is some sensorineural hearing loss, mixed with a conductive component." The words came out of his mouth sounding alien to him, formal, stiff, esoteric.

Detecting the confusion in her eyes, he switched to plain layman's terms. "A great part of the hearing loss is caused by the cold that's affected her middle ear function."

"What can we do, then?" she asked, eyebrows knitted into a soft knot.

He was suddenly moved by the concern in her voice. His mother had died when he was twelve, from a long-term kidney condition. His memory of her was vague, mainly revolving around prescription bottles, long days of bed rest, doctor's house calls, and the labored breathing in her last days. She didn't get to grow old, like Rain, to be taken care of by her child.

"Just need to monitor the loss for now. Bring her back in two weeks for a retest, when the symptoms of the cold have subsided."

That was not what he had intended to say, but the words seemed to have swapped themselves on their way out, from *one month* to *two weeks*. A moment of short circuit in the brain, for which he was almost grateful.

He didn't have to wait the full two weeks.

Five days later, Phoenix called the clinic to ask for a rush appointment, a favor, she confessed, for one of her students, an Afghan girl named Aisha. When Aisha came for her visit, George was surprised, pleasantly, to see Phoenix with her.

"She's a bit uptight," explained Phoenix, "so I decided to come with her."

Was this an excuse for her to come to see him? he wondered, with a swell of vanity more appropriate in someone half his age.

Later, when they became intimate, he pressed her for an honest answer. With a soft laugh, she dismissed him as being ridiculous. The exact phrase she used was *a water-soaked head*, a Chinese way, according to her, of saying "going bananas."

Clearly underweight for a nineteen-year-old, Aisha had little, if anything, to show for her six-month pregnancy. In a string of broken English, she tried to answer his questions when he took her case history. A few minutes into the conversation, both decided to abandon their efforts, turning, simultaneously, to Phoenix for help.

"Her hearing has never been the same since the bombing in her village two years ago. She lost her little brother, and her eldest sister became blind in one eye. She feels it's getting worse, her hearing."

Phoenix related the background to George while Aisha acknowledged, with eager nods, its authenticity. Phoenix seemed able to read Aisha's mind even when she was silent. There was some sort of tacit understanding between them that rendered words ineffectual.

Noise-induced hearing loss compounded by otosclerosis, George suspected.

Visibly uneasy about the attention directed towards her, Aisha never once raised her eyes during the conversation, her lashes fluttering like the wings of some frightened insect. During the hearing test, she grasped Phoenix's hand tight, as if it were her lifeline, without which she would be drowned in a pool of unknown terror.

"She has moderate hearing loss, may need hearing aids at some point." He explained the results to Phoenix who, in turn, translated them for Aisha. "We'll need to send her to an ear-nose-throat specialist for medical clearance, because of the deterioration during pregnancy.

"With the clearance, I'll write to the Refugee Board for funding for the hearing aids." He cast a sidelong glance at Aisha, lowering his voice. "There're food coupons available through Social Service. In her condition, you know, nutrition intake is crucial."

Phoenix immediately understood the delicate nature of the conversation and reduced her voice too in her response. "I'll talk to her about *that*, later."

She helped Aisha put on her winter coat and woolen scarf, a suit of armor for her tiny frame. After an affectionate round of goodbyes, they went their separate ways.

A sudden impulse propelled him, despite himself, to follow Phoenix into the corridor and stop her before she made the turn towards the hospital parking.

"I've finished my last appointment of the morning," he blurted out, while his mind, sober and rational, looked on helplessly. "Would you like to go for a bite with me?"

Turning around, she looked at him in a daze, as if he had spoken in a language totally foreign to her.

"There's this little Italian food place, run by father and son, two minutes' walk, serving the best pasta in town." His voice skittered around, sounding like a desperate sales pitch doomed to fail.

She stood in silence, waiting for the words to sink in while pulling on the tassel of her black cashmere scarf.

"Really?" she finally heard herself murmur.

He didn't know whether this was an indirect yes, or a polite no, both of which Chinese women are supposed to be very good at, as rumor has it.

"That is, if you don't mind," he quickly added, in total embarrassment, grateful to be out of earshot of the receptionist.

After what seemed to be a century, he finally saw the corners of her mouth lifting, a smile breaking through, lighting up her eyes and her face. He felt a vague need to squint against the sudden, overwhelming brightness of the universe.

"It better be good," she said, half teasingly.

They got to the restaurant just before the lunch rush and found a quiet corner spot by the window with a largely unobstructed view. The sky was a spotless stretch of a bright, cold blue. Through the closed window, dull splashes could be heard as the traffic raced through the half-melted snow. The heating in the room lacked enthusiasm.

"Can't believe my mother has actually got used to the winter here." Phoenix let out an audible shiver as she removed her scarf and coat and sat down across from George.

"She's never seen winter before?" he asked curiously.

"Where do you think we lived, Equatorial Guinea? Of course we have winter, but it's called rotten fall, or lazy spring." She chuckled at her own exaggeration, a little habit George would later call "embellished memory."

Their order came quickly, his pasta with meatballs, hers with seafood, and a bowl of salad to share between them. She moved her share from the salad bowl—lettuce, tomato, cucumber, olive—piece by piece, like a child moving her building blocks, piling them on top of her pasta, then with massive motions of her fork, stirring and mixing them together. The monstrous way of blending the pasta and salad shocked him a little.

Conscious of his stare, she paused for a moment. "Old habit dies hard. I was born around the Korean War. We were hardly over the civil war then, imagine two wars back to back. Meat was rare, so it had to be mixed with veggies, to feel more, that's my mother's golden rule."

Another child of war, George thought, while doing his quiet math about her age, using the Korean War as the reference point. She was probably in her early, if not mid, fifties, he guessed, but she could easily pass for a forty-year-old. *These Chinese women, the way they preserve themselves, the Eighth Wonder of the World.*

She hardly used her knife, as if dissecting food were an unthinkable act of disrespect. In big, hearty bites she gobbled what was on her plate, with the appearance of someone famished from a long day's work, licking, every now and then, the sauce smeared on her fingertips, paying little attention to table manners.

So different she was from the few women he had dated in his lackluster social life since his wife's death. She ate as though it were her last meal, and clearly didn't fret about her weight (not that she needed to).

"You are not eating." Noticing his silence, she spoke between two bites.

"I'm not that hungry," he replied, shaking off his thoughts. "It's just nice to see you eat."

"You mean, like a pig."

They broke into a roar of laughter.

He couldn't explain the irresistible gravitational pull he felt in her presence. He hardly knew her. For a very long part of their lives, they had lived on two separate continents, her sunrise being his sunset. The strangeness of the situation overwhelmed him.

"How many children do you have?" he asked, abruptly.

Immediately conscious of his bluntness, he started, without waiting for her reply, to buff off the edge. "It's just watching you take care of people, your mother, and Aisha, you're so natural."

"They've been through a lot," she said, avoiding a direct answer.

"Do you treat all your students the same way, as you do Aisha?"

She shook her head, laughing dismissively, as if he had asked an atrociously silly question. "Oh, George, no. There are twenty-five students in one class, and I have three classes. Who do you think I am, God?" Uneasy with the flinty cynicism in her tone, she quickly switched the mood. "But Aisha is special."

She put down her fork and knife, waiting for him to catch up to speed with his food.

"Aisha married her cousin Hafeez as they were fleeing. It's common for cousins to marry, in their country. It'd save them bride money and dowry, no future in-law issues to deal with—his mother is her aunt."

"I've seen patients from that part of the world," he said quietly, without sounding complacent.

She stopped short, embarrassed. What had he not seen, thirty years, day in and day out, in a clinic? *The salt he has eaten is more than your rice*, as her mother would say about a situation like this. Whom did she wish to educate, or, to impress? Damn it, that incorrigible teacher in her.

"And?" With a subtle effort, he steered the conversation back on track.

"They originally planned to marry when Aisha turns twenty, but her mother-in-law, that's her aunt, pushed for a rush wedding. She wasn't sure whether everybody could make it to safety, but as long as Aisha lives, and carries a life in her, then the family lives on."

She looked away so that he couldn't see the dent of emotion in her eyes.

"Did they make it?" He detected a slight crack in his own voice.

Phoenix nodded, then shook her head, as if to negate the nod. "All except her mother. Heart attack, in Tajikistan."

Silence fell. Neither of them was quite prepared for the gravity of the subject.

A spillover of war, that's what they had been seeing, he in his clinic, she in her classroom, both caught in the cleaning process of it.

She quickly recovered. "It'll be Aisha's birthday in two weeks, she is turning twenty. We're planning a surprise party for her. Guess what we're getting her?"

Of course he had no idea, and she wasn't really looking for an answer.

"Her wedding was held in the camp, no real ceremony, no photos—not the kind of weddings we see. She's sad that she won't have a proper picture to show the little ones when they grow up."

She paused briefly for a sip of water, creating a moment of suspense, which she soon broke.

"There's a guy from Azerbaijan in our class, an artist. He'll do a drawing of their wedding, based on the family photos she shared in class."

It suddenly dawned on him why this woman looked ageless, despite the crow's feet and the few fine gray hairs. It was that little glow in her eyes, the shimmer of childlike longing for good food, for a chance to know the world, for a moment to be kind, that had fended off the erosion of time.

Later, when he got more deeply involved in her life and grew wiser, he would look back on this day's events and realize he had made a mistake. It was not a misjudgment of her character, as that gush of enthusiasm was truly there. The thing he had missed, a grave miss indeed, was the driving force behind it: she was desperate to run away from a dark fear. Escape has many doors—drugs, alcohol, sex—but she chose the one that was more attainable and less risky.

She chose him.

This knowledge, in some peculiar way, would land his feelings for her on firmer ground. The sense of being needed by someone, absent for so many years, reinvigorated his stale existence. At fifty-eight (that was the age he married her), he was still naïve, thinking he could make a difference in someone else's life.

What a fool.

"I've got an idea." He grabbed her hand across the table, his voice communicating a thrill. "My friend Ted runs a little photo store in Pickering, a genius in computerized imaging. He can mix a nice wedding photo for them, a true Edwards Gardens royal wedding."

"Some brain you've got, George!" She squealed and then immediately stopped, embarrassed by the volume of her voice.

Nobody was really paying any attention, as the noise of the restaurant, now filled with lunch customers, nearly drowned out their conversation. It was 1:15 p.m.; he was late for his first appointment of the afternoon.

He stood up to pay the bill—he insisted—and they left together. The sun had started to tilt a bit. The street, with the traffic slowing down, looked a little languid, as if ready to sleep off a good meal. While waiting for the traffic light, she turned towards him and said abruptly, "No, George, I don't have any."

"What?" He looked at her in bewilderment.

"Children," she replied, averting her gaze. "I've never been married."

Still single. This woman could have her pick of men. A stream of emotions rushed through him—disbelief initially, that she hadn't been taken, followed by relief, for the same reason, and then disappointment, finally. At this stage of his life, he'd much prefer experience over innocence.

Was he being too harsh on her, and on himself? Marriage is just a piece of paper that one keeps in a file, like a degree certificate, or a conscription notice (he had both). An interesting mind stands on its own, with or without that piece of paper.

He had time to find out about her. There was a time for everything, a time for a traffic light to turn green, a time for streets to wake up, a time for trees to bud and a river to swell, a time for him to know her, and for her to know him.

All in good time.

Over the next three weeks, George saw Phoenix on a few more occasions when she brought her mother in for a retest (her hearing was getting better) and Aisha for a hearing aid evaluation. He had pulled a few strings with the resident otolaryngologist for a quick medical clearance and the Refugee Board for a speedy funding approval.

They went out for coffee twice at George's suggestion, "to discuss Aisha's care." At the end of the second meeting, he casually mentioned the name of another audiologist at Scarborough General Hospital. "A nice lady, understands some Mandarin Chinese. She can look after your mother in the future."

"Why?" She was a little surprised.

"Because"—he paused for a moment—"I'd like to ask you out. Can't see your mother anymore, not as a patient. Conflict of interest."

He walked away without waiting for her reply, smiling to himself while imagining her eyes wide open, lips parted, and her entire face a contorted exclamation mark.

Four months later, on his birthday, they got married. A quiet civil ceremony attended by her mother and a handful of friends from both sides. His only daughter, who lived in Japan, was unable to make it.

Their wedding vows, a far cry from the usual "for better, for worse," were discussed and drafted, for each other, over a dinner. His, in her neat teacher's handwriting, read "I vow to take care of my wife's mother, Rain Yuan, whatever the circumstances, till she leaves this world." Hers was simpler, a sentence scribbled in the typical sloppy hand of a medical professional, reading "I vow to tell my husband the truth, always." A marriage contract of some sort, dangerously close to a prenuptial agreement (except money was not involved), destined to be broken not long afterwards, as they would soon discover.

The best wedding present they received was a phone call from Hafeez, telling them Aisha just had a baby girl, a little overdue but fine, six pounds and three ounces, a good size for a tiny mother. A perfect picture of health, with all fingers and toes present.

They named her Phoenix.

3.

The suitcase retrieved from Pinewoods had remained in Rain's old bedroom, untouched for two days. Phoenix waited till George left town for a clinical seminar to open it. The time had come, she realized, for her to have *the* conversation with Mother. Alone, face to face, soul to soul.

Mother's room was kept exactly the same, as if she had never left. The last rays of the sun raged through the half-rolled curtains like a mad bull, smashing themselves against the wall, leaving behind a trail of angry dust. It was probably new dust, dust that had never seen Mother. The bed was neatly made, every corner of the quilt stretched out smooth and flat. Phoenix noticed a hair on the pillow slip, a fine thread of silver against the dark-blue fabric, left there before Rain's departure for Pinewoods. Still breathing, it seemed.

Can a hair live on when its root has expired?

Kneeling on the floor, Phoenix buried her face in the pillow, astonished at the dogged life span of someone's smell. It had been nearly three years since Mother had moved to Pinewoods. A faint mixture of sugar and sweat, like some overripe fruit. It was the smell, it suddenly hit her, of age and decay.

She felt strangely connected to Mother, though fully aware that they, the hair and the smell, were just what Mother had left behind, like the skin shed by a snake. The real Mother was lying on the dresser, inside the metallic urn glittering with a detached coolness made absolute by death, mocking the futile efforts of all the mortals who, regardless of how far they had fled, would all inevitably return to it in the end.

Rain's initial signs of dementia had been minor and harmless, an occasional mixing up of dates, a rare instance of a door left unlocked, or a pill-time missed. Then, one day, Phoenix found a shoe in the fridge. Standing before the fridge with its door open and cool air blowing at her, she began to shudder. She had finally found herself face to face with the beast.

Then George came along.

They shared everything, or he thought they did, the bumps and bruises in life. He let her into his memory of Jane, who had died of pancreatic cancer ten years ago, and spoke to her about their daughter, Kate, now teaching English in Japan, and of his father, a political science professor in Cincinnati, too liberal for his time, who taught him to read beyond what was taught in school.

Father's bold ideas had nearly cost him his teaching position at the university, when one day the FBI made a surprise call to his office, inquiring about a box of propaganda mailed to his home from the Soviet embassy, at the request of his son George, then an eighth grader. In a letter addressed to the ambassador, George had written that he didn't "quite believe what the history teacher says in class about your country." Father was astounded by George's reckless naïveté, but never, in any way, discouraged or prohibited it.

Several years later, when Vietnam started to drain the cream of the crop from America, Father helped George plan the move to Canada as a draft dodger. That was the last time they had seen each other. When the pardon finally came a decade later, Father had been dead for years.

Phoenix shared her story with him too. Her childhood in Wenzhou, a little town about five hundred kilometers south of Shanghai, the things her mother had endured while bringing her up, "three lifetimes' dose," in Rain's words, her father's experience fighting three wars, still winning no peace on his deathbed, and the heartbreaking spring night in 1970 when Mirs Bay, the body of water between Hong Kong and mainland China, took away the man she loved and left her a sudden adult.

She told him about everything *but* her fear.

She was driven to him by that fear. The fear of taking care of an ailing parent all by herself. The prospect of being a part of Mother's aging process, a realm totally alien to her, horrified her to her core. She had never witnessed a close relative growing senile before her eyes, as her father hadn't made it to his golden years and she never met any of her grandparents.

When they moved into George's house, Rain's symptoms had, for a while, seemed a little alleviated. It had done Mother good, Phoenix thought, this new living environment; Mother's every muscle had to tense up to adapt, as she had done for every major change in her life. It kept her alert and sharp.

Then, when they had finally settled in, over the course of a year or so, Rain's defense system gradually relaxed. Dementia, having ground its teeth impatiently, now launched a full-scale attack, leaving ruthless bite marks, first on her memory, then on her emotions, reducing her to a sodden wreck, forgetful, unpredictable, and impossible to reason with.

The first major incident, to be followed by many more, happened on a night close to Thanksgiving, during the second year of their marriage. After dinner, when Phoenix was marking student assignments in the kitchen, she heard a string of odd cries, more like the muffled wail of an injured animal, from Rain's room. Pushing open the door, she found Mother on the floor, curled into a tight ball, hands cupping her ears, shoulder blades sticking out sharp as blades. The TV was blasting, showing a miniseries drama about the Second Sino-Japanese War, on a new Chinese language channel Phoenix had subscribed to for Rain to view in the privacy of her room.

The first thought shooting through Phoenix's mind was a heart attack. "George!" she screamed frantically, blood rushing to her head, pounding it like a mad war drum. Hovering over Mother, she shook uncontrollably with fear, unsure whether it was safe to move her. Then the tight ball on the floor relaxed, squirming slowly towards her, cradling itself on her lap.

"Liars." Rain lifted a fist, feebly, in the direction of the TV, now showing a deafening battle scene. Something white and fluffy caught Phoenix's eyes: they were cotton balls stuffed in Rain's ears.

It suddenly hit Phoenix that this was one of Mother's little tricks, to wring the nerves of the household to extract attention. She remembered countless evenings of heated discussions hurled across the dinner table, between her and George, two damned gullible fools, about Mother's enigmatic hearing loss and the need for hearing aids, while Mother sat next to them, quietly listening, with an innocent smile and the occasional timid interjection of "me no English, not understanding."

"Ma, are you playing some sort of prank on me?" bawled Phoenix in exasperation, while reaching for the remote from the nightstand to kill the TV.

"What's up?" Hearing the commotion, George had rushed upstairs from the basement where he was doing his laundry.

Startled at the sight of George, as if he were a complete stranger, Rain became agitated again. Pointing to the door, she growled, in a strange tongue, "Get the hell out of the house, you!"

During the last few months, Rain had largely abandoned whatever little English she had picked up over the years in Canada, reverting, almost exclusively, to her local dialect. Dementia, like a plaster trowel, had scraped off the top layer of her memory, leaving only a base coat, the language of her birth, intact.

"Ma, it's *his* house," Phoenix reminded Rain, wearily, also in dialect.

"Out, him," insisted Rain, ignoring Phoenix's attempt at reasoning.

"She wants to be alone with me, for a few moments." Phoenix motioned George to leave, carefully picking out the barbs from Rain's tone.

"Tell them, you, tell them . . ." As soon as George had left the room, Rain clutched at Phoenix, sobbing like a child terribly wronged by some unreasonable adult.

"Tell whom what?"

"Them, the soldiers, on TV. They should have saved their bullets, not wasted them like this. They should save the last one, always, for . . ." Rain suddenly stopped, with a petrified look, as if she had just seen a ghost drifting around.

"For what?" Phoenix finally managed to get Rain up from the floor and sat her down on the bed. A little wrestling match, leaving her sweaty and drained. She wasn't even halfway through the marking due the next morning.

"For *himself*, the last bullet," replied Rain, stressing each syllable.

Later that night, while in bed, Phoenix told George about Rain's earlier behavior. "Probably a bad memory of the war," sighed George. "I know a Korean War veteran, once a POW, still can't bear the sight of an Asian face in a white coat, fifty-odd years later."

A dreadfully morbid way to comfort somebody. George immediately regretted it, but his occupational habit wouldn't leave him alone.

"What happened to her during the war, do you know?"

Phoenix shook her head in the darkness. "Ma says she doesn't remember much, but I know Auntie Mei joined the resistance forces at some point. They lost their mother in an air raid."

"We always remember what we want to forget, and forget what we want to remember," muttered George in reply, his breathing growing guttural and groggy.

Mother's room was dead quiet now, but the beast still lurked in the dark. That polymorphous, heinous beast, coming in the form of a refrigerated shoe, cotton balls, phantom soldiers and bullets, and perhaps, at some point, a house on fire. The world war was behind them now, but the war against the beast might have just begun. Phoenix's own war, fought alone. Sure, she had George, but how engaged was he? She wasn't sure.

Sleep refused to come. George's roaring snores poked hole after hole in her eardrums. Cotton balls—now she knew what they were for.

During the next little while, Rain seemed to succumb, more and more deeply, to the fear of being left alone. She would suddenly stop eating in the middle of breakfast, turn towards Phoenix, and gaze, intently and teary eyed, as if her daughter, instead of going to work, was about to embark on a journey of no return, and their parting an act of final farewell.

It rubbed a raw spot in Phoenix's heart watching Rain, once a fierce woman who would walk through fire to save her family, now a helpless child.

But Phoenix was fooled again by Rain, even with her Alzheimer's. That fierce woman was not gone but in hibernation, and she would suddenly leap to life when least expected, breaking loose from the shell of a meek child.

One night, feeling thirsty, Phoenix got up to fetch a glass of water. On her way downstairs, she stumbled into something and nearly fell. It was Rain sitting where the stairs turned, eyes glittering in the faint night light.

"I heard you, Ah Feng." Rain still called Phoenix by her baby name. "You and him, in the room."

Speechless, face throbbing with heat, Phoenix felt the sting of shame of someone standing before a crowd stark naked.

Groping at the wall for support, Rain slowly got herself up and put her arm around Phoenix's hip, her cold, gnarly hand against Phoenix's soft flesh beneath the nightdress, warm and moist from lovemaking. The air grew thick with Rain's foul breath, now on Phoenix's neck.

"Here," Rain hissed, pinching Phoenix on the fullness of her buttock. "You need to exercise, to be stronger. It'll hurt less when he does *that* to you."

Recoiling from her touch, Phoenix grew stiff. How many times had Mother sat here, outside their bedroom, with ears that grew eyes and a nose, so intent, that no hearing loss could impair? Phoenix fled as fast as she could without saying a word.

She didn't tell George about this incident, but sex was not the same afterwards. Whenever George made a suggestive move, she would see Rain's faceless eyes floating in the room, glittering, watchful, all knowing, instantly drying up the surging of her moistened womanhood.

A fastidious person till her last day, Rain normally took her shower around eight o'clock in the evening, with few exceptions. Over time, this fixed routine began to deviate—or rather, expand—from once a day to twice, sometimes even three times. Phoenix noticed, one Sunday, that it had reached a peak of four showers, spaced out through the day.

One evening, shortly after Rain slipped into the bathroom, Phoenix, while clearing away the dishes, heard her mother singing over the shower. Rain had a good voice. *A gift from heaven*, as Auntie Mei would say, not without jealousy, *even her first cry from Mother's womb was musical.*

Phoenix remembered falling in and out of sleep as a little girl, listening to Mother humming to her. Lullabies and nursery rhymes in the beginning, then revolutionary war anthems, Mao's praises, later popular love songs from Hong Kong, whatever Mother could pick up from the radio as the tide changed.

But this time it was a song alien to Phoenix's ear, with strange lyrics woven into a string of strange melody. Later, in one of Rain's more lucid moments, Phoenix asked her what it was. Rain, after a long pause, said she didn't remember.

The singing eventually stopped, but the water didn't. It kept running, splashing against the tiled floor, uninterrupted and sinisterly loud. Phoenix looked at the clock on the kitchen wall. It'd been over an hour since Mother entered the shower.

Rushing into the bathroom, she found Rain standing under the showerhead, frantically scratching her scalp, covered in a rich lather of shampoo, so hard that her body shook. Cold air bursting through the door thinned out the dense vapor, revealing a wet, thin figure with sagging breasts and a hollow belly creased by dark stretch marks.

The room suddenly grew quiet as Phoenix turned off the tap. Rain's lips opened in the smile of a child, knowing neither shame nor hurt.

"Filthy, so filthy . . . ," Rain murmured, a feeble defense.

Incidents like this happened over and over again, raising the level of tolerance, soon to be reached and broken, becoming the new norm. Then one day, came the last straw.

4.

In the summer of 2008, George's daughter Kate, her husband Yutaka, a Japanese engineer, and their four-year-old son Mark came to Toronto for a visit. It was their first meeting with Phoenix, since they were unable to attend the wedding.

Born and raised in Japan, attending a local kindergarten there, Mark was not yet fluent in English, so Yutaka and Kate (now in Japan for almost ten years) had to resort to Japanese when talking to him. Over the dinner table, their conversation in Japanese visibly disturbed Rain, who burst into a sudden slur of curses in her dialect, demanding Phoenix stop the "devil's sounds."

Too embarrassed to explain Mother's outburst, Phoenix had to take Rain to her room with a promise to "get rid of them tomorrow." A lie, like so many others, to buy a moment's peace.

The next day was a Saturday, a sweltering hot day. Kate went out to a high school reunion, leaving Yutaka and Mark in the backyard, cooling themselves off with a hearty hose fight. Phoenix was helping George prepare salad for lunch, while Rain stood by the window watching the father and son at play, her thinning hair a soft cloud of gold against the sunlight, a perfect picture of peace. *She's totally forgotten about last night*, Phoenix told herself, grateful, for the first time, for her mother's waning memory.

What if it was just an illusion, this peace, the mere purpose of which was to coax her into dropping her guard, and then *boom* came the real blow, harder than ever? Phoenix shivered, astounded by her own thought. Since when had she lost the ability to savor a moment of pure joy, not plagued by worry and fear?

Rain turned, giving Phoenix a vague smile. It struck Phoenix—like a bolt of lightning, right to her core—that Mother *was* a child, *her* child. Over the past thirty years, Phoenix had wrestled with God, going through denial, anger, bargaining, depression, and finally, acceptance, in a psychology textbook sequence, begging for a child, not realizing until now that He had already given her one, a child that would never grow up.

Outside on the lawn, Mark was totally soaked, voice hoarse from the wild running and screaming. Yutaka decided to bring him in for a cool drink. He stripped off their drenched T-shirts, leaving them out on the deck to dry before entering the kitchen, half-naked and dripping.

Yutaka had a well-toned body, triceps and pectorals hard as rock, sun-browned skin glistening with perspiration and waterdrops. Picking two bottles of cooled water from the fridge, he gave one to his son and offered the other to Rain, a mere gesture of politeness and respect. Seeing him approach, Rain turned, aghast, recoiling like a startled cat.

Before anyone could react, she grabbed a letter opener from the table, pointing it towards herself, growling, in dialect, "Any closer, I'll stab myself, kid you not!"

Flabbergasted, Mark rocked the house with a ferocious tantrum, refusing to be consoled. Yutaka had to carry him, kicking and screaming, upstairs to his room.

Downstairs in the kitchen, Phoenix was holding Rain in her arms, stroking her cheeks, calming her, again and again, with a vague reassurance. "Nobody is going to hurt you, nobody, nobody . . ." George stood by the counter, helplessly lost between a hysteric grandson upstairs and an impossible mother-in-law a few paces away, feeling suddenly old.

Later in the day, Yutaka took Mark to check into a hotel nearby. Kate joined them, and for the rest of their stay, they didn't come to the house again. George paid several visits to the hotel, sometimes with Phoenix, sometimes alone.

The night Kate's family headed back to Japan, the name of Pinewoods was brought up for the first time. "One of the best long-term care facilities in town, a strong Alzheimer's team. Built with Hong Kong money, so the staff mostly speak Chinese. Chinese menu, Chinese recreational programs," reported George, with a fluent command of the facts, "government subsidies available. Two blocks away from my hospital, visits are easy."

George's voice faded in and out, fragmentary and remote. "There is a waiting list, but I can pull some strings."

A sales pitch, well scripted and rehearsed, Phoenix thought, her feet a bit cold as the night air slowly thinned out the heat gathered through the day.

She had never been able to sleep, since she was a girl, when her feet were cold. Mother used to tuck her feet between her thighs, a deep, soft, moist haven where forbidden fruits are borne, lives bred, trade negotiated, and power exchanged. A land of copious pleasure, and a land of profound secrets. But Mother had wasted it all, on one plain, tedious task of warming her feet. She had believed, in those days, in the panacea of a mother's care.

"How long have you been planning this, George?" asked Phoenix, after a long pause of silence.

5.

Phoenix sat on the floor, the contents of Mother's suitcase strewn around her on the carpet. Most of the items were clothing, threadbare from rounds of laundry, with the exception of a new woolen sweater, navy blue with snowflakes embroidered on the front, still in a gift bag. Last year's Christmas present.

Save the best for the last, Mother had always told her, except Mother's *last* had now turned into a *never.* A penny-pincher and neat freak through and through. Phoenix was almost blown away by how Mother had packed her reading glasses, a cheap purchase from a dollar store. The lenses wiped spotless, arms folded neatly one over the other, wrapped in a smooth square of silky cloth, tucked away, with a stately air, in a silver-colored fabric box, like a body impeccably cleansed and embalmed, for its final viewing, in a casket.

Did Mother know that it was her last night when she went to bed?

Swiveling her head to relax her stiff neck, Phoenix caught sight of the urn on the dresser and its reflection in the mirror: aureole with silver trimming, intricate floral engravings, a beauty dignified and forbidding. It seemed to have shrunk a little, though, from the day she had first got it. Time spares nothing, not even death.

"Are you sure you want to keep it at home?" George had asked her that day, in the parking lot of the funeral home.

She had nodded.

They had driven home in silence, the urn between them. George, feeling the weight, had opened the window on his side for air. Dusk had just begun to gather. It was one of the few days in the year that both the sun and the full moon appeared in the same sky, far apart, pale and languid. Phoenix wrapped her arms around the urn, as if Mother were cold. Then she couldn't help but be amused. How ridiculous to think that Ma should feel cold, when she had just been through fire, burned to a heap of cinder, as white as beach sand.

Bringing Mother home was her idea, as she hadn't decided what to do with the ashes yet. George had thrown a few ideas around, but Mother's passing was still too raw for her to think rationally. She needed to wait till the dust settled. She had never been sure, even now, how Mother had felt about George. In the beginning, Mother had just been too shocked by the fact that her daughter, at fifty-two, would rush into the trap of marriage. For the last decade or so, Rain had grown comfortable with the assumption that it would be the two of them, mother and daughter, sticking together till the very end.

Then, when the initial shock had faded and she had a real chance of getting to know George, Rain's mind had been too far gone. Mother's final blessing, or disapproval, now lay in the urn, tightly sealed, to be imagined, and buried, forever.

What else did Mother take with her to the grave? Or rather, the urn?

In her final three years, Rain's mind worked like a malfunctioning camera lens, zooming in and out, producing long series of blurred images interrupted by a few fleeting moments of clarity. Those moments, moreover, grew fewer and further in between.

Initially, Phoenix asked the nursing staff to call her whenever Rain was in a clear state of mind, so that she could talk to her. The nurses did call on several occasions, but the timing had always been off. Phoenix was either in class or on the subway with no cell phone reception. The few precious moments had thus been wasted, turning into eternal regret.

Then Phoenix left a notepad in Rain's room, asking the staff to remind Rain to write down thoughts as they came. Phoenix later checked the pad, finding it totally blank, not even a punctuation mark. Mother had declared an eternal war of silence against the world.

Phoenix desperately wished to talk with Mother. One meaningful talk would suffice, before death shrouded her in an impenetrable veil. But the veil came sooner than death. Rain's mind, or the lack of it, rendered her entire existence opaque long before her life expired. *Five minutes,* Phoenix pleaded with God, a God she wasn't sure she believed in—just long enough for her to tell Mother one thing. She wanted it so badly that her body ached, waking her up in the middle of the night. But God didn't grant her the satisfaction.

Ever since Mother moved out, Phoenix spent every Saturday afternoon at Pinewoods, with two or three rare exceptions when she had taken ill. Most of the time she would go alone, as George often walked over to Pinewoods (two blocks away from his clinic) on weekdays to have lunch with Rain, in a way that was together but separate since they barely talked.

When Phoenix visited, Mother sometimes didn't recognize her. Even when she did, she would soon fall asleep, more like a slumber. Phoenix would sit by her side, reading a book or marking student assignments, while listening to her breathing fill the room, so deep, loose, and stale that one could tell the age from it. Phoenix felt strangely reassured by the lull of the sound.

Once, Phoenix dozed off but was suddenly awakened by a soft touch. Opening her eyes, she found Mother hovering over her, stroking her cheek with such tenderness that it made her feel like a fetus immersed in amniotic fluid.

"My poor, poor baby," crooned Rain.

Tears welled up in Phoenix's eyes. She almost believed, for a second, that she'd seized *the* moment.

"Ma, I have not abandoned you, you know that, don't you?" Phoenix grabbed her wrist, so hard that Rain moaned. A vacant smile soon swept over Rain's face, wiping out all the traces of emotion, and then she murmured something vague and incoherent, which had taken Phoenix a few moments to figure out.

"*Na*, sorry I am late," Rain said. *Na* was a term of endearment for a mother in Rain's dialect.

Phoenix had realized immediately that the moment of connection was behind them.

The memory of that afternoon became, in the days to come, a mixture of sadness and comfort: sadness because she, Phoenix, was not in Mother's last thoughts; comfort because Rain was finally reunited with her own mother, a mother she had long ago lost.

Then, early one morning, three weeks after the incident, the phone shrieked, earsplittingly loud, yanking both Phoenix and George out of sleep. "Mrs. Yuan-Whyller, your mother passed away last night in her sleep," the doctor on duty informed her.

There had been a little incident the day before, he told her, when the head nurse brought a male nurse to Rain's room, a routine practice to familiarize the new staff with all the residents. Seeing the new nurse, Rain had suddenly become agitated, tried to run away, and failing that, had locked herself up in the bathroom, until Yang, her favorite nurse, was summoned to the scene.

This nurse, Pinewoods' secret weapon, seemed to hold magic strings that controlled Rain's mind, like a puppet master with her puppet. She calmed Rain down, sweet-talking her out of her self-captivity, with a promise that the male nurse would "never be allowed in her room again." The rest of the day passed uneventfully, her dinner finished with a reasonably good appetite, some light TV for an hour and a half before bedtime, all in peace.

Next morning, when the early-shift staff came to rouse her and prepare her for breakfast, they found her curled up in bed, dead and cold.

6.

While sorting out Mother's clothing, Phoenix suddenly paused as she felt something in the pocket of one of Ma's house robes. It was a black velvet jewelry pouch, the size of a cigarette case, gathered around the edge with a thin ribbon tied into a knot. Before Mother left for Pinewoods, Phoenix had packed her suitcase, but this item did not look familiar. Mother had apparently slipped it into the suitcase right under her nose.

As Phoenix loosened the ribbon, a bottle fell into her palm. It was an old glass bottle with a translucent brownish tint, blown into the shape of a curvaceous female body. A printed label, or what remained of it, showed a few fragmented characters (looking like Japanese) against a backdrop of pale cherry blossoms, possibly pink when new. Holding it against the reading light, she could see a thin layer of dark powder, now crystallized, sticking to the interior wall.

Aisha might be able to identify the contents when she returned from her second maternity leave, Phoenix thought. She was a mother of two and a chemical analyst in a medical lab now.

There were other items in the pouch as well: a bankbook issued by the Industrial and Commercial Bank of China, last updated six years ago during a visit home, and two black-and-white photos with frayed edges and fuzzy images.

The first photo was of a man in his thirties, wearing a light-colored shirt neatly tucked into dark khaki trousers, sitting on a piece of decorative rock, a book open on his lap. She immediately recognized him as Meng Long, her high school English teacher.

She had first seen this picture in his room, pressed under a rectangular glass tabletop discolored by tea stains and littered with books and notepads. She squinted, as if stung by the edge of the light. His charm, after forty years, still hurt.

In the spring of 1970, after they returned from that cursed trip during which Meng Long was lost, Mother had drained the last drop of her energy to nurse Phoenix (then Yuan Feng) back to health so that she could finish the last leg of high school. Mother had carefully put away anything that might remotely remind her of Meng Long, yet Mother herself had, for all these years, kept his photo. Old memories rushed back, hitting Phoenix with such a mad force that it almost knocked her off her feet. She was shocked to find herself sobbing over a picture she thought long gone.

She waited until the surge of emotion ebbed to look at the second picture. It was a young woman in a nursing uniform—a complete stranger—standing, arms akimbo, in front of a shabby-looking hospital, wearing a tight smile that her eyes didn't quite approve of. Flipping the photo over, Phoenix discovered a line of faded writing in a skewed hand that read "Yuan Chunyu, Wuli Military Field Hospital, 1945.3.5."

A tingling, much like a slow-moving spider, was crawling up her spine, all the way to the back of her skull. It was the feeling that a secret was about to be unearthed. She had no idea that Rain, whom she had only ever known as a wife and mother, had actually served in a military hospital. No one in her family, not her parents, not even Auntie Mei, had ever mentioned it. She had stepped, it seemed, upon Mother's oyster. Was there a pearl?

With the thrill came doubt, and then, fear. Would Mother wish for her to pry? Once she opened the oyster, she would never be able to close it again. No one can disown a secret.

The phone suddenly rang, shaking her out of her reverie. It was George telling her he had just checked into his hotel in Victoria. The Fairmont Empress, spectacular harbor view, he just wished she could be there. Phoenix half listened, interrupting him after a few sentences with a vague question about the weather. He said something, she heard it, but it didn't quite register. *In one ear, out the other,* as Mother would say.

Sensing her absentmindedness, George switched gears, asking her what she was doing.

"Going through Ma's things, the memory box, you know."

"Anything interesting?"

She was about to tell him about the pouch, but changed her mind, suddenly annoyed by the faint trace of flippancy in his tone.

"Not much," she replied flatly.

There was an awkward moment of silence, then he said, hesitantly, "Nix, I hope you are not mad at me."

She could smell guilt a thousand miles away.

"What for?" she asked. A rhetorical question, of course, as she knew exactly what he meant. *Pinewoods.* Sending Mother there had been a mutual decision, but he was the one who had initiated it. *Orchestrated* might be a better word.

Another pause before George continued, "I just want to clear the air, Nix. We couldn't give her that kind of care at home, you know that."

"You mean *you* couldn't," retorted Phoenix quietly.

Before George had time to respond, she quickly concluded the conversation. "I've got to call Auntie Mei now, about Ma's ashes."

Hanging up the phone, Phoenix felt a sudden yearning for a drink. Walking down to the kitchen, she found an opened bottle of rum in the fridge. She filled her glass and moved towards the window. April in Toronto didn't fall into any season; it was just a nondescript gray patch of time between winter and spring. The only telltale sign of change it brought was the lengthened day—the night had to fight harder and longer to close in. Crickets were trying out their first song tentatively, but they would soon fill the sky with their tireless racket. A will of steel to make their voice heard. They only had a month or two, after all, to sing their life's song, as Mother told her when she was a little girl.

She lifted the glass, chin up, taking a huge gulp. Liquor shot down her throat to her stomach and spread, gradually, to her veins and nerves, icy cold initially, then burning like a thread of fire, turning her body into a flaming tree. She stood motionless, waiting for an explosion that never came.

It was ten to nine. Night in Toronto, but morning in Shanghai, between breakfast and lunch, a perfect time to call Auntie Mei about the ashes. And about the pearl in the oyster.

7.

The contents of Mother's memory box prompted frequent telephone conversations with Auntie Mei. Questions leading to more questions, doubts, further doubts, until Auntie Mei gradually opened the oyster. Auntie Mei dispensed the truth sparingly, as if it were a tube of toothpaste. A little each time, enough to shock Phoenix into losing a night's sleep, yet not enough to convince Phoenix there was nothing left in the tube. Eventually, Phoenix started to wonder whether there'd be enough nights of sleep left in her life to lose, in waiting for the final emptying of the tube. During one of the calls, her impatience got the better of her and she pushed Auntie Mei into abruptly clamming up. "Some things are not fit for telephone talk. I'll tell you when we meet."

Phoenix had shared with George some of what Auntie Mei told her over the phone, the bits and pieces of her mother's prehistorical existence that had been meticulously shielded from her. A clean slate to be handed over to the virgin memory of an innocent child, that must have been Mother's plan. With dispassionate composure, Phoenix handed George the missing pieces of the puzzle of Rain's early life, mixing them, unconsciously, with the loose ends of her own memory of events that happened later.

"I didn't know she was a nurse's aide. Five years, blood, open wounds, soldiers dying in her arms. I've seen her look away while gutting fish," she said, a flat statement of facts, no stinging smack of surprise, no display of blubbering and sniffling, and no signs of effort to seek solace. In her uttermost wretchedness, from the dual assault of bereavement and shock, she maintained the appearance of someone armored, tidy and untouchable. He attributed her heroic self-control to the nature of relaying a story secondhand: some raw emotion must have been consumed traveling through the same journey twice.

But he had an inkling that there must be a dent somewhere. A shock of this caliber could hardly pass without leaving a mark. It was not a thought to give peace and comfort.

"Nix, if you write her story down, I bet it would . . ."

Would help to root out the demons, that's what he meant to say. But he didn't say it.

"I bet it'll be a bestseller." He swerved at the last minute, screeching to a landing on a safer spot.

One night he woke up to find Phoenix's side of the bed empty. It was three in the morning. Room by room he searched the house and eventually caught the rover in the laundry room.

In the sliver of dim light from the half window was a blotch of shadow and a tiny flickering red dot. It was Phoenix, sitting on a laundry basket turned upside down, smoking a cigarette. Phoenix was not a smoker, to the best of his knowledge. She must have got the cigarette from his briefcase.

She almost jumped when he switched the light on. In her pajamas she looked half her size, the corners of her mouth twitching and drooping, yielding to the pull of gravity. He smelled a whiff of defeat.

She threw him a warped smile. "It's just the basement," she said, a lame defense immediately understood by George.

Phoenix had always hated people smoking, especially in the house. Once he had invited an old school buddy home for dinner. After the meal, the two of them slipped out to the balcony and lit up a casual cigarette, a juvenile attempt to relive their old school days. Phoenix completely lost it. As soon as the guest left, she hurled an arsenal of abuse at George that made the walls blush. A stark raving lunatic, as tactful as a bulldozer. This was a Phoenix totally alien to him. They didn't speak to each other for days, the longest dragged-out brawl they had ever had in their marital history.

He knew that she knew he remembered the incident. It would need nothing less than the Great Wall to defend her action of smoking in the house. But he didn't have the mean bone in him to corner her at a time like this.

"You have a morning class, better come back to bed."

Phoenix stubbed out the cigarette on the concrete floor and struggled to get up, resting against the washing machine to ease the pins and needles in her legs.

"What do you think it is that she has to tell me *in person?*" she asked, an earnest question needing an earnest answer, which he didn't have.

They returned to bed, but he couldn't go back to sleep, heart taut with the weight of the flickering red dot. Her breathing filled his ears, thin, tense, and distinct. She was wide awake too.

"Why don't you take the next semester off, try some writing maybe, and go home to see Auntie Mei? They can grab a substitute just about anywhere, it's not like you'll be leaving them high and dry." He turned sideways towards her, threading a leg around her thigh as he had sometimes done, before Rain's death, and certainly before the memory box. It felt a little strange.

She didn't answer, but she had already started, in her mind, to draft the letter she would write to the school board. *Six months no-pay leave, September–February, for personal reasons.* Her last visit home was more than six years ago, supposed to be a honeymoon, but she had taken Mother along with them.

Yes, it was about time for her to sit face to face with Auntie Mei and get to the very bottom of her tube of toothpaste.

Chapter II

The Memory of a Famine and a Dumb Head

Email from George to Phoenix, 2011.10.20 @ 20:17 Eastern Standard Time

Dear Nix,

Did you get any sleep on board?

This afternoon Aisha brought her daughter in for a screening test (the hearing is fine). Didn't get to see baby Eric as he stays at home with Grannie. Phoenix II has just started school. Lisa (the new receptionist) describes her as a munchkin with three mouths: her mom's, her dad's, and her own. Imagine Phoenix II grown to be an eighteen-year-old, walking in the streets of Kabul in distressed jeans, talking up a storm. She demanded to know the whereabouts of Phoenix I, so I showed her an atlas and pointed out Shanghai, telling her that's where you'll be in four hours.

Aisha told me the residue in your mother's bottle was potassium permanganate, a type of disinfectant. Her

Japanese colleague says the label on the bottle is for some sort of fragrance, nothing to do with the content inside. Wondered why Ma kept such a thing, but it's a very pretty bottle.

I'm almost through with the first part of your manuscript, the part about the famine and your dad. One can never be prepared enough to read about such an experience. More later.

Hope the jet lag won't be much of a bother and your lodging is clean and the food not too awful.

Your old George

Email from Phoenix to George, 2011.10.21 @ 22:17 China Standard Time

Hi George,

Landed safe and sound. Auntie Mei sent a driver to pick me up. The guesthouse is only half a block away from her facility, serves OK food, not expensive.

Didn't sleep a wink on the plane, a baby crying non-stop, my ears still hurt. Forgive my gibberish. I am going to bed this minute and hope to sleep till end of the world. When get up will do: 1. buy a local cell phone card; 2. talk to Auntie. I dread what I'll hear.

Nix

Email from George to Phoenix, 2011.10.21 @ 23:48 Eastern Standard Time

Dear Nix,

I didn't call your room number for fear of waking you up. Send me the cell number as soon as you get the SIM card.

I've finished reading the first part of your manuscript. The baby boomer generation all have a hard-time story to tell, but yours, good heavens, really hits home, especially the sparrow-hunting episode.

I know you've never been totally comfortable with your English (that's probably why you hid your writing from me till you booked the flight). Don't let it distract you. The core of the story and the way you tell it is clear and powerful. There are some problems with certain words and metaphors, and your love for commas is idiosyncratic to say the least. But in general, it's good. If we can find a publisher (I'm optimistic), they'll bring in a professional editor to fix them. For now, just trust yourself and pour your heart out.

BTW, I like the way you turn the story into a third-person narrative, to give yourself a little more freedom, a God's perspective, so to speak.

I'm attaching a casually proofread version of it, just in case you have a bit of time to work on a more polished draft while in Shanghai.

Love from George

P.S. Question: Did your mother have any relatives or friends around? She seemed awfully alone and cut off.

* Email attachment: Phoenix's manuscript *Famine*

1.

She was called Ah Feng, meaning little phoenix, when she was born, because Mother Chunyu (called Rain later) had dreamed, while seven months pregnant, of a phoenix perching on the mulberry tree in front of their house.

She didn't believe Mother's story, as she had later asked her, time and again, what the phoenix looked like in her dream and Mother couldn't quite describe it. It was not exactly rocket science to figure out Mother's intention behind such a name: Mother wanted her to get ahead in life. "There may be thousands of birds in the forest, but there is only one phoenix," Mother had said to her. "They all have to bow to that one bird. And you are going to be *that* bird, someday."

When she started school in 1960 at age seven (the age that marks the evolution from wild monkeys to remotely civilized little humans), she was then called by her full name, a school rule that everybody simply had to abide by. She became Yuan Feng, Yuan being her mother's family name. It was a deal, she was told, that her parents had struck before she was born, a prehistorical arrangement that the firstborn would assume Mother's family name, and the rest, Father's. But Father's family name, Wang, never saw the light of day, as they didn't have any other children. The end of the story.

Yuan Feng doubted the truth of this story too, the same way she had doubted the dream of the phoenix, since Father, as any two-legged fool could see, was incapable of striking a deal with Mother, or with anyone, for that matter.

Then, two lifetimes later, when she moved to Toronto, she anglicized her name, inverting the order of first name and last name, to Phoenix F. Yuan, an obvious attempt to blend in. And still later, at fifty-two, when she married George, her name went through yet another makeover, becoming Phoenix F. Yuan-Whyller.

Looking back on her life now, at the age of fifty-eight, she felt that her name, or rather, the course of the evolution of her name, was like a river that kept collecting tributaries along its way to the ocean—if there was an ocean for her to get to.

Yuan Feng had no siblings. Auntie Mei, her mother's older sister in Shanghai, was her only relative. Auntie Mei had no children, thus snipping off the last shoot of her hope for a cousin. On her street, boys and girls her age scuttered around with a pack of siblings, always fighting over something: a ball, an ice pop, a picture book, a slingshot, a dead bird. Stinky stupid baby stuff. She looked on with spite.

But at seven, who wants to be only a spectator, not an actor, when there's a never-ending drama unfolding right before your eyes? Their faces killed her joy. She ran away from them, alone and fast, towards home, a home so quiet that she could hear the dust whisper.

When she got home, Father was still at work and Mother was squatting on the dirt floor washing vegetables, the stove fire still too young to boil water. Sitting on the doorstep, chin in her palms, looking at the sky gray with afternoon clouds and birds flying by in a neat line, she could feel a hole in her heart.

"Ma, why can't I have a sister? Even a brother?"

Her mother, Chunyu, meaning spring rain, so named because she was born on a rainy spring day, lifted a hand to wipe the sweat off her eyebrows, breaking out a pale smile. "I thought you'd be grateful you've got your own desk, and nobody to share the rice in your bowl."

Yuan Feng stared at Mother, somewhat taken aback, as she had never thought about it that way. She wanted to say, *I really wouldn't mind, Ma*, but, after a moment's hesitation, swallowed it. The truth was she *would* mind. It was kind of nice to have her own desk, and her undivided bowl of rice. That gray, sunless afternoon taught her something the school never had: for everything she wanted, there would be something else she had to give up, as the price.

Mother came over, stroking the nape of her neck and messing up her hair, a soft, amorphous cloud. "You'd better change that sour little face before your pa comes home. He doesn't need to see that after a long day's work."

Father, again. When he was around the house, the mice needed to be on their tiptoes, the spiders to cease spinning their webs, and everything else to lose the use of their legs and tongues. One night she had the weirdest dream that Father was sealed in a huge bottle—aha, total peace, forever.

"All right, they do have brothers and sisters, but do they have a mother who can sing?" Mother's secret weapon, working like a charm every single time. Yuan Feng broke into a bright mood, pleading, "Ma, please, sing 'A Bright Sunny Day.'" It was a song from the wildly popular movie *The Story of Liubao*, Yuan Feng's favorite, about an early spring day filled with sunshine breaking through the end of winter's gray.

The lyrics and the tune were quite jolly, even leaning a bit towards flippancy, but there was something in Mother's voice that weighed her down. Yuan Feng didn't know then that it was Mother's apology to the world for the sibling she couldn't give her daughter, for the chipper home she couldn't build, and for a dreary course of life she didn't quite know how to avert.

"Why eighteen, Ma?"

"What?" Mother was confused.

"The lad, by the river, remember?" Yuan Feng reminded Mother. There was this eighteen-year-old boy in Mother's song who sat by the river, pondering how to confess his love—or was it torture—to a girl.

"Silly, it's just a song. Eighteen is the right age, I guess, to think about girls," answered Mother, with an unsure look on her face.

"But eighteen is *so* old!" grunted Yuan Feng.

Mother stared at her, a bit wary. "You aren't thinking about boys now, are you?"

Yuan Feng made a gagging sound, totally disgusted. "Ma, they are just a bunch of whiny babies, they make me puke!"

Mother was massively amused. "They are all fine boys, but it's not your time yet. You have a lot of learning to do, if you're going to be big and famous."

But she didn't want to be big and famous, or a phoenix. All she wanted was to rush through three forevers to get to sixteen, and fall in love, and then die at seventeen. Who wants to live to be eighteen? It's an age no number of forevers can lead to.

But Mother was too old to understand.

Mother had an extra pair of ears, alert to leaves falling, birds chirping, distant footsteps, and even the wind changing its course. Any street noise would drop her, in the middle of a song, into a dead silence. She seldom sang in Father's presence, not out of fear—she was quite at ease with Father around—but out of a desire to conserve. She wanted to save her songs for the right ears. Father's world had a door but it did not connect to Mother's; they moved in different orbits.

Father came home from work to a dinner ready and waiting. While washing his hands in a basin of water, a habit instilled by Mother in their early days of marriage, he would ask Yuan Feng, in simple, labored speech, how school was. Most of the time Yuan Feng just gave a perfunctory answer, a thoughtless word or phrase, as she knew full well that whatever she said, Father's response would never differ: "That's good, my little girl." The same lid for any pot.

Mother always served the food, first to Father, the only breadwinner in the family, then to Yuan Feng. Father moved, slowly and gently, something from his bowl (usually the cream of the crop) to Mother's bowl, without looking at her. Mother moved it right back. After several rounds of back-and-forth, much like the moves in a chess game, and a brief exchange of words, everybody began to eat, so quietly that the clattering of chopsticks against the bowls sounded like thunder.

A silence shared by two people could be contained, but the silence of three felt as though it would explode. Unable to bear it much longer, Yuan Feng quickly finished her food and fled to her own little corner of a room, to a desk that was her world, burying herself in her homework. Mother's unspoken words, meanwhile, were branded on her back, hot as an iron. *Study real hard, my girl, you'll be a phoenix one day.*

2.

Father's full name was Wang Erwa, meaning the second boy of the Wang family, but it was seldom used, except on important documents such as the household registration, his work ID card, his honorable discharge papers, and the marriage certificate. At the pinnacle of his glory, when he'd just returned from Korea with a near-fatal injury to speak for his undisputed bravery, he was addressed by the adoring crowds as Our Great Hero or the Most Respected.

Then, as time went by, the memory of the war started to fade, superseded by a swirl of new events. The clouds that once lifted him to the sky dissipated, landing him on the firm ground of everyday reality. People began to notice the dent the shrapnel had left in his mental and physical functions. This was a man, they realized, who couldn't even tie his shoelaces properly on his own, or complete two sentences without pausing and grasping for words.

This realization changed how they addressed him. In the beginning, it was subtle and tentative. The evolution from Great Hero to Slow Mind took a good six or seven years to accomplish, but it took only a moment for the nickname Dumb Head to grow the nerve to appear in daylight, all pretenses abandoned. The superman had fallen, in an instant, into the pit of contempt.

Mother was the last to know.

Mother shared a bed with Yuan Feng. Occasionally, when summoned, she would go to Father's room. The door would latch shut with a loud click, a clear signal to turn off all keen ears. There was little conversation behind the door. Yuan Feng, lying in her bed, could hear their breathing in the next room, heavier than usual, rise and fall, and Mother's moaning, so suppressed that it became hard to distinguish from breathing.

In half an hour or so, Mother would return, looking somewhat disheveled, cheeks flushed with pink fatigue. There were times Mother would pretend not to hear Father's call and he wouldn't insist. The head injury had dulled his nerve, wearing down his emotions into something like an overused elastic band, flaccid, slow to react, almost never snapping.

One night in bed, Mother noticed Yuan Feng was extremely quiet and suddenly recalled her poor appetite at supper. "Ah Feng, what's the matter?" She held her close, feeling her body, lean and bony, the young rib cage angular to the touch, the image of a string bean. *Whatever this girl eats goes straight to her head. She's got all the brains her father has lost.* Mother sighed, worried and proud.

Yuan Feng did not stir. Mother felt a patch of moisture seeping through the fabric of her pajamas, suddenly realizing that it was Yuan Feng's tears. *She is never a weepy child.* Mother sat up sharply, pushing her for an explanation.

"Ma, do you know what they call him?" Yuan Feng lowered her voice to a whisper, so that her father, separated from them only by a plywood partition wall, would not hear.

Around midnight, awakened by an urgent need to pee, Yuan Feng was about to get up, but held herself back abruptly when she noticed something glistening in the moonlight, like the eyes of a mother wolf that had just lost a pup: pensive, wild, burning with anguish and anger. It was Mother sitting against the wall. A chill ran down Yuan Feng's spine, making her shiver.

The next morning, when Yuan Feng was in her arithmetic class, Mother drifted into the classroom, like a legless ghost. Mother was wearing a new double-breasted blue jacket, with the collar of a yellow blouse turned out, her hair neatly combed back, curving around her ear with a turquoise plastic barrette. This was a mother she had never seen before, a stranger, young, fresh, with a light touch of fashion—if there was such a thing to speak of in those days.

There was something in Mother's eyes that unnerved the teacher, who surrendered the podium without a word. Mother's hands shook like skittering leaves while she fumbled through the contents of her string bag before retrieving a wooden box from it. Yuan Feng could detect, from three rows away, a muscle jumping in Mother's chin. After what seemed like a century, Mother finally managed to open the lid of the box, pulling out something hanging on a ribbon.

"I am Yuan Feng's mother." Mother bowed slightly, first to the teacher, then to the class, her voice feeble and faltering. This was the old Mother talking, the Mother she had known for her entire life of seven years. Yuan Feng could hear the roar of the blood rushing in her body and the sweat sizzling on her cheeks, wishing she were dead and buried.

"In case you don't know, this is a war merit medal, third class." The new Mother had slowly caught up and taken over, finding a tone that was cool, calm, and resolute.

"There's this young man, twenty-four years old, among the first to be sent to Korea, fighting the American devils." Mother's voice grew steady and clear. "He was assigned to work with a group of construction engineers, that's a big word, he was just a laborer, pure and simple, to fix the bridges blown up by the American bombs, to make sure things could move over the bridges smooth and fast, people and goods, you know.

"It's a tug of war, between them and us, blowing up during the day, fixing up overnight, round and round. Then one day, the planes came early, a surprise attack, the Chinese men were not prepared. This young fellow got hit by shrapnel in the head. He stood in the middle of a river, in water deep to his waist, with three other guys, holding a rock that's used as a bridge pile, for over an hour.

"Two degrees, freezing cold. It was his muscles that did the trick, not his mind, because the shrapnel had taken his mind. When rescue finally got there, they saw a half-dead man lifting a bridge, so to speak. They couldn't move him, he was hard as a rock, all frozen up. That's how he got this medal."

The class was so quiet, you could hear a needle drop.

"Now you call him Dumb Head to his daughter's face, you rotten, stinky, cruel bastards. Without him you'd all be minced meat in the hands of the Americans, understand?"

Mother put the medal back into its box, shut the lid with a loud click, gave the teacher a withering look as if he were the sole culprit, and then marched out of the room. Yuan Feng wasn't sure Mother heard the applause, which came a few moments later, shy and tentative initially, and then a lasting roar.

From that day on, nobody ever used the name Dumb Head in school again, not to Yuan Feng's face anyway. But she could never be certain about the whispers behind her back. Whispers, much like weeds in springtime, were something she couldn't possibly eradicate, even with three fierce mothers and ten shining war medals.

But time has a way of dealing with things. The hurt left a wound, then the wound grew a scar, and the scar, in turn, hardened into a callus. The mind became numb over time, and life went on.

3.

Father was conscripted, by force, from his home village in late 1943, when he was barely seventeen. The Japanese were bleeding the Chinese army at a rate even the harshest conscription law couldn't keep up with. As soon as he had finished buttoning up his uniform, he was put on the front line. It was nothing short of a miracle that he, a completely green soldier, survived the first few clashes unscathed. The bullets finally caught up with him, riddling his right leg in the fall of 1944. He had a nasty wrestle with death, drawing on his raw will to live and the full reserve of his youth, finally surviving a series of severe infections and narrowly escaping amputation.

The war against the Japanese, which dragged on for eight years, finally ended in the summer of 1945. He took a furlough back home, only to find his village in ruins and his family vanished. A fatal air raid, a deadly attack of cholera, a ruthless famine, siblings sold to different provinces . . . Over the years, he had heard quite a few versions of how his family ended up. Truth or fiction, he could never be sure. The only rock-bottom fact was he never saw any of his family again.

Upon returning to his army unit, he was almost immediately dragged into the civil war against the Communists. Another injury, this time a mere scrape on the left arm by a stray bullet, too trivial to be worthy of note. His battalion, led by an undercover Communist operative, soon fell apart, like snow melted by the sun, surrendering itself to, and becoming a part of, the Communist People's Liberation Army without putting up even a token fight.

He had briefly thought about leaving the military but soon dismissed the idea because of his fear: he didn't know how to fit into a civilian life, now a strange world to him, with no home and family to go back to. Little did he anticipate, when he made the decision to stay on, that a new war was brewing, this time in another country. A year after the Communist takeover in 1949, he woke up one morning to the order of an immediate departure. His unit, an untrustworthy remnant of the Nationalist army, although in PLA uniform now, was among the very first to be dispatched to Korea.

Three months later, he boarded the same train, traveling back to China to recover from his head injury. By the time he was basking in the glorious morning sun of southern China, on the balcony of a Wenzhou hospital ward, he had been a veteran of three wars, having served, at the age of hardly twenty-four, two governments, and been wounded by weapons manufactured in Japan, Germany, and the United States of America, in that order.

He stayed in the hospital for five months, until his medical team, the best brains in the province, reached the unanimous decision that nothing, no amount of extra therapy, medication, or fan mail, could further improve his condition. His only request, when the issue of release was brought up, was to be granted permission to work—any kind of job, he said, so that his mind, or whatever remained of it, could be occupied.

These words, by pure accident, reached the ears of a busy reporter, who, with his horns and trumpets, blared them into a noble, selfless, saintly statement.

Our hero expresses his sincere wish to continue to make contributions to mankind.

Next morning, when the paper was read to Father, he was mortified. The nurses guessed his thoughts, as they could all by now read his mood by way of his stare. "A man just has to work," he mumbled, with his jaw uneasily set.

"It's just a way of saying things. Besides, you deserve every praise for what you've done," they said, trying to calm him.

The war was raging on without him. As the first local soldier wounded in Korea, he had stirred the emotions of the multitude, and his wish, naturally, was no trivial matter. The Municipal Party Committee held a special meeting to review his situation, and a decision was made after rounds of exhaustive discussions. He was assigned, in the end, to work in the metallurgical plant, the largest state-run enterprise in the city, as a warehouse manager. A glorified nominal position, with no specific job description attached. There was a real manager serving as his "assistant," in name, of course.

An old bungalow in the central area of the city, with a bus stop right around the corner, would be cleaned out and fixed up, where needed, to be his residence.

His job assignment was not the only subject for discussion on the table. There were other, more pressing issues, such as how to make his return to everyday life a success, something the media and the public would love to hear. After all, who wouldn't want a bright sequel to a heroic but nevertheless grim tale?

He would also need, the committee became keenly aware, a cook to prepare his daily meals; a nurse to administer his medication and arrange for his hospital visits; a cleaning lady to take care of his house and laundry; an errand person to look after his daily shopping; a personal secretary to manage his salary, ration coupons, and various social appearances; and, most importantly, someone with inexhaustible patience, to serve as a handkerchief ready to wipe his sweat and tears and a bucket to contain his emotional trash, if any.

The issue of his daily care, seemingly so much more involved than that of his job assignment, was resolved almost instantly, as those attending the meeting, all men, reached a quick conclusion while looking at each other with smiles of tacit understanding. Such roles, complex and diversified as they were, could be readily filled, in reality, by one person.

A wife.

The issue of the Hero's marriage could be easily arranged, they believed, based on the fan letters he had received, in sacks, a ruthless assault on the vocal cords of the nurses who had to read them to him for hours on end. Young women from all walks of life—college students, teachers, opera singers, shop assistants, factory workers, farmers—poured their hearts out to him in letters, many with their photos attached. Some guileless and forward, others more reserved and tactful, all expressing one common desire: to worship and serve, to "clean the dust off his shoes," in their own words. It surely wouldn't be an impossible mission to pick one enthusiastic heart from a thousand.

But the Great Hero soon proved the plan wishful thinking. He stoutly refused, to the committee's great astonishment, to consider any of the women selected for him. "I don't know them, they don't know me," he said tersely, a simple statement rooted in sound logic and common sense, standing firm against any challenge or refutation, making his doctors wonder whether they erred in their evaluation of his mental capacity.

At their wit's end, the committee had no choice but to prolong his hospital stay, a makeshift solution to an impossible situation. Then one day, something happened, the nearest thing to a miracle, an answer to all prayers. A woman came to his ward, with a page torn out of a newspaper carrying a feature story about him.

Another admirer, the nurses thought, as they had seen enough of her kind. But they soon sensed their mistake, as this woman was somewhat different. Perhaps it was the way she walked, a sure-footed and agile stride, slicing through the stale air in the room, stirring up a fresh breeze. Perhaps it was the way she looked at him, with a calmness that could ease a storm, a familiarity, as if she had known him for her entire life, the way a mother knows her baby or a weaver knows her loom.

Unlike those barging into his room, calling him "my hero" or "my most respected comrade" in voices filled with tremorous adoration, she didn't even bother with a formal greeting. Surrounded by walls stained with water leaks and mosquito blood, she stood face to face with him, murmuring, "My poor, my poor . . . ," tears welling up in her eyes. She was tall, lean; her skin glowing with suntan, bones well structured, her look pleasant but far from beautiful. A smile cracked his face, and the air in the room suddenly became charged.

The nurses knew the moment had come for them to leave. A pretense, of course, for no one could really resist the lure of curiosity. They closed the door behind them, all trying nonetheless to stay within earshot, but the voices inside were too muffled to decipher.

She was obviously more of a talker than he was, but he wasn't silent either. Her flow of words was interrupted, every now and then, by his brief responses, often in the form of monosyllabic interjections. This was the longest he had ever talked to anyone since he came into their care. Nobody was sure exactly what they were witnessing, but everyone agreed that there appeared to be a dim light at the end of the tunnel.

The conversation went on for an hour or so, questions and answers exchanged, all in whispers mixed with an occasional chuckle. Then he opened the door, declaring to the shameless eavesdroppers, in a slow, awkward, but resolute tone, "I want to go home, with her."

A quick security check was run on the woman, whose name, they found out, was Yuan Chunyu. Twenty-three years old, from a relatively simple background, parents both dead, lived for a while with an older sister in Shanghai who was married to a high-ranking official, therefore politically reliable. A marriage certificate, expedited by a strong letter of recommendation from the brother-in-law, was issued, and a wedding ceremony was conducted right in the hospital ward.

The Municipal Party Committee sent their representative, Secretary-General Song, to attend the ceremony, bringing with him a Forever brand bicycle as a wedding present, a rare luxury in those days.

"Comrade Yuan Chunyu," Secretary-General Song said, shaking her hand warmly, with an obvious sense of joy, and—also—relief, "now we, the City, give you our hero. You promise you'll take the best care of him, for the City."

Chunyu recoiled a little, looking away at the pink oleander blossoms outside the window, saying softly, "I look after my husband, and the City looks after its hero. You promise me, in front of everyone here, you'll step in when I need help."

Silence fell like a deadweight, as the entire room was flabbergasted. They'd never heard anybody talk to a secretary-general in such a blunt manner, as if in a market haggling over the price for a chicken or a sack of yams.

Secretary-General Song gave Chunyu a long and steady look, more amused than offended.

"All right, you have my word," he replied, after a moment of thought.

Two days later, the Hero was discharged from the hospital, to a new home, a new job, and a new life free from war.

Two years later, in the fall of 1953, after two miscarriages and a very difficult labor, Chunyu gave birth to a baby girl whom she named Ah Feng, little phoenix.

4.

The first few years of their married life were uneventful, as they continued to bask in the glory of his war medal, which shielded them, to some extent, from the harsh realities of a young republic with old war wounds not yet healed and a new war raging along its northern border.

Until famine came.

Nobody had told them about the famine, not the radio, not the newspapers. Every day, they got deliveries of the major newspapers in the country, from Beijing, Shanghai, and their local area. Free subscriptions, a gift of appreciation from the City for the Hero and his family.

Father could be considered literate if the bar was not raised too high. His entire education consisted of two years of lessons given by a tutor in his home village, interrupted by the harvest when he had to help in the fields, and a few literacy training sessions during his service in the PLA.

With what was left of his brain, reading the paper was too draining a process for him, and headlines and photos were all that could hold his attention. Mother had to pitch in with the contents of the articles. "A morsel of meat to feed his empty head," she said to Yuan Feng, an apt metaphor alluding to the tight rationing of meat.

This idea of "feeding his head" began with a medical checkup when the doctor in charge pulled Mother aside. "Our hero has shown few signs of improvement. Now it's almost ten years since his discharge from the hospital," he told Mother in a lowered voice, face drawn with concern. "You need to give him more stimulation, since the medication can hardly do anything for him now." Sensing her confusion, he went on to explain, "You need to talk to him more, and make him talk too."

So Mother started to read newspapers to Father every evening after dinner. Mother and Auntie Mei had both nearly finished high school, a rare wonder for women in their time. Mother would quickly sift through the papers, picking out the news she felt suitable for Father to hear, interesting but safe. An editorial, for example, from *People's Daily*, the most authoritative voice of the central government, criticizing Khrushchev, the Soviet leader, on his erroneous statement about people's communes (harsh, but directed against a foreign government, thus safe), or a story from *Shanghai Evening* about an unprecedented harvest in some provinces north of the Yangtze, despite the adverse weather conditions (heartening), or a report from a local paper citing fresh numbers from Beijing about the national steel output greatly exceeding the target (uplifting).

With great effort the poor man tried, for the first five minutes or so, to focus, out of appreciation for his wife's kindness, but his attention would eventually dwindle to a string of yawns he could no longer hold back. "Eyes heavy," he would explain to her, apologetically. "Don't listen to those vets," he added, in a blunt reference to his doctors, "they are only good for pigs."

Yuan Feng couldn't help hearing, in her own room with her homework, her parents burst out laughing, which was suppressed, almost instantly, into barely audible giggles. The doctors were wrong, she told herself. Father had made huge progress: he had learned, or rather, relearned, how to turn disappointment into a joke.

It's true that there was little public knowledge of the famine, but in hindsight, there had been signs in the papers and on the radio, buried between the lines, too subtle for Mother to pick up. Some references, for example, to the drought on a scale unseen before in certain areas of the country, and a broadcast program calling for "the patriotic citizens" to be frugal with their daily consumption of rice and flour. But Mother's mind employed a different set of receptors, too dull to catch the oblique messages woven with nuance and ambiguity. She had her own antenna, nevertheless, sensitive to the pulses of the streets, a different world altogether.

The first thing Mother noticed was the shortage of rice in the stores. The maximum allowed purchase was now only five kilos at a time, even with the full monthly ration coupon. The rice grains, brownish in color, had a stale, damp feel to them, with sand and grit mixed in to bring it up to weight. It tasted rough and musty when cooked, and once a piece of grit nearly chipped one of Yuan Feng's front teeth.

Another day, Mother made a routine visit to the hospital to fill a prescription for cod liver oil, a precious nutritional supplement available only to a select few: the very important, the very sick, and the war heroes. The sight of a small crowd blocking the narrow corridor of the outpatients' clinic distracted and disturbed her, as she noticed that their faces and joints were swollen to a grotesque size and shape, their skin an anemic pale yellow, all typical signs of malnutrition—or, in plain language, hunger.

They were from a village about a hundred kilometers north of the city, a woman told her in a feeble voice soon turning breathless with exhaustion. Peasants, Mother immediately understood, outside the city residents' food supply range, not covered by the rationing system, a protection, however fragile, from total starvation.

They had hitchhiked their way to Wenzhou, over two days, the woman went on. They hadn't seen a bowl of rice for months, since the lion's share of the yield had been turned over to the state, and even the yams in stock had nearly been exhausted. Barks, roots, weeds, even edible soil where one could find it, mixed with the few yams left, now formed the nearest thing to a meal: whatever they could find to fool their stomachs into believing they had been fed.

The purpose of their trip here, explained the woman, was not for treatment, which they couldn't afford. All they wanted was a medical certificate issued from the city hospital, a document required by the commune, to indicate they were no longer fit for manual labor in the fields, and more importantly, to allow them to buy, outside the rationing system, a few slices of pork liver at a government price. Something, anything, to help tide them over the next little while, till the allotted rice seeds arrived for spring sowing. These seeds, she assured Mother, would be in their stomachs instead of landing in the soil, whatever the punishment.

A man, apparently the head of the group, came over, staring at Mother with a guarded coldness. "Save your breath," he warned the woman in a hoarse voice, too weak to yell, "what do they care, these city folks? We work like beasts in the fields all year round, they don't lift a finger, just sitting around looking pretty, and have a full bowl!"

Stung by their animosity, Mother flinched, stumbling away, totally forgetting about the prescription she was supposed to fill. She found herself lost on her way home. Town-head, that was her street, so named because it used to be, centuries ago, the location of the yamen (the feudal township office) when Wenzhou was still a tiny town. From Town-head to hospital and back: it was a route she had walked hundreds of times over the course of a decade. She knew every building and every tree by heart and had seen infants born and old men die along the road, a road she could follow blindfolded.

In a trancelike state, she began to run, soon out of breath, as if to escape a deadly shadow that would catch up and bite off her heels, her hair a flying mess, her feet stirring up a cloud of uneasy dust. A madwoman she was, not aware that she had taken a wrong turn, which led her farther and farther away from Town-head.

She heard her thoughts clambering in her mind. *The famine is real. It'll creep into my house before I know it if I am not prepared.*

When she finally got home, it was midafternoon, her daughter still in school and her husband at work. Locking the door and drawing the curtains shut, she rushed to her bedroom, rummaging through the drawers of the dresser, a wedding present from her husband's factory, looking for the box containing the war medal. It was there, almost ten years old, showing the first sign of aging, a few rusty spots around the tips of the star, now a dull red.

She crawled onto the bed, curling, like a cat in the winter sun, into a loose ball, holding the medal tight in her palm. She felt a tingling on her cheeks, and realized it was tears. She sobbed until she was aching, overwhelmed with a surge of relief. For every hideous hell she had been through in the past, Buddha had more than sufficiently made up with this medal.

The metallic edge chafed her palm, but with the pain came pleasure and assurance. As long as she had the medal, her daughter—the flesh of her flesh, blood of her blood, the sole purpose for her existence in this universe—would always have a bowl of rice, however rough and musty its taste.

Later in the afternoon, Yuan Feng got home from school, finding the fire unlit and the stove cold, and Mother curled up on the bed, fast asleep, one hand closed in a loose fist, a smile sealing up her lips, peaceful like sweet death. She opened Mother's fist and discovered her father's medal, the medal that had brought her embarrassment and pride all at once, not that long ago, in her school.

Two months later, a general notice was issued to reduce, province-wide, the supply of rice and vegetable oil, already tightly rationed, by a further 15 percent. The famine was now official.

Meat had been scarce for quite some time. Mother's last home-raised chicken, a white leghorn, was snatched away one night by a thief who climbed over the fence into their backyard, quiet and traceless, a skill only hunger could perfect. Next morning, Mother sat on the ground beside the empty coop wailing, like a dog with its tail chopped off, heartbroken over her silly idea of "saving the best for the last." *Best* indeed, but someone else's *last*. Mother didn't bother, from then on, with another flock, as she had nothing to feed them with.

Going through a growth spurt, Yuan Feng was forever hungry, her protein-deprived stomach perpetually craving food, or rather, the sensation of being filled. Mother's long list of household chores, once diverse and multiplex, was now trimmed down to one single task: to make food appear more abundant than it actually was, an arduous process requiring not only time and effort, but also creativity, and even a bit of magic.

She quickly learned how to make vegetable stew thick as paste, mixing it with a carefully calculated portion of rice to increase its bulk. She discovered, through trial and error, a hundred ways of altering the texture and taste of yam, still available from the street peddlers, unrationed, by adding different sauces, blending it with different vegetables, varying the ratio of mixture, cutting it into different sizes and shapes, or simply adjusting the strength and duration of the cooking heat.

Cooking rice was, however, a different game all by itself, a stark test of her skill, starting with a careful straining and picking process to get rid of the sand and grit. Once cooked, the rice would be spread out, in a flat, thin layer, on a sieve, to air-dry until the grains turned into solid crystals. Then, with fresh water added, it was cooked a second time, and then a third and final time, with a few precious drops of oil blended in as a finishing touch. When the final product, the result of half a day's work, was served at the dinner table, the mere sight of it—clean, puffy, plentiful, with a seductive sheen—would fool any stomach into believing the promise of a good meal.

Surprised to see some rice left in the pot even after the second serving, Yuan Feng made herself look twice, to ensure her eyes were not playing tricks on her.

"Ma, have we got extra rice coupons this month?" she asked, hands pausing in midair before digging in for her third serving.

Mother gave a monosyllabic answer, "Yep," quickly closing the subject. Same amount of rice, three times more bulk. Some might call this a lie; others, magic. What's truth, anyway? Truth is like water, assuming the shape of whatever it flows into. But Yuan Feng didn't need to be dragged into all that. Just let her be a child for a little longer. Mother smiled a vague smile, emptying the rice pot into Yuan Feng's bowl.

Hunger teaches us skills in a day that would otherwise take us twenty years to learn. A warm rush of pleasure washed over Mother as she dotingly watched her daughter let out a loud burp, face beaming with satisfaction after a good meal. A false sensation, as the stomach would soon tell.

A little while later, when Mother was wrapping up the "stimulation" session with Father, Yuan Feng came home from a visit to the public bathroom around the street corner. She sidled in, standing in the shadow of the dim light, her silent presence growing weighty.

"No homework today?" Mother asked curiously, shifting her eyes from the newspaper.

Yuan Feng looked away, head bent, face drawn with shame and fear, and muttered hesitantly, "Ma, I think there is something wrong with me."

Putting down the paper, Mother cast a closer look at her, a little worried. "What's the matter?"

"I just had two and a half bowls of rice, but I am, um, hungry again. Something's wrong, in my stomach, right?" said Yuan Feng, spiteful of that part of her body that knew nothing else but greed.

A sharp pang shot through Mother, twisting her heart into a tight knot. She walked over, standing face to face with her daughter, speechless, laden with guilt for the truth she couldn't admit, and for the lies she knew she would continue to fabricate.

"Sparrows."

Father's voice shocked them both, as they thought he had dozed off, bored with the monotony of the paper.

"Sparrows," he repeated, in slurred words, "they shoot them, Old Cheng and Big Yang, to eat."

Old Cheng and Big Yang were Father's coworkers at the metallurgical plant.

"My goodness, they aren't big enough to fill the cracks between your teeth," cried Mother in half disgust.

"They are meat," replied Father, impassively, "air gun, I shoot."

5.

The next day was a Sunday. At Mother's suggestion, Father took Yuan Feng to the woods.

"You better take her along, she needs some fresh air, that little bookworm." But Yuan Feng knew that was not Mother's real intention. While Mother had to stay behind to do the weekly load of laundry before the sunny day turned into the long stretch of rain typically seen at this time of year, she didn't like the idea of Father traveling alone, far away from her sight.

Yuan Feng wasn't exactly looking forward to the trip—not because of the woods, which she seldom visited, as Mother kept her on a tight leash most of the time, but because of the companion she was stuck with. She wasn't sure which she dreaded more, his silence or his disjointed speech.

Her excitement gradually grew when they drew nearer the Oujiang. The biggest river and the only one in the city that led, after a lengthy and treacherous journey, to the sea, it was hence the only gateway to the outside world, as trains and airplanes were still a long way away. They arrived at the dock after a good forty-five minutes' walk, and sat down on a bench, waiting for the ferry.

The morning sun, young and eager, was playing tricks with the water, setting one part against the other, the water closest to them a luminous blue and the rest an opaque gray, the division salient and striking, as if carved out by a keen blade. Boats came and went, all types and sizes—sampans, motorized boats, boats with black awnings—moving passengers, vegetables, and dried goods to and fro. One could see the faces of the boatmen in the clear sunlight, weathered and stern, carrying the world's cares on their shoulders.

The water was mostly calm, with an occasional swirl of undercurrent triggered by sudden gusts of wind, bringing rotten vegetable leaves and dead fish and waterfowl to the surface, to drift away to somewhere unknown. Yuan Feng watched in a daze, transfixed by the magnificence of the river and the life and death it carried, wondering if there was a world where water and sky met.

The ferry finally came, and the crowd waiting on the dock, obviously larger than the boat could hold, started to ruffle: peddlers with bulky baskets on their carrying poles, mothers with babies, boarding-school students going home for their weekend, everyone trying to squeeze on, as the next ferry would be another hour.

Father slung the canteen over Yuan Feng's shoulder and squatted, offering his back. "Up, you," he said. Her mind went blank for a second before realizing Father wanted her on his back. A flash of memory took her back to a National Day when she was three, or maybe four. Father had carried her on his shoulders so that she could gain a better view of the parade. It seemed that a lifetime had passed since then. She had crossed over the line of complete innocence and moved towards the edge of knowing. A hot flush surged up; she was half-embarrassed.

"Can't get in by yourself," Father hollered. Before she could give it another thought, she found herself on his back, her hands circling, without realizing, his neck. Despite his head injury, Father had a rock-strong set of bones. She could smell his unwashed hair with mixed scents of cigarettes and engine oil. What stories could a man's hair tell about his life? She was amazed.

With the smell came an unexpected sense of connection, a connection she had never experienced before. In an epiphanic moment, she suddenly understood that scent, like words and silence, was also a door, leading the way to knowing.

With the load on his back and a long gunnysack slung over his shoulder, Father elbowed his way, quietly but doggedly, through the crowd. Gradually, there appeared a crack in the tight pack for him to pass through, as people noticed his threadbare army uniform with the insignia removed, reminding them, with a chilling solemnity, that the war was not yet in the distant past.

Father was nearly 180 centimeters tall, a giant among the typical southerners with their petite builds. A string bean when he was taken away from home, Father had miraculously completed his growth in the army, despite long marches that wore through countless pairs of cloth shoes, endless nights sleeping in the open, cold and hungry, and a succession of battle injuries.

Father always slouched his shoulders consciously when walking, as if to apologize for his height. On his back, Yuan Feng gained a new set of eyes and discovered a new world. The houses along the riverbanks seemed, from a higher altitude, flattened out, the water a shade deeper in color, the sky a little lower, and she might be able, if she really tried, to grab the tail of a cloud in passing.

Slightly dizzy, she sighed quietly, remembering what Mother once said to her when she complained about the stringent house rules forbidding her to bring school friends over. *You'll see things differently once you are a grown-up.* The adult world was indeed different, now that she had a taste of it on Father's back, but she had yet to find out whether she liked it.

Once inside the ferry, Father set her down in a nook to give her a little more legroom. With a loud cough of the engine, the boat started moving, soon picking up speed, slicing the water open with a trail of foam gushing up. *The river is bleeding white blood,* Yuan Feng thought, half-amused by her wild imagination. Startled by the sudden motion, babies on board burst out crying, one after another, a chorus of hysteria. Mothers were busy patting and coaxing, all in vain. A basket of chickens, in a desperate attempt to break loose from the straw tying their claws, started a riot, flapping their wings frantically, beating up a horrendous storm of feathers and dust.

"Pa, am I heavy?" Noticing the beads of sweat gathering on Father's brows, Yuan Feng shouted her question over the noise.

Father took out his matchbox, trying to light a cigarette, unsuccessfully, with his shaky hands. Yuan Feng offered to help. The wind was picking up, and the flame flickered, sputtered for a second, but finally held. Father took a big puff in and then let it out, smoke forming a string of ringlets, reaching higher and higher, becoming loose, shapeless, and eventually lost.

"Not as heavy as your ma," Father said dreamily.

"You carried Ma too? When?" Yuan Feng asked, curious and excited.

Father looked perplexed, as if searching hard down a long and lost memory lane, then gave up. No answer came. A perpetual journey, back and forth, between clarity and fuzziness, that's how Father's mind worked. She could never be sure what to believe and what to ignore.

They landed ashore in a short while. Father seemed to know the way well, his feet guiding both his body and mind, picking out the shortest route, sure and fast. Yuan Feng had to trot to keep up. They passed a strip of partially paved land with clusters of wooden houses: a guest lodge, a teahouse, and two eateries, sparsely spaced from each other, dilapidated and ugly, true eyesores. The road then gradually narrowed down to a dirt path, leading into the woods.

"See that?" Father suddenly paused at the edge of the woods, pointing to a hillock on his left side, now visible as the road turned, with part of its slope scarred by quarrying. "My village, behind it."

Yuan Feng had heard, through Mother, bits and pieces about Father's family, but this was the first time he himself had brought it up.

"Do you have a picture of them?" she asked.

"Silly." Father cracked a smile. "Only city folks had pictures taken in those days. My ma would never throw money away on fancy things like that."

This was about the longest sentence Father had ever uttered, as far as she could remember, anytime, anywhere. He seemed to have left the foggy part of his mind behind, on the other side of the river.

"Do you remember my grandma?" she ventured.

There was a long silence. Father stared at the sun, squinting against its radiant glare.

"Before I went away, she made me bite my finger," he replied, slowly.

"Why?" Yuan Feng's curiosity was now fully roused.

"She wanted me to swear by my own blood I'd come back, but she didn't wait."

A lump seemed to swell up in Father's throat, cracking his voice. For a moment, she thought she had seen tears, but his eyes went dry and vague. The moment had passed. There was a division line, just like the water of the Oujiang, in Father's head. One part of it couldn't even remember what he had for breakfast, while the other could go back, all the way, to an incident when he was seventeen years old.

They didn't speak for a while, till they entered the woods. The trees, though thinned out by years of brutal logging, were leafy enough to darken the sky, subduing the sunlight into a few harmless dappled blotches, no longer a direct assault to the eyes. The chirping of birds could be heard, its sharp edge clipped by the breeze rustling through the leaves, bringing in the smells of the river, the wet mud, and the scattered mushrooms boosted by rain. A different world it was, in the woods, Yuan Feng concluded, with its own noises and its own quiet. The rules of the city didn't quite work here.

Father sat down on a tree stump, took his air gun out of the sack, rested it on his right shoulder, and started surveying the environment for his first feathered target.

He soon discovered a huge bird's nest cradled in a fork of a birch tree around fifteen paces away, half-hidden from view by thick leaves. A test shot. A flock fluttered their wings, darting, in a frenzy of panic, towards the sky—they were indeed sparrows.

Snap, snap, snap.

Father continued with more pellets, one after another, sharp and fast. Something dropped onto the ground with a faint thud. Then another.

"Go get them." Father motioned Yuan Feng, who was still recovering from the newness of it all, to a cloth bag sticking out of the gunnysack lying on the ground.

She picked it up and ran, like a hunting dog, soon turning around, waving the bag from a distance, breathless with excitement. "Three, Pa!" she hollered. "Pa, how could you shoot them when they were flying, faster than the devil?" She laid the trophy at his feet, panting heavily.

Father lit another cigarette, this time without help. "I was a sniper. I killed a few Japs."

"Your hands were steady when you aimed, not like when you hold a pen or a teacup," she observed.

"I hate pen, and tea," Father said, grimacing. "Count lead time, when target is moving," Father explained, brows relaxed, face shifting in and out of the shadow cast by the dappled sunlight.

This was not the father who had to struggle forth a greeting when a neighbor came to visit, and who dozed off every time anything remotely serious was discussed over dinner. Yuan Feng wasn't sure what had changed him—the outdoors, the gun, or being away from Mother.

The woods did him good, much more than the damned newspaper. Yuan Feng was determined to tell Mother that.

"Some people born smart with their eyes, others just dumb head," he added casually, totally unaware this was the name people called him behind his back, a name that had lowered Mother to the level of a street shrew, fighting a battle of honor with the weapons of her spittle and his war medal against a bunch of brats in school.

It was dead quiet. All the living creatures, stirred by the commotion, had now gone into hiding. The woods seemed to have fallen into a deep slumber, disrupted only by an occasional lonely pip of a cricket, startled and on tenterhooks.

"No more." Father heaved a sigh, slipping his air gun back in the sack and tying up the opening of the bag containing the sparrow carcasses. He weighed the bag with a hooked finger, disappointed, ready to leave. "Not enough for a mouthful."

Languidly, they headed back towards the ferry. About halfway, Father felt Yuan Feng tugging on his sleeve.

"Can we go back, a little deeper in the woods? Fewer people there, more birds maybe?"

In the years to come, whenever she looked back on her life, she would curse this day. How she wished to rewind her life, like a video cassette, so that she could erase the moment when she made this thoughtless suggestion that led, catastrophically, to their downfall.

6.

By the time they sat down to eat their lunch of cold yam bun, they had already collected fifteen dead sparrows in their bag, all one hour's work.

"Your ma's stolen chicken, here." Father lifted the bag, now half-full, beaming with pride, like a child showing off his good schoolwork, eager for praise and reward.

They could have packed and left, at that moment, with their trophy and glory, catching the ferry home in the sunshine, waiting for Mother to bring out a dinner with freshly roasted meat, or what came close to meat. But they didn't. They turned a deaf ear to the wisdom of sages passed from father's father to son's son, that joy begets sadness, and to quit while you are ahead. In a moment of foolish greed, they decided, instead, to stay until they hit the magic number of twenty.

Farther in the woods, with less human intrusion, the trees grew denser, their roots ancient, huge, half-exposed, and intertwined, forming an intricate web like an illustration of the blood supply system Yuan Feng had once seen in a doctor's office.

Father lifted his gun, beginning to search for another target, but soon put it down, distracted by something draping from a tree branch about twenty paces away. They realized, as they drew near, that it was a piece of fabric, the size of a bedsheet, half-torn and soiled by mud and bird droppings. Their eyes were stung, after they pulled it from the tree and spread it flat on the ground, by the image printed on it. Blue sky, white sun, and red earth. It was a flag of the Nationalist government, driven by the Communist forces, over a decade ago, to Taiwan, their last stronghold.

This was something Yuan Feng had been taught to loathe and spit on, ever since the dawn of her memory. She let out a cry of horror, bolting away as if near a bomb ready to explode. They eventually calmed down, as they became aware, to their huge relief, that they were the only living human souls in the woods. Having regained their composure, they ventured on and spotted, a few more steps away, something half-buried in the tall grass. It was a balloon, largely deflated, tied to a crate.

It suddenly dawned on them that it was one of the airdropped packages from across the Taiwan Strait, the enemy front. A part of the psychological warfare, "sugar-coated poison," as the papers had warned them, to mock, to entice, and to win over their ex-subjects now struggling to stay afloat in the brutal waves of an unprecedented famine.

This was a situation, Yuan Feng understood, even at her tender age, that she should run away from, as fast as her legs could carry her, and report to the authorities. But she didn't, and neither did Father. Seized by curiosity, and maybe greed, they kept wandering, farther and farther, along a path so black that no war medal could ever whitewash it.

Slowly and cautiously, they approached the battered crate, its planks shaken loose by the impact of landing. A careful inspection through the cracks revealed no signs of weapons or a human body, dead or alive. Thank God.

With a sharp-edged rock, Father pried open the lid, a surprisingly easy job. Kneeling on the grass, they started to go through its contents. Stacks upon stacks of printed material: posters, books, postcards, pamphlets, written in old-style characters now no longer taught in school. But the pictures spoke to Yuan Feng plainly enough: pictures of women and children playing together, of men working in well-lit offices, neatly dressed, of families around dinner tables, smiling, with plentiful food. A picture of joy and contentment, all too obvious.

"Damn lies." Yuan Feng threw away the propaganda in disdain, finding, buried underneath, things that she couldn't name out loud, as the very sound would entice her stomach to growl. Sacks of rice and flour, packages of dried noodles and popped popcorn, cans of lard, preserved fruits, and peanut oil, and, at the very bottom, dozens of white shirts made of fine cotton.

She sat back on her heels, gasping for air, hearing her blood rushing in her ears, succumbing, helplessly, to a craving that no principles, however noble, could damp.

She looked up at Father but he turned away, his face blank and vague, a vein, faintly purple, squirming along one side of his temple. There were two armies, she figured, in his mind (if he still had a mind) that were fighting a fierce battle: one led by craving, the other, fear. Father saw them both but couldn't decide which side to take.

There was, in fact, yet another army in his mind that Yuan Feng was too young to recognize. It was this third force, a father's love for his daughter, that clouded the judgment of an already cloudy mind, urging him to cross the fire of hell, to lose his war.

Father started to sort out the goods, discarding items too bulky to carry or with labels impossible to remove, eventually deciding, after rounds of picking and choosing, on two cans of lard, one tin of peanut oil, and one package of dried noodles, all small enough to fit in the bag containing the dead sparrows. Then he tore open a sack of rice, scooping out, with his palms, enough of the grains to fill each of their pockets until they bulged.

"Pa . . . ?" Yuan Feng's eyes brushed, ever so briefly, over a package of popcorn, and then dodged away sheepishly. Without saying a word, Father emptied one of her pockets, refilling it with a handful of popcorn.

She took a piece, holding it in her palm and sniffing it suspiciously, as a cat would unfamiliar food. A scent of sea salt, of faraway fields, of fire and oil, slithered into her nostrils, lifting every lid on every pore, and she felt a weird urge to sneeze and yell. She chewed the piece slowly, savoring the texture and taste, but her stomach, having known only yam and stale rice for months, rebelled against the calm pretense of her teeth and tongue with a heinous racket. In an instant, she had finished the entire contents of her pocket, and still wanted more.

Father finally broke the silence: "Getting late." After a refill of popcorn, they started on their journey home, wobbly and staggering with the full load in their pockets. The thought of bleak consequences, if caught, did cross their minds, but it was a sense of luck that ruled the moment. Hunger defeats fear, every time.

"Wait, Pa." Yuan Feng stopped him and ran back towards the crate, returning, triumphantly, with a white shirt. "You've got to have this."

Father, after a moment's hesitation, took it from her, putting it on underneath his old uniform.

The ferry arrived on time, much less crowded than in the morning, with empty seats here and there, but they didn't sit down, for fear their pockets would burst. They couldn't help smiling whenever their eyes met. A secret hung in the air between them, so filling that it was impossible not to show a crack. But they didn't speak.

When they got ashore, it was a little past five. The sun was still hanging there, burning up bright-pink patches of cloud, the wind stirring up a sultry air. Yuan Feng could smell Father's perspiration three miles away. After making sure that all the pockets were securely buttoned up, Father decided to remove the uniform jacket, wearing only the white shirt, his new loot, with the sleeves rolled up.

They walked side by side, exhausted but exultant, impatient to get home to a meal they would never forget, in this life, or the next. While crossing an intersection, she suddenly felt a strange tingling sensation on her back. Turning around, she noticed, to her utter confusion, a growing crowd trailing them, closer and closer, eventually forming a circle around them, blocking their way. A man in thick glasses, a complete stranger, pointed at Father, yelling in a screaky voice: "How dare you!"

Following the direction of the man's finger, Yuan Feng saw two lines of words on the back of Father's new shirt, now visible through the moisture of his sweat.

Wiping out Mao Tse-tung and his gang,

retaking our lost mainland!

It took a few seconds for the meaning of the words to sink in. What happened next was all blurred in her memory, scenes fading in and out, blending with each other, a riot of motion and sound. Shouts, a siren, a police car, handcuffs, Father knocked down onto the ground, spitting blood from his wounded lip, looking up at her, imploring silently for help, as if she were the adult, and he, the child.

"He is just a dumb head!" She heard herself yelling at the top of her lungs, knowing, from the taste of blood in her mouth, that she had torn her vocal cords.

By the time Yuan Feng finally got home, alone, it was completely dark. Mother was pacing, back and forth, along the dimly lit street outside their house. Yuan Feng began to shake at the sight of Mother, so violently that she feared her bones would break. Sensing a catastrophe, Mother quickly took her inside, bolting the door. Between hysteric fits of sobbing, Yuan Feng finally managed to deliver a rough account of what had happened, skipping, of course, any mention of the popcorn.

Mother didn't say a word, her face set as stern as a rock, but Yuan Feng could hear Mother's thoughts jostling in her head.

"Save your tears for later. We'll need them when the time is right," Mother finally told her.

Mother went into the bedroom, soon returning with a box that Yuan Feng immediately recognized as the one containing Father's medal. This time, Mother didn't bother to bag it. Instead, she held it up stark naked, as if it were a torch or a flag.

"Let's go, right now, to Mayor Song's house," Mother said flatly, wrapping Yuan Feng's hand in hers. "Once we get there, you can cry your eyes out, but not before that."

Yuan Feng stumbled along, watching her own shadow cast by the dingy streetlight trampled upon by her feet, again and again, hungry, hurt, and full of guilt.

Father was released from prison two weeks later, haggard, lost, smiling blankly at anything moving, a child, a shadow, or a street dog. With the intervention of Mayor Song, formerly the secretary-general, Father avoided a gruesome prison term corresponding to the nature of his crime, but his war medal, together with his disability allowance, was stripped away.

An average Joe now. No, not really. An average Joe was someone without a medal, but Father, with a medal publicly stripped away, was less than an average Joe.

Father never talked about what had happened to him in prison. When asked, his answer was invariably "All right, I was." No longer able to sit through the paper-reading sessions, he spent most of his spare time lying in bed, staring at the ceiling, or fast asleep. He seldom called Mother over to his room now, but one night, out of the blue, he burst into her bedroom and grabbed Yuan Feng's arm, muttering huskily, "I lost your sparrows, my little girl, I'm so sorry."

Mother got him into their bed, holding him in her arms, stroking his hair, trimmed into a crew cut since prison, eventually calming him down. That night, the three of them lay in the same bed, with Mother in the middle, crowded, but feeling, strangely, safe.

7.

They survived the famine, but Father's situation had further deteriorated. When he walked, it was more like sidling, as if afraid of crushing the dust under his soles or disturbing his own shadow. When he talked, which was rare, his voice was between a whisper and breathing, as though afraid he would, out of carelessness, agitate the air. When he sat, he barely perched on the seat, in case he broke the chair with his body weight. Any sound would startle him—a clock ticking, plates clattering, children kicking a ball outside their door, footsteps passing on the street, Yuan Feng's stationery box clicking shut. Bright lights and colors made him cringe.

Mother learned to adapt, over the years, to Father's impossible habits, like water conforming itself to the contour of a twisted riverbed. Before Father came home from work, Mother would switch off the radio, any unnecessary lights, the whistling kettle, and Yuan Feng's tongue, to prevent noises not yet made. Yuan Feng was convinced Mother would have turned off the sun, the moon, the wind, and the rain too, if she could. The house was quiet before, but now a morgue.

"Do you want me to live the life of a rat, like him?" snapped Yuan Feng one day, when she was shushed, in the middle of memorizing a Tang poem for school, by Mother anticipating Father's return.

"But this rat brings food to the table," said Mother sarcastically.

"That's why you married him, wasn't it?" snorted Yuan Feng, unmindful of the abrasiveness in her words.

Mother was flabbergasted, realizing, for the first time, that her daughter, now twelve, had reached an age with ears open for gossip and a tongue to lash her own mother. But Mother remained silent.

The real answer revealed itself to Yuan Feng (then called Phoenix) almost half a century later, when Mother had been reduced to an urn, an ocean away from where the question had originally been asked. Too late, death outruns everything, including truth.

That evening, before going to bed, Mother gave Yuan Feng two fifty-cent bills. "For your swim camp registration," she said, turning off the bedside light. "Just come home right after." Yuan Feng had talked about joining the winter swim camp for months, but Mother had held off her approval till now.

Yuan Feng was a good student in all subjects, but not exceptional. The difference between the two might not be all that striking, but enough to make her a constant second choice, a most convenient *just-in-case*, a forever ready but seldom implemented plan B in any school event that called for preeminence.

School work was easy, leaving lots of spare time, much of which she devoted to reading. There weren't enough books around: Gorky, Mayakovski, and a little Pushkin and Balzac, in addition to a handful of national writers, were about all the names that could pass through the sieve of revolutionary ideology, its mesh getting finer each year. The excess energy, plentiful for a child her age, she decided to squander on swimming.

It was a casual pastime in the beginning. During summer months, when there was no school, she would go with a handful of girls from Town-head to a river called the Nine Hills—she never understood why a river should be named after a hill—within walking distance from home, for a dip to cool off. Nobody had ever taught her how to swim, but everything came naturally the minute she plunged into the water, as if she had been born for it.

The water of the Nine Hills was calm and translucent almost all year round, turning muddy only occasionally after a severe storm. Most parts of the river were narrow and shallow, making crossing a breeze. She could do laps and laps very early on, each lap, it seemed to her, easier than the last. She wondered whether she could have been a fish in a past life, though the idea of a previous life was a bad thought, as her teachers would say. For the atheist proletarians, which she thought she was one of, there was no God or Buddha, therefore no past life, or next.

As soon as she was in the water, she found her limbs quickly dissolved into fins and tail, and her body, boneless and weightless, free from traction, friction, and the pull of gravity that restrained her on land.

The water gave her a different set of eyes as well. She saw the blue of the river, the green of the reeds, and the white of the pebbles in the riverbed, but they were not the same as observed from ashore. They had an added pureness to them, as if freshly created, seen from an infant's unspoiled eyes. But creation, of course, was a wrong thought too.

The water was her own world, a world away from the other one onshore that she had to share with a mother who constantly shushed her, a father absent even while present, a sibling never to be had, and a featureless multitude she couldn't tell apart. The Nine Hills was a world of solitude, removing her from an uncaring and officious crowd, and giving her the peace that she couldn't find ashore.

She soon outgrew the Nine Hills, finding a far more exciting world in the Oujiang, the city's main river, compared with which the Nine Hills was a drooling baby. A casual summer pastime had, unexpectedly, evolved into a more regular routine as she joined the winter swim camp sponsored by the Youth Palace, with a group of kids, some her own age, others much older, nearly high school graduates.

During the years when Yuan Feng found solace in water, swimming had quickly become a national sport. Unlike basketball, tennis, baseball, or even football, which required a court, a bat, a stadium, or at least a pair of running shoes, which the populace, just emerging from a famine, found hard to scrimp and save for, swimming carried little cost other than for a swimsuit—if you were a girl. No pools were needed, as one could find water almost anywhere—a brook, a canal, a lake, a river, a sea—in a country with an abundant and intricate network of waterways.

Besides, their great leader, Chairman Mao, an enthusiastic swimmer himself, had set an illustrious example for them. Over the years, he had crossed the Yangtze quite a few times, and written a poem of such power and eloquence about his swimming experience that it soon found its way into school textbooks and various musical programs. Like a magic wand, his radiant smiles captured in photos turned a cheap pastime instantly into a national patriotic passion. *Build up a strong physical constitution to defend your country,* he said. One was either *in* or *out*.

In July of 1966, while Yuan Feng, turning thirteen, was approaching her target of a hundred laps across the Oujiang, the Great Leader, at age almost seventy-three, had just completed yet another crossing of the Yangtze. His eighteenth—the most sensational, final crossing—became an instant headline for every newspaper in the country. *Excellent health, vigor, stamina, extraordinary ability to lead, an immortal legend to be passed into posterity*, et cetera, et cetera.

Only in hindsight, when the dust finally settled, did people realize that the zealously celebrated crossing was a gesture, a fully charged but unspoken pep talk. A revolution, long brewing and unsurpassed by any before, was on the horizon. That was the message the Great One was delivering to the nation, from the swift water of the great Yangtze. Fair warning was given, but unheeded.

Revolutions were a frequent occurrence in those days, most of which bore a name with a clearly defined target: anti-feudalist, anti-imperialist, anti-revisionist, anti-rightist, anti-three-evils . . . But this one, by comparison, was a bit fuzzy: *the Great Proletarian Cultural Revolution*. Less harsh sounding, perhaps even faintly poetic, but in reality it was a superstorm, to be endured for the next decade to come, a general sweeping away, sparing nothing and no one.

Unlike the famine that had crept quietly into the house, the Cultural Revolution was a declared war, well publicized through every radio, every loudspeaker, and every newspaper. Mother was, nevertheless, still not fully prepared.

Can anyone really be prepared, though, for a revolution any more than for a famine? If anything, famine was more predictable, with its battlefield restricted to the kitchen, stove, and dinner table. But a revolution may ambush anyone, just about anywhere. A wrong hair style, a wrong choice of clothing, a wrong conversation with a wrong group, a wrong smile, a wrong parent, or a wrong past—one could find it waiting right around the corner.

One day Mother, on a routine trip to the vegetable market, ran into a man who stared at her, followed her around, and asked her hesitantly, "Have we met before?" With a vehement denial, Mother quickly fled, her shopping mission half-accomplished. The shadow of the revolution had since marched into her dreams, vivid, amorphous, but always in the same color, the color of blood.

Mother kept her nightmares to herself, not telling Yuan Feng (still too young) or Father (still, if not more, dumb headed). Besides, Father had his own hell to deal with. The revolution had broken into his dreams too, digging up his long-buried dirt: his early years of service in the Nationalist army. This, combined with the incident of his blasphemous shirt, was a sin no amount of reasoning or good deeds could cleanse or atone for. His forced conscription, his loyalty to the PLA army, and his war wounds, once a gleaming record of endurance and valor, now doubted, ridiculed, and negated. The start of the revolution found the great war hero turning, ignominiously, into an utterly despicable rotten apple.

8.

Father died a very slow death, losing his life in bits and pieces over a long course of years. When the Japanese bullets riddled his right leg, they took a scoop of his vigor and half an inch of his manhood. Then the American shrapnel scraped off a piece of his brain, leaving it behind in Korea. His pool of self-respect was depleted, on a separate occasion, when he was knocked down on the ground, bleeding, pockets filled with Taiwanese rice. The loss of his pride was, by comparison, a swifter act, when his war medal was stripped away before an audience of three thousand coworkers.

The seed of death had been sown perhaps much earlier, when he was taken away, at seventeen, from his family and the land where he, his father, and his father's father were born and raised. That he had managed to live for so long, as a rootless plant floating on the surface of thin soil, was a miracle by itself.

The Revolutionary Committee at the metallurgical plant, a new power structure that had sprung from the revolution, locked on to Father as an easy target but soon discovered, to their chagrin, that their eager sweeping broom had erred in its choice.

When brought in for rounds of interrogation, Father wore, invariably, a vacuous smile often seen in a child, accompanied by a uniform answer to every question asked: "I guess not." His interrogators didn't know it was his fear reflex at work. It took them a while to realize that what they wrung out of him was nothing but strings of disjointed utterances, devoid of meaning or logic.

The time spent in the interrogation room was not a total waste. While it yielded little information, it produced age—Father gained a year or two each time he was let out. There was no point in Mother seeking intervention this time, because she had neither the old medal nor any new tears to speak for her. Besides, Mayor Song himself had sunk lower than Father, having recently been put under house arrest. After months of fruitless efforts, the committee finally lost interest in Father. What fun could one derive from kicking, however fiercely, a sack of cotton? Reaction, which Father was incapable of, was necessary to fuel a lasting zeal. One couldn't squeeze blood, after all, out of a stone.

Father's file was eventually sealed in a big brown envelope and put away in a cabinet to collect dust, waiting for a new set of hands spawned by a new revolution to unseal and disturb it.

The day Father came home from the last round of interrogation, the only part keenly alive in him was his stomach. Sitting down at the dinner table, quiet as usual, he wolfed down two huge bowls, both filled to the brim, of the steaming-hot egg noodles Mother had freshly prepared. Yuan Feng could smell, across the table, the odor of his body, unbathed for days, and of his mind, too long in disuse, growing rotten and foul. She didn't speak, but the loathing in her eyes said it all.

"A living dead," she said to Mother, with all the cruelty of a four-teen-year-old, when they were alone in the kitchen clearing away dirty dishes. Mother stared at her in a stupor of hurt, then hurled the dish towel against the wall. With a dull smack, the towel stuck to the wall like a battered flag, water dripping, pit-a-pat, onto the dirt floor, forming a small, dark puddle.

"Do you think he wants to live, like this?" Mother blurted out, in an undertone. "He wanted to die when he came back from Korea. I begged him to live, for me, because I wanted a child. Where do you think you'd be without him, eh?"

Yuan Feng felt a tingling chill traveling down her body, all the way to her toes, shaking her with a new awareness of the weight on her life: the original guilt.

9.

Father hung on for another year, thinner than air, drifting around in a gray zone of subexistence. During the last few months of his life, people at his workplace no longer paid any attention to him. He was half-invisible; even the wind sweeping through the street would bypass him, for lack of interest. Mother noticed, one sultry summer night, that Father no longer needed a mosquito net, as the insects were repelled by the rancid smell of his blood.

However, he managed to shock them—his wife and daughter—with his last act before death, leaving one final, indelible mark on Yuan Feng's memory. A dead cat bouncing, in the words of the commonfolk, or the final radiance of a setting sun, if one chose to be melodramatic.

Father died in the winter of 1968, three days before the New Year.

It was a gloomy day, turning to snow in the afternoon, a rare event for a subtropical city like Wenzhou. Was it a sign from heaven, Yuan Feng would later wonder, to mark Father's farewell to this world? Not even forty-two years, a brief life of dramatic rise and fall. Tragicomic, as one might say.

The snow was getting quite heavy towards the evening, the city soon losing its color and contour to a fluffy cover of glistening white. Onto the streets, houses disgorged kids, most of whom had never known snow before, now having one hell of a time running around throwing snowballs, generating a dreadful racket. Mother was out there too, helping Yuan Feng and two of the neighborhood girls build a snowman.

Every now and then, Mother would pause and simply watch them play, overwhelmed by the mere fact of their young, exuberant existence. *This cursed year is finally coming to an end,* she thought, savoring a moment of peace so rare that she felt almost dizzy.

A neighbor, who happened to be a photographer, took a picture of the girls and their half-finished snowman. This picture had miraculously survived a long succession of years and moves, following Yuan Feng—or Phoenix as she later came to be known—all the way to Toronto. Every time she laid eyes on it, now turning brown and fuzzy, she would almost automatically recall the day it was taken.

It was the day she lost her father.

Father got home around the usual time but dinner was late, as Mother and Yuan Feng had just returned from their wild excursion in the snow. He went straight to his own room, lighting his first cigarette of the evening. Smoke crept out of the door that was left ajar, a signal to announce his mute presence.

"Did you get wet from the snow?" asked Mother from the kitchen, while fanning the stove to boost the fire for the rice.

Father mumbled something back that they didn't quite catch, but neither of them pressed him further. Silence fell, a silence they had got so used to by then.

Suddenly, Mother felt the growing weight of her fan and became aware, a moment later, of a shadow cast on her hand. Looking up, she saw a man emerging from the space between the kitchen and the eating area where the lamplight was dim. She jumped as if seeing a ghost, remembering that this was the man who had followed her in the vegetable market a while ago.

"Who are you? How did you get in?" Yuan Feng paused in the middle of peeling carrots, her brows knitted with suspicion.

"Well, your door isn't locked. Who am I? You'd better ask your mother." The man smiled forth a greeting, with an air bordering on familiarity. "I bet she remembers me, Little Tiger, the errand boy, but not so little anymore."

"No, I don't know you," replied Mother, a slight tremor in her voice.

"Come on, Fumie, you've got to remember me, you and your sister, after what they did to me." The man invited himself into the kitchen, splaying his right hand before Mother, three fingers missing, their stubs dark with craggy scars.

Turning away from the gruesome sight, Yuan Feng let out a whimper, but was immediately shushed by Mother.

"I don't have a sister," retorted Mother, eyes cast sideways, increasingly uneasy about having lied in front of her daughter.

"Yes, you do. Sachie, that's her name," the man insisted.

The pot started to boil, the broth spilling over, sizzling noisily on the brim of the stove, permeating the room with the fragrance of half-cooked rice.

"What do you want from me?" asked Mother feebly. Her fan dropped to the floor but she didn't bother to pick it up.

"With my hand, it's a right hand too, I can't get any job. I've lived like a beggar for years. You can surely lend me a hand," the man said, pleading.

"Do I look like somebody loaded? I don't even have a job." Mother stood up, moved the peeled carrots over to the cutting board, and started chopping.

"I've done some digging. Your man served in the army, has a government job. For sure he can spare a few pennies, for an *old* friend like me." He put extra stress on the word *old*, as if it were too flimsy to stand on its own.

"Leave him out of it!" roared Mother, throwing herself without the slightest warning against the man, who, blindsided, staggered and nearly fell but quickly regained his equilibrium, grabbing Mother by the wrist to keep her still.

"Calm down, Fumie. I've lowered myself to begging, you sure don't want me to tell your daughter . . ." He stopped short as he felt a nudge on the small of his back. Turning around, he saw a man, tall but hunched, with graying hair smelling faintly of engine oil and cigarettes. As they locked eyes, sizing up each other, he saw the tall man's eyes melting like wax in a blaze of wrath.

The thing the tall man was holding against him was an ax, Little Tiger soon realized. He began to shake, soaking in his own cold sweat.

"If I see you again, this is what you get." The tall man swung the ax at the dinner table with the force needed for a sledgehammer. With a loud thud, its pinewood top—worn smooth by years of use—swallowed the grave insult, suffering a raw, gaping wound.

The intruder's eyes, nearly blinded by the flashing blade of the swinging ax, darted away, skipping around the room aimlessly before finding Mother's. He looked at her imploringly, petrified and deplorably lost.

"Get out!" Mother hissed between her teeth, motioning him towards the door.

The man, taking his cue, leaped away as fast as he could, leaving an echo of hurried footsteps in the snow-covered street.

Mother doubled over as if in searing pain, burying her face in her hands, a trembling mess from head to toe. Father rubbed his hands hopelessly after trying in vain to help her up.

"Gone, Chunyu, him, safe, all past." Father muttered the string of words, blurred and incoherent, as much to himself as to Mother, waiting for a response that never arrived. Neither Mother nor Yuan Feng noticed his disappearance, quiet as usual, back to his own room.

Silence returned, not the same one, though—nothing would be the same after Little Tiger. This new silence, like liquid cement, seeped in, filling every crack the commotion had caused.

Yuan Feng slowly emerged from the corner and began to chop the carrots left by Mother on the cutting board. The knife slipped, paring off a small piece of skin on one of her fingers. She stuck the wounded finger into her mouth and sucked it, a bit salty and metallic, the taste of blood. Gagging with disgust, she spit out the saliva, dipping her finger into a basin of water intended for rinsing the sliced carrots.

A thin red thread appeared in the water, dancing and swelling into a coral-colored stream, then blossoming into a pink flower. She couldn't help but be mesmerized by the wild images the bloody water conjured up in her mind. A setting sun, a blotch of spilled tomato juice, a petal falling from a blooming peony, a blushed cheek, everything but the glistening cold knife blade that had bred them.

"Who's that man?" asked Yuan Feng.

"I don't know," Mother managed to say between half sobs.

"Why did he call you Fumie?" she persisted.

"I don't know."

Yuan Feng stopped asking questions, knowing she would get the same answer.

Dinner was finally ready, but Father didn't come out of his room despite Mother's repeated calling. Yuan Feng was sent in to check. The room was dark and dead quiet, her footsteps bouncing around the walls, startling her. Switching the light on, she saw Father lying in bed, foaming at the mouth, eyes shut tight, unconscious.

Hearing her scream, Mother burst into the room and tried to shake Father awake. Failing at that, she rushed out the door without bothering with her cotton-padded jacket, towards the community clinic two blocks away, hoping to fetch a doctor on duty.

Yuan Feng was left alone with Father and the shadow of death she was too young to recognize.

She sat at his bedside, holding his hand in hers, watching his body convulse slightly, his breathing growing more labored. A numbness washed over her, with no sense of sadness or fear.

"Pa, please wait for Ma, please wait." She heard herself repeating, over and over again, the same words mechanically, as if going through a rigid drill in an English grammar class.

Suddenly, she sensed a slight twitch, a finger moving in her fist. Father's eyes popped open abruptly, so wide that they seemed to have held all of her in them. "Blood, swear, your ma . . . ," he mumbled, nearly unintelligible.

She was perplexed, only for a second, then suddenly understood. She leaned over, showing him her wounded finger that had been hastily bandaged, with a speck of dried blood on the gauze.

"Pa, I swear by my blood, I'll look after Ma." She squeezed his hand tight.

A dark cloud spread over his face, and his eyes dimmed.

Chapter III

THE MEMORY OF A YOUNG TEACHER AND TOSSING WATERS

Email from George to Phoenix, 2011.10.22 @ 22:17 Eastern Standard Time

Dear Nix,

Called your cell several times, it kept telling me the number is not in service. Called your room too, no answer. Guess you're at Auntie Mei's. Give me her number just in case, I need to hear your voice. The night is long and the house is big.

This blue, mopey man tried to kill time by reading more of your manuscript, but I had no idea what I was getting into. How much do I know you, Nix, if I know you at all? We've talked a lot about "the pearl" in your mother's oyster, but little did I know that you have your pearl in your oyster too. Maybe we all have our own pearl in our own oyster. In searching for other people's pearls, we might inadvertently open up our own shells. Revelation can be cruel. Reading about your earlier life hurts me A

LITTLE, because of what you were put through, and also because I wasn't there for you.

There is another layer of hurt I was debating whether I should tell you about. I've been made aware of the precarious position I am in: a pair of shriveled arthritic feet trying to fill some giant-size shoes. That handsome, young teacher came out so vividly in your writing: one can smell his charm from three miles away. He ushered you into the world of English. From the grandiose "long live . . ." to the small talk about weather, what an evolution! He opened your eyes and led you through so many doors that I wonder whether there are any left for me to open and for you to enter? I can feel the pain of your loss, the flinching and burning kind, as if it were just yesterday. Can anyone (except Job maybe) ever get over a loss like this? But you did.

Did you?

Please excuse my rambling. All I am really trying to say (and I don't know how to say it properly) is that I hate myself for having missed so much of your life.

George

P.S. If your jet lag is still bothering you, just get out of bed and do something totally stupid. Watch a boring movie, read a computer manual, smell your stinky socks, whatever tires your mind out, then sleep will find you.

Email from Phoenix to George, 2011.10.24 @ 01:17 China Standard Time

Dear George,

Did I hear a little cry somewhere? I didn't expect a reaction like this. Was there a trace of jealousy too? One never fails to discover new traits, even in an old dog. My dear dear old George.

Meng Long is my memory. I kept him alive for decades until I put him in words and lines, then I killed him. Writers are murderers: we give life and then take it away, in a most premeditated way. Did I say "we"? How shameless—I haven't published even one book. The minute I put Meng Long in writing, he leaves me and becomes a part of whoever reads these pages, you included.

Wise men use their memory as if it were some sort of fertilizer. "We grow from our past experiences," they would brag. I am a fool and I use my memory as if it were a pillow, to sleep and to dream on. If I ever need fertilizer, I run to Canadian Tire. Besides, I've done my growing, for the most part, anyway. Does it sound like consolation?

However, the idea of filling somebody's shoes sounds vaguely intriguing to me: it keeps you in line. If I have to pick a vice to fight, I will choose complacency over insecurity, every time.

Did you add the area code when you dialed my cell? It's a local number so needs area code. Auntie Mei's number was left on the fridge door on a sticker (with a bunch of appointment dates), you probably overlooked it. Use her number sparingly, she hates to answer the phone— telephone fraud is rampant here.

I visit Auntie Mei every day. She is in good shape and keeps herself busy. It's amazing to see the way she enjoys food—I remember you said the same thing about me when we first met. She talks about Ma and their young days, but on her terms only—she doesn't like to be squeezed. The more I learn, the more I feel I've been left out of something important. I can't figure out what's holding her back. Revelation is indeed cruel, and truth is expensive. At times I wonder whether I can afford it.

It's your Sunday, so call me now, I can't sleep anyway. I have a feeling that somebody is in dire need of comforting, although I am supposed to be the one that's bruised and heartbroken.

Nix

Email from Phoenix to George, 2011.10.28 @ 16:11 China Standard Time

Hi George,

I can't call you since it's your 4 AM, besides, the international airtime is a killer. But I really need to talk to someone before I explode. So I write.

I just found out that Ma and Auntie Mei have thirteen half sisters from the same father and one half brother from the same mother. Imagine the number of cousins! A day ago, I had none, now I have a kingdom. What math is this? Sounds like a weird story in Arabian Nights. Shake me awake. Remember you asked me why Ma was so alone and cut off? Only Auntie Mei holds the key to the answer. I am coming awfully close to it now, if my poor nerves can hold up. I've been diligently writing down everything she tells me.

I've booked a train ticket to Wenzhou tomorrow to arrange for Ma's interment. Auntie Mei is getting edgy with the urn in her room (to be precise, in her closet).

Nix

Email from George to Phoenix, 2011.10.29 @ 19:49 Eastern Standard Time

Dear Nix,

I'm still recovering from the shock. Even Aisha can't compete with you re: the size of the extended family now. There has to be a better reason for the cut off than just "do not like each other." Fourteen siblings, that's a lot of falling-out to do.

Part of me feels relieved hearing you talk about it— you were awfully quiet in Toronto, which worried me. Wondered what kind of bomb Auntie Mei would drop next. We were so engrossed in the subject on the phone that I forgot to tell you I've done more proofreading on your manuscript. Here I attach the finished part just in case you want to work on it further. Will talk more about it. Soon.

George

* Email attachment: Phoenix's manuscript *Teacher*

1.

The post-Father era wasn't much different from a post-war era, starting with a tallying of losses, what's gone and what's left, to be followed by a redivision of territory and a regrouping of resources. A new balance sheet.

Father didn't take much with him, really: a presence at the dinner table, a scent of smoke and unwashed hair—not in its entirety, though, as some of it had already seeped into the pores of the plastered walls and needed a bit of time to dissipate. Of course, there was the loss of that small envelope containing his monthly salary, a minor detail, hardly a worry.

What he left behind was much more substantial, a house suddenly bigger (you'd hardly have noticed him taking up much space at all when he was around), a bed his daughter Yuan Feng could finally call her own, a silence to be broken at one's will, and two sets of vocal cords growing bold and versatile, for bursts of anger, wails of grief, and occasionally, tunes mimicking the radio music.

Father's death changed the math of all things—his past, his wife's present, and his daughter's future, the sum total of the three amounting to a new reality, grim and fuzzy. Father's monthly salary had been forty-five yuan and was now reduced to a fifteen-yuan widow's allowance until Yuan Feng turned sixteen, the legal working age.

Hearing the decision, Mother burst into the canteen at the metallurgical plant with her daughter tagging behind, stopping the Revolutionary Committee chairman in the middle of his lunch. "Fifteen yuan, who do you kid? Not enough to feed a bird. Never mind an old mare like me, but he's got a daughter, a revolutionary youth, ready to take over the torch one day, and you dare to starve her!"

A crowd started to gather, just the kind of audience Mother was hoping for. Her black armband of bereavement, like a warrior's fire-licked flag, was burning a hole in their eyes, she was fully aware. She knew exactly what she was doing.

"Poor thing." Someone heaved a sigh, audible but unechoed, while the rest slowly formed a circle around them in silence. There was a smell to their silence, which Mother's nose quickly picked up. A smell of sympathy, or rather, pity—Mother liked to call a spade a spade. A pity mingled with fear, the fear of ending up the same way, or worse.

Father, the dumb head, had never struck up much of a friendship with anyone in the plant and, by the same token, he had no real enemies either. His absence didn't break any hearts. He was forgotten, until now, when the dust was stirred up by his widow, a woman with her looks fading but not totally gone yet. She came to disturb their lunch, and their peace of mind.

"Ma, don't make a scene, please," Yuan Feng begged in a whisper, suddenly envying Father, who no longer had to be a part of the theatrics.

A scene indeed, but that's exactly what Mother had intended. Yuan Feng was too young to understand the tricks of a dogs' land where barking was the only language that was heard.

"He fought two wars, in blood and sweat, to save us, shame on you, to treat his family like this!" Ignoring Yuan Feng, Mother decided to ride along on the tide she knew was in her favor. She hadn't totally lost her mind. There was enough sanity left in her for her to subtract, at the last minute, the wrong war, the war against the Communists, from Father's military record.

The chairman, long used to unchallenged authority, was utterly unprepared for such an assault, his neck turning scarlet under a face that was chalk white. In a rage fueled by shock and humiliation, he ranted at Mother at the top of his lungs. "Count yourself lucky, woman, that he didn't die in prison. He's not entitled to anything, *nil, zero, zilch*, with what he did! It's a gift of mercy—you take it or leave it." He stormed out of the canteen, leaving behind a lunch unfinished and a trail of angry dust.

Mother left shortly after, dejected, without saying a word to Yuan Feng on their way home. For the next few days, she was on pins and needles, uncertain whether she would lose the allowance, meager as it was, altogether.

But on the first of the month, she received her first allowance. Eighteen yuan, a real surprise.

Barking had, after all, worked, gaining her an inch if not a foot.

Keeping the eighteen yuan going till the end of the month required creativity combined with precision.

Mother came to learn, very quickly, that 4:30 p.m., half an hour before the market's closing, was the best time to shop, as the peddlers, some from afar and reluctant to walk home with a load, were willing to sell their leftovers at half price, or even a third. Rare treasures could be found too, among the refuse disgorged by a tired market. Bean sprouts with rotten roots, for example, potatoes that had grown eyes, fish with their bellies burst open, and even a box of moon cakes with a few spots of mildew.

Nothing in this world is totally spoiled, if one thinks about it. There is always some part left worth salvaging. A vigorous rinsing will take care of it, Mother argued, with a philosopher's wisdom, a scientist's cool, and a beggar's pride.

Amid all the chaos, there was at least one certainty, some might even call it a blessing, that made Mother's monthly budget not utterly impossible. It was the absence of inflation, as the state held the padlock to the supply-and-demand chain. There was no need for hoarding; the money she had spent yesterday for a postage stamp would get her the same stamp today, tomorrow, or the day after, only with a prettier design.

Shopping and cooking put only a small dent in Mother's time, the rest of which she spent, lavishly, on her newly procured assortment of odd jobs—piecework mostly, including, but not limited to, pasting envelopes and matchboxes, knitting children's sweaters, and babysitting neighbors' kids.

These tasks wormed into her time as well as space, filling every corner of the house with an entourage of tools and accessories. Bottles of glue and milk, jars of paste, balls of yarn and wool, brushes and knitting needles of every size, scissors and blades, a bamboo baby walker, several basins to hold soiled diapers, bags of saponins, et cetera. If she got really lucky, by the end of the month, her odd jobs might add eight yuan to her purse.

This was Mother's life, in the post-Father era, overlapping, only partially, with that of her daughter, as Yuan Feng had her own mess to sort out, new skills to learn, old habits to get rid of.

Yuan Feng had quickly become, through diligent practice, a good letter writer, letters addressed to different offices but with the same kind of purpose: a waiver of fees for schoolbooks and incidentals, swim camp registration (she still swam), field trip program enrollment, et cetera. Letters she would compose, in neat and respectful handwriting, invariably starting with "As a devoted patriotic youth from a poor proletarian family . . ." A bit theatrical, perhaps, but a savvy way to get things done. The first tear into her adolescent pride was painful, but she was surprised to discover how soon the scar stopped stinging.

There were things, however, one couldn't get a waiver for: an ice pop on a scorching summer afternoon, for example, or a new jacket for New Year's Day, a tradition she had to cheat with one of Mother's hand-me-downs, or a school outing with a small lunch fee, which she would dodge by sundry excuses (a headache, an upset stomach, a bereaved mother, or a sick cat).

It'd be soon over, all this, she consoled herself. She would turn sixteen in the fall, old enough to be a working girl, earning a living, however meager, that would help to dig them out of the rathole.

"Over my dead body you can quit school," Mother declared, face set with a resolution that only death could thaw. Mother was still delusional, Yuan Feng figured, refusing to shake off the pathetic damn nonsense of a phoenix rising from ashes and leading a glorious flock.

Yuan Feng's post-Father era had a magnificently smooth start, as she had—or she thought she had—shed her old skin and grown a new one immune to feelings. A spill of blood, a quick fix, a thorough makeover, then a clean slate: those were terms she would use, if asked, to describe her process of metamorphosis. When there was no shame, there was no fear, hence no hurt.

On the occasional nights when sleep refused to come, she had imagined herself marching into her sixteenth year of life, dirt poor, but free as a bird—a sparrow, not a phoenix—with no anticipation, and therefore no disappointment.

Until she met Meng Long.

2.

Down with the imperialism and all its running dogs!

Long live Chairman Mao!

Meng Long put down these two lines, slowly and elaborately, on the blackboard, every letter a work of art. The arc of his arm when he wrote, the care with which his fingers held the chalk as if it would melt, the swaying of a stray strand of hair to the undulation of his voice, the gentle nature of every move he made. So out of place, but so fascinating.

English as a subject had been recently added back to the school curriculum to replace Russian, not because the Americans were hated any less, but because the Russians were loathed even more. Learning the alphabet could wait, as could grammar. In the era of revolution, ideas had no patience to stand in the queue, behind such trivial matters as phonetics and conjugation rules.

The curves, lines, and dots, with their alien fluidity, mesmerized Yuan Feng. What kind of a language, she wondered, could these strange letters build, and what ideas could they carry? It reminded her, by some freakish association, of petals on the surface of calm water, slow dances in soft moonlight, and *love*. The very word made her blush, suddenly conscious of her drab clothing and short, tomboyish hair—Mother chopped her braids off in the summer for fear of attracting lice. How long would it take to grow it out? Two months? A semester? She would be long dead.

She was a little surprised when Meng Long, their English teacher, wrote the Chinese translation beside the English words on the blackboard. This new language, with all its flourishing, foreign looks, could actually be used, in much the same way as her native tongue, to build the same roaring statement, a declaration of war. *A new bottle for old wine*, as Mother would say.

If Yuan Feng had been asked to remember one thing, and one thing only, about Meng Long, she probably would have singled out his eyes. Large, deep set, and prominent, glowing with experience not quite tarnished by cynicism, inviting and deterring all at once. This guarded charm drew her to him, almost instantly, like a moth to the flame.

She would, without a moment's hesitation, have thrown herself at his feet, laying bare her young guileless passion, all of it, to be consumed in a flicker of brilliance, and then to end in a wisp of smoke. To live in a moment of splendor, and then to die forever. At sixteen, death is spelled differently.

But she had to mention his voice too. How could she not? Blue ocean waves rubbing, titillatingly, against the gray folds of her brain—that's how she came to think of it. An ocean that could be choppy at times, but mostly calm, transporting her to a shore she knew, by instinct, to be safe. His voice came, in time, to rescue her from a world inundated with screaming, roaring, clapping, and stomping, fanned by a crazed enthusiasm, all in the name of revolution.

It was also hard not to notice his clothes, or rather, his style of clothing. While the whole nation was taking pride in faded olive and navy-blue cotton outfits, a cheap imitation of military and police uniforms and an ardent cry of hero worship, he wore a demure gray cotton jacket in a traditional style, with a straight collar and rounded shoulders, a safe territory between blending in and standing out, far enough from *them*, yet not so close as to rouse the suspicion of *us*.

He couldn't entirely suppress his desire to be different from the madding crowd. A faint gesture, for example, in the form of a black woolen scarf, casually slung over the shoulder, fluttering, as he walked in the wind, against the solid gray of his jacket. His fashion statement, subtle, but there. It was a birthday present knitted by his late wife, according to a reliable source, which he wore throughout the long months from fall to spring, as if his neck was the part of his body most vulnerable to the assault of the elements. You might find chalk dust on the scarf, but never dandruff.

And his scent too, of fresh soap, when he leaned over to ask her a question, reducing her, instantly, to tatters, face burning like a kerosene lamp, tongue tied into a dead knot.

No, it was simply impossible for her to pick out one thing about him, from the intricate web of all things. The memory of Meng Long was all in one, and one in all.

Many years later, when she, as Phoenix, sat in a classroom at the University of Toronto, taking a course in poetry, the distant past, out of nowhere, launched a fierce attack, hitting her so hard that it almost jolted her out of her seat.

If there was ever such a thing as Creation in the way Milton described in his poems, then Meng Long must have been created on a fine spring day, the fairest of the fair, when God had just awakened from the nap of the century, completely refreshed, with the sweetest cup of nectar beside him, in the bestest of moods. There wasn't a soul before him, in Yuan Feng's eyes, that was quite like him.

She cursed him, throughout her adult years, with a bitterness that only love could brew, for he had molded, inextricably, her taste in men. A brother she had never had; a father whom she had lost before she was old enough to understand his struggle to live in the shady space between a pea brain and a cosmos-size heart; a lover she so intensely desired that her body ached and her soul went blind; a thorn in her flesh she could never remove, he was all of them.

In the long years after him, she had searched for him, from bed to bed, relationship to relationship, in other men. Time and again, she led herself to believe that she was almost there, so close, until she realized, with chilling despair, that it was just a dream away.

3.

A week before Meng Long reported for his teaching duty in Wenzhou, a thick brown envelope containing his personnel files—a track record, one might say—arrived in the school, leaving enough time for rumor to ripen and reputation to rot.

His records were intended exclusively for the eyes of the Revolutionary Committee, but every member had a friend or a cousin. A secret was meant to entice and be shared, always for the next pair of ears to keep. The day Meng Long walked into the reception office with a pathetically slim canvas bag, which was all he had as luggage, he didn't know he was naked. Everybody in the school held a piece of his life; even Yuan Feng, a lowly student—and there were nearly two thousand of them—had grabbed hold of a corner of his sensational past.

Very few people had a chance to read the contents in the brown envelope, but who wanted the official version that bored you to tears with dates, signatures, and red seals while there were vivid and spicy unofficial accounts to be had? So the moment the first detail from the envelope leaped into the first pair of ears, the journey began, from tongue to tongue, each adding its own dye and flavor. In no time, a story was born. It kept evolving, as time went on, with a few more twists and turns here and there. The anecdotes of Meng Long's past, a blur of fact and fancy, stirred the stagnant air of a stagnant school, like good sex.

Meng Long had graduated from Peking University, the best school in the country. He stayed on after graduation, first as a lecturer, then a professor, one of the youngest, until 1957, when he threw himself quite literally, as one version went, into the swirl of the Anti-Rightist Movement. The story of his fall was quite dramatic, or melodramatic, depending on your taste.

Rumor had it that there was a plan, implicit and unstated, from high above: a targeted percentage of people had to be branded as Rightists. This put the chair of the Party at the university, who was a slow thinker and an awkward time server, between a rock and a hard place. On the one hand, a quota had to be filled and, on the other, there were innocent people to be spared—they were arrogant, stinking assholes maybe, but no enemy of the state.

At his wit's end, he called a general staff meeting to lay the issue on the table, hoping some hotheads would volunteer themselves for the journey to hell. But there was a dead silence. The air grew so thick and brittle that any sound, a burp, a sneeze, or a fart, might cause a crack.

In the middle of the deadlock, as fate would have it, Meng Long felt the urgent call of nature and made a trip to the bathroom. Upon returning, he found himself, at twenty-three, the newest and one of the youngest members of the Rightist club. He was removed, instantly, from his teaching position and demoted to a community-run library as a staff worker, a relatively lenient punishment.

What happened to him—if the story had any merit to it—could very well be described as pure bad luck, but he was not totally blameless either. He had said things, in his literature class, that were dangerously close to getting on someone's nerves.

"A true patriot does not need to limit his love for mankind to his own nation, because truth has no geographical boundary," he once proclaimed to a large audience of students. "Lord Byron is more fondly remembered in Greece for his fight for their independence. Elizabeth Browning wrote *Poems before Congress*, a scathing criticism against her own country for its indifference to the sufferings of the Italians. No one views them as unpatriotic."

He met his wife at his new job, a young physicist from the Academy of Sciences before she became a janitor in the library, another member sentenced to the Rightist club for making derogatory comments about the tilting of the scale in favor of engineering (which she considered a working tool) over science (the truth about the universe). "Science is a universal language," she asserted, fervently, "it's not a possession of any class, capitalist or proletarian."

Later, when they compared notes on the nature of their sins, they couldn't help but be amused. A poetry lover and a physicist, from two paths of life that couldn't have been any further apart, were brought together by a freakish turn of events for a belief they didn't even know they shared. Neither of them had expected their internationalistic views, casual and half-minded, would lead them to their common doom.

Very soon they were granted permission, by the committee at the library, to marry. "It's better for birds of the same feather to stay in the same nest," declared the chair, "instead of poisoning other innocent minds."

She worked a long shift beyond the regular hours, sharing with another janitor the duty of cleaning thirty-six rooms located on three floors. Arriving home exhausted, she no longer read, wrote, or engaged in anything remotely intellectual. He made love to her, every now and then. She'd fall asleep, at times, right in the middle, leaving him hanging with a desire half-quenched, and full of guilt.

She quickly picked up the hobby of knitting and crocheting, filling their dorm with mittens, hats, sweaters, scarves, string bags, socks, enough to tide over ten winters. Observing her engrossed in such a mindless and repetitive task before dozing off in the chair, a close image of a contented wife, he almost believed that she had made her peace with the world.

What a damn fool he had been, so deaf, and so blind.

He still read—Shakespeare, Wordsworth, Byron, Milton, Whitman—not from physical books, as they were banned, but from the lines etched into his memory, which he could retrieve, in meditation, accurate to the last punctuation mark. His continued intellectual interest surprised and irritated her all at once. She would, in the midst of knitting, pause and stare him in the face. *How can you, as if nothing had happened?* He suddenly understood her mute outrage, and was stunned by her bitterness and ashamed of his lack of defense.

"Just look at Puyi, selling door passes," he murmured, a smidge of shameful uncertainty in his voice. He was referring to the last emperor, now a commoner working in the Peking Botanical Garden, earning his bread with a pair of royal hands born for gold, silk, and worship. *What can't be cured must be endured* was the answer at the tip of his tongue, but finding it a cliché, he decided to swallow it. He had borne his fate as it came, with a quiet, almost submissive acceptance, until he met his wife, who made him feel uneasy for the first time about his resigned state of mind.

Then, a decade later, when he met Yuan Feng's mother, Yuan Chunyu, he suddenly saw a clear reflection of himself in her. Bad luck didn't just happen to them by chance. It had, in some freakish way, spotted them and picked them out of the faceless crowd, by the mark fate had branded on them, like an ear-tagged cow or a tattooed horse. Born conservationists, they knew, in their blood, how to minimize the consumption of life's sap, saving every drop for the most needed moment. They wore out the bad luck, in the end.

His wife, on the contrary, did not share his attitude, finding it debilitating and morbid. Only after she was gone did he realize that they were truly from two different planets.

The world, to a physicist's eye, came in the form of lines, numbers, and equations. His wife was contemptuous of adjectives, emotions, and poetry, dismissing them as fuzzy, unreliable, and therefore on the verge of absurdity. She had little faith in conclusions not derived from data and statements that couldn't be quantified. The lever that sustained the delicate equilibrium of the universe, according to her, was truth and truth alone. Any acceptance or even acquiescence to a lie was more heinous to her than a prejudiced opinion, because the latter was the result of ignorance that could be redressed through knowledge and time, while the former was committed with full knowing.

One morning, she was found in a pool of blood outside the library, dead. A thirty-minute police investigation yielded the quick conclusion that she fell from the roof of the building, by accident.

But their doctor revealed something quite shocking to him. A few weeks later, upon a visit to the clinic for a persistent cold, he found out that his late wife was four months pregnant at the time of her death. She was hesitant, the doctor told him, about whether to bring a life into the world from the pit she was in.

All the dots suddenly connected.

That night, he brought home a bottle of sorghum liquor, the cheapest kind from a cheap corner store, and invited her to a drink—or rather, her picture, now in a black frame of mourning. Their first time ever, and their last. It struck him, in a moment of insight, that the three years of their marriage must have been the loneliest days of her life, so lonely that she would tear her heart out for a stranger rather than her own husband.

When she stood on the rooftop, looking down on the street that changed little from day to day, she must have thought about flying, an attempt to free herself from the grip of gravity, her last and loudest cry against the world of nontruth unheard.

He buried her and returned to work the next day, quiet and impassive, but his coworkers noticed his hands shaking while he was working on the index cards. His grief, and the way he bore it, opened the door to a few tender hearts. Invitations started to come his way, to weekend basketball matches, an occasional group outing, a New Year's gathering, and even a wedding. He never pushed away any gesture of friendship, but everyone knew, deep down, that he was not one of them.

When his Rightist label was twelve years old, a chance for a pardon floated in the air, so close that he could almost smell it, but it slipped from his fingertips at the last moment because of a wrong letter arriving at the wrong time.

It was from his mother, who, while fleeing the Communist takeover in 1949, had abandoned her husband and son, then fifteen, and boarded one of the last boats with her lover to Hong Kong, a British colony, a rotten *imperialist land*. In her letter, his mother asked him to join her in Hong Kong and then leave together for Canada. He never wrote back but didn't turn the letter over to the all-knowing committee either, until too late.

The punishment for a repeat offender came in harsher terms. He was banished to Wenzhou, almost a village compared with the national capital, to teach English to a bunch of middle-school kids who had never even seen the alphabet.

4.

It had been a while since Yuan Feng last swam in the Nine Hills River. The water had a different feel. October in Wenzhou was not to be trusted; it was a tug of war between the tail of summer and the beak of winter. A gust of wind, a drop of rain, or a passing cloud could tip the scale in an instant.

It was really a fine day, to be fair. The right dose of sun, light, breeze, and cloud, just the vibrant sort of day to convince you that the world wasn't out to get you. If you had the right frame of mind, you might even think that you were out to get the world. But Yuan Feng didn't have the right frame of mind then. She was sulking.

Actually, her sulky mood had started last night. In the gray zone between sleep and waking, the list—the same old list of the things she needed—popped up again, gnawing away at whatever was left of the peace she had brought to bed. While the order of things might shift from day to day, the top item had always been consistent.

A new swimsuit.

Her sixteen-year-old body had been trapped in a suit meant for a thirteen-year-old. Her breasts were the first to rebel against the oppressive fabric, which was now losing much of its color and elasticity and becoming a mere rag. She hated her beastly breasts more than she did the swimsuit. But she could do nothing about them, other than adopting a slouching posture, as if to apologize for the attention they drew, much the same way as Father did for his height. Too ashamed of her body, at the mercy of a mocking swimsuit, she withdrew from the swimming program at the Youth Palace.

She also needed a new bra, two sizes bigger, and a new pair of socks. Most of her class, including the two girls from the outskirts of town, had changed into nylon socks, the new invention, the *in* thing, but she still wore the antique socks knitted with cotton threads salvaged from Mother's worn-out sweater.

A new school bag would be nice too. The one she was using now, a gift when she entered middle school, had a hole around the corner, through which her favorite ballpoint pen had made its bold escape. The new bag, nonetheless, could be moved around on the chessboard of her mind as "needed but not essential." A good mending might easily add another six months to its life.

She had been to the department store a hundred times to check prices. A swimsuit in solid blue without a floral print, the most basic style, was 3.20 yuan. It was 1.30 yuan for a bra made of cotton, no fabric rationing coupon needed. A pair of nylon socks was 2.50 yuan, a little pricy, as they were made in Shanghai. The subtotal came to 7.00 yuan, or roughly 39 percent of Mother's monthly allowance. If she removed the socks, a corner she was prepared to cut, then it would come to 4.50 yuan, 25 percent of their dispensable cash. If she cut a bigger corner by keeping just the swimsuit, an absolute must, it would round off to 18 percent.

She'd done the math over and over again, a chess game played and replayed in her head. All the corners, her corners, had been cut. Now it was Mother's turn to cut hers. There was always something that could be done, somehow. She rehearsed the conversation with Mother, different words, different tones, until she worked herself into a full-blown headache, and then, a tattered sleep.

Waking up in the morning and putting on the old, stinky knitted socks, she found herself with a colossal hangover. Her misery, with nowhere to go, was ready to explode. They had just been told by the Revolutionary Committee at the metallurgical plant that, next year, upon her graduation from high school, they would cease to pay the widow's allowance, as she would start to work and fill the vacancy Father's death had created. No one had told them this before. Her starting salary, as an apprentice, would be fifteen yuan, one swimsuit less than now. She had thought, when Father was around, that their days were hell. What an ungrateful brat she had been, now that she knew real hell.

The water in the river was different, but she wasn't sure how. Maybe it was the consistency. It seemed a little thicker, her limbs measuring the resistance with each stroke. She felt like a fish moving in a pool of runny jelly.

Or maybe it was the temperature. It was definitely not cold, and yet she was shivering. The shivering seemed to come from her bones, and no matter how often her skin and flesh told her the water was not cold, she couldn't seem to stop.

Or perhaps it was the color? When she dived deep and looked around—she was one of those swimmers who could keep their eyes open underwater—she saw a piece of red glass above her, huge, smooth, and translucent, as if the sun had shed its skin on the river. It was the color of blood, from Mother's vein, flowing to vials and bags, drip, drip, slow and creepy.

That morning, she sat at the breakfast table, eating her porridge in silence and brooding over the right moment for her conversation with Mother about the corner—Mother's corner—to be cut. She could almost hear the sound of her thoughts churning.

Mother was silent too. Yuan Feng couldn't guess her mood. Since Father's death, Mother had been quite thrifty with dispensing emotions, as if there were a price tag on them. The headache from last night grew tenfold worse, as Yuan Feng's nerves stretched taut.

The morning sun, now gaining strength, threw an obtrusive glow on the dining table, exposing the beastly truth that the darkness tried to hide. A few scratch marks, a blotch of blistered paint, a fine fish bone, some dried rice crumbles, a smear of dust escaping the dish towel, and the gaping wound left by Father's ax a mere ten months ago. The sunlight had stained the table a sickly yellow, suddenly ten years older.

No, she shouldn't wait any longer. In a household running on an eighteen-yuan monthly budget, there would never be a right moment.

"Ma, I need a new swimsuit, three yuan, a little over," she blurted out, stunned by the audacity she didn't know existed in her. What a waste, all the mental chess, the guessing, and the headache.

She got a silent nod from Mother, a mere acknowledgement, completely neutral, with no indication one way or another. Mother stood up, pushing aside her emptied bowl, leaning over to fetch the string bag hanging on the wall.

"I've got to go out now, cutting us some fresh pork liver."

"Don't you need a certificate for that?" Yuan Feng was a little surprised. Pork liver was a rare luxury, outside the rationing system, supplied only to people with a medical certificate verifying their state of malnutrition or a severe sickness.

"You need meat" was Mother's terse answer.

Halfway out of the door, Mother turned back, pointing to a basin with a load of soiled clothes in it. "They've been there a few days. It's

Sunday, no school, you might as well help me with it. Rain in the afternoon, they say."

Breakfast was finished listlessly. Yuan Feng picked up the textbook for her English class, her new favorite subject, and leafed through a few pages but found herself unable to focus, the swimsuit still hanging large in the air.

But the swimsuit was not alone. A plate of pork liver was in her mind too. It was more than six months since they had last tasted it. Mother had begged Auntie Liu, their neighbor three doors down the street, for a certificate, as her son was a doctor in a local hospital—that's what Mother had told her.

Yuan Feng imagined her mother slicing the pork liver, the little pieces opening up in the hot oil like flowers, the meat turning pink, then brownish purple, against the white garlic and the long stalks of green onion. The vivid colors, brought out by a quick stir in strong heat, nearly knocked Yuan Feng over—and that was before she remembered the smell. The smell was the longest-living monster, dormant maybe but never completely dead; the mere thought of it revived it instantly, with its full power. Her stomach gave a shameless growl.

The money going to pork liver could, quite easily, be spent on her swimsuit. Pork liver or swimsuit, which should she pick? But she wasn't given a choice. She was never given a choice, on anything. At this very moment, she felt the liver a little closer at hand, a difficult pleasure.

She put down the book and moved towards the basin containing the soiled clothes, starting, absentmindedly, to go through their pockets before soaking them in water, a habit Mother had taught her when she was a little girl. A handkerchief in her jacket pocket; a five-cent coin, what a marvel, in one of Mother's pants pockets; a fifty-gram rice ration coupon too, the smallest unit. She was overwhelmed by her unexpected discoveries.

Mother must have lost some of her marbles, Yuan Feng thought, otherwise she would never have left anything anywhere. The likelihood of a cat finding a shred of fish meat on the bone left on Mother's dinner plate—ha ha, what a joke.

Finders are keepers. Every kid on Town-head knew that. But she wasn't a kid anymore, was she?

Yuan Feng stood still, mind split between yearning and fear: the yearning for a piece of flatbread, freshly baked, bought with what was in her hand, and the fear of being caught. Who can say for sure it was not some sort of a trap, the type that mothers like to lay? Just as her yearning for the flatbread was about to win the upper hand, she suddenly noticed, out of the corner of her eye, something white with a blue border buried between Mother's blouse and a bath towel, possibly fallen from a pocket.

She pulled it out. It was an airmail envelope, a letter from Auntie Mei, mailed from Shanghai a week ago. Auntie Mei and Mother had kept, over the years, a steady flow of correspondence. Auntie's letters were mostly about her job, apparently a draining one, in the office of a district school board, and about Uncle Chen, her husband, once a senior official with the municipal government, demoted, since the start of the Cultural Revolution, to a much inferior position in a branch office. His depression, and her struggles, nothing new. Auntie Mei had, on several occasions, wired them money that Mother stoutly refused.

Then she found another piece of paper, folded into a square, stuck in the same envelope but obviously not a part of the letter. She didn't know why it was there. She spread it out on the table, trying to read what was on it. It was a page torn off a prescription pad, two lines of handwritten notes, in typical doctor's scrawl, with a seal on the lower right corner.

Type O, 400 ml, 40 yuan paid in full,

one day bed rest, nutritious meal, do not repeat for six months.

These words, familiar and clear when standing alone, became fuzzy and strange when lined up in a sentence. The only explicit part was the seal. In red ink, the color of authority beyond dispute, it read "The Accounting Office, Five Horse District Hospital."

A thread gradually started to emerge, linking, bit by bit, these disjointed words, forming a hazy line of logic. The ceiling tilted a little, and the shards of light through the window became as sharp as needles. Feeling dizzy, she closed her eyes, but the dust, made silver by the light, was still raging even in darkness.

When she opened her eyes again, she found herself in the street, running like a mad bull, not remembering when and how she got out of the house. It was not until she had covered the entire block that she became aware of something in her hand. It was her swimsuit, the pathetic little rag. Her body was a furnace, burning through every pore. The white-hot heat of regret, of guilt, of anger. There was nothing in the house, or in the street of Town-head, that could cool her fire. She had to find water, a river, a sea, an ocean, before she was consumed to a pile of cinders.

Why?

She had never asked to be born, to be thrust into this absurd world, a world where to have a piece of pork liver, you had to give up a swimsuit; to keep a swimsuit, you had to forfeit a school bag; and to have pork liver, and a swimsuit, and a school bag, your mother had to sell her own blood.

She plunged, headlong, into the Nine Hills.

5.

Yuan Feng sat on the back rack of Meng Long's bicycle, feeling the wind graze her lips and lift her hair. She had, it seemed, just swallowed nine suns, every fingertip glowing with a light that could illuminate five nights. A sour morning could turn itself, in the snap of a finger, into a fresh and gleeful afternoon, a miracle only possible when you were sixteen. Not before, and not after.

Two years ago, she'd been promised a bicycle once she turned sixteen. A two-year-old promise growing stale, even rancid by now. Father had forsaken his ultimate duty of bringing her up and delivering her, safe and sound, into the land of adulthood. What's the point of holding him responsible for breaking a promise, so trivial in comparison, about a bike? Death left all the strings untied.

Besides, why would she want a bike of her own when she could ride on Meng Long's? A swimsuit, a school bag, a pair of nylon socks, a plate of pork liver—she would, in a wink, give them all up for a bike ride with him. She would *die* for such a moment of ecstasy. Death and ecstasy, weren't they the same thing? The scent of the flesh underneath his shirt sent a swoon of warmth to the base of her legs, a weird sensation she'd never experienced before and didn't have a name for.

In no time they arrived at Town-head, right before Yuan Feng's house. It was one of the old bungalows built around the turn of the century, between the last days of the empire and the first of the republic, on a very solid foundation set two stone steps above street level to protect it against frequent flooding in this area. There was a clothesline in front of the house tied between two tree trunks, one mulberry, the other sycamore, both old enough to have probably seen the laying of the first stone of the house. The washing on the line was flapping noisily in the wind, partially blocking the street view.

The door was open. The light inside, at this time of day, was a little harsh, turning everything it touched translucent, digging out blemishes you didn't know existed. Mother was sitting at the dining table, head bent, nose wrinkled, working on a pile of matchboxes, four hundred milliliters of blood paler than before.

"How much is 400 ml?" Yuan Feng had asked Meng Long, a Mr. Know-All. "A normal-size bottle of soy sauce is 500 ml," he said, giving her a reference point, so she knew it was a bottle of soy sauce that had been used a little. It suddenly kicked into her that the pork liver she had had six months ago, and probably the one before that, was really Ma's blood. Salty, metallic—she recalled the taste of blood from her injured finger the day Father passed away. A retching sensation shot through her stomach.

Just as she was about to get down from the bike, Meng Long stopped her, his attention drawn by a sound coming from inside the house. Mother was humming. Her voice, soft and tentative as it was, had drowned out, strangely, all other sounds. A wordless tune, looping round and round, like distant ocean waves, enticing but bashful. Something in that voice poked a hole in the heart. Meng Long, caught unawares, was wounded and his breathing, Yuan Feng could tell, grew damp and ragged.

Mother stood up, leaning over to fetch a bottle of refill paste from the other side of the table and noticed, to her surprise, the eavesdroppers at the foot of the steps.

"Ma, this is my English teacher, Meng Long," Yuan Feng stammered, unsure of Mother's reaction. It was uncharted territory as she'd never brought anyone home. Not allowed, as simple as that.

Mother threw a searching look, from two steps above, at Meng Long.

"Is she in trouble?" yelped Mother, the tingle of alarm in her voice reducing Yuan Feng, by the mere tone of it, into a toddler just out of diapers.

Please, Yuan Feng begged with her eyes.

"I worry about her, every moment," Mother went on, oblivious to Yuan Feng's silent plea. "Sixteen-year-old body, three-year-old mind."

No matter how fast a daughter runs, a mother can always catch up, Yuan Feng realized, with a bitterness bordering on despair. A mother's love knows neither timing nor boundaries and will always make itself known—one can rest assured—in the wrong place and at an inopportune moment. An ice pop in winter, as one might say, or a cotton-padded jacket in summer. Yuan Feng was boiling mad but decided to swallow it, as she was sure the worst was yet to come.

"She is more mature than you think," replied Meng Long, rescuing Yuan Feng from the swamp of humiliation just before she was engulfed. She got down from the bike. Mother shifted a little, to give them room to pass, a vague and guarded gesture of welcome.

"Well, what are you here for then, if she's not in trouble? Her head teacher has never darkened this door . . ." Mother caught herself, noticing, suddenly, that Yuan Feng was hopping on one foot.

"What happened to her?" Mother's volume turned up a notch, from worry to panic.

"A little cut on the foot, disinfected and bandaged, nothing to worry about." Meng Long helped Yuan Feng sit down, steadying his tone to settle the dust agitated by Mother. "People leave stuff onshore they shouldn't. Yuan Feng, next time you'd better put shoes on as soon as you're out of the water."

"So she went swimming? No wonder the door was left unlocked. Were you there with her, Teacher Meng?" Mother asked, her fear gradually easing into curiosity.

"I ran into Yuan Feng on my bike ride."

"She's not going to get sick from the cut, is she?" Mother lifted her brows, seized by a new wave of concern.

"No, she won't. Yuan Feng, you need to stay away from swimming for a few days." He turned towards the daughter while assuring the mother.

"You are good with her. She talks about you, you know," said Mother, choking with relief.

"Only the good things, I hope, Yuan Feng?"

Yuan Feng sat quietly, watching Mother and Meng Long playing a shadowboxing game, with Mother pushing her into eternal infancy by talking *around* her as if she didn't exist, and Meng Long countering by pulling her back, deftly, *into* the conversation as an equal, or some

111

semblance of it. The old alliance of *us*, Mother and daughter, against *them*, the world, was disintegrating, and a new alliance, daughter and Meng Long, was forming against the world, Mother included.

Yuan Feng was fascinated by the economy with which Meng Long dispensed truth. He didn't lie, he was just cursory with facts, leaving out a vast area of details, as vast as Siberia on a world map. So many doubts could have been raised, but Mother was too overcome by Yuan Feng's safe deliverance to bother.

"Comrade Yuan, what kind of a song was that? I heard you sing, like . . ." He halted, searching for the right word, brows drifting towards each other, joining in a thoughtful knot. "Soul." When he eventually found the word, a smile broke, touching the corners of his eyes, a pool of genuine delight.

Mother's face turned scarlet, all the way down to her neck, and her fingers, smeared with paste, seemed to catch fire. The lost blood, all of the four hundred milliliters, every drop, had returned. Yuan Feng gloated secretly as she watched Mother unravel before her eyes. A fortress that had stood through hurricane and tsunami, crumbling, all in a flutter, at the mere touch of a compliment.

"An old nursery rhyme, I'm sorry you had to hear it," Mother stammered, in utter embarrassment.

"What's it about?"

"Some silly spider spinning a web, each round for a family member. But I would never get past the third round, my mother told me, I'd fall asleep." Mother chuckled, caught unawares by the memory of her childhood.

"Let's hear it. Shouldn't we, Yuan Feng?" he urged.

> *Tiny little spider spinning web,*
> *round and round,*
> *round and round.*
> *The first round is for precious mother,*
> *she needs a rose of red color.*

Mother stopped, unable to keep a straight face.

"More, please," he begged.

Tiny little spider spinning web,
round and round,
round and round.
The second round is for dear father,
tell him I want a baby brother.

Mother wouldn't go any further, with the rest of the words all mixed up in her mind. Yuan Feng and Meng Long quickly caught on and started their own loop of "round and round," giddy with mirth, until utterly exhausted.

"Ma, how come you've never sung this one to me?" asked Yuan Feng hoarsely.

"Silly baby stuff, you are too grown-up."

"Wouldn't you run out of family, Comrade Yuan, when you come to the tenth round, say?" Meng Long was still gasping for air.

"You always find somebody, a nephew's mother-in-law, say, and something silly to give," replied Mother and all three of them burst into another roar of laughter, offending the walls that were so used to quiet.

He winked at Yuan Feng. *See, everything is under control.* This was their Morse code, she immediately understood.

"Call me Chunyu, *Comrade* is a big word. You just give me a minute to clear this up." Mother pointed her chin towards the pile of nearly finished matchboxes. "Teacher Meng will stay for supper, I insist. I have some fresh pork liver, you don't get that sort of thing every day."

He fell silent, struggling to find a proper answer. He knew the story behind the pork liver. Once he had been let in on the secret, he could no longer feign ignorance.

6.

Earlier that day, Meng Long took his bike to a deserted section of the Nine Hills riverbank. It was a part of his Sunday routine, a bike ride or a dip in the river (he was an excellent swimmer too) to steal a few moments of peace and quiet so that he could deal with the madness of the week. Quite unexpectedly, he ran into Yuan Feng sitting under a banyan tree, waiting for assistance, with her foot bleeding from stepping on a nail.

Teaching ten classes spread over two grades, he couldn't remember all of his students, but he recognized her. Not because she was shy and blushed easily, an adolescent epidemic the revolution couldn't quite cure, but because of her unparalleled devotion to the subject matter. Her homework was exceptionally neat, often including questions she wasn't brave enough to ask in class. He had no idea that his casual responses, written next to her questions, would be her bible, to be digested and worshipped, each letter and punctuation mark.

The truth would come to him later that she was no more interested in English than in math or physics (Industrial Basics, as it was called in those days). She loved the subject simply for the sake of the one who taught it. *Love him, love his dog.*

He took her on his bike to a nearby hospital to have the wound treated. Disinfection, dressing, and a tetanus shot, the whole nine yards. It was past lunch hour when they were finished, so he brought her to a little eatery on the roadside, buying each of them a bowl of fish ball noodles, something he'd never done for a student.

The shop was pretty dead, with a portrait of Chairman Mao, brown with grease and smoke, smiling at them from the wall, a genial smile made possible by age, untouchable authority, and a gratifying meal. Flies were buzzing around fiendishly and undeterred, a big fat one landing blissfully on His Majesty's nose tip, giving him an extra royal nostril.

A bloody hilarious sight. They avoided eye contact for fear of igniting into wrong laughter.

He was hungry, but she was famished, plunging right into her food without a word. Slurp, slop, smack—a quiet girl with noisy table manners. "When was the last time you ate?" he asked, intending it, full-heartedly, to be a joke. But the humor went catastrophically wrong, prompting a pool of tears. Big, fat, uninvited tears, digging holes in the table.

Blindsided, he quickly delved into his lexicon of comforting words from his collection of dead poets but found it useless, as the dead could only console the dead. The air was ripe with recent hurt and nobody could come to his aid. The shopkeeper was rustling through some old newspapers, totally oblivious and undisturbed, and Mao's smile on the wall had, at some point, turned into a sneer. *What an imbecile!* Meng Long couldn't believe the mess he had got himself into, stuck with a weeping sixteen-year-old, too old to be treated as a child, yet not old enough to pass for an adult.

Eventually, she calmed herself down and pulled him out of his plight by telling him a family tale—the shame, the battles, and the wounds. It was not planned, the whole situation, the words simply dug their own escape route out of her, as much to his surprise as to hers. Once they found the exit, they rushed out, in a stream, a river, and an ocean. She couldn't stop them any more than she could stop a monsoon or an earthquake. There wasn't a dam tall enough to contain such a torrent.

The torrent finally dwindled to a trickle, and then passed.

She felt cleansed and light, having shed her rotten skin on the table that was so used to hearing people's secrets. Vulnerable, exposed, but no longer afraid of him. He had heard the worst of her life. The torture was over and done with, and the shame lost its hold. Truth left her naked, free, and bold.

He listened in a stupor, struck by the squalid world this sixteen-year-old opened up to him. He was a political outcast, so to speak, but he wasn't poor, not in the strict sense of the word. His university education, a rarity in those days, earned him a relatively easy living, and his understanding of poverty was always centered elsewhere—a remote frontier town, a village without a water source—but he didn't know until now that a city could have its own paupers too.

He fought hard against the urge to hold her and tell her something reassuring. Silence fared better than lies, he decided, in a world he could neither improve nor alter. Besides, he found himself suddenly unable to talk to her the same way as before. Some sort of metamorphosis had just taken place in her, right in front of his eyes.

She was no longer a child.

Mother had no idea about what had happened earlier, other than the bare facts Meng Long chose to tell her. She didn't pry further, simply pleased to see the change in Yuan Feng, the willingness to open up to and show respect for her teacher, an adult. Lately Yuan Feng had been going through an impossible stage, building walls and declaring war against the entire adult world, including, and especially, her own mother. This young teacher, a godsend, might become a timely buffer between an angry daughter and a lost mother.

A supper with pork liver might be a way to nourish the rapport. A history-making move, though, as this house had never before seen the face of a dinner guest.

Mother began to clean up the mess at hand. These matchboxes were almost done, needing only the finishing touch of a label. The content of the labels, varying from batch to batch depending on the political mood, was a slogan this time, artistic calligraphy against a screaming red background: Prepare the People against War and Famine.

"Only if you'd allow me to chip in, Chunyu," Meng Long said, after a brief hesitation.

"What?" Mother was perplexed.

"If you want him to stay for supper, he means," Yuan Feng explained to Mother.

"Three pieces of flatbread, I'll buy," added Meng Long.

"What nonsense." Mother seemed offended.

"The ones with pickled veggie and minced pork filling," Yuan Feng said, grinning.

"Ah Feng!" In disbelief Mother berated her, wondering whether, by some unexplained fluke, her child had been swapped.

"Agreed!" With a wave of his arm, Meng Long concluded the subject. His mind was elsewhere, dazzled by the speed and fluidity of Mother and Yuan Feng as they worked together. The labeled matchboxes passed from Mother's hand into Yuan Feng's and soon formed a line, then a square, each close to another with a precise distance in between, to save room and simultaneously allow space for the paste to air-dry.

"Chunyu, how much do they pay you, the match factory?" he asked curiously.

"Five cents for a hundred" was Mother's reply.

"How many matches in a box?"

Mother was taken aback, then laughed. "Nobody has ever asked me that. They take care of it at the factory."

"Eighty to a hundred, whatever fills the box," Yuan Feng offered.

How many boxes would it take to reach fifty-six yuan, his monthly salary? He did some quick mental math.

"One hundred twelve thousand," he heard himself murmuring.

"What?" Mother was again puzzled.

One hundred twelve thousand boxes or 8,960,000 matches at least in a month, enough to blacken half of the lungs and torch all the forests in the world. Twelve months in a year, but how many years in a life, the devil only knows? This tunnel has no end. *Round and round.* A despair swept over him, like a long dreary night.

Mother lifted her eyes, looking at him and smiling, knowingly. "I've got a phoenix to feed, every box is closer to a cent," she said calmly.

He couldn't look back, too ashamed.

The conversation between Mother and Meng Long faded in and out, in waves. Yuan Feng sat there, listening absentmindedly but completely content. Her life, all sixteen years of it, was a cancellation process, love canceled out by guilt, pride by shame, the future by the past. She had seen enough to know that the chance of her stepping on a piece of dog shit around the street corner was a gazillion times more likely than finding a five-yuan note.

But today, Buddha must have dozed off, allowing such a pure, good moment to slip through. Would there be some sort of cancellation lying in its wake? So be it. She just didn't want to spoil the moment. Love had slowed her senses, like the sun dulling a candle, leaving her mind a puddle of blind, lazy joy.

Of course, she had heard the story, in several versions, of his past: the Rightist label, the dead wife, the unborn child, and the letter from Hong Kong. It was just mud, she was convinced, flung at people, the good ones, the smart ones, the fast ones, the ones hated by a few and envied by many. It might soil his clothes, and even his skin if he was not careful, but not his soul. A soul was beyond smearing and assault. At sixteen, she didn't understand that the skin is the house of the body, the body the house of the soul—all in one, one in all.

Even if she had, she wouldn't have given a damn. He could be an angel or a devil, a gentleman or a villain, for all she cared. He could sweep her off on his bicycle, to heaven or to hell. All she wanted, at this moment, was the ride. She didn't want to become Mother, spending the best of her years practicing conservation and economy, shushing emotions as she did noise, dispensing a pitiful trickle of love when summoned, forever fearful of overspending and bankruptcy. She wanted to love, with a love so intense, so mad, and so mindless that her innards would hurt. For that she would give everything and hold nothing back.

It would take twenty more years for her to wise up and accept the plain truth that every daughter in the world loathes but nevertheless ends up living: the life of her mother.

"Chunyu, I'll come every Wednesday and Friday after school to tutor Yuan Feng in English. She's really into it," she heard her teacher saying to her mother.

Meng Long began his visits, as promised, to Yuan Feng's house twice a week, but he would arrive at 7:30 in the evening, to avoid the awkward invitation to supper. The story of the pork liver had jostled his stomach out of place, making him for a long while see blood in every dish.

Every now and then, he'd bring something with him on his visit, a piece of freshly toasted flatbread, a packet of pickled olives, two apples imported from North Korea. Small, casual items Mother would find hard to reject. He couldn't save the world. He couldn't, in fact, even save himself. All he hoped for was to push back the next blood-trading date by a month, a week, even just a day. It was a thin line he had to tread, between his goodwill and Chunyu's pride. No amount of goodwill could dull the edge of pride, he sadly realized.

The book he used to tutor Yuan Feng was, in the strictest sense of the phrase, one of a kind. The cover might fool someone into believing it was a standard textbook, the type commonly used in school. The first few pages carried, indeed, standard lessons like *I am a little driver. I drive a long train. My train runs very fast. It is running to communism.* But if you persisted, it would jump, a few pages farther, into dialogue quite different, such as *I like hot weather best. Really? Personally, I prefer winter.*

"It's *English 900*, an American English textbook," Meng Long explained to Yuan Feng. A camouflaged copy, of course.

Then one evening, he carried a bag into the house, bolted the door behind him, and asked Mother, in a whisper, to draw all the curtains tight and switch off any unnecessary lights. An impish smile broke and spread, as if he were about to set out with a new toy to trick the world. The clock on the wall held its ticking in breathless anticipation. He extracted from his bag a rectangular box, lifting it ceremoniously high before laying it, delicately, on the table.

"My new radio," he declared, beaming with a delight that he soon came to regret. Thank heaven, the price tag had been removed. How many matchboxes to get to such an amount? He dared not think. Math had ruined everything, reducing every pleasure to guilt. Since when had he got into the habit of measuring the value of all things against the unit of matchboxes?

Yuan Feng's mouth opened, turning into a big frozen O. She was growing up in the age of wire broadcasting and loudspeakers, and had seen, a year ago, in a classmate's house, a crystal set assembled by her father, who was an electrical engineer. A transistor radio was something she had vaguely heard of, but understood almost nothing about. It might as well be a dinosaur or a comet. *Shock* was not even the word; *awe* was maybe a smidge closer, but still no way near how she felt when face to face with the real devil.

He switched the radio on. It was the national news from the Central People's Broadcasting Station, the same program they usually heard from their wire broadcasting system, except with crisper reception. Then he lowered the volume until it became more vibration than sound. "Not a word," he warned them, while motioning them closer, his voice charged with suspense.

Rapt, he started to adjust the dial ever so slightly, from frequency to frequency, as if searching for a fine fissure on the perfectly smooth surface of a steel plate. Static, static, and more static. Rain, ocean waves, distant growl of thunder, rustling of trees, and crackling of fire, all suppressed, fuzzy, running into one another.

Then, suddenly, a clear stream of music. Startled by the foreignness of it, the ear tensed up. Shivering moments of suspicion and circumspection passed, and the ear, deeming the sound safe, gradually relaxed before eventually warming to it.

A female voice came on, in Mandarin Chinese, rendered strange by its tender and peaceable tone and inflection.

Voice of America broadcasting . . .

Mother stiffened, aghast and turning pale, as if she had just lost another four hundred milliliters of blood.

"You know what they'll do to you, if they . . ." Mother swallowed the tail of the sentence, lest the words, once in the air, should turn themselves into reality.

"How? Unless you report on us, then you're an accomplice," he retorted, the corners of his mouth twisted into a *you dare not* grin.

"Ma, it's just us, nothing will happen," implored Yuan Feng, hopelessly caught up in his contagious, creepy delight.

A male voice came on now, uttering a long string of sentences of which Yuan Feng could only make out a word or two, here and there.

"It's English spoken by a native speaker. *Their* world news, a Chinese translation right after," he explained. "If you want to learn *real* English, this is the way to go about it."

"Daredevil," protested Mother futilely. Two against one, a battle lost.

That night, Yuan Feng had trouble falling asleep, her bed suddenly too small.

7.

Meng Long changed a little since these visits started. There was an added layer of politeness, Yuan Feng soon felt, in his way of greeting her or even glancing at her when they met at school. A public declaration of distance, to acknowledge a secret hanging in the air between them. She welcomed it, kind of.

Then the fear came, like weeds, cropping up in places least expected, in the middle of supper, or before dreams tearing into her sleep, or when the morning light first licked open her eyelids, or simply when she was turning around a street corner. There were only three months left of her student life, then he would no longer be her teacher, hence no more excuses for his visits. She would start her job at the metallurgical plant, three years' apprenticeship, to be followed by permanent employment as a fully trained worker. *Permanent.* Forever and ever, until she became too old, or dropped dead, whichever came first.

A life inexorably predictable.

This bleakness would have been a little more tolerable if she had never known him. He had held up a candle, giving her a glimpse of the world beyond hers, and beyond the limits of Wenzhou. He left a mark on her soul when it was soft and most impressionable, and in so doing, he took a piece of her too.

But people leave people, that's a law of nature and mankind, like day leaving night, spring leaving winter, fruits leaving trees, and father leaving daughter. They, she and Meng Long, might part ways forever the day she left the school. The very prospect made her shudder. How much did he know, or did he know at all, about the feelings throbbing in her heart, growing too big for her frame, ready to burst into the broad daylight?

She must tell him. She simply must.

One night, just as he began shifting the radio dial back to the Central People's Station, a routine cautionary measure when they had finished listening to VOA, she said to Mother that she needed some air. Mother was surprised because of the hour but didn't object, merely asking her not to go too far and to stay in the area with streetlights. Since she had started high school, Mother seemed to have relaxed the leash a little. So the two of them left together.

He offered to take her for a bike ride, something she would be, in normal circumstances, elated about, but not tonight. She needed time to ease into the right start (which she didn't have yet) of a conversation she had in mind.

She insisted on a walk.

It was almost a full moon. The light was ruthless, digging out blemishes on every surface, making a mockery of every shadow it created. April was a month of restless contention, every creature trying to claim, by voice, its nocturnal territory, the frog the loudest, then the cricket, and then the katydid, all from the nearby bushes and water. Wenzhou was a city traversed by an intricate network of waterways, small inner-city rivers older than the city itself, longer than living memory, but soon to be filled in and disappear, in the decades to come, beneath highways and apartment buildings, the paw prints of modernization.

But they didn't know that yet. They had no idea that what they heard that night was one of the dying cries of the old town, soon a site on an obsolete map as the new landscape was carved out against the changing tide. What revolution leaves behind, commerce will readily pick up. Nothing ever goes to waste.

"Look at you, how tall you've grown," Meng Long marveled, as Yuan Feng walked next to him in his shadow, unusually quiet.

She'd grown quite a bit in the past year, so much that the head teacher had moved her, at the beginning of the semester, to the last row, to be seated with the tallest boys in class. A giant among the girls, her very presence was a threat, reminding them, they sensed, of their inadequacy. A misfit, to be distrusted and ostracized, naturally. Or perhaps, it was the willing exile of a self-made loner. She harbored the secret of a woman, whereas they had just been weaned off their dolls—if they could afford a doll.

"Get it from my pa, I guess; he was a tower. Ma says I take up too much of the fabric ration, now she has to wear my hand-me-downs," said Yuan Feng, her mind adrift, as she was contemplating her next move.

"Has your mother ever told you that you've become so"—he hesitated, rummaging through his mind for the proper words—"grown-up?"

Her mirror, the mirror on Mother's dresser, had told her what he held back in that brief pause. She was no longer a bag of bones, and the sun rust had largely faded from her cheeks. There was a sparkle in her eyes, an unsophisticated and stubborn fire—she knew what had fueled it. She plodded through the week in a half daze, waiting, languidly, for the two evenings of his visits to leap into life, every fiber charged like a high-voltage wire.

His eyes were her mirror too, less exacting and more responsive, whose reflection concurred with the fact already revealed to her by the other mirror, the real one, that her looks weren't an affront to any mirror in the world. But the faint hint of *you cute little girl* in his way of speaking suddenly rubbed her the wrong way, goading her to fight back, by asserting herself with all the 174 centimeters of her existence.

"I'll move out to a dorm, as soon as I start working," she said, her face stern.

"Have you talked to your mother about it?" He was surprised.

"No need," she replied, but immediately felt uneasy about the grinding edge in her voice and decided to concede, just a smidgen. "Later, maybe."

He laughed, a soft, almost indulgent kind of laugh.

"You've got a lot of growing up to do. Don't worry about the fabric coupon. I'll save mine for you. Next season, though, this season's all gone," he said, with a tenderness not seen before.

She paused in disbelief. "You mean, you'll come to see me even after my graduation?"

He paused too, waiting for her to finish the burst of euphoria. "Silly, of course I will. You'll have to kick me out."

A wave of relief swept over her. For the last few days and nights, she had been planning for this evening. Thoughts and words had come, in bouts and snatches, abundant and chaotic, waiting for the right opening to string them into a meaningful conversation befitting adulthood.

In a time when sex was practiced but not discussed, she was ignorant, at sixteen and a half, of the mechanism of the human reproductive system, with all its pain and pleasure, other than the memory of her vague surmising as a child when woken by the suppressed moans behind Father's closed door. Surmising, however, couldn't go very far alone without a helping hand from, say, a book, a movie, or an experienced girlfriend. These simply didn't exist for her. But hormones had their own way of finding the path to her.

A kiss, that was what she had intended, if the right opening in the conversation failed her or went catastrophically astray. She had been so tense about the idea that her palms were soaked in perspiration, and her teeth had begun to rattle.

His assurance of a continued contact unexpectedly relaxed her. She didn't have to go through with it, the talk, the kiss, at this dismal nerve-racking moment of utter misery and torture. She would have plenty of time to do her growing up, to wait for his fabric coupons to turn into a new blouse, apple green preferably, and for her words to grow roots of style and confidence.

"Ah Feng," he said, calling her, for the first time, by her baby name, "I've got something to tell you after the midterms. Something very important." The air was tremulous with implication, and she was alarmed by the weight, at once, of his voice and of her own suspended hope.

The math was simple, seven days and six nights: that was the distance between now and the midterms, her journey to heaven or to hell.

Many years later, she could still trace the track this imagined kiss had burned in her memory. Her first kiss not given, but forever remembered. The torture, the anticipation, and the delirium, of something coming so close to reality, but slipping away in the end, as fate would have it, into fantasy.

Midterms came and went, but *the* talk never occurred, the content of which would remain a mystery forever. Right around that time, an unexpected event took place, leaving in its wake plans disrupted and lives derailed.

In one of his classes, Meng Long absentmindedly wrote "Celebration of *Nationalist* Day" when it should have been "Celebration of *National* Day." The right praise sung to the wrong party, a minor spelling error resulting in a grave political offense.

Yuan Feng couldn't be sure, when reflecting on this incident, whether her conscience was completely clear. A discreet person, taking such pains always to cover his tracks, he wouldn't have made such an elementary mistake in black and white, and worse yet, left it on the blackboard when the class was over. Unless he was preoccupied with the proposed talk. *Very important,* he said.

Of the three major mishaps in Meng Long's life, the first two were, more or less, some sort of a situational comedy that went absurdly wrong. But as far as the third one was concerned, no sensible case could be made in his defense. It was his own doing, plain and simple.

The punishment, a severe one, came a few days later. He would be banished, as a repeat offender twice over, to a village three hundred kilometers north of Wenzhou, on a mountaintop, at the highest altitude in the province, and therefore the poorest. No electricity, with the closest bus station three and a half hours away by foot. He was to set off before the end of the summer and report to a commune-based primary school, where he would teach Chinese and arithmetic, as English would not be needed there, not for another hundred years.

He had no intention of going. For the first time in two decades, he thought about his mother, a longtime resident of Hong Kong, now dividing her time between Kowloon and Vancouver.

One night, he came to visit Yuan Feng and Mother. A few sentences into the conversation, he astonished himself by revealing to them an escape plan that he had brooded over for days. He brought it up as a gesture of farewell initially, without any intention of involving them. At this stage of his life, they were all he had in this world.

"This is for you. Just be extra careful, remember to switch the dial back always." He turned towards Yuan Feng while placing his radio on the table, together with *English 900* in its camouflaging cover.

But the bomb he dropped didn't explode as he had expected.

"Why not sell it?" interjected Mother flatly. "We'll need the money on the road."

"Sorry?"

"We'll go with you. It's a dead end for Ah Feng here."

8.

They had imagined this body of water in a thousand different ways, but when brought face to face with it in the wee hours of the night, they found all their prior imaginings skeletal and pale. The distant roar of the breakers on the shore spoke of its expanse and power, the power to give and to take life at will, and the raw scent of the sea brought in by saliferous wind held in store unknown dangers and unforeseen opportunities. Its magnificence and mystery struck them silent and breathless with awe.

There was a thin slice of moon in the sky, its light, sieved through the faint mist in the air, a dim shimmer on the surface of the water. Just the kind of light for their purpose: dark enough for them to blend into the background yet not lose their bearing. The boatman, who made his living by smuggling people and goods across the water year in and year out, decided on this night just as their patience was wearing thin, having spent four days hiding in a nearby village.

Years later, in the 1980s, when the country started to open its door to the rest of the world, Yuan Feng found a detailed map of this area in a bookstore in Shanghai, with the name of this body of water noted: Dapeng Wan, or Mirs Bay in English. But in the spring of 1970, such a map, a handy tool to facilitate an exodus to Hong Kong, was not available, at least not to the general public. However, Meng Long could always dig his way through to the things that he really desired. For twenty yuan, a little over Mother's monthly allowance, he got hold of a hand-drawn local map from a fisherman. While the revolution still ruled supreme in the rest of the country, in these southern frontier areas of Guangdong, money talked.

Underground routes from Guangdong to Hong Kong had been operating for two decades, growing more varied and creative over time, through trial and error. Lives lost and experience gained.

Three main routes, each with its pros and cons, had been laid out in detail. To go mostly by land, one needed to cut through a barbed wire fence erected along the border. If successful, then there was a short swim across a river beyond the fence before you hit the other side. Among all the alternatives, this was the shortest and least expensive route but with the greatest risk, as border guards and patrol dogs were a constant presence. An exceptionally keen nose was needed to sniff out a weak link along this mini Great Wall.

Other alternatives included a much longer journey combining land and waterway. A ten-day walk, give or take, through the dense forest, led by a local guide familiar with the trails blazed by the early pioneers, followed, then, by a distance of swimming, around five kilometers, to the final destination. This was the safer but most strenuous option, requiring extraordinary patience and muscle power for long hours of hiking, in silence and the heat, with little possibility of bath or shower, while carrying the weight of swimming gear, a two-week supply of dried food, and a first-aid kit for malaria, cuts, and bites by bugs and snakes.

These two alternatives were quickly abandoned for the simple reason that Mother wasn't a strong swimmer, not the kind you could count on when in need. They soon found themselves focused on the third one, the safest—if *safe* could ever be used to describe such a daring adventure. This plan involved a passage on a fishing boat, crossing the sea on the deadest night. Three hundred yuan a head, an exorbitant price, half paid upon handshake, the other half in the form of an IOU note, to be honored by their relatives in Hong Kong upon landing.

They started running around, as busy as bees in nectar season, purposeful and tireless, working towards their boat fare. The idea of more matchboxes had never crossed Mother's mind. It would take half her life, if she burned enough midnight oil and practiced the most stringent economy, to earn the needed amount—but the boatman didn't have half a life to wait around, nor did the tide.

Blood trading couldn't assuage the urgency of the situation either. She could drain herself into a mummy if she wished, which would only bring her a sliver of the fares. Besides, she needed to conserve all her energy to endure such a journey—one couldn't burn the candle at both ends.

The only option left, they concluded, was to sell what they had. Meng Long's watch (an old Enicar inherited from his late father), his two-year-old bicycle, and his fairly new transistor radio, when combined, made him 215 yuan richer.

The Yuan household, on the other hand, had little, if anything, worthy of a trip to the secondhand store. Father's old bike had been traded months before for Yuan Feng's new winter jacket, but Father had left behind a domestic-made watch—old and battered, with a crack on the crystal—and several army uniforms, threadbare and faded. The shop assistant, who had seen all kinds of rise and fall, stunned Mother with a rare crack of emotion as she, braving his scrutiny, laid those relics hesitantly on the counter.

"My my, the real thing. You don't see them often . . ." He lifted his eyes from the uniforms, casting a knowing glance at Mother, but quickly curbed his enthusiasm. A hasty expression of interest was a blunder perhaps seen in a young apprentice, but not something he, a man who had long since learned his trade, would allow himself to indulge in.

"Forty-three yuan altogether, a good deal," he said expressionlessly.

Mother stood in silence, feet shifting uneasily between leaving and staying, hesitation written all over her face.

"Forty-six yuan, take it or leave it," he concluded.

Mother took the money, rushing out of the door as fast as her legs could carry her, for fear he would change his mind. Four years into the Cultural Revolution, the worship of military glory was still red hot. Her husband, the dumb head, had saved her repeatedly over the course of his life, and he was still trying to save her from his grave.

Then another thought hit them: to sell the furniture, theoretically the property of the metallurgical plant, but a minor detail to fret about at such a time.

"My crazy sister in Shanghai wired me some money," Mother explained to neighbors who caught her moving out a bed and a table. "She insists I should replace the old stuff, it's not good for Ah Feng to lie on the bed her father died in. Bad luck, she said. Superstition, what can you do, heh?"

Distress spawns the best con artists. Mother was half-amused by her effortless skill, freshly crafted, of improvising ostensible excuses, or rather, genuine lies, when the situation demanded it.

It was not a total lie, to be fair. A check was in the mail, as the old saying went, except it was a *real* check. Mother had telegraphed Auntie Mei, asking her to wire two hundred yuan, *in urgent need*. The money she had refused, all these years, to take from her sister and her brother-in-law, who owed her in more ways than one.

In a week's time, they put together every penny they'd gathered, 535 yuan, plus a few coins, enough for the first payment on their one-way crossing to the rotten imperialist land.

Special travel permits to the southern frontier areas, an absolute must, were meticulously counterfeited, with a fake official seal made from a bar of laundry soap, a flawless match to the authentic version, and a glorious testimony to Meng Long's craftsmanship, perfected by burning necessity.

They were put in a fishing boat powered by a small engine, holding ten people—nine passengers plus the boatman. It was the best size of engine, the boatman told them, as the level of noise it generated would be easily masked by the roar of the wind and the splashing of the waves. Everybody needed to lay low all the way across, no cigarettes, no talking, no sound. Period.

It was a perfect night, according to the boatman, everything looking exactly right and no children on board. It couldn't have been any better. But all the right things combined, he warned them, could still lead to a very wrong end, as the patrol boats, manned by the most seasoned water police, knew all the tricks inside out—it takes a diamond to cut a diamond. A night like this would put the hounds on extra alert.

The boat slipped through the water in darkness. As the sea opened up, the wind gathered speed, rocking the boat violently from side to side. Mother felt sick shortly after, her strong mind losing its grip on a weak stomach. Subdued by fear and a sudden attack of dizziness, Mother retched, choking with tears and vomit. The boatman, repulsed by the sound and the smell, threw a towel to Meng Long, motioning him to gag her.

"Almost there," Meng Long whispered to her, helplessly watching her labor with breathing and nearly faint from the stench of the towel stuffed in her mouth.

All of a sudden, Mother's stomach ceased fussing. Something in the air was trying to communicate with her. She was not sure what it was; she simply sensed its presence. A moment's stillness made her aware that it was a sound, hardly distinct from the noise of the sea. Her blood rushed to her head, pounding ferociously, like some mad, hot summer waves, and then it ran icy cold as she noticed, in terror, a blotch of light in the distance, gradually swelling into a beam, ripping a ragged hole in the dark fabric of the night.

The boatman uttered a deep-throated curse, spinning the steering wheel to escape the searchlight. The boat jerked sharply, making the women on board shriek.

The consequences, if caught, had been explained in detail before the group boarded.

"You will be put in a detention center," the boatman had informed them, "anywhere from a day to several months, depending on your luck and their mood. Admit you're wrong, make it honest and real. Tears work wonders sometimes.

"But don't sell anyone else out. Remember you've acted alone because you've lost your freaking mind. Never talk back—they, not you, always know better. You may get a reprimand in your record, but very seldom a prison sentence. There isn't a prison big enough to hold all the rotten apples like you."

When they had first listened in their hiding place to the boatman talking about the chances of success versus failure, their ears, preferring luck over the truth, naturally picked up the easy part. The likelihood of leniency if caught, a slap on the wrist, was what they chose to believe and to remember. The face of imminent danger altered the course of memory, reminding them of the much grimmer reality at the hands of the hound dogs.

"How far along are we?" Meng Long asked abruptly.

"Halfway, about," the boatman replied.

Meng Long quickly collected the plastic bag containing his underwear, what remained of the dried food, and some tiger dung wrapped in a piece of tarpaulin purchased from a zookeeper in Guangzhou, the scent of which, they had trusted, would deter the patrol dogs. The bag, tied tightly at the end, could be used as a makeshift float if needed.

With the bag slung over his neck, he pressed Yuan Feng's arm, so forcefully it hurt. "Sorry about the fabric coupon I promised you," he whispered before plunging, headlong, into the water before she had time to respond.

He couldn't risk being caught. A slap on the wrist perhaps for others, but not for him, a fourth-time offender. They'd want his entire limb, if not body. The water split itself to make room for him. He turned around from a few strokes away, grimacing, his eyes glittering, a lone wolf's chilling glare.

To the present day, Yuan Feng wasn't sure if it was just her imagination—the final sight of him before he was engulfed by the dark expanse of water.

"You can't stop people who wanna die." The boatman shook his head, speeding his boat away like an arrow.

9.

He swam towards her, so close that she could see his hair swaying softly in the water like seaweed, his fingers splaying, their souls almost touching. Night after night. Even in her delirium, she was fully aware that they lived in parallel planes. He was fighting his way, through dark layers of time and space, towards her, but they were like two fish separated by a thin glass wall, always close and always apart.

He could have picked a different route, alone, and got away safely. He took them on, a burden that cost him his life, she thought between two strata of consciousness.

All those laps of the Nine Hills River and the Oujiang, all the time and money spent on winter swim camp. What a waste. Her entire youth, it seemed in retrospect, had prepared her for that *one* swim, the swim to love and freedom. But when the moment came, she balked. She chose Mother.

There was a sound weighing on her eardrum, like the distant droning of bees or the lingering vibration of thunder. She knew, at the edge of consciousness, that it was Mother crying.

She struggled awake, finding herself lying on a floor mat, her pillow smelling of disuse and dust. It was an empty room, familiar yet strange. Not totally empty, though, since there was a stove standing next to a smudged wall, waiting for food to breathe life into it. A world of fog, blearier than the one she just came out of. Where was she? She felt the urge to scream, but the voice didn't come.

"Ah Feng?" Mother crawled over from the other end of the mat. The sun also rose, like any other day, raging through the window glass, glaring on Mother's face mottled with bugbites, bugs that thrived on the blood of southern soil. Her eyes totally dry, no trace of tears. Self-pity was something Mother loathed.

"How long have I slept, Ma?" she asked, her eyelids still sticky.

"Two days." Mother was a smooth liar now, an adept weaver of the fabric of alternative truth. It was the fourth day, in reality, after their return from the detention center in Guangdong, and Yuan Feng had been running a fever, sleeping fitfully for the entire time.

The sunlight did something funny with Mother's hair, sprinkling on it a thin layer of dust. Yuan Feng leaned over to give it a closer look, realizing, to her shock, that Mother had turned gray while she was asleep.

"You haven't eaten much, just some rice soup, between fits of sleep," Mother said.

Yuan Feng had no recollection, whatsoever, of it.

"Did you buy rice?" She stared at Mother, groggy and unseeing.

"Yes, enough to last us till the beginning of the month."

With what? Yuan Feng intended to ask but changed her mind. The answer was obvious: Mother had traded in more blood. They had spent every penny and sold every item sellable around the house. Mother would continue her bloody business till her veins dried up, like her milk many years before.

"Lock away the receipt," Yuan Feng heard herself thinking aloud.

"What?" Mother asked in bewilderment.

10.

The tide began to turn, as the Cultural Revolution, growing weary of itself, finally ground to a halt. The harsh winter of 1977 brought thawing news of colleges reopening after a decade of being closed to the public. In the summer of 1978, Yuan Feng, an experienced lathe operator at the metallurgical plant, passed a tough entrance exam with the English Meng Long had taught her and was admitted into a big-name university in Shanghai, leaving home for the first time.

Several years after her graduation, a Canadian professor who had taught English poetry to her class sponsored her to study at the University of Toronto. A master's degree, a part-time job, then a second master's degree, a full-time job. Amid the chaos of settling in, she invited Mother over to Toronto, first as a visitor, then as a permanent resident. They lived together for nearly twenty years, until Mother moved to Pinewoods and eventually died there.

One day in January 2003, Yuan Feng, now Phoenix, took her then boyfriend, an artist / poet / musician / pizza delivery guy from Singapore, and her mother, now called Rain, to a Chinese restaurant in downtown Toronto for a Lunar New Year dinner. It was there she spotted Meng Long, whom she had thought long dead. A bombshell encounter, to say the least, which she wished had never happened. Three cruel decades apart had turned him into a man no one would look at twice, with a receding hairline, hunched shoulders, and a deeply furrowed, lackluster face.

The real change in him lay much deeper, when she thought about it. He no longer had that shimmer of controlled rage and the laser-sharp focus, the wolf's cold glare, in his eyes. A docile, harmless, dull old man, that's what he had become. *Common*—it wasn't the exact word, but close enough.

The one thing that had never changed was his voice, still gentle, magnetic, sending a ripple of waves through the thick layers of thirty years, hitting her hard.

She sat motionless, watching him immersed in the festive company of his family. His wife, apparently older than him; his daughter, plain looking, wearing a pair of huge, dark-rimmed glasses, without a male companion; and two young girls, about five and sevenish, running wild and screaming, exultant with red envelopes in hand, Grandpa's New Year cash present.

Damn it. She cursed the fate that wouldn't cut her any slack, denying her the few fragments of a happy memory, the rare, guileless moments of youth made immortal by his presumed death, now killed a second time by his survival. A true death, this time.

She left without going over to greet him.

It remained a question in her mind, for many years to come, whether Mother saw him too, but she never asked her about it.

Chapter IV

SISTERS

Email from Phoenix to George, 2011.11.3 @ 02:07 China Standard Time

Dear Old George,

My visit to Wenzhou feels like a French absurdist drama. I tried to look for the school I attended and the metallurgical plant my dad and I both worked for. The school is gone, and the site of the plant now a shopping mall. Town-head, the street where I was born and raised, has been expanded to a thoroughfare, all the houses along it eradicated. I don't have any DNA left in the city to prove who I am. Can someone staying in a hotel honestly claim she's come home?

The real climax came yesterday when I ran into an old schoolmate. We were in the same class for four years and trained together at the Youth Palace, she in table tennis, I winter swimming. But her version of school life differs so much from mine that I wonder whether someone has drilled into my brain and replaced a chip. She had no recollection of me ever in the swimming program, and she told me the reason for Meng Long's downfall was "he couldn't keep his dick in his pants"—he screwed a female phys ed teacher whose husband kicked up a huge stink with the committee. Holy cow, her details are juicy.

I was in a daze for much of the day. The scenes I wrote with such a sense of reality in my manuscript, are they not even my actual experience? Did I create a childhood and youth purely with my imagination? Or have I fallen prey to some sort of gaslighting? The one person who can verify my history is silent in an urn. But I have decided to trust my own memory—this is all I have. My lost town has no place to go except in my memory, so I have to stick to it regardless.

More bad news. It may not be a viable option to inter Ma's ashes next to Pa. The situation is complicated, I'll give you the details when you call.

Don't bother proofreading the section named Sisters. Auntie Mei has added a few new details and switched the sequence of some events. She says Ma and she had several long heart-to-hearts before Ma left for Wenzhou to marry Pa, during which Ma told her things she had had no idea about. I am trying to knead in Ma's perspective, so just wait.

Nix

P.S. I am taking the noon train back to Shanghai.

Email from George to Phoenix, 2011.11.4 @ 12:55 Eastern Standard Time

Dear Nix,

It's good to hear your voice (don't look at the phone bill for this month). As much as I miss you, I must say your trip has done you good: it stirs up emotions in you I didn't quite see in Toronto. People believe what they choose to believe. Memory is subjective, so in that sense we are all gaslighting others somewhat when we assert our version of the past. But we have to trust our own memory, otherwise we crumble.

As soon as I hung up the phone, I realized I had forgotten something—my memory is a sieve now. The other day in the cafeteria I ran into Yang, your mother's favorite nurse at Pinewoods, who came to visit a hospitalized friend. She mentioned something new to me. Remember your ma had a fit the day before her death when she was introduced to a new nurse? Nurse Yang told me she kept crying, "Little Tiger go away." I remember in the section about the famine, you mentioned a guy called Little Tiger coming to your house asking your ma for money. Do you know who he was?

It's a good thing we've interred part of Rain's ashes in Scarborough. If you aren't sure about the situation in Wenzhou, you can bring the urn back and have the two parts merge.

I'll wait for your revised version of Sisters. I have a lot of questions with the current draft. I infer both sisters run away from home but have no idea why. What has kept them apart before their reunion in Shanghai? Who's Kiyo? She reads like someone with a story, but she never returns to the scene after a brief mention in the beginning. The sisters seem to have gone through some horrific experience that I am anxious to learn about. Who's responsible for

Chunyu's accident? Where and how do your parents first meet? Hope to find some answers in your next draft.

Another question: Why didn't you arrange the different sections of the book—"Famine," "Teacher," and now "Sisters"—in chronological order? It may make it an easier read.

Sleep tight.

George

Email from Phoenix to George, 2011.11.10 @ 17:28 China Standard Time

Dear George,

Here it is, the revised version of Sisters. The last round of reading shocked me a little—the few tweaks (I thought they were minor) have unexpectedly moved Ma to the forefront while pushing Auntie to an obscure corner. I felt guilty, but not for long. After all, I only got Ma's perspective through Auntie's recounting of their long talks, which Ma is not around to confirm or deny. Ma only breathes through whatever space Auntie allows her. In that sense, I've been more than fair to Auntie.

To answer your question about the chronological order, the first two sections—"Famine" and "Teacher"—are my own memories, whereas the events in this section are "prehistorical," before I was even a whiff in the air. I decided to place my voice before anybody else's. Does it make sense?

Unfortunately, this version still doesn't answer some of your questions (I have them too). Auntie has finally yielded to the mounting pressure from her doggedly relentless niece, promising that she will give me "the thread that

connects all the dots," but she wants to wait for a day when she feels fully rested. "I'll die in peace afterwards," she says. I am terrified at the prospect of an earth-shattering revelation, but until then, curiosity reigns.

I don't really know who Little Tiger is, but he seems to be a ghost that appears now and then. In Grandpa's letter (which you'll see in this section), he also mentioned a man who lost three fingers. Putting all the clues together, I have a feeling Little Tiger is someone who once played some sinister part in Ma's life, although she denied ever knowing him.

Nix (on tenterhooks)

* Email attachment: Phoenix's manuscript *Sisters*

1.

What a change! The trace of shock in each other's eyes triggered a covert cry from both of them in silent unison.

It was September 1949, four months after the Communist takeover of Shanghai.

When they parted in the fall of 1944, Chunyu (Rain, as she would later come to be known) was sixteen, and Mei, a year and a half older. The whirlwind of events had left them with patchy and disjointed memories and derailed them from their normal tracks of life. They hadn't had the mind, at their hasty departure, to entertain the idea that there was still a lot of growing up ahead of them, in a biological sense if nothing else.

They had been through long journeys of life to get to this point: Chunyu a nurse's aide at a military hospital in a town not far from their home, and Mei, freshly demobilized from the Communist New Fourth Army, now a local government official in Shanghai.

Growing up was something that had just happened *to* them, catching them unawares and inattentive. Five years and two wars later—the Anti-Japanese War and the civil war—face to face at the train station in Shanghai, they were stunned to recognize the fruit of the growing process in each other.

They were both a good half a head, if not more, taller. Chunyu had a sick, almost anemic, pallor to her face. The straight, steady gaze that had made many a heart jitter was gone from her eyes, replaced by a tiny, timid flutter of uncertainty, like a frightened animal. Her feet, having been confined for the last five years to the narrow dirt path between her dorm and the hospital wards, reminded her that she was in unfamiliar territory, somebody else's world. Oh God, no—Shanghai was a different universe altogether.

She remained in a mental haze for days before eventually simmering down, easing herself into the right frame of mind to scrutinize the life Mei had invited her to share.

Of the two, Mei was the one who had changed more. The storm of war had swept over her face, sanding off the pale, tender, moistened, and southern smoothness, leaving a raw surface that was bronzed, coarse, wind cracked, and glowing with passion and purpose. Her braids gone, she now wore her hair short, boyish short, to match her army uniform with its patched elbows, every wrinkle crisp. A belt, a canteen over her shoulder, and a white towel tied to the strap of it—the typical image of a soldier, despite the freshly removed insignia. A combination of female delicacy and muscular power, a perfect morphadite.

It was a style that Shanghai, the epitome of sophistication, hadn't seen before and didn't know yet how to react to. Enigmatic and alluring to Chunyu, nonetheless.

"Four months, only four months ago, we took the city when no one thought we could. The first night our soldiers got into Shanghai, a hundred thousand of them all slept in the open, in the rain, not a sound made! The first of the locals to open their doors in the morning found entire streets covered with our boys, fast asleep, wet, snoring—just imagine the shock! Nobody, not even one soldier, tried to get into the residences, even to pee. We won their hearts over in an instant!"

Mei's Mandarin had also gone through a revolution: the thick local accent, her birthmark, was largely gone, replaced with a smooth, near-perfect Peking tone, carrying, in passing, a slight *r* sound at the end of nouns.

Accompanying the change in her accent was a reformation of her diction. The princessly *I* and *my*, Chunyu had noticed, were usurped by the common band of *we* and *our*. In Chunyu's mind, there echoed Mei's girlish voice from before the catastrophic events that had derailed her course of life: *I am the first to finish the quiz in class today; it's **my** calligraphy that got picked for the exhibition; I've decided to become an artist, when the war is over; I think Hsu Chih-mo the absolute best poet of the Crescent Moon School . . .* The theatrical assertion of self-importance and self-opinion, the trademark of Mei's adolescence, was now beveled by an unconscious yet proud identification with a faceless multitude.

Cascade of fresh impressions, inundating and overpowering. Chunyu wondered whether she had, in confusion, imagined a different past of a different sister. She eyed Mei with the beginning of envy. *You scare them: you've got that fire on top of your head, fire of life, bright as hell.* The face of Kiyo, the Japanese woman who came into her life five years ago, barged into her mind out of nowhere; it's what Kiyo used to say about Chunyu. *You've got that fire on top of your head.* And of all the people in the universe, why did it have to be Kiyo who discovered that mind-boggling truth about her? Where was her flame now? Why wasn't it burning five years later?

Where was Kiyo anyway? Was she dead in a land not her own, with the gold earrings Chunyu gifted her? Or was Kiyo still alive, back in Japan, managing another "household," as she liked to call it, supplying the goods this time around to the defeated, the war trash?

Chunyu shuddered. They had never been far away in her consciousness, Kiyo and the rest, a capricious presence lurking in the memory grotto, leaping up at her in the most inconvenient moments when she was least alert.

Was she the only one haunted by them? There was no shadow in Mei's eyes. Mei's memory grotto—everybody has one—must be safeguarding something entirely different. Victory, conquest, sleeping in the rain while dreaming about a starry sky?

She's stolen my *fire, that's why she has no trace of fear.* Chunyu brooded in silence. A wave of bitterness surged up despite herself and beyond all reason. In the five years that she hadn't heard from Mei and imagined the worst, Mei was out there gallivanting, seeing the wild, wild world, winning two wars, and gaining a man on the side. The tide had turned, and now it was Mei who was calling the shots.

Mei's Mandarin suddenly sounded harsh and jarring, pushing Chunyu to the very edge of eruption. She felt a wrenching urge (which she soon came to regret) to ask Mei to switch back to their dialect, the tongue they had used for girlie chats and secret little battles for parental favor. Can one outgrow the language of birth, simply casting it aside like a pair of shoes that no longer fit?

Chunyu didn't know then that Mei would come back to their shared tongue one day, when life's cycle brought her closer to where she had started out. But that would happen later. Much later.

They shuffled out of the train station, merging into a boisterous crowd. A squeaky honk from a rickshaw passing made Chunyu jump. There was a white man in a hat and suit peering out from under its cover waving at her, muttering something vague, maybe a *good morning*, maybe a *guten Morgen*, she couldn't quite make out. The driver cut through the traffic with such savage impatience that one of the wheels nearly ran over her foot.

A left turn removed them from the crowd, ushering them into a much wider and quieter street flanked by sycamore trees with mottled trunks, whose tall, strong branches were pruned to embrace each other across the road, forming an arched canopy. Leaves were losing their green to the crisp breeze of fall, turning yellow and brown against the pale blue of the sun-bleached sky, wretchedly vivacious.

Later Chunyu would come to know that a street like this, in a city like Shanghai, was called by a different name. *Boulevard*, an alien word.

Several women, obviously of the leisure class, brushed past them, all dressed in silk cheongsam, a style Chunyu had never seen before with her dismally limited exposure to the world of fashion. The side slit was cut so high that she could almost see the edge of their panties. She looked away, feeling the heat rising to her face. In the corner of her vision, Mei walked straight ahead, perfectly calm, perfectly natural, indifferent and undistracted.

There were only so many *first times* that could be stuffed into one day. Chunyu's head was overstocked, swelling and spinning, her cloth shoes hopelessly tight.

"When we get home, you probably won't meet Comrade Chen right away. He is *so* busy, a thousand loose ends to sort out. The world is watching and waiting for us to fail. They don't believe we can run the city, just like they didn't believe we could win the war. But we did, didn't we?"

Comrade Chen was Mei's husband. They had met four years ago in a military training academy, she a literacy teacher, he the Party secretary. It was her first marriage and his fourth.

His first wife had been a child bride, a free helping hand around the house, forced upon him by his parents when he was seventeen. He left his home village in Shandong three years later, walking barefoot for two days, to join the Communist forces active in the northern mountainous region, turning his back, for good, on his loveless marriage, a two-year-old son, and the bottomless pit of a poor peasant's life. The next two wives were his own choice, his comrades, companions of love, as one might say, but both died during the war, one from a miscarriage and the other typhoid.

Chunyu listened to Mei talking about her husband, trying hard to silently unravel the mystery of Comrade Chen's job that could, apparently, cause a stir in the world. Curious as she was, she didn't dare to pry. She hated to sound more ignorant than she had already made herself out to be. It suddenly hit her, sharp and hard, that the real change in Mei had little to do with her growth spurt, her different skin texture, her modern haircut, or her altered accent. The earth-shattering change had taken place in Mei's heart. The place where Mei had once stored poetry, writing brushes, and attention-seeking tactics had been emptied out, yielding space for something much bigger than herself.

How much can a heart grow in five years?

"Once you settle in, we'll get you a job. This is a new Shanghai, no longer a haven for opportunists and parasites. Everybody has to work to earn a living, and contribute to the society," declared Mei, loud and resonating, pushing back a strand of hair displaced by the wind.

Mei had been recently assigned to work in the office of a major school district and was soon to be appointed its Party secretary, in charge of training the staff for the transition to the new educational system. A podium, a crowd—that was what Mei was born for. The words out of her mouth fell naturally into the form of a lecture or pep talk. Mei's poetry readings at Father's birthday parties when she was a child, and the fantasy stories she had told their half sisters with such verve, had all been, in retrospect, perfect preparation for the role she was playing now.

But who would have imagined that it would take two gory wars for Mei to get here? The time had finally come for her to capture a real audience with a real interest in what she had to say.

Chunyu sighed, torn between admiration and misery. A sister lost and a sister found, but she wasn't sure the one she recovered was the one she had lost.

She had been waiting for Mei to mention their hometown, East Creek. Shortly after Mei broke the five-year-long silence and called her sister out of the blue at the hospital, Chunyu wrote her a letter explaining the story she had fed Father and their half sisters about Mei and Chunyu's disappearance, a story she hoped Mei would corroborate and repeat.

Mei wrote back three weeks later, telling her of a potential plan to visit Father sometime before the year was out, as there was "too much going on" right now. But Mei didn't make any reference to Chunyu's story about their disappearance. It was insignificant, irrelevant, and microscopically trivial compared with the great course of events that were currently unfolding, on which Mei was hoping to leave her very own fingerprints.

Mei had since steered clear of the topic. The conversation between them dried up.

2.

Was Comrade Chen's existence a myth, like one of the tales Mei used to spin from her unbridled imagination to impress their half sisters? This incredible thought ambushed Chunyu one night as she lay awake.

In the first few days after her arrival in Shanghai, Chunyu didn't see Comrade Chen around the house. He wasn't home when she went to bed and wasn't around for breakfast when she got up in the morning. She didn't know when—or whether—he got home at all.

"He's been really busy lately, held up in long meetings. The big heads from Peking are here."

"He's taken a trip to Chongming Island, to meet with the local cadres."

"He's signed up for a course in the history of Shanghai workers' movements."

Chunyu's curious glances at the empty seat at the dinner table invariably prompted an explanation from her sister. Comrade Chen lived in Mei's words.

However, there was circumstantial evidence pointing to his existence. One morning Chunyu found two cigarette butts in the kitchen sink. Another time, she spotted men's clothing mingled with Mei's in the laundry basin as the housemaid, provided by the Party, was doing the washing.

She heard of him often, and saw *of* him sometimes.

His full name was Chen Tiansheng, or Chen Tianchen—she wasn't quite sure of the exact characters as Mei only mentioned it once in passing. He was always Comrade Chen around the house, and became Director Chen over the telephone when Mei or the maid picked up the line. Director of the Industry and Commerce Bureau in the municipal government, a pivotal department according to Mei, to keep the wheels of the city, and to some extent, the country, rolling.

"Does he know enough about commerce, you think?" Chunyu asked Mei innocently, remembering his background as a farmer boy and then a soldier.

Mei looked at her as if stung by a bee.

"So, you are one of them too," she said coldly.

"What?" Chunyu was puzzled.

"You don't believe we can run the country."

Chunyu immediately realized her mistake. There are things in the world that can't be questioned, a victor's confidence, for example, and a wife's pride. Mei was much more Mrs. Chen than Yuan Mei now.

The safest way is for each of you to marry into a different Party, so when things get messy, one can watch over the other.

Mother's wish, a parting gift of wisdom from a woman who had, or thought she had, got the rules of the world figured out, had been partially fulfilled through Mei, her favorite daughter. Mei, the prettier and more quick-witted of the two, had chosen the right Party to give herself to. In Comrade Chen, Mei had found a steel roof that could withstand any rainstorm. Mother would be pleased with herself and proud of Mei in heaven—if there was such a thing—for the right half of her wish materialized and the wrong half, the alliance with the Nationalist Party, dodged.

What a wise gambler Mother had been, by placing a well-calculated bet in the game of man against fate on the most secure spot: the sibling connection. Blood is always thicker than water.

Isn't it?

Chunyu's new life in Shanghai came with a bombardment of new vocabulary that Mei introduced daily, tossing Chunyu into a perpetually confusing, and almost infantile, cycle of learning, retaining, relapsing, and relearning.

"A *domestic assistant*, a *comrade*, that's what she is," Mei repeatedly corrected her sister, more sternly each time, whenever Chunyu slipped into the term *housemaid*. "Only the bourgeoisie class has *maids*. She is assigned here to help Comrade Chen with his work, as simple as that. In this new society, we are all equals working towards the same goal. What better word to use than *comrade*?"

Did any of the words she learned in school have the same meanings? Chunyu wondered. She felt, with a crushing despair, that she was shrinking, intellectually, back to a grade school girl, lost in words elusive and specious. Memory could no longer be trusted; neither could experience. There existed a shimmering hostility between present and past, the boundary of which was increasingly volatile, as every new day was eagerly pushed into a new past in the spirit of a general negation of anything that had come before.

Liberation. Land reform. Landlords. Poor and lower-middle peasant class. Bourgeoisie class. Proletarian class. Capitalist. Comprador. Exploitation. The oppressor and the oppressed. Chunyu recognized every character of the phrases, but their accumulative effect generated a fog in her mind. What a waste, the previous twenty-one years of her life, since everything she had learned now needed to be unlearned. In bleak moments of doubt, she started to question whether she had lost her marbles, a dog's instinct to scent out new surroundings, to survive and thrive.

"What's the difference between a capitalist and a bourgeoisie?" One day after dinner, catching Mei in a rare moment of quiet relaxation, Chunyu ventured to ask, "What do you think our father is, then?" Their father was a well-to-do tea merchant in a town called East Creek, about eighty kilometers from the city of Wenzhou, where Chunyu would later come to settle.

A soft knot started to form on Mei's brow where her thoughts traveled.

"Big money and small money, I guess," the answer came, slow and hesitant in the beginning, but quickly gathering confidence as it rolled on. "Our father is bigger than a bourgeoisie, but not quite to the scale of a capitalist. He is a sure oppressor, though. Their marriage was purchased, there was no love in it."

Chunyu listened quietly, not totally convinced. It didn't need a genius to see that Mother hadn't been happy in the marriage, but was she oppressed, honestly? Father's provision had seemed, in general, to keep them comfortable and there had been moments, rare and fleeting as they were, when Father had tried to put his best foot forward to win Mother's smile. The true and final answer was buried with Mother. *A marriage is like a pair of shoes: only the wearer knows whether they fit,* went the old saying.

But Chunyu, a silent dissenter in the making, restrained herself from a rushed comment. Her instinct whispered to her, loudly, to let Mei have her say. The gush of Mei's self-conscious rectitude had to find a pair of willing and receptive ears, if she, Chunyu, wished to share a corner of Mei's roof in peace.

3.

Still settling in, Chunyu tried to make herself useful in her idle time by helping the maid. An assistant to the *domestic assistant*, she was amused with her new role.

The city was still in a chaotic stage of transition, with the new power treading its way—tentatively in the beginning but growing bolder with each step—through the old patchwork of the governing system, establishing its new roots as it gradually advanced. A salary system was yet to be established for government employees. At the time, every need was provided for by the Party: food, lodging, furniture, medical care, schools, marriage, divorce, burial, daily essentials, and especially, the needs of the soul.

The residence provided for Comrade Chen was a two-story French-style villa with a sizable backyard, located in the southwestern part of the city. The building, split into two equal halves, was now shared by the Chen household and another family, each having a separate entrance. Its previous residents, Chunyu was told, were two brothers, joint owners of a textile manufacturing plant who had fled to Hong Kong at the fall of Nanking, the seat of the Nationalist government.

Having lived for so long in a hole of a dormitory with two other nurse's aides, Chunyu found the house, even split in half, confusingly large. Days after her arrival, she still got easily lost in the labyrinth-like pathways connecting the cluster of rooms, made more dazzling and complicated by glass walls and mirrors with gilded frames of elaborately carved wood. She hated mirrors. She wondered how Mei could breathe, trapped in the hell of kaleidoscopic reflections of herself.

"This house will be used as another office for Comrade Chen." A whiff of uneasiness flitted through Mei's eyes as she tried to justify their living space. "In the future, he'll receive important guests here, foreign reporters, local and international capitalists—of course they have to be willing to work with us to begin with. It's the façade of our city, the window of a shop, to show the world the new republic is not a beggars' state, not anymore."

But he is never home, refuted the silent dissenter in Chunyu, unconvinced but mute, as usual. *We are all equals, sure, but not everyone gets to live in a French villa.*

One day, Chunyu got herself lost again, stranded in a storage space closed off from the rest of the rooms where there was nothing but a rattan baby crib. The dim midday light revealed a pink flannel sheet spread over the crib, fresh, soft, and fluffy, waiting, in eagerness, for a warm little bundle to breathe life into it.

It appeared to be brand new, the crib. Was this provided by the Party too, in anticipation of a new addition to the household?

From the base of her thighs came a sudden surge of warmth, shooting up to her breasts that swelled so full she began to feel pain. In a trance, she saw herself turning into a gigantic cow, ready to produce an unimpeded flow of milk, a creek, a river, an ocean, enough to feed all the babies in the world twice over. The swoon of delight nearly paralyzed her, filling her ears with a joyful humming of thousands of buds in gestation, in an imagined faraway garden, impatient to break out in a riot of blooms. She forgot, for a moment, that it was October.

A child, Mei's child. Not her own, but close enough.

That evening, Chunyu caught Mei alone in the living room reading a newspaper. After a few awkward attempts at conversation about the weather and local food, which triggered a string of yawns from Mei, Chunyu was propelled, by her deplorably obstinate curiosity, to the land-mine zone of the crib. "I found the crib. Is it happening?" she asked, carefully suppressing the excitement in her voice.

"If you are too busy, leave her with me, I'll raise her for you. There's nothing much for me to do anyway," she quickly added to the question that still awaited an answer, not knowing why she picked the word *her* instead of *him.*

She was expecting a tirade, an indignantly righteous lecture, about the titanic importance of the liberation of mankind versus the infinitesimal insignificance of one's personal desire, but Mei surprised her with a long pause.

"What do you think we've been doing for the last few years?" Her voice, devoid of any inflection, finally shattered the silence. "His son hates his guts, refuses to come to live with us. Who can blame him? Twelve years, not a letter, a word, from his father."

"But you are only twenty-two, you still . . ."

A faint sneer around the corners of Mei's mouth put a sudden halt to Chunyu's efforts at consolation.

"You've never been with a man since *then*, have you?" Mei said. She fixed Chunyu with a soul-chilling stare. "How naïve of you to think we can get pregnant, after what we were told to take."

It was the first time since their reunion that Mei had made a reference to *then*, the first crack in the hardened crust of a battered heart. Of the myriad of emotions, relief and comfort floated to the surface, seizing Chunyu with an unforeseen force as she stretched out her arms, without realizing, to hold Mei to her. In that very moment, she was certain that the person in her arms was indeed the sister she had lost. Vulnerability sealed their renewed bond of sisterhood.

"He knows nothing about *it*," murmured Mei, chin resting on Chunyu's shoulder, in muffled sobs.

4.

Then came Sunday. Mei was called away for a meeting and the domestic assistant took the day off to visit her mother on the other side of the city. Chunyu was left alone in the house.

It was dreadfully quiet. Every sound she made—the rustling of her clothing, the rubbing of her feet against the hardwood floor, a little sniffle, even her breathing—became audible, dragging out an echo that

chased her from room to room, dreadfully eerie and unnerving. She
slowed down in the middle of the hallway, just to dampen the omi-
nous trail of echo. But the flowers on the wallpaper popped open with
eyes, dark, deep, prickly, stinging her with cold scorn. *Imposter.* A chill
crawled up her spine: she recognized the blame.

It was the soul of the house, thrusting into her the lingering memory of its masters, generations of them. It had waited for days for this
very moment, alone, face to face with her, to show its bitter resentment.

Yes, the resentment, blame, and rage, from the restless ghosts of old
masters who had earned their right to be here with their lifelong labor
and care. What had she done to deserve a share of this splendor and
comfort? Nothing. Naught. Diddly. Zilch. Her presence here was a gift
pillaged. A plunder, a theft.

This new awakening horrified her. In fright she fled the house, running towards the backyard, unaware that she didn't have her shoes on.

It was deep into fall now but the lawn was still lush and lively. The
first frost was still a few weeks away in this mild subtropical climate.
Under her bare soles were the dew-softened blades of grass, ticklish,
cool, and strangely calming.

The first thing that jumped into her vision were the sunflowers.
Tall, zealous, regal, pure yellow flames, reaching up and out, dauntlessly.
No apology for the space they were taking. No intention of blending
in, inconspicuously, with the rest of the garden. A proud world of their
own. She had seen plenty of sunflowers in her hometown of East Creek,
almost anywhere, any little corner of an idle strip of land, common as
weeds. But they were nothing compared with what she saw here in this
garden. Shanghai could make gold out of any stone it touched, and a
prince out of any commoner.

A little distance away stood roses, in their last bloom, showing
visible signs of weariness. She had never really cared much for roses,
not because of their infamous thorns, but because of their crooked,

unshapely limbs and shoots. What an ugly plant if not for its blooms, its only saving grace.

But she was not alone, she suddenly became aware. Around a far corner of the garden was a man working on the lawn, huffing and puffing rhythmically to the rise and fall of his hoe. The ease with which he handled his tool was obvious; one could almost see a smile in the arch of his back, the raw, hearty pleasure in what he was doing. It was a gardener, probably provided, just like the domestic assistant, by the Party.

How should she address him? She quickly raked through the new collection of vocabulary instilled in her by Mei, finding no ready answer. *Comrade gardener? Comrade groundskeeper? Landscape assistant?* She was hugely amused by her wild improvisation.

Her gaiety quickly dried up as she realized, to her astonishment, what the man was doing with his hoe. Instead of weeding, as she had thought, he was actually tearing up the turf.

"Hey, you, stop right there!"

She rushed over, lashing out breathlessly at the man. But it was too late, the damage was done. A corner of the lawn, the size of a bed, was already dug out. A rectangular patch of dark and moist earth lay bare, mixed with clusters of uprooted grass. An ugly scar on the expanse of green next to it, a mocking insult.

The man rose, turning around and sizing her up with eyes narrowed against the glaring sunlight, his receding hairline glistening with perspiration. His face showed a few more years than his back, square, ruddy, with wrinkles running towards each other in some sort of dark mirth. His shirtsleeves and pant legs were both rolled up, exposing a network of bulging veins underneath the skin, like lines of rivers on a detailed map.

"Ever seen such rich soil? You plant a chopstick, it gives you a tree in no time," he exclaimed joyously, propping himself against the handle of the hoe.

"What the hell are you doing?" Mortified by the damage done, she let her anger get the better of her.

Taken aback, not so much by her words as by her tone, the man paused, remaining quiet for a few moments. Setting down his hoe, he reached into his pocket for a cigarette, lit it with a match, inhaling slowly and deliberately, as if working on an answer to a difficult question.

"Little comrade, what do you think I'm doing? Such good soil, lying in waste. Why not grow something useful, like vegetables?" he said slowly, between two puffs.

Little? What a shameless, flagrant flaunting of age and experience. She was anything but *little*.

"You mean to rip up this garden for *vegetables*?" Her face flushed ruddy with disbelief; she was unaware, until later, of how she uttered the word *vegetables*, as if they were flies or maggots on a piece of rotten meat.

"Why not? Half of Shanghai can't find food to fill their dinner plates. You have no idea how people live outside these walls, little princess, because everything you need is provided for."

His harsh mockery, totally unexpected, struck her speechless. It took a good long moment before the words eventually found her tongue.

"How much do you know about me?" She returned his unflinching stare and retorted bluntly. "For things you have no clue about, better shut the hell up."

The man didn't know he'd just rubbed a raw spot.

"Did you get the permission from *Director* Chen, for this?" Her battle, which had begun with a half-minded defense, was now blown into a full-scale offensive.

"Why do I need his permission?" responded the man with an inscrutable smile.

A simple question, to which there was no easy answer. The work of the last few days hadn't been totally in vain, as she had learned not to fall into the booby trap of social status.

How should she explain Chen's role in her argument? A quasi owner of the villa? A fancy director in a fancy department that runs a fancy city? Why did she pick, after all, the epithet of *Director*? She was ashamed, deep down, of the new snob she had quickly become, and her inability to win a fight on her own without borrowing an extra hand, a hand that carried weight.

"Because he lives here" was the best she could come up with.

A roar of full-throated laughter. "So, my wife has never shown you a picture of me, heh? Am I too old for her, you think?"

It suddenly dawned on her to whom she was speaking. A weakness ran through her knees, and she lost her tongue.

"Sorry, Director Chen, I didn't know, didn't mean, so wrong, so very, sorry." She found herself entangled in a web of flustered apology.

The man watched patiently, like a cat toying with a captive mouse, until he finally got bored with the game. "The hell with *Director*, that's for fools. Just call me Old Chen when there's nobody around."

A hand was thrust out for her to shake, and her thin-boned palm quickly disappeared into his bearish paw.

She gradually relaxed as she noticed tobacco stains and the wet mud stuck in his fingernails. However paramount in importance his position, he was a peasant through and through. Nobody and nothing, not even Mei, not even Shanghai, could alter the cold, frigid, naked truth of his breeding and blood.

"I still think it's a pity to rip up the lawn and flower bed. It takes so much hard work to put together," she muttered quietly, fully aware of the waves of subdued disapproval she radiated. Her mind, now cleared, allowed a smooth passage—that'd been denied before—for the right words to walk to her tongue. How much worse could it be, to top off a flagrant offense with a trivial impropriety?

Old Chen didn't respond. He took off one of his rubber-soled canvas shoes and sat down on it, then removed the other one, tipping it over to shake the mud and grass out of it, and then repeated the process with the first shoe. When he stood up again, there were two dark, wet patches on the back of his pants where the shoe hadn't covered them. He didn't feel them, or he didn't care.

"Little comrade—can I call you that? You're a slip of a girl to an old man like me. Do you know what these bastards are doing to us? *Hostile forces*, polite words—to me they're just bastards. They put their stinky heads together and fix the price in the market. The money you paid to get a basket of peas yesterday, today you get half. Tomorrow, just a handful. They try to clear out their rotten meat and seafood for the price of gold. *Sleeping* crabs. That's the fancy name they've cooked up for their dead crabs!"

His tone grew a shade gruffer as he went on. "They want to starve the new government to a slow death. I wish I could shoot them, one by one, making a pile of *sleeping* men. My poor quartermaster's hair turned gray in a week. Who'd envy his job, trying to feed everyone with an empty basket? You're damn right I won't let this good land lie in waste, for *roses*, when my fellas have bloody mouth sores because they don't have enough vegetables on their plates!"

The silent dissenter in Chunyu didn't quite die, but grew less sure. The roses in her mind faded a shade (they never had much vigor to begin with), whereas the peas were growing stronger and more vivid.

"You are not an old man, you've just turned thirty-two. Mei told me." That wasn't exactly what she wanted to say, but she didn't know exactly what she did want to say either.

"All right, my little comrade, you let me grow my vegetables here in the backyard and I'll let you keep your roses and all that nonsense at the front. Never a word more to bother each other, hear me?"

Chunyu couldn't help but smile forth a half-reluctant agreement. Maybe, just maybe, there was another reason for Mei's choice of a husband beyond what Mother had wished for. Perhaps Mei liked this man, even just a little.

"Do you have to do this by yourself? Don't you have help, people you can boss around?" Chunyu asked Old Chen in a more relaxed, almost chatty manner.

"Sure, I can gather an army, if I want to. I'm a damn director, am I not? But this is my own fun, the best kind of rest. My work has cost me too much hair."

"You call this rest?" She chuckled, casting a skeptical glimpse at his sweat-streaked face and the dried mud flakes on his sleeves.

"Nothing better," he replied, almost gleefully. "The dirt relaxes me. It's my baby milk, no one can wean me off it, the smell of it."

Just as she thought he was ready to resume his land reform project, he suddenly pointed the tip of his hoe towards her, as if it were a long-barreled gun.

"Don't know what's in your womenfolk's mind, always putting looks before your stomach. Can't hard times teach you anything? Can roses feed you when your stomach is empty, heh?" he mumbled while wiping the beads of sweat off his forehead.

Every inch a farmer.

He threw himself right back into his work with such joy and energy that every move of the hoe was charged with an unsung song. Chunyu no longer existed, nor did the rest of the world.

A weird thought struck her, watching him working. Was this whole business of food shortage a convenient excuse for him to justify his caprice, so that he could relive, in his backyard, his childhood and youth? A part of life he hated so much that he had to break away at the first chance available, leaving everything behind? Don't people always love the things they hate?

"Director Chen—Old Chen, I mean, can I ask you for a favor?"

Feeling a tap on his arm, he paused. "Shoot."

"Mei said she would find me a job when I settle in. I've been here a little while now. My bones are growing mold doing nothing all day long."

Chunyu's vivid exaggeration sent Chen into another roar of boisterous laughter.

"What's your working experience, tell me?" His face instantly grew serious, an expression he probably wore every day in his office when talking business.

"A year short of high school, because of the war. I worked in a hospital, for a while, doing"—she hesitated, feeling the weight of her memory—"odd jobs."

A twist in his brows suddenly alerted her to a possibility she wanted to avert at all costs.

"I can do anything to earn a living, anything but the hospital," she pleaded, a tremor in her voice.

"Why? Is it beneath you?" There was a curt edge in his question, a mixture of vexation and displeasure.

A strange man, inscrutable and unpredictable, Chunyu warned herself. Underneath the coarse, weather-battered skin there lived a childlike, sensitive soul, every change in mood rising to the surface, instantaneously visible. No subtle sophistication, no social finesse.

"No, that's not the reason," she protested, with a flush of hurt. "It's just I've seen too much sickness and dying. I want to do something that lets me see a little *life*."

A flicker of satisfaction, an *I see* smile, quickly dissipated the gloom that had gathered a moment ago, as if he just discovered a redeeming quality in something he had deemed beyond saving. He closed his eyes, a muscle shifting slightly across his forehead. A thought, or perhaps several, was in gestation. When his eyes opened again, a decision had been born, full term.

"Why don't you work right here, in charge of this little farming thing? I can send you whatever help you need. I'll be around to give you a hand if I can get away from the meetings—some people just need to learn when to shut the hell up. You can do peas, garlic sprouts, radishes, spinach, cabbage, all year round."

Chunyu didn't know what to say. This certainly was not what she had considered, before today, to be a line of work.

"You can raise chickens, even pigs, if our dandy neighbors won't kick up a stink. Enough life for you to see. My quartermaster will thank you for the rest of his life." The excitement burned on. "I'll put you in the roster of my department. We run on a provision system, I don't have cash to pay you a salary. But what do you need money for, anyway? Everything you need is provided for, just like for your sister; now you'll have your own provision."

With those words, a deal was sealed.

"Now move and make yourself useful." Old Chen gave a sideways toss of his head, motioning her to the small bare patch. "You pick out grass from the soil. It's not dead, it'll grow right back if mixed in. Don't throw it away, just give it a good sunning to dry out. It'll be your next load of fertilizer."

A lot to learn, for the next while.

"You are a bit different from your sis," noted Old Chen, seeing Chunyu, across the path of his vision, plant her bare feet into the wet mud and proceed with her assigned task, slowly, awkwardly, but without fuss.

"What do you mean?"

"You don't mind getting your hands dirty," he said impassively. "Some schooled folks think they are above others—the sour air they carry, you smell it from three miles away." He snickered.

She lifted her face towards him in confusion and with curiosity. "Are you talking about my sister?"

He replied with a cough.

5.

Chunyu's new job altered her perception of time, the calendar now a useless display on the kitchen wall. The passage of days and months was now measured by the little stages that constituted the growing cycle. The time to sow, the time to weed, the time to fertilize, the time to set up trellises, and the time to harvest.

In the next year, with the help of the man that Old Chen sent, a seasoned vegetable grower, Chunyu's garden became a reliable mini source of vegetables and poultry for the canteen where Chen and his comrades ate lunch and sometimes supper.

Then there came the occasional knock on the door, usually a neighbor with a complaint. Originally an outrage, suppressed and then suppressed again on his or her way here, until it sounded like nothing more than a casual neighborly chat. Always the most carefully chosen words, delivered in the most polite and respectful tone, about the crowing of the cocks at the most ungodly hours, or a *slight* smell of something (they carefully avoided the word *manure*) that crept through the cracks of their windows on certain days—of course, the wind was to blame.

Rumors traveled fast. The entire block had by now guessed the status of the new occupants of the villa. Those a little slow and less connected in the gossip department had also reached a similar conclusion by a different route, from the sight of the cars pulling up every now and then into the driveway, disgorging important-looking visitors (once or twice even foreigners, a fast-disappearing species nowadays).

Chunyu, as the one who usually answered the door, handled the situation with delicate care. No high-handed lectures about petty personal inconvenience versus the grave needs of a new nation, et cetera. Not once did she drag the name of Director Chen to her defense, not even a passing reference. In fact, there was no defense—though rightfully expected of her—presented in any shape or form. Instead, she plunged right into a torrent of naked apologies that took the visitors by surprise, easing them into the right frame of mind for peacemaking.

Her apologies, however, were not accompanied by any promises for corrective measures, but instead, by a gift, *a humble token of gratitude* as she called it, in the form of a few fresh eggs with the harvest date pencil-marked on the shell (her way of keeping track of their freshness), a few tomatoes or cucumbers or a slice of pumpkin, depending on the season, often with fresh mud still on the skin.

By the time the visit finished, usually within a brief span of ten to fifteen minutes, hostility (never overt to begin with) had subsided into a placid neutrality leaning towards a faint possibility of friendship. Grievances were quelled much better with food than with words in this chaotic time, with everything in short supply and inflation burning a huge hole in every pocket.

Mei and Old Chen listened with dropped jaws when these anecdotes, all in past tense by then, were related at the dinner table.

"What a pity you aren't in politics, a lot fewer wars" was Chen's reaction.

"Looks like you've learned a few ropes here" was Mei's remark, referring, not too subtly, to Chunyu's awkward callowness when she first arrived in Shanghai about a year ago.

The edge of condescension in Mei's tone chafed Chunyu sharply, and she replied with a mute sneer. It seemed that Mei had forgotten the many schemes Chunyu had contrived, on various occasions in their past, to dig Mei out of her hideous pit of misery. What a selective and convenient memory. There weren't any tactics that Chunyu hadn't always known. She could conjure up her tricks, absorbed from Mother's amniotic fluid, even in her sleep. For Mei to brush off a natural gift as some cheap lessons learned under *her* wing—how flagrant, and how dare she.

Since the start of the miniature farm, Old Chen had spent more time at home, for supper and almost certainly on Sundays, his only day off. The minute he got into the house and set down his briefcase, he would rush to the backyard, now refenced and well sectioned off for different purposes.

With his jacket discarded and his shoes kicked off, he would squat, barefoot, on the stone steps leading to the garden, a cigarette in hand, lost in the colors of the vegetable patch. The green of the beans, the deepening crimson of the tomatoes, the pale yellow of the pumpkin flowers, all the plants an extra inch taller than in the morning, he was convinced. His wrinkles faded in the pure pleasure and satisfaction of a farmer at the prospect of a foreseeable harvest.

"It makes you so happy, that little patch of land," Mei said to her husband at the dinner table, not without jealousy. "If that's all you want, you could've got it without leaving your village. What's the point of marching ten thousand miles through all the mud and blood?"

He put down his emptied bowl, starting the first cigarette of the evening in silence. No offense taken, no response given. He was a very different person in the garden; the good earth made him chatty.

"Comrade Chen wants his small world in this big world. One won't fill his heart without the other," Chunyu ventured—she never called him Old Chen in Mei's presence.

Immediately she regretted it. How dare she put herself in the position of knowing him better? She hated the undue responsibility she took upon herself, for breaking an awkward silence that she didn't create and wasn't hers to break.

Chunyu's patience with the vegetable plants, for some weird reason, just couldn't be duplicated in her care for the livestock—namely the chickens. In the first few weeks after she brought the freshly hatched chicks home from the market, forty of them altogether, she was fascinated by the liveliness of these little fluffy, tumbling balls. But her enthusiasm quickly waned as they grew into their gawky adolescence, with thin, long stocks of feet, ugly half-fledged bodies, and squeaky voices asserting their farcical existence.

Then her distaste turned into disgust when one day, a few months later, she came across a horrifying scene in the chicken quarter of the yard. A cock, the fastest growing and strongest one, launched a savage attack, totally unprovoked and unannounced, on a young hen. He was all over her, crushing her nearly flat on the ground with his entire body mass, aided by the viselike grip of his claws, his beak pecking, brutally, at the back of her head, like a nail driven by an insane hammer.

In a desperate attempt at defense, the hen flapped her wings hysterically, trying in vain to jerk herself loose from his grip. His wings, visibly stronger, overpowered hers, quickly neutralizing her. Four angry wings entangled, beating up a sky-darkening storm of dust and feathers, a true battle scene from hell. Chunyu felt a twist of pain as the shrilling shrieks of the hen pierced her eardrums.

Something suddenly snapped in her, severing her body from her mind. She watched herself grabbing, with both hands, a nearby spade, not thinking of what she would do with it. There came a loud bang, followed by a whirlwind of colors, motion, and noise, but she had no clear recollection of what happened.

When she finally came to herself, she saw, in astonishment, a smashed cock's head on the ground in a puddle of frothy blood, among feathers and bits of crushed bones. A nauseating rush of repulsion propelled her gaze away from the eye remaining in the mutilated head. Glassy and wide open, it stared at her with an icy force of disbelief and fury. Drained and breathless, she leaned against the fence to regain her composure, feeling an urgent need to pee.

Later that evening, Mei and Old Chen were surprised to see a pot of stewed chicken among the few routine vegetable dishes on their dinner table. A rarity in those days that usually needed a justification, such as a family reunion, a New Year's gathering, a birthday, or a special guest—people didn't just cook chicken for no reason.

Chunyu's face tightened when Mei asked, out of curiosity, what the occasion was. "Do I need a reason to enjoy a bite of chicken after all I've put in for the garden?"

Chunyu's gruff eruption, unexpected and nameless, put an abrupt end to any further inquiry into this matter. But it didn't go unnoticed that she didn't touch the chicken throughout the meal.

6.

Orange came to Chunyu on a cold winter day, close to the Lunar New Year. It was the second Lunar New Year since the end of the civil war, the coldest winter in Chunyu's memory, with the washing on the laundry line stiffening into an armor of thin ice.

This winter found Chunyu curled up in bed quite often, in a sunny spot if the sun was out. The last batch of vegetables had long been collected, with the major part sent off to the canteen and whatever remained—usually radishes and cabbages—pickled for family consumption in the next few months before spring arrived.

It was the idlest period in the year, but there were still things to do. Mending the holes in the fence, for example, before they became big enough for chickens to find their gleeful freedom in the street, and rearranging the contents of the toolshed for more space to store extra kindling wood and charcoal. But she found little drive to get out of bed. The daily care of the chickens had been delegated to her helper, which gave her more free time to waste. She was pulled out of bed only by her need for lunch, and the presupper fuss to get her armor ready before Mei and Old Chen came home.

A general sense of purposelessness, the same lethargic feeling she had experienced in the last days of her time at the hospital, returned in full force. She didn't know it was depression, which wasn't even a word in those days.

Father had died three months ago and her tie with East Creek, feeble to begin with, was now no more. Since Victory Day, which marked the end of the Anti-Japanese War, she had only been home once. There was no strong motivation to repeat the visit. Her father had five wives and fifteen children, all before the Communist takeover, of course, as polygamy was not allowed anymore. What amount of fatherly love could remain, being split up among five households and fifteen daughters? A son, whom he had never had, might have taken up a monstrous chunk of his attention but made them less divided as a family.

She would come to appreciate, in the years that followed, Father's timely death and the blessed lack of a brother, a legitimate heir to Father's entire fortune, which was now divided among four households and thirteen daughters (she and Mei had gladly chosen to remove themselves from the abstruse game of math). The dispersion of the assets, as if orchestrated by a mysterious unseen hand, inadvertently shielded the family from the whirlwind of the joint state-private ownership movement that would arrive a mere five years later.

The feeling of remoteness was mutual, as she had discovered, which assuaged her sense of guilt to some extent. A few months after they settled in Shanghai, Mei had written home suggesting, lukewarmly, a possible reunion for the New Year, the first one in more than five years, which Father refused in a surprisingly firm tone. "The Communists don't like people of money, and we are by no means their favored flock. So it'd be wise for you to keep a distance from us, if you and your husband want to stay safe and secure in your position," said Father in his reply, weirdly echoing Mei's sentiment.

From then on, the two sisters had kept a very thin trickle of correspondence with East Creek, until one day Chunyu received an unexpected letter from her eldest half sister bearing the news of Father's sudden death. Passed away in his sleep, no warning signs whatsoever, at seventy-two, an age that could be entered into a lustrous record of longevity in those days.

Enclosed in the letter was another letter, tightly sealed, "For Chunyu's eyes only, to be posted after I am no longer around" in Father's big, slightly tilted brushwork on the back of the envelope.

Father had, after all, foreseen his end coming. The letter was dated two years ago, and in it Father wrote:

> *A certain young man with only two fingers left on his right hand came knocking at my door, around the time when victory was announced. He'd been here once before to deliver a message for you, about your mother's sad passing. He demanded money from me, as a 'compensation' for his hand injury that he blamed you for. If I didn't give him what he wanted, he'd start to 'spread the word around.' I gave him some, but no way near the astronomical sum he asked for, and told him 'my two daughters have never contacted me, most probably both dead, somewhere. So do what you like for all I care.' This seemed to work, for he hasn't come back since, though I don't know for how long.*
>
> *Do NOT come home in case he gets wind of it. He seems to know your Japanese names only, which makes it a little harder for him to track you down, but your whereabouts aren't a top secret if he really wants to dig.*
>
> *Mei's husband, whom I've never met, holds quite a position in the new government by the sound of it—your mother should rest in peace knowing that. You need to make sure not a smidge of dirt gets to his ear . . .*

So Father had known, all along, the horrid truth about their disappearance but kept a calm and cool face—never a crack to indicate otherwise—when listening to her carefully crafted lies. Unsummoned tears suddenly blurred Father's words. That sensitivity, that concern, which she had never known existed in him until too late. His decision not to see them was, after all, not for the reason she had suspected. What a despicably narrow mind she had that had doggedly refused to recognize the rare but true shining moments of unselfish generosity in the dull, selfish, shrewd man that was her father.

But Father didn't mention whether her half sisters and their respective mothers knew about *it*. The relationship between the Yuan children had always been volatile, today an ally, tomorrow a foe, in a constant battle for Father's approval, affection, and ultimately his wallet. Any secret in the hands of her half sisters would be as secure as a pile of running sand. Father's death left Chunyu more determined than ever to sever her ties with East Creek, once and for all.

Ever since Father's letter, every knock on the door, every stranger wandering in the street, made her jump. Her secret was no longer safe.

She kept the letter from Mei. Mei could handle, with ease, an ardent crowd of followers, but would be totally unraveled by a faceless shadow behind. They each had an allotted role to fill: Mei a flag bearer and trumpet blower, leading the marching and pageantry, Chunyu a cleaning lady to clear up the mess of a seedy, conniving underworld. While there was more than enough mess to warrant the existence of multiple Chunyus, there might not be enough spotlights for two Meis.

One day, Chunyu stayed in bed till nearly suppertime, skipping breakfast and lunch altogether. Sitting up half-dazed, she peered out through a gap between the curtains, noticing that the tailor shop across the street had hung a pair of red chiffon lanterns. The soft, warm glow of festivity knocked an icy fact into her: another year had drawn to its end. New Year was the cruelest thing that had ever been invented in human history, especially for the homeless. Yes, she was homeless with Father gone, although she hadn't been aware till now that Father had owned a place in her heart.

It was weird that she had never considered where she was home. In fact, she wasn't even sure that this building was *Mei's* home. Mei was just as much a drifter. A childless house could never be a home.

Lately, she had heard Mei talking to Old Chen about finding her a *home*, to which he gave a vague nod, his oblique yes, she surmised. The prospect of dating a man, a total stranger, sent her skin crawling. Sensing her apprehension, Mei tried in the best way she could to give her a little boost. "They don't have to know about *it*, ever," breathed Mei behind Old Chen's back.

How could she carry a secret of such size into a shared life, and still sleep at night? A shadow, a glance, a whisper, even a breath of air would make her jitter. To keep the secret was hell; to lose it, death.

In the lowest of her low moods, she found Orange. Or, as one might say, it was Orange who found her. Their dire mutual needs drove them to each other.

She got up, making her way, listlessly, to the backyard. She was the only one around the house, as the yard assistant and the domestic assistant had both left earlier in the day for their New Year's holiday. The chickens had been let out, cooing and clucking on the bare vegetable patch, digging for roots and seeds left in the dirt while leaving their droppings everywhere, a natural fertilizer for next season.

It was so cold, the coldest day in the coldest month. The sun was hanging low—pale, remote, worn out. Winter in places south of the Yangtze, brief as it may be, wore a straitjacket of humidity, clinging to one's bones until the blood turned to ice. Chunyu's hands and feet were swollen from chilblains that tortured her alternately with itchiness and pain.

She went to check the chicken coops for eggs laid during the day, but there weren't any. Before leaving for the holiday, the yard assistant had replaced the hay, now smelling of a mixture of last season's sunshine and this season's damp. Just as Chunyu was about to rise, she heard a sibilant hissing that made her pause. A further look inside revealed two bulbs of light, round, grayish green, flickering with a fierce fear and distrust.

It took her a few moments to realize that it was a cat hiding in the corner. In the dim light, its fur shimmered, a glow of yellow with a hint of orange, woven with stripes of brown. A miniature tiger, a startled and vigilant one. It jumped as her hand approached, its back arching high, hair exploding into a ball of needles.

"Poor, poooor little thing, must be soooo cold out there. Isn't it a good thing I didn't patch up the fence?" she crooned, surprised by the gushy tenderness in her voice. "It's them chickens' house, they wouldn't like you here. You better come over. I won't hurt you, I promise. Let me find you a good place, poooor thing. Come, not to fret."

The cat backed itself against the wall while sizing her up, shaky, confused, and wary. There was something, maybe in her voice, maybe in her posture, maybe in her smell, that made it decide, slowly and gradually, to lower its armor. After what seemed like a century, its hair settled and it inched over to her, sniffing, shyly and tentatively, her outstretched fingers.

Orange, that's the name she decided to give her—she had an inkling that it was a girl cat.

She didn't know at the time that cold weather wasn't the only reason that drove Orange, a street cat, into her backyard.

7.

With firewood and hay, Chunyu built a little bed for Orange in a corner of the toolshed, the warmest option short of bringing her indoors—she couldn't honestly turn Mei's house into an animal playground. Then she rushed to the kitchen to scavenge water and leftover food, setting them right next to the bed, a feline haven thus completed. The door of the toolshed was left slightly ajar, just in case Orange needed to go out.

Later in the evening, she checked on Orange to find the water level down but no dent in the food.

"You picky thing, don't you like my food? You've got to eat." She picked her up, a little surprised by her weightiness for a street cat. Orange didn't fight her. Instead, she snuggled against her, purring as if she had known those arms forever. The soft suppleness of Orange's body warmed Chunyu, making her feel drowsy. "Don't you dare run away. A night like this, even the mice won't leave their holes," she warned her, half teasingly.

Just as she was about to leave, she felt a soft weight on her wrist. It was Orange's paw pulling her hand. There was something in Orange's eyes, two clear pools of moonlit water, sad, fearful, helpless, pleading for companionship. Chunyu felt a twinge in her heart. "Silly girl, I can't be with you for long. You don't want me to turn into an icicle, do you?"

During the night, she heard a few faint meows but quickly went back to sleep, feeling strangely reassured. Orange didn't go away. She was in her little bed, and everything was all right.

She rose very early in the morning, before Mei and Old Chen were up—she hadn't been up awake this early for quite a while. Bundling herself up and grabbing a flashlight, she tiptoed downstairs, unlatched the door, and slipped quietly into the backyard. It was still dark, the sky just starting to show the first signs of cracking. The ground was barren, open, and flat, shimmering with a thin layer of ice from last night's drizzle. She rushed to the toolshed and shone her flashlight onto the bed.

Orange was there, startled by the sudden assault of light, eyes narrowing with confusion and annoyance against the unannounced intrusion. Chunyu turned the light away from her eyes, noticing that Orange had grown visibly bigger overnight. A second look nearly dumbfounded her: nestling against Orange's belly, now swollen pink, were three tiny ratlike creatures with sparse wet fur, twitching and suckling.

Kittens.

It suddenly dawned on Chunyu that Orange had come to the yard knowing she'd soon be in labor. She had begged her, in cats' language, to stay with her last night. Of all the houses on the street, Orange had chosen this one to bear her young in; of all the humans she might have run into, Orange had picked Chunyu to entrust with her life. A mother's mortal fear, an animal's instinctive trust. But she had left Orange all by herself, in dire need.

"I've let you down, poor thing," Chunyu murmured, filled with guilt. Orange had strangely revived Chunyu's desire, lying dormant for years, to be needed, and to be alive.

Chunyu dipped her finger into the food, still largely untouched, trying to feed Orange with it. Orange gave a perfunctory lick before turning away and resuming her grooming duty on the newborns, whom Chunyu could see a bit clearer now. One white with a few gray and black spots, the other two both ginger colored, more like their mother, one with a white chin, the other a shade darker with more pronounced brown stripes. Spot, Ginger, and Leopard, she quickly named them.

Orange's tongue was patient and tireless, leaving no spot uncovered—the kittens' ears that were more like two tiny holes with no flaps yet; the pink bellies with the umbilical cords curling up like withered vines; the tiny paws with claws that didn't know yet how to retract; and the private areas covered by the largely unformed tails. One by one, round after round. Squirming and nudging, the little ones gave out occasional meek, squeaky sounds of contentment.

A surge of nameless emotion washed over Chunyu's womb, where she felt the universe's emptiness originated. She broke down into a sudden fit of sobs.

A void, a huge void in her life, that could only be filled by a Spot, a Ginger, or a Leopard of her own. A wild dream, that's what she needed for it to happen. A miracle.

The care of Orange and her clan became a new purpose in life, pulling Chunyu back into her regular daily routine, her schedule now charted around their mealtimes and bedtimes.

After a brief bout of diabolically cold weather, the mild days returned, all signs pointing to an early spring. She and the yard assistant, now returned from his New Year's holiday, started to prepare the soil for the spring sowing. Meanwhile, with astronomical speed, the kittens grew. Their eyes opened and their irises assumed their permanent color: six tiny pools of melting blue. The ear flaps appeared, some awkward thin stubs initially, soon turning into pointy, wiggly miniature trumpets constantly alert to sound and motion. The fur grew thick and fluffy, taking on a lustrous sheen, the claws became firm and retractable, and each tail, a bush.

But nothing could compete with their exponential growth in curiosity. No longer confined to their den, they thrust their wild rollicking farther and farther into every corner of the yard, wallowing delightedly in mud, trusting wholeheartedly in the omnipotent cleansing power of their mother's tongue, and totally impervious to the flock of chickens skittering around.

It was the chickens, giants in comparison and more formidable, that were confused and nearly terrified by these strange, tiny, dauntless furred creatures that ran faster than devils. There wasn't any point behaving in a territorial manner, the chickens soon realized, to their dismay, as *territory* was not a word in the lexicon of kittens. The kittens' dictionary, at this stage, contained only four words: *mother, food, play,* and *sleep,* in that order. With a tacit understanding among themselves, the chickens quickly learned to keep their distance whenever the furry devils came near.

Never for a second did Orange let her young ones out of her sight. She was always close enough for an emergency rescue, if needed, yet not so close as to interfere. Alert but lazy, and almost genial, Orange seemed at times more a grandma than a mother.

"Don't grow up, not so fast," murmured Chunyu in blissful, pleasurable languor, watching Ginger nibble Leopard's ear on a sunny, breezeless afternoon and Spot chase the shadow of his ghostly, brisk tail. The rest of the world seemed to be standing still, in a hypnotic trance.

But there was a phantom voice at the back of her mind warning her, in a prescient whisper, of something about to happen. *It's all a sham,* the voice echoed, *nothing good will last, just like peace is ended by war, life by death, and love by betrayal.*

She waited, in fearful suspense, for *it* to happen. Yet time went by and nothing happened. What an absurd folly, the uncalled-for apprehension and panic, she observed in a fit of self-derision. A sign of aging, that's what it was, she felt sure—she probably was the oldest twenty-three-year-old in the world. The kittens would grow into healthy cats, and there would be a time when Ginger, the only female of the three, would bear her own kittens and perform, like her mother, a dandy grooming job on her young, who would in turn grow up and have their own young. The cycle would go on and on, till eternity.

Just as she was beginning to relax, *it* suddenly struck out of the blue, on a very normal day in late April. In fact, it was more normal than most normal days. The hens didn't lay square eggs, there were no three-legged cocks in the flock, the cucumber seedlings were going through a normal growth spurt, Mei, now a doting feline lover, came home at a normal hour with no complaints about work, and Spot, the strongest and wildest of the three kittens, was taking his adventure a step further into the new world of height.

Using a stool as a stepping-stone, Spot climbed onto a tree stump, then a lower tree branch, then a higher one. After a series of tentative advances, he got himself onto the wall separating their yard from the neighbor's. A new view, a new world, allowed by a freshly achieved height, elevated him to cloud nine, his head swelling with the vain notion of his own immensity versus the diminished size of everything else.

A self-anointed prince and conqueror, Spot wasn't aware he had just let go of a lifesaving chance to make his second mistake, as his first one, which he was about to make, would soon prove to be fatal. At three months, no cat is humble.

Orange's attention was directed, at the time, to Ginger, who was playing peekaboo with Leopard, disappearing into a mini cave created by two intertwined tree roots above the ground. When she became aware of Spot's absence, it was too late. The princely conqueror, in his unbridled boldness fueled by curiosity, didn't notice a hole made by a missing brick. In a flash of a second, he slipped into the sandwich wall.

At Spot's heartrending cries from inside the wall, Orange sprang up, the panther in her suddenly awakening. Following the trail blazed a few moments ago by her young and reckless son, she leaped, light as a feather, to where Spot had fallen. On top of the wall she paced, perilously close to the edge, back and forth, in endless rounds, meowing plaintively and hysterically, trying to locate her son lost in the labyrinth of the layers of brickwork.

In blank anxiety Chunyu watched, feeling the daggers in Orange's deranged eyes, an icy, accusatory stare charging her with being useless and unfeeling. *A despicable windbag,* Orange hissed in her contempt.

A hectic rescue plan soon ensued, with wild ideas thrown together by everybody around, including Chunyu, Mei, the yard assistant, and the domestic assistant (Old Chen was away on a business trip). Tools and weaponry were gathered in a rush: a ladder, a bamboo pole, a long knotted rope, an iron hook, a basket, and even a small goldfish net, all of which inevitably failed to generate any positive results.

It was getting darker and darker as the night closed in. Hope was waning with each passing minute. Soon everyone realized that Spot was lost, in his foolhardy juvenile adventure, to an unassuming foe—a sandwich wall.

Spot's bloodcurdling cries, echoed by his mother's sorrowful howls, lasted through the night. Chunyu had to find cotton balls from Mei's emergency kit to block her ears, but a mother's woeful plea to a deaf god and a son's desperate wish for deliverance could always find a way through the densest cotton. Chunyu didn't sleep a wink.

Early in the morning, Chunyu got up, rushed to the predawn yard, and found Orange still on the wall, in a prone position now, too weak to stand. Spot's voice had diminished to a feeble whimper and, towards the later part of the day, was completely silent. Chunyu mounted the ladder, trying to get Orange down. Scrawny and shriveled, Orange was a different cat, her eyes dark, deep, dull, a pile of mournful ash and cinder.

It was then that Orange did something that petrified Chunyu—she bit her, a raw, hard, sharp-toothed, relentless bite. Never before had Chunyu seen so much repulsion and loathing in the eyes of another human, let alone a cat.

Orange remained an unflinching and unapproachable fixture on the wall for two days, refusing any offer of food or comfort, not heeding the needs of her other two children. The third morning, when Chunyu got up to check on her, Orange was gone, together with Ginger and Leopard, leaving no trace whatsoever, as if their prior existence were the mere delusion of an insane mind. A roar of silent protest, the ultimate declaration of condemnation, against a trust breached and love betrayed.

Chunyu's days of true, bottomless depression had just begun.

8.

In the year of Orange (the cat had come to be a major reference point in Chunyu's mental chronological record), several events occurred, all contributing to the pivotal turn in her life.

First of all, the Korean War, the third major war in a short span of ten years, was raging along the northern border. Director Chen was among the first to volunteer his service for the battlefield. He missed the feel of rifles and grenades in his grip, but his nostalgia wasn't, in any significant way, reciprocal, as the weapons, much like women, preferred younger and more responsive hands. He didn't pass the first round of physical inspection. At thirty-three, he was nearly obsolete by military standards.

In the nationwide supporting-the-war frenzy, Mei donated her twenty-four-karat gold ring, the only memorabilia of Mother left behind in the world, thus rendering Chunyu and herself orphans through and through.

The second change, inconsequential by comparison, took place within their home, involving an abrupt termination of the vegetable garden project. An anonymous letter had mysteriously found its way onto the desk of the mayor's office, complaining about certain behavior "running counter to the new government's promise to protect the traditional characteristics of the city."

Old Chen's hazy ambition of replicating his home village in the backyard of a French-style villa was crushed, to his humiliation, with a harsh reprimand from his superiors. The yard assistant was sent packing, and a new team of two old-school gardeners was dispatched in his place to restore the turf and the flower beds—a reflection of the general cycle of destruction followed by restoration, to be repeated every few years for several decades to come.

Shortly after the departure of the yard assistant, Old Chen had a chat with Mei at the dinner table, in a near whisper so as to be outside the hearing of the domestic assistant busy in the kitchen. "Now another war. The country is really bleeding, more hard times ahead. There're talks about thinning the list on the provision system. She is more needed by families with kiddies to look after."

Mei didn't know how to take this conversation. Was it a real concern, perhaps inordinately profound, for the well-being of the nation? Or was it a personal regret in disguise, for the wrong choice of a wife who, despite all her alluring exterior qualities, was not much more than a piece of barren land that no diligent tilling could turn around? Or a mixture of both, with no particular order of importance?

"If we have to let her go, then what about Chunyu? She's on your roster too." The prick in Mei's voice told Chunyu that Mei was giving her husband a soft little hard time.

It was his turn to be reticent. The crunching of food got on one's nerves. After a few rounds of hard and awfully loud chewing and swallowing, he droned out a response without looking at either of them. "Chunyu can stay as long as she likes, but not on the roster. We split our rations for her." His words had a dull finality.

Chunyu flushed ruddy with humiliation, mortally offended by the way they talked about her as if she were invisible.

As long as she likes. How? In what role? An unofficial replacement maid, like a boy born out of wedlock, a bastard, doing a son's duty without a son's title and reward?

But what other choices did she have? Going back to the hospital as a nurse's aide, dealing with the sick, the dying, and the wounded, now there was a new war raging? She had become so used to staying within the confines of a home. Crowds made her dizzy.

The *official* domestic assistant was let go a week later and Chunyu, naturally and seamlessly, slipped into her shoes. No eyebrows raised and no questions asked, she filled the role tacitly expected of her.

One day, Mei got home a little earlier than usual while Old Chen was delayed at work. It was eerily quiet around the house, no signs of Chunyu, and no sounds from the kitchen indicating a dinner being prepared. The floor felt strange under Mei's slippers as she advanced farther into the hallway, a sticky, squeaky sort of weight to them. She looked down at her feet and her scalp jumped.

It was blood, fresh, wet, emitting a metallic scent, trickling from underneath the bathroom door, gathering itself around a lower spot on the floor into a small scarlet puddle.

The first thought that burst into her mind was a crime, a murder, committed when Chunyu was alone at home. But everything around the house seemed to be in neat order: the furniture in its right place, the floor shinily clean, drawers properly shut, not the slightest sign to suggest any rough intrusion or pillaging.

She held her breath and pushed open the bathroom door. The room started to spin like a huge, hazy wheel as she looked in.

Chunyu was lying on the granite floor, limbs spread out like the wings of a giant, lifeless bird, unconscious, white as chalk.

"Ectopic pregnancy," the doctor told Mei hours later, in the waiting room adjacent to the surgical unit. "The embryo landed on a wrong spot, in one of her fallopian tubes. It grew too big, causing the tube to burst—that's the reason for the bleeding." The doctor tried his best to give her a popular-science version of the incident.

"I need to talk to her husband," added the doctor.

"She has none." Mei struggled to come up with an answer.

"A fiancé? A boyfriend? Somebody, anybody?" pressed the doctor.

A stubborn silence ensued.

The doctor eventually stopped pestering Mei. From his evasive eyes Mei could sense the pity he felt for this young patient, a pity mingled with a trace of contempt. He must have taken Chunyu as one of *those* women. A sweeping closure of brothels in the city was in the works recently, spitting out, in the process, a stream of unclaimed and unwanted pregnancies through the hospital doors. But Mei was not in the mood to set him right. There was no point quibbling with someone who wasn't anyone in your life.

"You'd have joined Mother, if I hadn't got home in time," Mei told Chunyu, when the latter finally woke up late at night. The effect of the anesthetic was still heavy, driving Chunyu in and out of drowsy spells. She heard every word Mei had said, but it took quite an effort to pick out the thread of meaning buried in the sounds. She lay in frigid stillness, head sunk in the pillow, a faint tinge of pink on her cheeks from a low-grade fever, and a placid, blank smile giving her lips a slight twitch.

This indifference, in the face of a situation that might have overturned a ship, shocked Chunyu herself no less than her sister. *A skin as thick as a chopping block.* Mother's jealous invective hurled at Father's favorite young wife left nothing to the imagination, and her words were just as handy when describing her own daughter. *How much lower could one sink?* Chunyu wondered with no particular emotion, neither sorrow nor regret.

There was an abysmal gulf of silence between them, which she didn't feel an urgent need to fill. Quietly she waited for Mei to ask the first question, but Mei's patience matched her own, right to the last ounce. Then they broke the silence at exactly the same moment, their words clashing against each other in midair.

"Did they say anything about my future chance . . . ?" asked Chunyu groggily.

"Did he force you?" was Mei's question.

Neither of them answered. They understood each other perfectly well, in silence as in words.

Chunyu stayed in the convalescent ward for three weeks. During one of her daily strolls along the little patch of green at the back of the hospital, she stopped before a board where the daily newspapers were posted. The headlines nowadays were mostly about the war, a subject she'd rather avoid if she could, but today, a picture caught her attention and made her pause. It was a feature story about a young soldier's heroic action in Korea.

Instantly she recognized the soldier in the picture—it was Wang Erwa.

Seeing no one else around, Chunyu quickly tore the paper off the board and folded it into a square to fit the pocket of her hospital gown. She didn't realize she had just kicked off on a journey beyond her usual orbit.

9.

Chunyu had no idea what she was doing when she boarded the ship for Wenzhou with a thin string bag containing a few articles of clothing and a toothbrush. *Severe head injury*—that's what the paper had said about Erwa. She wasn't even sure he could recognize her. It had been quite a while since they parted, seven years and two wars, to be exact.

With the same uncertainty, she walked into his hospital ward and found him standing in the middle of the room surrounded by a group of people. The center of attention, a status he seemed to be unconscious of but at ease with. The unmistakable light of surprise in his eyes when he saw her immediately told her that he was not totally out, as the paper had described. A part of his mind was still alive and kicking.

To the people in the room, the newspaper clipping in her hand naturally identified her as one of his many admirers who crowded into the hospital every day. To get a handshake, a word, an autograph in a notebook or on a scarf, or to feel his war medal, anything that was a part of him and his glory.

The nursing staff had spent a lot of time, beyond their usual clinical duties, screening the visitors and rationing the visiting time so that they wouldn't wear him out. But they, the staff, didn't mind. Aside from the warmhearted desire to find the hero a good wife, they found these extra-curricular activities a delightful diversion from their otherwise mundane daily routines.

This woman, though, had bypassed the defense of the hospital reception and hence their exacting sieve, infiltrating straight into the confined space of his room. No one in the room, even the dreadfully insentient doctor on duty, missed the glimmer of a smile in Erwa's eyes at the sight of her. He had always been polite to his visitors—polite in the sense of not rude—but smiling, that was something else. His smile was a present that he doled out only once in a very long while.

However, he smiled at her, a woman who seemed to have traveled a long way to see him, judging from the dust in her hair and the wrinkled and soiled clothes she was wearing. Unlike the others, she didn't wear a typical timid and flustered eagerness on her face. She seemed calm and in control. There was something in her that kindled a spark of warmth in him. He liked her, a blind man could see that. The staff sensibly left them alone.

Chunyu almost wished for them to stay a while longer, so that she could take the temperature of the room well enough to handle his questions, if they came. *How* was an easy one, *why* would be a little tougher. "Just wanna see how you're doing" was her official rehearsed version. There was quite a bit of truth to it, but it wasn't totally true. What was the part that wasn't entirely honest? She couldn't answer.

The room grew quiet. The initial surprise had worn off and the weight of daily despondence had returned, crushing him unexpectedly. "I can't, just can't do this anymore," he muttered, in a fit of subdued sobs, broken like the shattered pieces of China.

This was not the first time she had seen him break down. The last time he did so was seven years ago, on another hospital bed, over a potential amputation of his leg. This time, it was his head. No matter where he went, war always found him. Poor thing.

"You got your leg back, last time, remember? This time, you'll get your mind back, trust me," she said, tenderly and firmly, but deep down she knew her words lacked a bone to prop them up. She was no longer that sixteen-year-old girl who could walk through fire to save a man's leg and his pride, and believe, foolhardily, that a miracle was possible.

He ceased sobbing, a little ashamed of his weakness, but the fear was still there in his eyes, growing shadowy. "I was knocked out totally in the beginning, but it came back after a while. My mind all clear now but I haven't told them yet, because"—he grasped her hand, so hard that she could hear the joints crack—"because I don't want to be sent back . . . awful things there . . ."

A deep cough stopped him from going any further. She jerked her hand loose, stepping back to check on the door and window before returning to him.

"Did you tell anybody about *this*?" she asked in a voice three floors below a whisper.

He shook his head.

She felt dizzy with relief. The purpose of this trip suddenly presented itself to her, crystal clear.

"You suffered severe brain damage, the *doctors* say so. You are here to be looked after, not to be sent anywhere, hear me?" she said, with a firm and authoritative air. An order to be followed, no room for bargaining, period.

A sudden awakening, a flash of enlightenment—he understood her.

The seven-year separation hadn't washed away his trust in her. He handed to her, on their first reunion, a cosmic-size, life-and-death type of secret without the slightest reservation or doubt. A simple, guileless, absolute, infinite, total trust.

She was moved.

"Erwa, let's get married." The words came suddenly, but they didn't sound rushed. There was a cool poise to them, as if she had thought about it for a long time, the entire seven years while they were apart.

Never once—not then, not after—did she ask him why he had stopped writing to her or why he hadn't come back to visit, as promised. What was the point of risking a tangle with feelings and emotions when there was trust? He held her big, dark secret of the past, and now she held his. There is nothing safer than keeping the key to someone's secret. It wasn't a great love story by any measure, nothing to stand out and tickle one's heart or to lose nights of sleep over, but it was a fine story of trust. Trust rises above emotions and mood swings, so it would last.

"And start a family," she added. "Now you go and tell them."

Chapter V

THE MEMORY OF A CATACLYSM

Email from Phoenix to George, 2011.11.11 @ 16:35 China Standard Time

> *Hi George,*
>
> *Just returned from Auntie's, utterly drained. She finally made good on her promise to tell me THE story that connects all the dots. Every piece now falls into place. I had to stop her several times to give her a break, which I needed as much. This is not something I can tell you over the phone or in a rushed email. I'll put it down in manuscript—that's the only way I can handle the retelling of it. You'll be the first to read when it's ready, but until then, do not squeeze me.*
>
> *I doubt there'll be any sleep tonight.*
>
> *Nix*

Email from George to Phoenix, 2011.11.19 @ 08:07 Eastern Standard Time

Dear Nix,

You've been awfully quiet lately (I've kept my promise not to pry). Every time you shut down, you make me worry. Probably you are just working hard on your writing, which I hope is the case. One needs an exit before exploding.

It's been a month since you left, that's the longest we've ever been apart. I am counting the days until I can join you in Shanghai.

A note: I kind of remember you telling me Auntie Mei has kept some contact with her eldest half sister. Any plan to visit East Creek, as a distraction, you think?

Will call you after dinner.

Love from George

Email from Phoenix to George, 2011.11.20 @ 02:18 China Standard Time

Hi George,

I received an email from my students today (forwarded here). It brought tears to my eyes—I have grown pulpy. So often we work just for bread, and mine is a thin slice, but one may find a surprise reward in it sometimes. From now on, I'll complain less about my paycheck.

Do worry a little about me just to keep you on your toes, but not too much. We Yuan women aren't just pretty faces, we bark, bite, and live. Wait till you read my mother's war story on which I am working quite hard. So far, it has progressed well. I'll try to finish the first draft before you come over—it's possible.

Auntie did resume contact (very minimal) with her eldest sister after Uncle Chen passed, but for some reason

she's never made up her mind to visit. A few of her siblings are still around, including the eldest who has just turned ninety-nine. I'll see whether I can convince Auntie to take a trip to East Creek with me. It's been too long, people grow used to their ways, hard to change.

Eat well and smoke very little.

Nix

Email forwarded: greetings from students

Dear Mrs. Yuan-Whyller,

You took leave this semester, but we didn't know why. Today, Vittorio heared in office about your mother. We are very sorry. Why didn't you tell us? Last week Mrs. Khan (our substitute teacher) asked us talk about mother. Five people have no mother (war and sick), eleven cannot see mother (divorce, abroad). We know how hard without mother. Please take care and feel better.

Everybody in class asking me to write you, wish you come back soon. Mrs. Khan has much accent, hard to understand (please do not tell office, we don't want her lose job). You are the best teacher, and you really try your best help us. We miss you very very much. I hope you do not upset with my poor grammer.

Ansuya on behalf of everybody

Email from Phoenix to George, 2011.12.21 @ 13:46 China Standard Time

Hi George,

You didn't answer my previous two emails, so out of desperation I called your cell, but went straight to the

voicemail. From diarrhea to stroke to burglary to house on fire to another woman, horrible thoughts traveled at the speed of light. I even checked the weather network to see whether there's a tornado around your area, then realized it's not even the right season (watched too many Hollywood movies). Where the hell are you, at this ungodly hour? Please contact me ASAP before I have a heart attack.

Insanely yours, Nix

Email from George to Phoenix, 2011.12.21 @ 01:09 Eastern Standard Time

Dear Nix,

You sabotaged my plan for a pleasant surprise. When you called me, I was going through the security at the airport. Now I am in the lounge waiting for my red-eye connection flight to Vancouver. I managed to move my holiday schedule forward by four days (no need to bother you with all the logistic details), as I simply can't wait any longer. I was planning to surprise you at your hotel door, but the concern over your sanity got the better of me, so I decided to spoil the surprise.

Will see you in less than a day.

George

Email from Phoenix to George, 2011.12.21 @ 14:25 China Standard Time

Old man, you nearly gave me a heart attack. I was thinking crazy things such as whether I'll be able to open my

house door with the same key, or if I'll find somebody else's lingerie in my bedroom when I return home.

Glad you are coming sooner. Good news: I've finished the first draft (see attached) of Ma and Auntie's war story (I named it "The Memory of a Cataclysm" for now). This is the most difficult section, but I completed it in the shortest span of time. In this section, I still draw on Auntie's perspective and her version of what Ma has told her. But Auntie is no longer my exclusive source of information. There are some blind spots in the story that no one can shed light on, so I've tried to fill in with my own eyes. This is a "prehistorical" mother that I have NOT seen but am sure of knowing, from the bottom of my soul, through ALL my life with her.

Hope you get this mail before the plane takes off so that you may read some of it during your flight (if you are not too tired).

I'll change to a better hotel now that you are here. I stay in this one mainly for convenience, and for the heavy discount—its owner is the son of Uncle Chen's army friend.

Nix

* Email attachment: Phoenix's manuscript *Cataclysm*

1.

Chunyu felt a weight on her eyelids and opened her eyes to find it was the daylight edging through the window—or a hole in the wall, rather. The sky, reduced to the size of the hole, was blue, bright, and brutal.

After a dazed moment, she gradually became aware of where she was.

Every night is a tiny death, Mother used to tell her, *and every morning a tiny rebirth.* But last night was not a tiny death. It was the grand total of all the tiny deaths of three lifetimes. Yet however astronomical the size of last night's death, it still led to the same tiny rebirth this morning.

She was alive. No death could kill, or save, her. The realization came to her in a cold sweat.

The rest of the room, untouched by the sun, was still dark. She could, like a hound, sniff out her surroundings. An old, musty, dismal, soulless, rotten rathole.

Mei was still sleeping, fitfully, on the other side of the straw mat. Her legs twitched, hands thrown overhead in loose fists, holding a nightmare.

It was September 1944.

The war with Japan was by then seven years old, and didn't bite quite as sharply as when it was younger. The occasional sight of the northern refugees wandering along their street did not stir up as much blood now. Mei still talked, every now and then, about leaving for Yan'an to join the Communist forces, a crazy idea she got from her contagious school friends. But her plan never grew feet, the kind that could carry her beyond the limits of East Creek, their town.

Seven years was the government's version of events, to convince the seething masses that things weren't totally out of hand. The fall of Manchuria, however conveniently excluded from the war narrative, took place thirteen years ago. It was thus a much older war, senile and dilapidating. Many skies had fallen, each fall bringing them a numbing terror, followed by a wave of secret and almost evil relief that their sky—the tiny one over East Creek—was still intact.

Until yesterday.

It was hard to imagine that the sky, Chunyu's sky, holding steady for sixteen years, could crumple in the narrow space of a day and then reappear, innocently, in the morning, all in one piece, like a cat awakened from its eighth death. No memory of yesterday's hurts.

Bastard.

An urge to spit at the face of the sun didn't gather quite enough strength, abating instead into a feeble slur of profanity.

She tried to sit up and found herself shivering from the pain that assured her the shame was real.

Memory started to return, in bits and pieces.

2.

It was Sunday, the day before, so Chunyu and Mei, both attending high school in the county seat, were home for the weekend. Just as the maid was setting the table for lunch, the air raid siren sounded again. The third time that morning; the previous two both false alarms. *Crying wolf.* Mother was not in any hurry to leave the house.

"I am not an old stick-in-the-mud, I know some educated girls no longer want an arranged marriage. If you meet someone nice in school, no hanky-panky, just bring him home for me to see. One rule, no bargaining: never agree to be a junior wife like me. Hear me?" Mother was still talking about her daughters' marriage prospects, a topic she had started earlier. "If the war ever ends, it's hard to say who'll be the next ruler. The Nationalists, the Communists, or the emperor—no difference to me, they all suck your blood. The safest way is for each of you to marry into a different Party, so when things get messy, one can watch over the other. You know your father, how much you can count on him."

Nobody knew, at the time, that this would be Mother's last wish.

Their conversation was interrupted by the security head of their block, who came knocking, urging them to run for the air defense trench. Over the past seven years, East Creek had been bombed only once, which left a little scratch on an unattended rice paddy. A full-scale shelter, therefore, remained a plan on the town magistrate's desk.

Halfway there, Mother decided to turn back to fetch the jewelry box she'd left behind, dragging the maid with her.

I can't live without it, Mother had said before, in less distressing circumstances. But when she said it, she hadn't thought of the flip side of the coin: she might die with it.

Mother never came back to join them.

An hour later, when the alert was lifted and they were finally allowed to return home, they discovered their portion of the street reduced to a pile of smoldering rubble. They had heard the explosions and thought the worst, but the actual scene was worse than anything they had expected. It took the neighbors and rescue workers two hours to dig out Mother and the maid. Mother was found curled up, her entire body wrapping around the jewelry box, as if protecting a baby from an unforeseen assault.

It was East Creek's turn, finally, to have their sky fall.

Chunyu could have cursed the Japs for what had happened, the bombers with the emblem of a filthy sun, or the sky that remembered no pain, but they were a little too far out of her grasp. The closest thing to spit her venom on was her father, who lived on the other side of the town. If Father had sent their monthly upkeep in time, Mother would never have risked her life for that rotten box holding the loose ends of their future.

Father was a tea merchant, rather well-to-do. His tea was sold as far away as Manchuria, Hong Kong, Singapore, and Ceylon. Even in wartime, people needed tea, a soothing reminder of peace and comfort. The worry that wormed into Father's sleep was not so much about his income as about where his fortune would end up. When he was forty-eight (the year he married Mother), nearly ancient by local standards, he still had no son, hence no heir to his assets and the family name.

A tireless stud, Father had sired a long string of offspring with his five wives, each of whom, with one exception, was a good few years younger than the one before. They jointly produced an impeccable collection of fifteen daughters, a specious army that could fight no war but would leave, in due course, bite marks on his fortune in the form of dowries.

The girls, between the ages of five and thirty-two, lived (with the exception of four married ones) in separate households with their own mothers, meeting twice a year, on Lunar New Year's Eve and Father's birthday. During the New Year's Eve dinner, Father would, invariably, hand each of the unmarried girls a red envelope containing a small cash present. Exactly the same envelope and exactly the same amount, no chance for mistakes—he often mixed up their names or their households.

Chunyu's mother was the fourth wife, an incredulous, and almost appalling, choice at the time, as she was not only five years older than the previous wife, but also had been married once before. Mother's first husband, a schoolteacher, had died of typhoid fever, leaving behind a son, then four years old, to be raised by his grannie.

Father paid Mother's family the same bride money as for his other wives, a move understood by very few but ridiculed by many. When compared with the proven track record of having produced a male child, virginity was a petty and irrelevant detail. The shrewd business-man in Father prevailed.

Mother let Father foster hope, a very palpable one, which turned, upon delivery, into a searing disappointment. Not once, but twice— two girls, eighteen months apart. A seasoned farmer before becoming a successful merchant, Father surprisingly didn't quite seem to understand the basics of farming. When the harvest didn't yield the desired crops, he blamed the soil, never the seeds.

Over the years, his visits to Mother's household grew fewer and farther between, and lapses started to occur in their monthly allowance.

Chunyu, the younger daughter, less shy, more daring, a born negotiator, was sometimes sent to visit Father, asking (not begging) him to loosen the purse strings.

After finding Mother underneath the rubble, Chunyu and Mei ran for Father's to deliver the bad news. But they never made it to his house.

Chunyu had no clear recollection exactly where on their way they were stopped. Grief had dulled her senses. Throughout the day, she and Mei had moved around with numb efficiency powered by muscles alone. When they became aware of the footsteps behind them, the men had been practically at their heels. A group of seven, perhaps eight, in bedraggled yellowish-green uniforms. There was something glinting on their shoulders. She knew what they were, but her mind went blank, suddenly unable to recall the word.

A sweeping gust of wind—that was the first thing she felt before she was knocked down onto the ground. Her shoulder blades, pressed hard against the dirt road, sent the warning signal to her mind, instantly awakening the full range of her faculties to pain and danger.

Bayonet. She remembered the word.

Where is Mei? she wondered.

She ought to think about Mother too, a few hours deader now, lying in the open, on a strip of ground cleared of the rubble, wrapped in a straw mat, alone, hungry, and cold, waiting for one-fifth of a husband. Maggots might arrive sooner than the Buddhist monk needed to say a round of soul-saving prayer. But she didn't think of Mother. Her sentiments had been stripped, at this moment, to the bare minimum; the needs of the living always precede those of the dead.

The man on top of her had the weight of a dead log, his foul breath sending her stomach tumbling towards an urge to retch. She tried to turn her head away, but he pinned her chin with his claws, demanding eye contact. With his face forced onto hers, she noticed his bloodshot eyes, pores filled with road dust, neck dotted with scabs of mosquito bites, nose wings flared with desire ready to burst, and a dark spot, in the vague shape of a butterfly, on his left cheek.

He stared at her with a cool, morbid wonder. A flicker of hesitation came into his eyes and faded, all gone in a matter of a millisecond. His body started to writhe, growing hot and stiff. Then a violent thrust, a dagger between her legs, deep and stirring, tearing her insides to shreds.

She let out a cry, but immediately stopped, as she heard a shriek, more piercing than her own, almost bloodcurdling, from a little distance away.

It was Mei. She hadn't got away.

The inside of her body was turning, she could tell, inch by inch, into a gutter as the stranger on top drained the grimy sewage of lust into her. No amount of water could ever cleanse it. Not a river, not a sea, not an ocean. She would need an entire new body to be clean again.

A second stab came, from another man, followed by yet another. And another. Each brought a different layer of pain, shearing, gut-wrenching, grinding, burning . . .

Then the weirdest assault came, not against her body but against her eyes. It was the sting of the predusk sun, in its last moment of righteous glory, frowning upon her shame. She couldn't bear its excruciating glare.

Mei was still wailing, her shrill scraping Chunyu's ears like a sharp blade. A surge of rage swept through Chunyu, gathering the remaining embers of her strength into a fireball. "Stop it, Mei!" Her yell quickly shriveled into a muted groan, as she realized how futile it was. Mei couldn't hear her. Buddha might have, but he didn't care. He had long ago washed his lotus-shaped hands, since the fall of Manchuria, of the evils of mankind. He could have easily lifted a finger, a tiny one out of his thousands, to put a stop to all this: Mother had told her that there was a bodhisattva that had a thousand hands.

Everything around her grew fuzzy and dim, closing her in a seamless void of darkness.

She passed out.

3.

The door was elbowed open. A woman edged her way backwards through the frame, a tray in her hands containing two bowls of porridge. She paused for a few moments until her eyes grew used to the darkness inside. The mossy stone walls, having seen so many deaths, sucked the life out of all light, blurring the division between day and night.

The woman set her tray on the floor, fumbling in the pocket of her apron for a match to light a candle. The little flame flickered, then held, bringing her face into focus. Ruddy, wrinkled, weather beaten, but not old.

"A damn icy hole." She hissed the curse between her teeth in a detectable Manchurian accent, resting the candle in a corner safe from the draft.

"Still sleeping?" She pointed her chin inquisitively towards Mei. "Better rest well before they come back."

"Who?" Chunyu asked sharply while sitting up. The pain almost held her back, but she didn't let it.

A queer grin spread over the woman's face, narrowing her eyes. "Don't tell me you don't know. Consider yourself lucky. They often kill the women they're done with, to avoid questions from their own police. Dead people don't talk, not as witnesses. But they pick you to serve here—pretty faces get to live."

The truth, vaguely suspected, was confirmed. The worst nightmare, now a reality. A chill crawled up Chunyu's spine, not so much from fear as from despair. Death, a gift, would have been sweet.

"No use thinking about running away. It's the highest spot on the hill, three sentries, twenty-four hours on duty. No matter which way you take, they see you, clear as day."

A sob crept its way to their ears, almost voiceless, but the air was agitated by the forlorn hysteria it implied. Mei curled up at the edge of the mat, half-awake, struggling to break free from a coil of confusion, her face, swollen with overnight tears, wearing a blank smile of numbed terror.

"Of course, you can always put an end to it all." The woman, unheeding, stared hard at Chunyu, as if reading her mind. "Nobody can stop someone who's set her mind on dying. There's the sheet, the wall, the beam, you know what to do. You can starve yourself to death too. I don't have all day watching over you. They can grab another girl from one of the villages, just as easy. Might not be as pretty, but serve the purpose."

The sobbing continued, like a frail thread, threatening to break at any moment, but still lingering, getting on Chunyu's nerves.

Mei was Mother's toy to show off at family gatherings. Improvising a poem for Father's birthday, cleverly rhymed with witty metaphors; writing a New Year's scroll, in flourishing brushwork; sharing a story of adventure from some fancy books she had read, talking her half sisters into a stupor. Mother could have used Chunyu's voice too, a song or two to relax her husband's knitted eyebrows, but Chunyu wasn't quite as manageable as Mei, having a silly idea stuck in her head against singing for any purpose other than self-pleasure.

Father, a fox, saw right through Mother's little tricks, but tolerated them with good humor, convinced, more than ever, of the pointlessness of schooling for girls. Mother, the only educated one of his five wives, failed to grasp the most rudimentary truth of life: a hundred accomplished daughters couldn't fill the role of one most mediocre son.

Mother had looked on, beaming with genuine pride. "Your sis, oh, your sis," she murmured, in doting adoration. "All the fourteen brains put together, you girls, are no match for Mei." Mother's sweeping statement went largely unheeded, but crushed Chunyu, inadvertently, into dust.

But Mei bloomed only in fair weather, when the wind was blowing her way. There was a reason, Chunyu now understood, for Mother to have two daughters: one for shine, and one for rain.

"Could you just stop, for a moment?" Chunyu turned towards Mei imploringly.

"If you want to go *that* way, I'll leave you alone to finish off your business." The woman lit a cigarette, drawing with it an imaginary line across her neck, a mimed gesture of hanging. The pungent smell of cheap tobacco negotiated its way through the overused air.

"But do me a favor, leave the porridge behind, life is hard." She talked between two puffs, to Chunyu alone, as if Mei didn't exist. She had been around long enough to tell who was calling the shots here.

The options were laid bare before them, crystal clear. To live would be a prolonged torture for sure, and to die, a quick bliss, perhaps. It was the fear of the unknown that tipped the scale. Sixteen is an awkward age, too young to die for honor, but too old to live with shame. The naked, raw, flaming, hideous shame, every pore of which was oozing pus.

Outlive. Chunyu suddenly remembered Mother.

Outlive was a word Mother used, casually, about almost anything she didn't like: the war, the marriage, a delayed allowance, a sour remark from one of the other wives, a bad meal, a headache, a rainy cold day . . . Mother, in the end, didn't outlive the bomb. Yet the bomb didn't outlive Mother either. They perished together, in an instant splendid blast.

Quietly, Chunyu picked up a bowl of porridge from the tray, handing it to Mei before moving on to her own, without bothering with the chopsticks. Her stomach greeted the first sip with a fierce growl, a loud protest against the many hours since her last meal. Between the last meal and this one, she had been reduced to a rat.

A rat of all rats.

With a few noisy slurps she finished it all.

"More." She stretched out her emptied bowl to the woman.

"Little Tiger, move your ass over here, I haven't seen your shadow since sunrise," the woman yelled towards the door.

A boy appeared, his head shaven clean, wearing a tunic way too short, with his hands dangling out like chicken claws. He stood at the door quietly, stealing a furtive glance at Chunyu and Mei, a little shy, and a little bold.

"Get another bowl of porridge, some pickled radish too," the woman ordered.

With a mute nod, the boy took the empty bowl from Chunyu and sped away, fast as the wind, shoulder blades bouncing underneath his tunic like dancing sticks. A big twelve, or a small fourteen, Chunyu guessed.

"I know you'll live through this, believe me, it takes one to know one." The woman bared her tobacco-stained teeth and let out a raspy chuckle. "There's an extra eye, right here." She knocked the middle of her forehead with a knuckle. "I see things you don't. There are people in this room, trapped here, can't find home."

Chunyu's skin started to crawl. Turning around, she saw the porridge bowl in Mei's hand quiver.

"But they stay away from you, you scare them, you've got that fire on top of your head, fire of life, bright as hell. You'll live."

"What about me?" Mei asked timidly.

The woman shifted her gaze, for the first time, towards Mei, sizing her up with a cold pity.

"You'll never make it without her," she said, after a pause.

The cigarette was nearly finished. She threw the butt across the room, watching it land in a corner, glowing with its last breath.

"Try one, works better than opium, kills pain." She fished out another from the pocket of her apron, lit it, and passed it over to Chunyu.

Chunyu took a hesitant first puff. It tickled and then rasped her throat, burning a scorching trail as it traveled down her body. Blue veins jumped on her temples as she fought to tear the rocking fit of coughing out of her lungs.

"You'll get better at it, Fumie." The woman gave a quick hiss of a laugh.

"Her name is not Fumie," Mei interjected in a meek whisper.

"I don't give a shit. Here, everyone has a Japanese name. She is *Fumie*, and you are *Sachie*." The woman said the names slowly, with a drag between the syllables. "It's just a name, you don't lose an arm or a leg over it. It helps to smooth things out."

Mei turned towards Chunyu, seeking, in vain, reassuring eye contact.

"Then what's yours?" asked Chunyu, finally recovered from the savage assault of tobacco.

"You call me Mama-san. No need to know my real name, that's my mother's business," the woman answered, in a tone between mockery and sneer. "I take care of things here, but I'm not your servant. Little Tiger, the boy, runs errands and brings you meal. No fancy food, but you'll be fed."

The boy returned in no time with a bowl of lukewarm porridge filled to the brim. In the shade of the door he stood, listening, stealthily, to their conversation. Misplaced curiosity had knocked the child out of him.

It had to be the cigarette, Chunyu thought—the first one in her life, to be followed by many more—that had altered her eyes. Everything felt old and crinkly: the boy, the sun outside, her lungs, and her soul. Everything but Mei, who was busy dividing the refill of porridge, half and half, no more and no less, between their bowls. A baby, that's what Mei, or Sachie, had become.

"They are building a warehouse nearby. More men to come. Twenty? Thirty? Six women so far to *serve*, you do the math. Make them busy, a card game, a song, so they won't be onto you all the time. If they are onto you, make it quick. There are tricks to be learned."

Aware of the lingering presence of Little Tiger, Mama-san burst into a fit of outrage. "Why are you still here? Is this something a boy should hear? Go and suck on your mother!" she snarled.

The boy was booted out, tail between his legs.

Chunyu caught herself snickering. A most heartless, despicable, mother-shaming laugh, but she just couldn't help it. Fear of hell? No need, she was already in it.

"For you." Mama-san dropped two coins on the tray holding the bowls, again emptied.

Mei looked up at her, baffled.

"Stick it between your butts, squeeze hard, and harder, till it no longer drops. You need muscle to handle the beasts," Mama-san explained flatly.

A pause of dead silence.

"I can't," Mei muttered, in a renewed fit of sobs and snuffles.

Mama-san's face congealed into an ugly look of contempt.

"Yes, you can," she said curtly, then left.

4.

"Fumie, your water!" It was Little Tiger's voice, outside the door.

The well was ten minutes' walk away, Mama-san had told her. They could wash there. But if they had a *bad* day, Little Tiger could fetch the water for them, one bucket a day, for each in the "household"—that's all he could carry.

"Just leave it there," she answered in a feeble murmur. An overwhelming surge of inertia washed over her, leaving her with no desire to stir, let alone get up.

He was still there, she could tell. Imagining him on tiptoe, pressing his thin frame against the door, holding back breath, peeping and listening in. Every presence carried a different kind of weight, and his was light but slimy. It was the sliminess that had rubbed her the wrong way. Charged by an impulse of anger, she leaped up from the mat, bolting towards the door.

"What do you want?" She flung the door open, snarling.

Little Tiger, unawares, nearly fell into her arms. Under her flinty glare he began to wither, flustered and tongue tied.

She noticed a bruise on his forehead, with a blotch of half-dried blood.

"What happened?"

He regained his breath and composure and carried the two buckets of water over the threshold, setting them beside the mat that Chunyu and Mei slept on.

"A slip, fetching water, no big deal." He grinned, a faint twitch around the corners of the mouth.

She felt a faint sting of conscience. A rat's world—that's where she had sunk to, a world ruled by the law of rats. Even a rat knows, from birth, how to pick out its target, a weaker rat.

She took out her hankie, dipped a corner in the water, and helped him clean the wound.

"What was this house used for, before all this, you know?" she asked casually.

"A prison, from Emperor Qianlong's days. You can tell from the windows and the walls."

"How did you get here?" she continued, half-mindedly.

"My village is only three *li* away. They came rounding up coolies. I have two older brothers, they skipped conscriptions, by luck. Uncle Yang, the village head, said to my pa, 'None of your boys are fighting the Japs, so it's your turn to give one out to them now, a sacrifice for the village. If this one dies in their hands, you still have the other two.'"

She listened in silence. She was supposed to say something comforting, but she didn't. No more pity in reserve to offer to any men, or any rats. She was all dried up.

"Who is that woman, Mama-san?" She quickly switched the subject.

"Her name is Kiyo, half-Japanese, half-Chinese. She ran whorehouses in Manchuria, quite a few, and made a load. Then her man died in the war, so they brought her to the south, to run a new whorehouse."

Whorehouse. Brutally honest. Yes, a whorehouse, no amount of whitewash could change the base coat. One might use the word *household*, as Kiyo did, but it's a household of whores.

"How come you know everything?" she asked curiously. The shrewd blood inherited from her father, lying dormant for sixteen years, suddenly leaped to life, opening a new eye she didn't know existed in her. She now saw a vague crack that a loose tongue might lead to, somewhere, in this tightly sealed rathole.

Her interest in him, an unexpected flattery, filled his heart with raw delight. An unquenchable eagerness gushed up, pushing him to pour out what he knew, to keep their conversation alive and rolling.

"I have the ears of a dog, my pa says," he claimed, in tremulous excitement. "I hear things, even mice chatting. I bring water to Kobayashi a few times a day; he uses water a lot to keep himself clean. The rest of them live like pigs, they don't care. He speaks Chinese with Kiyo sometimes, when they don't want the others to know. I hear them talk, but never make a sound."

"Who is Kobayashi?"

"Their head guy, the one with a big birthmark on his cheek."

Chunyu's heart skipped a beat. The dirt-filled pores, the bloodshot eyes, the sinister dark butterfly on one cheek, the foul breath, and the first searing stab into her half-formed womanhood. *What's remembered gets a life,* she read once in a book. She didn't want to give that beast a life, but she couldn't kill her memory either. Memory exists on its own terms and decides what life to give.

"Do you get to go out, from here?" she asked abruptly.

"Sometimes they send me to get supplies."

"Do you have a chance to go in the direction of East Creek?" She hissed out the name as if these words gave her a toothache.

"If they want a fish meal, East Creek has the best seafood market."

Chunyu took a deep breath, slowly exhaling, to steady her voice.

"Do you think you'll go that way again, soon?" Her lips quivered.

"I can always suggest a fish meal, the cook sometimes asks my opinion," he replied with a self-important air, suspecting she would probably want him to bring in something from the store, a pack of cigarettes, a bag of saponins, like the other women did.

A crack, or even a path, too easy to be trusted.

"Can you go to 25 Prosperity Street, on your next trip to East Creek, to deliver a message to my father?" she asked tentatively.

He turned pale. He might not recognize the unfamiliar face of adrenaline, but he certainly knew the age-old face of fear when he saw it.

"I don't know how far it's from the fish market. I have to make it back in time, you know." He averted his eyes, stammering, "They'll kill you, if they find out."

True. Nothing is worth the fight when one is dead, man or rat.

But one still tries.

She removed her earrings, a birthday present from Mother when she turned fifteen, and placed them in his hand.

"Take them to your mother, gold," she said wearily.

He held the earrings as if holding a scorpion ready to sting. Slowly, he steadied his hand and moved the earrings towards the window for a close inspection in better light. They fought the sun off fiercely, emitting a strange yellowish glow, at once warm and cold. Much to her astonishment, he put one of them between his teeth, and nipped at it. A large grin of satisfaction split his face, baring his huge brown fangs.

"It's real gold. Uncle Yang told me real gold is soft, will leave a tooth mark."

Suddenly he grew quiet. Thoughts were parading through his mind, she could tell, one after another, humming with audible doubt.

She waited in silence, with a slow patience that could wear through a rock, for the line of thoughts to run its course. The innocent curiosity of a child, superseded by the self-complacency of an adolescent, then by the growing greed of an adult, and finally, by the rancid fear of an old man, all in his head. What a marvel that her eyes had grown so sharp in such a short span of time. Two days, in everyone else's calendar. Two lives, in her own.

"I don't have any use for them, my ma is dead, and I don't have any sisters." After a long moment of hesitation, he gave the earrings back to her.

He finished talking, yet was not quite finished, a trail of unfinished thoughts lingering in the air.

She tried to determine which was doing the mute talking: the greed, or the fear. The answer eluded her, so she placed her bet on greed. What more could one lose when she had already lost it all?

"Maybe I'll come back later for them." He looked up at her, halfway between a dribbling dog and a wishful toad.

She heaved a sigh of relief. Her instinct had led her to the right bet.

Mei was still sleeping, snuggled up to her own warmth, her only way to kill the dreadful time before the night of terror struck. The beginning of their rat life.

Chunyu threw a knowing glance at Little Tiger as she moved towards the door and closed it.

The room became dimmer, the air ripe with suspended possibilities. She started to undo her buttons. Her naked body glistened in the dull light, a cold, dangerous, grayish-white mass defined by a few soft, sinuous curves.

He recoiled in shock, his breathing quickened and messy. The space between them congealed into a thin filmy wall, vibrating nervously until he decided to break it. A slimy warmth pressed itself on her breast, a shaky hand eager to feign experience, yet deeply ashamed of its ignorance. His lips parted, sounds slipping out, a string of muffled and unintelligible mumbles.

"You tell my father that his wife, the fourth one, has died. Ask him to give her a decent burial. Hire a good Buddhist monk to say a soul-saving prayer."

She wasn't sure if he was listening, or if her words registered, so she repeated it one more time, adding, "Don't tell him anything about me and my sister, here."

It was a long while before his response came.

"They say she's pretty"—he pointed tremulously at Mei—"but I think you're prettier."

5.

Night plodded in. From the end of the corridor, noises rolled: shouts, curses, cigarettes tossed around, and the clanking of boots, belts, and weapons being removed.

It was an old, ugly stone-walled jailhouse, with two rows of dingy cells facing each other, connected by a shared corridor. The bigger rooms were all on one side, now the living quarters of the Japanese, the higher-ranked officers at one end, and the lower ranks the other. In the smaller rooms lived the Chinese coolies, the kitchen and laundry staff, and the *women*. The end of a working day for some was the beginning of a busy shift for others.

Threaded through the seething sounds was Kiyo's calm, managing voice, a voice that had seen the world fall and pick itself up. From the fog of a language that was choppy and decisive, with a sudden rise in tone at the end of a sentence that was altogether foreign, Chunyu guessed that information and money were changing hands.

It was deadly quiet in the room. Mei seemed to have drawn, with her silence, an inviolable circle around herself that shielded her from being seen, heard, or touched. There was a piece of dirty, wrinkled fabric draped between them, now fully drawn, to prepare the space for the men who would come at any moment, to each of them. The drape, like the sun, divided their time. It closed to usher in their night of separate ordeals and opened to start their shared day of rest—if there was rest to be had.

Kiyo told Chunyu and Mei not to scream, or fight back, when they came to them. "What's the point of kicking?" she said, matter-of-factly, as if talking about a mosquito bite. "A month? Two? As soon as the warehouse is finished, they'll be gone. Have you ever seen a war that doesn't end? They move on and you move on. It's just mud on your body, a good hot bath will take care of it. Change your name, move to a new place, marry a man that doesn't ask a lot of questions, a new life, all over again."

How many lives had Kiyo left behind, before this one?

Chunyu could feel Mei's presence, through the pores of the fabric that made the drape. The smell of perspiration, running hot and cold in turn, and the muted shudder that agitated the thick and unforgiving air.

"Sis?" she called out, tentatively.

Mei didn't answer, or stir.

"At least, Mother will rest . . ." She felt a snag in her voice and stopped. She meant to say *in peace*, but Mother was not in peace, and would not be.

Footsteps drew nearer and eventually paused before her door. The door was a mere display, a lie, as the latch and padlock had been removed. Anything could intrude—ants, roaches, wind, a snake, a penis, or a ghost. No, a ghost doesn't need a door. A ghost is a door by its own right, leading to another world.

Then she heard her name, the strange, fake name, spoken outside the door.

"Fumie and Sachie, the sisters, the best, I save for you, Kobayashi-san." Kiyo's voice was lowered, hardly above a whisper, subservient, yet slightly teasing. "Ask your men to go easy, they are young, and a bit *broken*."

Chunyu's heart gave a lurch as she realized whom Kiyo was talking to. The man with a butterfly on his cheek.

"New, those earrings, gold? You must have made another load," Kobayashi said, in a half-mocking tone, but not harshly. His Chinese was fluent enough, with a tiny tinge of an accent.

"A gift, pretty neat, aren't they?" Kiyo responded. There was a thin, girlish giggle kneaded into the words, approaching coquetry, but not quite. Would this woman, Mama-san, as she liked them to call her, open her thighs to these men too, when the lust outran the supply of women? Chunyu wondered.

Chunyu closed her eyes, whispering a wish to *it*, the dark, amorphous shadow she had seen in the twilight zone between layers of consciousness, drifting around from wall to wall, light as a wisp of smoke. She immediately knew, from the first moment *it* entered her sight, that it was a ghost, one of the many in this house, the unwilling and undying dead gathered from generation to generation. A collective ghost, one might say, for lack of a better word.

At first, *it* kept its distance, vigilant, hesitant, unsure of itself, but not entirely uncommunicative. She felt its presence, its breath behind her, around the nape of her neck, tingling and chilly. *I am afraid*, *it* was saying to her, in the language of the dead. From the fuzzy recesses of her mind, Mama-san's words popped out, *the fire on top of your head*, and she immediately realized what stood between the ghost and her: the deterring force, the strength of the fire, in her.

An impulse seized her, propelling her to pass her thoughts over to *it*, through long, deep, slow, calming breathing that intimated safety and assurance. *It* gradually stopped fidgeting, growing still and peaceful, even though *it* would not come near her.

A conversation started between them across the room, in complete silence. Tense and distrustful initially, gradually growing more relaxed, but at no point unkind. They struck a deal, right there and then, a deal to be put to the test when night fell. Among all the monstrosities that filled the day and the space, this deal was the easiest and the least cruel.

The door was thrust open. Two men burst in, leaving a queue of others outside, waiting impatiently for their turn.

"私の名前はサチエです。" (*My name is Sachie.*)

Mei's voice drifted over, from the other side of the drape. This was the only Japanese sentence she had learned from Kiyo, to be repeated over and over again, in the course of the night, in quivering, dreamlike slowness. A dose of sedative, to be refilled every few moments, to numb her senses.

A man plodded over to Chunyu's side, a candle in his hand. There was a lantern hanging from the ceiling, shedding a dim, yellowish, diffuse light. A full measure of light was really not needed for an act that animals could perform anywhere, in the dark or in the light. But this man demanded his own designated light. The straw rustled uneasily as he bent down on the mat. A black butterfly flitting on his cheek left a burning sting in Chunyu's eyes. It was Kobayashi, a name that could make it snow in summer, turn flowers into spiders, and all the butterflies in the universe into a nightmare.

He was different from the man on top of her two days ago on the roadside. Freshly out of a shower, he smelled of soap not completely washed away by water, the water Little Tiger had brought to his door from the well, bucket by bucket. He looked filthily clean tonight.

Between then and now, he seemed to have grown a morbid patience. Slowly, he stripped her, and parted her legs. Holding the candle close, he started to examine her, intently, studiously, as if she were a map to be thoroughly studied before a battle that could decide a war.

All of a sudden, she found herself weightless, drifting around the ceiling, bouncing from corner to corner, looking down, with a vacant apathy, at a girl naked on a mat and a man sniffing her, inch by inch, like a dog would unfamiliar prey.

She realized, with an overwhelming rush of relief, that the deal she had struck with *it*, the ghost of all the dead, had been honored. They had traded places, as agreed. She had assumed its form, a soul without a body, and it had entered hers, a body without a soul. Her soul, in its bodiless form, was too battered to cook up a boiling rage or a fuming disgust at the sight of the man-beast. The only energy it had left was barely enough to simmer weary scorn at the absurdities of it all. How could such a soul, a century-old fossil, have once inhabited the young body of a sixteen-year-old? She was baffled.

Kobayashi's candle tilted, dripping hot tears on her. Not the real her, but what she had left behind on the floor, a heap of flesh and bones, a skin shed. The pain was every inch real, but not hers, because she wasn't there, in that body.

The inspection could have dragged on longer, but his body started to rebel against his mind. The beast grew tumescent and weepy between his legs. With violent, farcical jerks, he entered the empty shell of her.

He wasn't in any hurry to leave even after his beast had been appeased. At the top of the pecking order, he operated on his schedule, and his alone, unmoved by the anxious queue outside the door, and undisturbed by the repeated greetings from the other side of the drape by Mei, in a fainter and fainter voice, stating her phony Japanese name: "私の名前はサチエです。"

Slowly he rose to his feet, buttoning up his breeches. Unexpectedly, their eyes locked. The whimsical deal with the ghost was over, as Chunyu became aware of the regained burden of her body that she had so readily and rapturously discarded. She had nothing but her own reserve of resistance to draw on now.

She didn't withdraw her stare, long, deep, and unwavering, demanding an answer she would never get. To her surprise, she discovered a sudden crack in his fighter bull's eyes, revealing a razor-thin line between conscience (if he had one) and a fury that might be easily provoked with one tiny misstep.

But there had to be something, amid all the insanities, that would stand on its own ground, untouched by the slaughter and destruction. She just had to find it, in a quick second, before his conscience was totally consumed by rage.

Rage was, perhaps, just the voice of a wretchedly waning conscience. The thought struck a spark of sudden inspiration.

She decided to act on it.

"How is your mother, Kobayashi-san?" She heard her own voice, soft, quivering but calm, knowing that she had managed, narrowly, to put forward a foot.

The butterfly stopped fluttering as he stood still, utterly stunned. From Manchuria to south of the Yangtze, he had covered thousands of miles of the map of war. A veteran war-hand, he knew killing, pillage, and rape were all part of war, but conversation was not. He had overpowered many women, young and old, pretty or ugly, some too terrified to utter a sound, others weeping and begging for their lives, still others screaming, kicking, and biting in desperate attempts to break free, but there had never been a single one who dared to venture into a conversation with him, about his mother or about anything.

He looked at her, dazed, dubious, and lost.

6.

Chunyu entered the room to find Mei still asleep.

Chunyu had recently been moved to Kobayashi's room, at his request—or his order, to be more precise. "This is the best a girl can hope for, in this situation," Kiyo congratulated her, with a genuine delight, as if Chunyu were about to marry a prince, or had just hit on a bucket of gold. Mama-san had a way with words and tones, not exactly lying, but just twisting the truth a little, adding a gloss, here and there, to the dull surface of brutal facts.

There was a reason for everything—a reason for war, a reason for peace, and a reason for a Mama-san to make her loads. The plain truth was, in Chunyu's own unpolished words, she was to be thrown to one beast instead of the whole jungle.

She spent her nights now in Kobayashi's room, returning to her old cell in the morning (when he left for the construction site) to be with Mei and, most importantly, to get some sleep, the kind where she wouldn't have her heart in her mouth. Who could get any real sleep lying next to a man with a pistol and a bayonet at his bedside every minute of the night?

Last night, she had felt a sudden blast of heat and woke up to find, to her horror, Kobayashi holding a kerosene lamp so close to her face that she could hear the sizzling of her hair. Kobayashi had a morbid interest in her body, every unthinkable fold and corner, the same interest a surgeon might have in a cadaver. It made her shudder to imagine that, one day in her sleep, he might cut her open so that he could study her interior, with the same detached microscopic meticulousness as he did her exterior.

Mei slept a lot, getting up just to eat. In slow, uneventful abundance, time dragged on during the day, like a long, endless sentence, from page to page, with no punctuation marks. The safest and most effortless way to squander it was to kill it with sleep. Mei seldom got out of the door even on a perfectly fine day, when the other women would stand against the stony wall outside their cells for a good sunning, chatting nonsense, enjoying a moment of imagined freedom in captivity.

Mama-san had asked one of the coolies, a village carpenter, to make two beds for them. Unchanged, from day to day, was Mei's way of spreading herself out in the bed while sleeping, legs parted and hands thrown over her head in loose fists, as if she had fallen into sleep while the last man was still on top of her. She looked thinner than the day before, a little thinner every day. Her cheekbones cast a seedy shadow on her face, the corners of her eyes lurching slightly, fighting the first pull of gravity at seventeen going on eighteen.

Mei didn't even bother to wash herself, or change the sheet. When Chunyu pushed open the door, the crisp morning breeze sliced through the rancid air in the room, revealing the smell of perspiration, snot, saliva, and the slimy remains of men's lust. Mei didn't care. There wasn't enough willpower left in her to get up and move around.

Everybody suffered, but Mei suffered more because her soul wouldn't cut her any slack; instead, it was forever watching, judging, and blaming, even in her sleep. Heartlessness was heaven's gift of mercy in troubled times, but Buddha had bypassed Mei in his round of gift giving and she didn't get her share.

You can end her pain.

Suddenly Chunyu heard a faint voice—a vibration, rather. Looking around, she found *it*, the dark, amorphous presence, in the corner, a blind spot where daylight couldn't penetrate. *It* was always somewhere in the room, sometimes revealing itself to her, sometimes not, at arm's length, never coming near.

Her hands started to shake uncontrollably, not out of fear—she had long warmed to its presence—but out of excitement, at the fresh revelation brought to her by a ghost.

Yes, she could. She was the only one who could end Mei's suffering.

How beautiful Mei used to look. Mei was born in the wrong time, Mother used to say, regretfully, as if it were her fault. If the emperor still ruled, Mother had once joked, who's to say that Mei wouldn't have been chosen to hold an exalted spot in the Forbidden City next to him?

Among his three thousand wives, Chunyu had meant to interject, but she managed to hold her words back. She had been enough of a thorn in everybody's side.

They were so different, it all became clear now. The Chunyu in her could bear the intrusion of Fumie and manage to breathe in the skin of Fumie, but Mei had to kill the Mei in her to be Sachie. It had always been either/or with Mei, no one-and-the-other, no alongside. Killing Mei to become Sachie was a slow and hideous process, which Mei didn't have the guts for.

But I have, Chunyu told herself.

Mei's neck was long and slender, a swan's neck, now marked with faint veins underneath the pale, translucent skin. A grisly bag of bones. Chunyu's heart sank. Her hands could form a perfect loop around it. One minute? Three? Mei might not even have to wake up to experience the slaying of Sachie. A flower's death, quick, clean, and beautiful.

Just as Chunyu was about to stretch out her hands, Mei abruptly opened her eyes and sat up, panting heavily, face bleary in a mist of numb confusion.

"I saw Mother." She clutched at Chunyu's hands, murmuring in a voice that was trusting, and almost kind.

This was the first time Mei had spoken to Chunyu since the day Mama-san came to deliver Kobayashi's message that Chunyu was wanted, in his room.

Mei was not the only one that shunned Chunyu. The entire "household," the cook, the laundry maids, the coolies, all avoided her. Even the eyes of Little Tiger, the eyes that had learned their first lesson of female anatomy from her, avoided hers when they met in the dreary corridor or when he brought water to Kobayashi's door.

To serve the jungle made one a victim worthy of pity, but to serve one beast, a despicable whore. They built a wall of contempt around her, and her own sister was one of the bricks that made the wall. But Chunyu pretended not to notice. One doesn't need to apologize for a wish to live any more than for the desire to eat or breathe. With slow, penetrating patience, Chunyu had waited for the first crack to appear in the wall.

The first crack had come sooner than expected, in the form of her sister.

"What did Ma say?" Chunyu asked, carefully working down the snag in her throat.

"Gibberish, something about being cold," Mei vaguely remembered.

"I'll get you out, to sweep Ma's grave." Chunyu was astonished to hear her own voice, speaking these thoughtless words.

"How?" Mei looked at Chunyu, baffled, as if still in a dream, then suddenly awoke. "*Him*, of course." She didn't try to hide her disdain.

Chunyu didn't have an answer. The idea was freshly hatched, way too young, with a lot of growing to do. Probably she would have to sell to Kobayashi the idea of Mother again, whenever she could find a hole in his mood. An abstract idea of motherhood to begin with, and then working towards a more specific version of one mother. Her mother. A mother is a safe commodity to sell, an assured pity-monger, most appealing, least risky, with almost no possibility of offending. A mother's usefulness lives on, beyond death.

"Wash up, now. They can get rid of you as easy as a piece of junk if you smell," Chunyu warned Mei with a ponderous gloom.

With her foot she maneuvered a basin half-filled with water nearer Mei's bed, then fished out a bottle from her pants pocket. It was potassium permanganate powder Mama-san had given her, for her to "clean the men off" at the end of the day, or rather, the night. She carried it with her wherever she went, and used it more often than was instructed.

What an exquisite bottle. Chunyu had been utterly mesmerized, at first sight, by its unusual shape and design. Made of translucent, sedate brown glass lightened by a tinge of orange, with a long and slender neck gradually curving into a rich roundness of a belly, the perfect profile of a naked woman, sensual, but not at all obscene. Most stunning was the artwork on its label, a twig of cherry blossoms, fresh, dewy, and almost angry, against a stretch of spotless azure sky. Such pink! Such blue! It almost took her breath away, making her forget about what was contained in it. How can anyone loathe the flesh but love the skin?

Using the unscrewed lid, she measured out a dose of the powder and dropped it into the basin. In the water there appeared a deep pink bud, slowly and languidly opening into a full bloom, the petals loosening up, floating, and eventually fading into an amorphous body of lighter pink. Chunyu watched abstractly as the calm pink melted.

"Come." She motioned Mei to the basin, handing her a clean towel, unaware of how close she resembled Mother in her demeanor. A mother she had become, in the past few cataclysmic days, long before a real daughter was conceived in her.

With a renewed strength fueled by the vague hope of escape, Mei got up, stripping off her pants, squatting over the basin to clean herself. Chunyu didn't look away. Far more unsightly things had taken place in each other's presence. No secrets between them, and no need for privacy.

"If you ever get out, go see Auntie Lin straight, offer her half of the jewelry. Don't begrudge it, you'll just give her an excuse to deny she's got it. There's no witness around, it's your words against hers." Auntie Lin was their neighbor with whom they'd entrusted Mother's jewelry box.

"What's left is still enough for you to go wherever you want. Just find a good old big shot to marry, so that you'll never sink again into where we are now," Chunyu said, with complete peace and composure, unaware she had just echoed Mother's last wish. Mei had no notion that the plan had just found Chunyu's tongue as she spoke.

"What about you?" Mei started to sob.

What a relief, the old Mei was back—the weepy, lost, fragile, helpless damsel in distress. This time, Mei's tears were shed for a different fear, the fear of losing her sister, her only reference point in the world, with whom she had formed a double bond, by blood and by shame. Shame bonds people more than love ever will.

"I kill him, or he kills me, or we kill each other, depending on who acts faster," replied Chunyu, in a casual, almost dismissive manner.

Mei burst into a fit of convulsive wailing.

"Come on, you can cry up a flood, it won't help. I'll live, I know it." Chunyu lowered her voice, wiggling her ears like a wild rabbit in full alert, surveying the surroundings. "Little Tiger told me the warehouse site is in a village called Five-boys, one li from here. Only two sentries on duty for night shift. If this gets to the right ear, you know what can happen."

It took a while for Mei to connect the dots in Chunyu's words. She looked up at Chunyu, aghast and pale, her upper body twisted into a rigid, almost ludicrous, arc.

Chunyu was unseeing and unheeding, her mind a thousand miles away. A myriad of ideas, eager and premature, was pushing its way through her head, making her dizzy. She managed to hold it all back, only saying, tersely, "Now finish up, let me get some sleep."

The clear pink water in Mei's basin had turned into a muddy pool.

7.

For the last few days, Kobayashi had been working late.

They were building one of the largest warehouses south of the Yangtze, to store supplies for the coming winter months. The village of Five-boys, on a piece of bowl-shaped land nestled in a range of hills, was selected as the site due to its seclusion and, hence, safety. But the incessant rain, in this usually dry season, hadn't been in the plan. The delay, the death of three coolies and several mules due to overexertion, and a harsh telegram from his superiors in Shanghai had all together pushed him to the limits of his patience.

Along his way back to the dorm, the image of Fumie popped up unexpectedly. The thought of what he could do to her, his most handy exit to oblivion, if not pleasure, pushed its way through the tangle of frustration, filling his heart with a queer agitation.

When he reached his room, he found the door ajar, a string of soft sounds leaking through the crack and making him pause. It was Fumie singing, in a subdued and indistinct voice.

> *Tiny little spider spinning web,*
> *round and round,*
> *round and round . . .*

Fumie was sitting at the table, stitching her torn tunic. The *women* had been brought here with only the clothes they were wearing, so they had to take turns with their washing, some of them staying in bed, naked, while the others did their laundry for them, usually on a clear and breezy day for quick drying. Mama-san had lent Fumie an old tunic, thus allowing her to do some mending. The light was dim, and she had to get quite close to the kerosene lamp. The flickering flame cast an orange glow on her face, creating a close resemblance to a figure in a quaint vintage oil painting. This was a Fumie he had not seen before.

He couldn't make out most of the words. A jolly song, it seemed, rendered unbelievably tender by a sad voice. He felt an uncanny lurch, realizing, uneasily, that something inside him was hit, and on the verge of being broken.

"What's this?" He heard his voice shaking the room.

A dead silence. Every sound froze.

He seldom talked to her. He entered her body whenever he liked, and in whatever manner, sometimes in her sleep, sometimes when he first woke up, sometimes in the middle of a meal. In complete silence she endured him, her body expressing no emotion, numbly compliant, like a piece of risen dough. Silence was powerful; they both knew that and used it to unsettle, but not to be unsettled.

As long as she was kept outside his wall of communication, he felt no sting on his conscience. If the silence was broken and she was let into his loop of thoughts, he would have, inadvertently, granted her the status of some sort of equal, with her own feelings and will. The faintest suggestion of her being an equal would prove him an instant animal. His father, a farmer in Hokkaido, had once told him, from his own experience, that a butcher should never look into the eyes of a cow when it's being slaughtered.

She glanced up, startled, her needle dropping to the table. In her glazed eyes, he found the reflection of his awe-inspiring existence.

"A nursery rhyme my ma sang to us," she muttered timorously, "to draw me and my sister to sleep, when we were little girls."

His mind was sheathed in armor, but she had once discovered a pore through which she gained a brief glimpse into his emotions, and found a soft spot.

It was his mother.

He carried a picture of his mother with him wherever he went. Once he left it at his bedside, and she had spotted it when making his bed. A farm woman in her early forties, ruddy faced and markedly wrinkled, rising, halfway, from a rice paddy, too exhausted to feign a smile for the camera. There were two teenage boys beside her, one of them looking like a younger Kobayashi, although Chunyu never asked him.

He stood in the shade of the door, drenched from head to toe with rain, motionless, as if transfixed by her words.

"What does she do, your mother?" he asked huskily, utterly shocked by his attempt to converse, something so alien to him that he felt a dreamlike uncertainty hearing the words out of his mouth.

"Dead, the day I was . . . I came here. I don't know when and where she was buried."

This was the line she had rehearsed during the day, over and over again, so she was cool, collected, and emotionless when she actually said it out loud to him. The moment had come, she immediately recognized, a fleeting moment for which she had waited for days, and she couldn't afford to let it slip. Not through her own carelessness.

No response.

She wasn't sure whether her words had left a dent in his armor-plated mind. He plodded over to her, his presence filling the room with a sullen menace. Without warning, she was picked up and thrown onto the bed. Scarcely undressed, he entered her, direct, forceful, but not brutal. She thought she had grown used to his unpredictable eruptions by now, but every fear was a new fear. The only difference between then and now were the layers of callus she had gradually developed against any unexpected affliction.

It was over very quickly, but the burning memory of the pain lingered. She curled up with her back to him on the bed-mat now soaked with rainwater and perspiration, head turned slightly, listening for and gauging his move and mood. He had spread himself out, very still, panting like a heat-struck dog, exhausted but awake.

Outlive.

From the depths of the unfathomable darkness emerged Mother's face, staring at her, eyes deep, forlorn, glistening, full of concern. Mother didn't come to her often, but every time she did, she would come with this word, as if her sole mission, in the haphazard plan of this chaotic universe, was to deliver a message to her daughter: *outlive*. To outlive the rain that dug holes into the skin, to outlive the bayonet that hissed in her dreams, to outlive the long nights infested with mosquitoes, bedbugs, and penises, and to outlive the gawky, cruel age of sixteen.

If she couldn't, Mei must. Then she would be, in a biological sense at least, living in Mei, through the blood they shared. She'd rather have Mei live in her, if she had a choice. Guilt might bite later when her conscience came to find her. Who can go through a war unscathed, after all, without suffering some sort of sickness of the soul?

But at this moment, she felt no need to apologize for a selfish wish that had no chance of materializing. There wasn't a choice to be faced, as Mei could never be able to carry out her grand scheme of escape. The stronger of the two, she, Chunyu, was more fit to die to save the world.

"It would be kind of you, Kobayashi-san, if you'd allow my sister Sachie to find out where my mother was buried and pay respect to her grave," she said quietly, holding her breath for his response, which didn't come.

They got up. Little Tiger brought in the meal, which they quickly finished in silence. Then she prepared the bathwater and towel for him, and cleaned up the bed. They didn't speak again, for the remainder of the night.

Early in the morning when she woke up, he was putting on his boots, ready to leave for the site.

"Three days. She must return in three days, your sister." He didn't look at her when issuing the command.

Mei left the same morning.

"He doesn't really expect you to come back," Chunyu told Mei when they parted at the gate. It was a lie, smoothly told. So calm, not a muscle out of place in her face. Did Mei know it was a lie? Perhaps she didn't really want to find out. If one had to travel a long way, why not travel light?

The wind was gathering, wild, desolate, and chilling, blowing up their hair like weeds. They said a goodbye that was more like a farewell, as neither of them was sure of a reunion in the near future, or ever.

Chunyu had staked her own life, in a promise made to Kobayashi, on Mei's timely return. Reckless, but not totally stupid; she had assessed the risk the way a shrewd businessman like her father would have. In the game of mind wrestling, her odds against Kobayashi were no more than pure fluke. She had struck the right chord that led to Mei's escape, and the rest was up to heaven's unpredictable mood.

8.

The night was soggy and depressing, putting Kobayashi in a damp mood, so damp that one could almost wring water out of his brows. He had always been sullen and quiet, but tonight, he was more so than ever. Chunyu could smell the devil in the air.

Supper was finished in silence. The meals for the Japanese were prepared separately, mostly chicken, eggs, sometimes pork, and occasionally beef, with whatever local vegetable available. The home-raised poultry, from villages in a one-li radius, had largely been rounded up here. Soon the radius would have to expand to fill the needs of the kitchen, but these were petty details, to be easily ironed out. Whatever the Imperial Army set its mind on, it would get in the snap of a finger—food, coolies, women, et cetera.

Chunyu's meal was just a mix of rice and boiled cabbage, tasting of little else but salt. She hadn't had any meat since the day she was brought here.

Kobayashi sat on a stool, starting his nightly cleaning ritual, something between a bath and a shower, with a towel and a full basin of water. During the day, fresh water had been brought in from the well, bucket by bucket, to be stored in a vat for him to use in the evening. Lavishly he scooped the water onto his body, making noisy splashes, little puddles everywhere on the dirt floor.

"Not good enough for you?" he grunted, lifting his chin in the direction of his dinner bowl left on the table. On an overcooked yellowish spinach leaf there sat a braised chicken wing, a mere leftover, she had thought. She didn't realize, till now, that some leftovers could be a gift.

"Eat," he said tersely, a decree, with irrefutable finality.

She picked up the piece demurely. Her stomach greeted the long-absent scent of meat with a brazen growl, but her throat stood in the way: the wing seemed to have bones that stuck. His gaze grew heavy, every blink a hammer stroke, driving the chicken bones down like a nail. She flinched. Fear, all too familiar, had by now lost much of its edge and authority, but tonight's fear had a new set of teeth, and she had yet to prepare for its untried bite.

Mei was supposed to return today, as agreed upon, by noon at the latest, but she hadn't. The air was charged with the question of Mei's whereabouts. Chunyu remained quiet, staying, as much as she could, out of Kobayashi's radar, every nerve taut as a fiddle string. It might snap at any moment, but she didn't want to be the hand that plucked it.

With the used bathwater, Kobayashi tried to wash his boots, well worn and massively warped, covered in dirt, sawdust, and mule dung. The water in the basin quickly turned into a gruesome pool of mud, which disgusted him.

"More water, quick!" The building was vibrating with the volume of his yell.

"Right away!" Little Tiger's voice echoed, from the other end of the corridor.

It was pitch dark out there, with a storm brewing on the horizon. A ten-minute walk to the well, in such a night, could easily become fifteen or twenty. Little Tiger's "right away" would be half an hour at the least, Chunyu calculated.

She took out a deck of cards, shuffling, and reshuffling, a silent invitation to a game. He liked to play a round or two, some nights, of a card game called "who's the general," in which each player would show a card, the bigger card eliminating the smaller, until one party had no cards left. A simple game, child's play really, no rules to remember, no moves to plan ahead, and, most importantly, little communication needed between the players. Kobayashi picked this mindless game to relax, and to forget. Tonight, of all nights, distraction was what he needed—or rather, what she needed for him, desperately.

By now Mei would have joined her school friends, a resistance group with a fervent desire to fight the war, on their way to Chungking, the wartime capital of the Nationalist government, or Yan'an, the Communist headquarters. The mud the war had smeared on her could only be washed away with blood. Water was too mild. But Mei could never face blood, or shame, alone. She needed a crowd.

Kobayashi came over to the table, smelling of soap and tobacco, watching Chunyu dealing the cards with an owlish stare, his face brooding and inscrutable.

"Have you ever thought about killing me, Fumie?" he asked, out of nowhere.

The flame of the kerosene lamp flickered, filling the room with eerie shadows that chased and bit the tails off each other. The air grew stiff, making breathing a task.

Beside the cards scattered on the table sat Chunyu, all her senses screeching to a halt. A few brief moments passed and her brain woke up, running like a high-powered processing machine, to sort every random thought coming its way. There was no right answer, no safe middle ground. To deny it would be a lie, all too obvious and hence infuriating, but to own up to it, an incriminating truth, costly and *fatal*.

The dust gradually settled, and her mind became clear.

"Yes, I've thought about it, sometimes," came her voice, cool, calm, and detached.

He froze. Some truths, though plain as day, are still shocking when stated face to face.

"Then, why didn't you?" he asked, following another pause of silence. This time, his.

"I want to live, I guess," she said softly, with a slight hesitation. A tiny smile, more of a grin, shy and almost apologetic, spread over her face. For a moment she looked like a little girl fretting over something she had said, thinking it improper and blunt, but knowing, deep down, she just had to say it.

He was speechless. She never failed to astonish him with truth, the simple, plain, childlike truth. Not because she didn't know how to lie, but because she knew that a lie, however adept, would do her more harm than the crude truth, as in this case. Lurking beneath her silent, supercilious compliance were her vigilant eyes that never went to sleep. She knew his mind better than he himself.

Among the range of emotions stirred up by her words, he found, to his stark disbelief, envy. He was jealous of her. So much younger and weaker than him, yet with such a quiet but enduring reserve of resistance, matched only by water. He could bend steel, but he couldn't bend water. It was hard to decide whether he was enraged or awed by her ruthless honesty.

"You know what I'll ask you next, don't you?" He spoke between his teeth, in a controlled, chilling tone.

It finally came, *the* question.

"Yes, I do" was her slow answer.

"What do you say, then?"

Thunder rumbled on the horizon, then rolled nearer, setting the windowpanes rattling. Following a blinding flash of lightning, the rain poured down, driven by fierce gusts of wind. In the threshing tumult, the building and road moaned in pain.

A night of annihilation, Chunyu thought, while sitting motionless, fully resigned to the final resolution of her fate. She had done what she had done, and said what she had said. There was no going back and undoing it. Even if she could, there was little room for improvement. Mei was out there, somewhere, most likely alive and safe. One death—if she had to die—for one life; no ostentatious victory for Kobayashi to flaunt, and no humiliating defeat for her to swallow. It was a tie, fair and square.

"I don't know what happened to my sister," she replied, hardly above a whisper.

The door was suddenly flung open and a shadow fell in, knees first. It was Little Tiger, totally soaked and shivering, with a bleeding nose. He had had a terrible fall on his way back from the well, spilling much of the water in one bucket, the other one almost empty from a leak.

He picked himself up and staggered towards the corner of the room where the vat was, emptying what was left of the water into it, hardly enough to soak a dry bath towel.

"Go and get more," said Kobayashi sternly, his jaw set skewed and firm, and the butterfly on his cheek flushed dark.

Little Tiger glanced imploringly at Chunyu, but she averted her eyes. In a night when all hell had broken loose, no one could pacify, let alone reason with, an angry god, or an insane beast.

"Can I do it early in the morning, sir, real early? The lightning, the rain, too hard . . ."

Little Tiger suddenly stopped himself in the middle of the sentence, as he saw Kobayashi walking towards the wall where his uniform was hung. And his gun.

No shot was fired, but the building was split by a shrill, infernal howl that woke up the sleeping village, babies and dogs all joining in a cacophony of hysteria.

Chunyu turned around to find three severed fingers on the floor, still twitching like big fat earthworms accidentally cleft by a reckless hoe. It had been the bayonet. She felt a tightening of the throat, then she gagged. Before she could utter a word, she threw up violently, chicken wing, spinach, rice, and all.

"*Baka*, you all think I am a fool, don't you?" came Kobayashi's voice, sepulchral, forlorn, worn out, as he leaned against the wall, standing over a thickening trickle of blood.

9.

Chunyu slept fitfully through the night. There seemed to be holes in the fence dividing her layers of consciousness. Images, scenes, and thoughts lost their shape, drifting, like wisps of smoke, from the deepest recess of awareness to the upper surface of near reality, crossing all the shadowlands in between.

Towards the early hours of the morning, the weirdest dream came to her: the scene of an earthquake, it seemed, interwoven with some sort of a storm—a hurricane, perhaps. Earth-shattering noises, the sky falling like a huge piece of glass, smashing into slivers, wind and flames, heat and cold, men and women in dark shadows trampling on each other while fleeing, shrieks of panic and confusion. A kaleidoscopic picture of hell. Waking up, she found herself drenched in cold sweat, her heart in her mouth, racing like an untamed horse.

Kobayashi was already up, half-clad, standing before the window, looking out fretfully. Through the window frame there appeared a little piece of trimmed sky, weirdly colored, rippling yellow mixed with streaks of gray and black. Crackling sounds, distant and muffled, could be faintly heard.

"Baka, the warehouse!" muttered Kobayashi, in dark fury.

An explosion, it suddenly occurred to Chunyu. Her dream was a concave mirror, a distorted reflection of reality—but reality, nevertheless.

Across the corridor commotion rolled: voices, half-asleep and baffled, heavy footsteps, doors opening and shutting. A guard burst into Kobayashi's room, reporting something in choppy Japanese. While listening, Kobayashi got fully dressed, weapons ready. After a brief exchange of words, the guard rushed out. A few shrill whistle blows ensued; now the building was fully awake.

Kobayashi sped out of the room right after the guard, yelling, on his way out, "Run, you!"

It took a moment for Chunyu to realize he was talking to her.

Slipping on her cloth shoes, she ran, in confusion, out the door. The corridor, narrow and dimly lit, was filled with soldiers in various stages of dress and undress and a strong odor of unbrushed teeth. They pushed her aside to gain their way. She caught a glimpse of Mama-san and two other *women* at the far end and waved, but they didn't see her. In a flash they disappeared, merging into the flow of people rushing towards the gate.

The early morning air stunned her with a slap of crispness, alerting her to the fact that she was now outside the jailhouse. For almost a month, she hadn't set foot beyond its confines. How strange it all looked to her, the trees, the road, the dim sky tinged with streaks of gray smoke, and the mountain range lurking in the shadowy light of dawn. In a dreamlike, fatuous blankness, she followed the movement of the crowd, soon finding herself lagging farther and farther behind.

"Fumie!"

Suddenly she heard her name yelled out from the crowd ahead. It was Kobayashi, around twenty-some paces away, turning towards her, rifle lifted, aiming.

"It's Sachie, isn't it?" he shouted, every syllable charged with rage sprung from a new awakening.

Her legs were the first part of her body to snap themselves out of the trance, yanking her, fiercely, towards a narrow zigzag trail blazed by the local herbalists. The rest of her body simply gave in to the pull of those two stalks, thin and weak, deprived of sun, protein, and sleep. She didn't know where the trail would lead, but she didn't have time to think. Every fiber in her was tensed up in a desperate desire to get away, from the men, the rage, and the gun barrel.

It's no use, her common sense was telling her, *no flesh of men can outrun a bullet of steel and lead.* But another voice snapped at her from the very core of her existence—"the fire on top of her head," as Kiyo put it—commanding her to ignore common sense and thrust ahead.

There is always a chance—the voice was gaining volume—*a slim one, a miracle, that Buddha may be awake and actually watching.*

She didn't know how long she had been running, as time had lost its measure and authority. Then she heard a report from behind, a dull one, duller than the New Year's firecrackers on her street, the street where she and Mei had lived. Then an impact, a feeling of tingling numbness, but not pain. Pain came later when she noticed a dark blotch of wetness seeping through her tunic.

It was blood. She was shot, she realized, in the shoulder.

She staggered on a few steps farther before falling, facedown, onto the ground. Dogs were yapping, roosters crowing, sparrows chirping. Gradually everything grew quiet, so quiet that she could hear her own breathing stirring up dust. The road was clear now, and the crowd had disappeared without a trace, as if it had never existed. On the trail leading to God knows where she lay, alone, bleeding, and *free*.

Did she fall into yet another dream? she wondered.

Kobayashi missed his target, such a grave miss for such a fine marksman. She remembered he had once shot, from his window, a hare a long distance away in the yard. They couldn't find the bullet hole when the carcass was brought in, because the bullet had gone into one eye and out through the other.

Somewhere there was a Buddha indeed, who made Kobayashi's hands, if not his mind, waver.

10.

Never in her life had she been so close to the earth, the rain-permeated black earth that smelled of rotting leaves, bird droppings, and the muddy claw prints of poultry, the silent, all-knowing, all-embracing bed of last year's death and next year's birth.

She was conscious, but just a little, maybe more than a little, tired from the blood loss. This bed of soggy earth was coaxing her to surrender her willpower to the sweet promise of a timeless sleep. In the rathole of the jailhouse, she was awake even in her sleep, every fiber of her body bristling like a dog's hackles, forever alert and scanning. This bed removed all the weight attached to sleep, and she could hear the sounds of her nerves turning into pulp.

Let go, just let go, tenderly and reassuringly, the bed breathed to her.

All of a sudden, she felt a lurch in her heart and was fully awakened by a thought that chilled her to the bone.

This sleep, unlike any other, was a poppy flower, enchantingly beautiful but harboring a poisonous seedpod, luring her onto a path of no return. She wasn't going to relinquish, without a fistfight, her first morning of freedom to *that* eternal sleep. She willed herself to get up but was too drained to move, the mind willing against a body indisposed.

Then, on her eardrum something tickled, a slight vague vibration, a stir, perhaps, of the tree roots or a yawn of the leaves. Gradually the vibration grew into sounds, nearer and louder. They were footsteps, she soon figured out, of people running. A new fear seized her, pumping adrenaline into her depleted veins. She managed, with all the strength she could muster, to get up onto her knees. The sky was spinning, as were the trees, the rays of the first daylight sharp as glass shards.

From the depths of the trail appeared a group of men, in muddy, torn uniforms, bearing sundry firearms that looked decrepit and mismatched. Even an untrained eye could tell, at first sight, that they were poorly equipped. Her apprehension eased to some degree when she caught bits and pieces of their conversation—they were not Japanese.

They slowed down and paused cautiously when they noticed, a few steps away, a young woman (some might say a girl) kneeling on the ground, one side of her body covered in blood, an arm stretching upwards, as if in supplication to some unseen deity. In her eyes there appeared an intimation of relief and hope, and in theirs, suspicion.

"Who are you?" A man, older than the rest and apparently their head, approached her.

Only when in close proximity did she notice that he had only one ear. The other side, where an ear had been, was a dark, rugged scar centered around an unnerving pea-size hole.

"Take me with you," she said imploringly, but she only found half her voice, the other half too feeble to survive the journey to her tongue.

"What happened to you?" A soldier, the tallest of them all and apparently the youngest, made a vague gesture of bending over, a hesitant indication of inspecting her wound.

Thrown off not so much by the question itself as by the tone in which it was asked, a kindness so unexpected, she found herself suddenly unhinged, trembling all over. It would take quite a reserve of emotion and energy, which she didn't have, to relay the cataclysmic tale. How could anyone explain hell, in a few cursory words, to someone who hadn't been there? And the shame.

"A long story." She gave up trying.

"Move on, Erwa," said the one-eared man to the tall soldier. "The Japs will be here in no time."

It suddenly dawned on her who they were.

"Did you just blow up the Five-boys?" she asked, half-excited about her discovery.

With the speed of lightning, the one-eared man drew a pistol from his belt, aiming it at her.

"How did you know about this?" he hissed between his teeth, his brows knitted tight with distrust.

Chunyu was taken aback, realizing, in despair, that whatever she said, or didn't say, would be equally a mistake. An insect caught in a cobweb, she would only get herself deeper in the snare, whatever move she was about to make. What a cursed day. Even before the sun was fully up, she'd already found herself, twice, in the paths of two groups of men, mortal enemies of each other, yet both wanting her dead. The enemy of an enemy is not necessarily a friend.

"The Japs shot me," she replied, feeling the newly recovered strength draining from her.

"Sir, she doesn't look like a spy."

She heard Erwa, the tall soldier, speak to his superior in a timid and deferential manner.

"Why did they shoot you?" demanded the headman, poising his gun.

"My sister . . ." Chunyu suddenly paused, conscious of yet another plight. She and Mei were strung together by a common thread of shame, the oldest kind since the beginning of man, and she couldn't possibly drag Mei out in the open without revealing the thread, and hence, herself.

"We really need to move . . . It'll be too late . . ." A contagious air of anxiety swept through the group. The one-eared man caught it too but managed not to show it.

"The villagers will be up and around in no time, somebody will help you." Tucking his pistol back in his belt, the headman was ready to depart with his men farther into the woods on a well-planned escape route.

"My sister, Mei, is the one who sent the message around, about the warehouse," blurted out Chunyu, in pure desperation. It was only a guess, she knew, but a very intelligent one.

The secret was finally in the open, placing her before them, naked. They—all of them—now knew she was one of *those* women.

"Take me with you, please." Tears rolled down her cheeks, drilling hard little holes in the ground. She had no intention of crying, but the tears came on their own, as if from another mind, just borrowing her face for pure convenience.

"But you can't walk in your condition. We need to run, fast." The young soldier Erwa divided his glance between her and his headman, visibly torn.

The eyebrows of the headman twitched, suspicion relaxing, giving way to impatience.

"If we take her, we all die," he told Erwa shortly.

Silence fell. A dreadfully antsy kind of silence. They all knew time was not on their side.

In a desperate impulse, she pulled at Erwa's sleeve, pleading mutely to him and him alone, drawing on the trailing power of silence.

"Please."

By now she was sure that out of the nine men—she had counted them—this man, Erwa as they called him, was the only one she could possibly count on. She saw it in his face, a sun-browned, unsophisticated peasant boy's face, knowing little else but fields and toil, not yet corrupted by the meaner spirits of the human race.

"Sir, we can't leave her here to die, her sister helped us," begged Erwa, in one last earnest attempt to convince his superior.

"How?" The headman was not moved, but his face started to lose its armor.

"I'll carry her, I've carried sacks of yams and butchered cows for my dad since I was nine," Erwa insisted.

"All right, if you want to take her, then take her. You know what's going to happen if you lag behind. Nobody can save your ass." The headman waved his arm decisively, chopping off all further discussion.

"Come, you!" said Erwa to her, in a tone that was more of a command than a request, while lowering his upper body for her to get on.

Stunned, Chunyu was speechless. In her entire life, since her earliest memory, she had never been carried by any man, not even her own father. A cold-blooded desire to live, for sure, but not in this way: her weight on his back for sure, and his death on her hands, most likely.

Was there another way, though?

Calling on the strength of her shock, she stood up, leaning back a little as if to shake herself loose from his sway, then, to everyone's astonishment, she grabbed hold of his rifle.

"Shoot me, and you leave. I just can't fall into their hands, ever again." Her voice broke.

They all looked away, evading the icy, corrosive sorrow in her eyes that could turn anything it touched into a glacier. The vulnerability, the solitude, the shame, and the fortitude, this woman had it all—a cold, cold heroism that made them shudder.

"Get on with it, woman, if you don't want us all to die here!" snapped the headman in a final dismissal of her nonsense. "Do as we planned before. Two of you will stay behind as cover if we can't shake free of them. Go easy with your bullets, no wasted shots. Save the last one, you know what for." He turned towards Erwa. "In your case, save two."

Before she had time to utter another word, she found herself on Erwa's back, moving, despite herself, like a dead fly carried along by an ant.

11.

The Japanese came after them with a lightning speed fueled by unchecked fury, at their enemy as well as themselves. It was not totally unexpected but still hard to believe that the resistance force could infiltrate so deep into such a secluded area.

It all went up in a column of smoke: a nearly finished warehouse, a month of drudgery in rain and mud, the laborious efforts to maintain the daily supplies and round up the local coolies (the pool of able-bodied men had been heavily bled by the conscription law). The thought of a long queue of trucks loaded with military goods waiting for a place to unload before the wet winter set in filled them with exasperation and rage, turning them into fiery wolves.

The entire group rushed to the site, now in rubble, sorting themselves into two teams. A small team of three was left to assess the extent of damage, while the rest were engaged, expeditiously, in a frantic search for signs left by the saboteurs. A trail of wet footprints soon pointed them in the right direction.

The Japanese could have caught up with the Chinese much sooner if they hadn't got themselves lost at a crossroads, where exuberant undergrowth made the footprints less visible. The land, distrustful and wary, clammed up tightly, refusing to yield clues to the intruders.

Pausing at the crossroads, the Japanese hesitated briefly before deciding, by instinct, on the road less traveled. They only wasted five minutes—a cosmically insignificant smidgen of time during peace, but a pivotal delay in a battle of escape and pursuit that could separate life from death. By the time they set themselves on the right track with regained speed, the miniature army of nine, led by the one-eared chief, was close to Black Circle.

Black Circle was a name the locals gave to a pocket of land tucked away in a hilly area where three counties shared borders. It was an area occupied by several packs of outlaws, among whom were bandits, thieves, opium peddlers, firearms smugglers, and even a small tribe of currency counterfeiters. In Black Circle, *government* meant something quite different and books of law were mere toilet paper. Ever since the days of the Qing Empire, it had been a no-man's-land, a most dangerous place, and hence the safest, like the eye of the storm. That was the very reason for the one-eared chief to pick it as a refuge against their pursuers.

The Japanese, insolent as they were, still had enough common sense left to understand the tricks of jungle warfare. The gangs in Black Circle fought like mad dogs among themselves, but the divisions would fuse the minute the government forces, their common foe, stepped into the scene, changing the fight into small dogs united against the big dog. If the Japanese, the commonest of common foes, were blunt enough to throw themselves into the fray, they would flip the fight, instantly, to all dogs united against the wolf.

The Japanese didn't want to offer themselves as a piece of meat in the dogs' fight. Once the saboteurs got into the no-man's-land, the game was over.

Ahead of the Japanese, the little army sped on. The sun by now was up and high, rain cleansed, spotlessly fresh, throwing, whimsically, a glorious spatter of bright light through the cracks of the trees. The blades of grass rustled and parted at their feet, and the bushes bent over and flew past, as if on wings. They gave Chunyu the illusion that she was the only stationary object amid a world of speed and movement.

Erwa's unobtrusive and dogged strength amazed Chunyu. Later he would boast, in a jolly and dismissive manner, that she was lighter than a half-filled sack of yams he had carried as a little boy. A lousy liar he was, as she had sensed, the entire way, that the added burden had pushed his muscles to their very limit.

For most of the journey on his back, she closed her eyes, too weak to handle the thrill of the speed and the panic of losing it. With every passing moment, she was seized with a new fear that his strength would run out and snap at some point, like a good but overstretched elastic band.

So far, he had managed to keep up with his comrades. She had turned him into a beast of burden—no ordinary beast, and no ordinary burden, one life responsible for another, a responsibility he took on himself for no other reason but a raw kindness.

As the journey dragged on, she started to feel his exhaustion seeping through the fabric of his uniform, warm, sweaty, and macho. The jolting of his body chafed her wound, the pain now fully grown. However, she felt the bite of her anxiety more keenly than that of the bullet wound.

Mother's voice was echoing in her ears. *Stop thinking your bad thoughts. Bad thoughts lead to bad luck, they are the root of all the bad things.* Mother used to nag Chunyu and Mei whenever they started to fret about things. But Chunyu's mind was now numb to the preaching of the wise; it was wide open to the flood of bad thoughts that were drowning out the bashful, little murmur of good hope.

Her fear turned real as the Japanese were quickly gaining speed. Closer and closer they drew, but still not close enough to be within clear shooting range. It didn't prevent them, though, from shooting randomly. With the coolies carrying boxes of ammunition alongside them, they didn't have to ration their bullets, as their Chinese counterparts did.

The one-eared chief decided not to shoot back. An active defense at this point, he believed, would not only deplete their limited stock of ammunition but also slow them down. With the warehouse obliterated, their mission had been accomplished, one glory to last through the day, and their goal now was nothing but a smooth withdrawal.

All of a sudden, Erwa began to lose speed. A bone, a tendon, or a muscle seemed to have snapped on its own, surrendering to overexertion. His body became a little flaccid, she felt, like a punctured tire.

Finding him lagging behind, a fellow soldier tried to give him a hand by offering to carry his rifle, but he stoutly refused, as if it was a mortal insult. Within a few brief moments he regained speed: his broken parts, whatever they might be, appeared to have reconnected themselves by some freakish trick. He moved on, keeping up but no longer the same powerhouse, his feet dragging a little. In their frantic attempt to break away from their pursuers, nobody, Chunyu included, had noticed the bloody footprints marking his trail.

Then there came a sudden agitation among the men, as their captain, the one-eared man, was hit by a stray bullet in the chest. They all stopped, hovering over him, helplessly watching him writhe in a spout of blood, knowing, in silence, that it was his end. In his eyes there was a reflection of the sun, pale, tarnished, cracked, and glazed over. The valve of life was being turned off by an unseen hand, but pain stood in its way, delaying the process with a cool and detached indifference.

With strenuous effort he lifted a finger, pointing in a vague direction, lips quavering, but no sound coming out. His deputy was the only one who guessed his mind.

"Marching on, he wants us. We must go!" He issued the order in the captain's stead, with an undisputable authority that they all acknowledged and obeyed. A second later, there came a muffled gunshot behind them as they resumed their speed, and then a string of heavy, squashy footsteps. It was the deputy running to catch up with the group, two pistols, his and his captain's, in his hands.

"Black Circle, only five minutes away, speed up," he said hoarsely, now abreast of them.

A few minutes later, they came to a stream, rather narrow where they stood but gradually widening at the next turn. As they started wading, cloth shoes in hands, everything grew quiet—the Japs had stopped pursuing. They were finally in the jurisdiction of Black Circle.

It was not until they reached the other side and collapsed, breathlessly, on the rocky bank, that the thought of their captain hit them relentlessly hard. Their comrade, the one they had left behind. Abandoned, rather. The immensity of the loss set in, a void so huge that no words could fill it.

A victory indeed in the morning, when the warehouse went up in flames, but a victory they were not in the mood to celebrate now, a mere few hours later. Was the victory worth the cost? It was a question they never asked. They didn't dare to.

In solemn, profound silence they sat on the riverbank, listening to the water rushing forward, making a lively trill of splashes whenever it hit a rock, like a silly frolicky girl. An uneasiness in each other's presence, and an inexplicable need for solitude, washed over their general mood, as they became aware of the blood on their hands and the stain on their consciences. They were different people now from when they had started out in the morning.

It was then that they noticed the absence of Erwa and Chunyu, who had not made it across the water. A further search discovered them on the other side of the stream, lying on a patch of squashed foxtail grass, a step or two apart, one apparently thrown off the back of the other.

They were quickly retrieved, ashen and unconscious, she from excessive blood loss, he with bullet wounds in one leg.

It was nothing less than a miracle, everyone marveled, that Erwa could carry a woman all that way, nearly to the end, with three bullet holes in his leg. But he didn't hear any of their fuss, as he, together with Chunyu, was immediately transferred to a nearby field hospital and thus separated from the rest of the team.

Later, when Erwa was well enough to talk, he brushed off Chunyu's gushy expressions of gratitude, declaring, with all the seriousness of someone not even eighteen, that it was she who had saved his life. Without her added weight of responsibility, he claimed, he would have given up at the first bullet shot, which had caused the most severe injury.

12.

Kobayashi's bullet started Chunyu on a long cycle, for the next three decades, of unusual incidents of blood loss. Never before had she been so aware of the existence of her own blood—something up till now she had simply taken for granted, much like breathing, or air, for that matter.

It was the angel of death, her blood, keeping a diabolical rein on her life. In her eventful and unsettling lifetime, she had three experiences of serious and near-fatal hemorrhages, one from a bullet wound, one from a miscarriage in Shanghai, and one from childbirth. It was the angel of mercy too, as her blood, in vials and bottles, would later on, when she became a mother, turn itself into food on the table and clothes on her daughter's back. It wouldn't be entirely preposterous to suggest, in a more theatrical rendition of the events, that her daughter Yuan Feng (alias Phoenix) was raised steeped in her blood.

When she came to reflect upon the episodes of her wretched life, Chunyu was quite ambivalent about the roles her blood played in them. Love, awe, respect, gratitude, disgust, and fear: they all had their fair share, with fear floating on top. Fear of its eventual depletion one day, leaving her a shriveled, wasted, useless, lonely old hag, with no more life to give and no more life to save.

They would come, these emotions, all of them would, in the next chapter of her life, a chapter with blood as a running theme and a lasting link connecting all the loose ends. But right now, in a hospital bed, she was simply resting, waiting for her depleted blood level to rise, like tide, in time.

The wound on her right shoulder from a single bullet was a simple one, complicated only by the excessive blood loss over a lengthy period of time. They didn't give her a blood transfusion, as they didn't have much left to give her. It was a makeshift field hospital, with its priority, naturally, for wounded soldiers and other resistance fighters.

They stanched, sterilized, and dressed her wound, giving her a bowl of egg-and-spinach soup and a plate of boiled pork liver—an iron-rich meal to purportedly promote the blood regeneration—and, finally, a dose of sedative to aid her sleep. The rest was left to chance, and her young, resilient constitution.

The next day, she woke up to a racket of birds chirping. A stealthy glance, out of pure habit, at the other side of the bed brought her no sight of the *other* pillow, next to which a pistol was usually placed. Memory started to return, in bits and pieces, after a dizzying moment of confusion. A surge of disbelief, and then relief, flooded through her, giving her a tingling sensation, a thrill. The dressing on her shoulder drove home the fresh and undisputed fact that she had *outlived* Kobayashi's parting bite.

It was another day, another world, and another life. A life away from that dingy, filthy, grimy, little piss hole of a jailhouse. A world without Kobayashi.

The glaring sun told her it was near noon. She had slept for nearly an entire day on this cramped hospital bed, hardly the size for a fully grown adult. A day of wrinkleless, dreamless, heartless sleep. Despite what the nurses might tell her, it was the sleep, she firmly believed, that had pulled her away from the door of death. Every part of her body was turned off, in a protracted state of deep rest, easing the insatiable demand for blood. Her veins, reinvigorated, now resumed the duty of pumping and irrigation in full force. Up until the day she lay dying (as Rain) seven decades later at the Pinewoods nursing home in Toronto, she always harbored an unwavering faith in the panacea of a good sleep.

From the adjacent trauma wards came the moans and groans of wounded soldiers, scraping her nerves like a dull razor blade. The thought of Erwa barged into her mind. The young man who carried her on his back, running for hours with bullet wounds in his leg in a desperate attempt to escape and to live, then collapsing at the first glimpse of safety. A preternatural, heartrending, earth-shattering feat of gallantry, to be repeated, only a few years later, in another war and another country named Korea.

She got up and asked the nurse for directions to his ward.

13.

Erwa didn't share Chunyu's good luck in his bumpy journey to recovery. An infection soon set in, which the hospital, in a dire hiatus between shipments of antibiotics, could do little to help. Unabating fever and large doses of painkiller threw him into an endless loop of delirium and fitful sleep.

While recovering from her own injury, Chunyu took upon herself the task of his personal care, freeing the nurses of such menial tasks as washing and feeding him and attending to his toilet needs. Erwa, in his few lucid moments, would refuse her care with the uneasiness of a young man whenever her hands approached the private territory of his body. She would shush him, with a posture and tone soothing but commanding. "There, there, don't be silly, it'll be over in a wink. A good cleaning will kill the germs."

In amazement, the nurses watched, utterly captivated by the cool, almost apathetic efficiency with which Chunyu handled her tasks, without so much as a wince at the sight of naked blood, a full bedpan, or a soiled sheet. Such maturity, such composure, such skill, from someone without an iota of medical training, at such a tender age typically marked by brittle sensitivity and bashfulness, which would have deterred her from a job much less awkward and cruel.

Only at night, when she returned to her own ward, did she confront the depths of her sorrow and despair. Kobayashi and his pack had robbed her of an intrinsic part of her youth: the innocence, the modesty, and the right to blush at scenes not suitable for her eyes. The war had jabbed its finger, with tumescent ferocity, into her adolescence, messing up the natural progression of life's cycle, making her an imperturbable mother to all men before she was a shy girlfriend and a callow wife to one.

In these moments, how she longed for a cigarette, a habit Kiyo had taught her to enjoy, the only thing that calmed her nerves and made her forget. But she couldn't; no *decent* woman of her age and upbringing would smoke.

Erwa's fever persisted as the infection worsened. One day, while helping a nurse change his dressing, Chunyu held back—with effort—a scream of shock on seeing two maggots squirming on the surface of his infected flesh. Amputation quickly became the only option to save his life. When the decision was explained to him, between two doses of morphine, Erwa dropped his armor, totally unhinged.

"How can I give my old man a hand in the field with one leg?" Using whatever strength was left in him, he propped himself up on his elbows, shaking the room with a volcanic eruption of anger.

"Nowadays, they make good strong wooden legs. You'll learn to work with one soon enough," said the doctor, worn out from the succession of surgeries he had performed that day.

"What woman in her right mind will marry a stick, you think?" retorted Erwa, with a derisive laugh.

"But you want to live, don't you?" The doctor ended the conversation with a trauma surgeon's unwavering factuality, too drained to venture onto another round of counseling. "Get the team ready first thing in the morning." He issued his terse order to the head nurse and then retired for the night. War had cut short everything: niceties, empathy, psychology, philosophy.

A gulf of silence.

Erwa remained still, staring into the vague, unknown distance, vacant, deranged, and uncommunicative. His teeth chattered audibly, as if he were going through feverish chills. A door was shut—Chunyu could hear the loud clanging of it—so tight that no dynamite could blow it open; it closed him in, alone and helpless, against an indifferent world. The despair in his eyes struck her to the core.

"It's not the end of the world," she said softly and carefully, ashamed of the lack of conviction in her words.

"How?" he asked in a stupor of bitter resentment.

Guilt swelled up, nearly choking her.

On the day of the air raid, if she had insisted on going with Mother to retrieve the jewelry box, there would've been one more quick death to kill all the future slow torture; if she and Mei, on their way to Father's, hadn't taken the shortcut, Kobayashi would've been someone else's nightmare; if at the jailhouse, she hadn't planned, with such cunning and calculation, for Mei's escape, the maggot-infested wounds and the prospect of a stick leg might not have been the ordeal of Erwa's life and the weight on her conscience.

So many what-ifs, so many probable causes and unpredictable effects, the fate of man tweaked by an unseen, enigmatic, whimsical—some call it divine—hand with which no one can reason or negotiate. But one thing remained clear: she was his ultimate undoing, leading him, in the course of half a day, to his miserable doom.

"I'll marry you, if it comes to that. I mean, I wouldn't mind your stick leg." She said it calmly, as if talking about the weather or their next meal. It was a bomb, nonetheless, shocking him as much as her. Never before had she been made to understand the true power of guilt and gratitude, compared with which love was a pale, insecure, untrustworthy, pathetic wimp.

For a while they couldn't see each other clearly, because of the dust of confusion between them. His lips parted, twitching and quavering, but no words came out.

His silence was ill taken. However armored she felt she was, she still had one raw spot, and the merest touch to it could make her jump.

"I know, in my situation, no decent man would ever want me," she murmured, near tears.

It suddenly struck him that the conversation was heading in the wrong direction, a direction he had never intended, but the damage was done.

"That's not what I think, I mean, I mean, not this way." Flustered and lost, he was desperately trying to find a quick fix he didn't have the wit or finesse to contrive.

They dropped the subject and never picked it up again. She fixed his pillow, helping him to lie down in a comfortable position. She slipped back into her role of meticulous caregiver, as natural as breathing. The latest dose of morphine soon started working, numbing his senses and releasing him into a deep coma-like sleep, all thoughts lying in limbo.

Chunyu didn't return to her own room but instead spent the night in Erwa's ward. A thought, in all its absurdity, fortuitously darted into her mind, as if a message from some unknown deity, far above and beyond her comprehension.

She thought of a home remedy that Mother had used on her and Mei ever since they were babies. It was saliva. Mother used to apply her saliva on an insect bite, a little cut slow to heal, a blister on a toe, or a skin rash. "The best medicine, costs you nothing, kills all the germs," Mother used to declare. The scrapes of modern ideas learned in school had driven Mei and her to laugh, ruthlessly, at Mother's blind faith in such a notion without any *scientific* basis. It was something she would ridicule and dismiss under more normal circumstances, but now she was ready to try, as one final, desperate resort before the fate of amputation was sealed.

As the night deepened, with the patients in the ward all fast asleep, Chunyu started to lick Erwa's wounds, smearing them with as much saliva as she could generate.

Swallow's nest.

She remembered a tale Father told her and Mei about swallow's nest, an expensive delicacy he brought home from his business trip to Malaya. "The swallows there use their saliva to bind seaweeds, feathers, and plant fibers to build nests for their chicks," Father said in one of his more relaxed moods, making them taste the soup made of the nest, a pale, yellowish-white broth with a few faint red threads floating around.

"It's their blood," Father explained, to their astonishment and then disgust. "The mother swallows, poor things, sometimes run out of saliva—that's why you see their blood." The soup had tasted bland until Father spoke the word *blood*, at which point they felt an immediate need to throw up.

"Such work, such love," Mother marveled, eyeing Father plaintively.

Does guilt work as hard as love, if not more? Isn't guilt a part of love, and love guilt?

Licking, smearing, gagging, and spitting. Inch by inch, round after round, she worked and worked, until she was totally dry and washed out in fatigue.

Towards dawn, Erwa was awakened by a monstrous weight on his body. Snapping out of a trance, he realized it was Chunyu throwing herself upon his chest, sleeping like a log, with a soft, babyish wheezing bouncing in the air.

Stung by his intent gaze, she suddenly woke up, stretching out, and muttered a blurred apology for her lapse in duty. Against the first dim light of daybreak, he saw a stranger—scrawny, pallid, leathery, devoid of the juice and suppleness of life.

14.

The wretched fate of a stick leg didn't catch Erwa in the end, as his fever subsided in the morning.

Never would Chunyu have imagined, even in her wildest dream, that the story of her saliva remedy would snowball, from mouth to mouth, ward to ward, into a legend. Something the head nurse would repeat, year after year, to nurses in training, as an example of dedication and care, though to the uneasiness of a few younger physicians who read different textbooks and believed in a different god.

Following the armistice in the summer of 1945, the hospital was turned into a local medical facility, but it soon found itself treating trickles of wounded soldiers again, this time from the civil war. With its original tang fully preserved and new flavors added through wild rounds of retelling, the legend was passed from one war to another, until the arrival of the 1950s, with a new government firmly in place.

The tale of miracle saliva didn't quite blend in with the sentiment of the new establishment, who deemed it backwards, uncivilized and nonscientific, an image unfit for a modern hospital ready to serve a new era. The decade-old legend was finally shushed into whispers, and then silence. By then Chunyu had left the hospital, only too happy to see the ashes of her war memories dispersed and disappear. A new chapter of life, a new start.

After two months' stay in the hospital, Erwa had fully recovered. Towards the end of 1944, he returned to the front, joining his old military unit. "When the war is over, if I still have all my limbs, I'll come back." Those were his parting words to Chunyu.

Come back for what? A little opaque, he seemed to her at that moment. *How opaque could a peasant-boy-turned-soldier be?* she wondered, but she had no intention of pressing him for clarification. Truth always hurts, but her truth hurt more than others'. With a past like hers, she had to turn her sensitivity down by quite a few notches, to be numb and dumb to live. In such a gallant way he had saved her life, but she had saved him right back, with no less blind courage. The debt was paid, the sting of guilt assuaged, but the shame remained. Nothing could take away the edge of such shame, not bravery, not kindness.

There was a tinge of sadness in the air when they bid goodbye. A flame of warmheartedness, a kind light on her lonely path, brought to her, and then cut short, by the same war.

But soon, to her surprise, a sense of relief ensued. Erwa was the only one around who held a key to her dark secret. "We ran into her on our way to Black Circle," she had heard him answer the nurses' questions about how they met. "She was hit by a stray bullet." The truth, but not the whole truth. He was tight-lipped, leaving out the part that needed to be left out. No one seemed to cast any doubt on his account of events.

But at the back of her mind, there was always that tiny voice warning her of an unpredictable moment when he might loosen his tongue. With him departing, probably never to return, the version of facts he had given now congealed into permanency. Her secret was hers, and hers alone. She was officially safe.

The hospital decided to keep her on as a nurse's aide. Her devotion to the work, her calmness in crisis, and her willingness to be called on duty at any hour soon made her an indispensable asset, and the cheapest kind in addition. Despite the pitiful wage, this job secured her a place to stay and three meals a day.

Erwa did write to her, as promised, in the beginning. Letter writing was a strenuous task for him, with what limited schooling he had. His letters, hardly a page, usually dry and insipid, were barely more than a skeletal account of his daily activities, in vague terms to avoid intel leaking, devoid of any expression of feelings.

Then, his trickle of correspondence came to a full stop following the announcement of the armistice. Death was a natural assumption, perhaps in the last round of the bloodiest battles. Returning to his home village was another possibility (he had always talked about it), to help his dad in the fields and to be married with children of his own who would, in turn, help him in the fields. The predictable life of a peasant boy. In either case, she didn't expect to hear from him again.

There remained the real mystery of Mei's whereabouts. Not a word from her since they had parted at the gate of the jailhouse. Soon after the armistice, Chunyu reconnected with her father and her half sisters. By then she had worked out an elaborate tale to explain away her mysterious disappearance. The timeline, the places, and the sequence of events, carefully woven into a plausible narrative, so complicated that she had to write it down in a notebook to keep her story consistent. But her story didn't include Mei. For years she worried that Mei might, one day, barge into her newly established track of life and blow up her lies on the spot.

At the family reunion, after the initial snuffling and slobbering, Chunyu and her half sisters found little to say to each other. The war had cut a line—or rather a gulf—between them, so wide that it rendered the crossing a fantasy. Her half sisters on one side—even those older than her—remained innocent children somewhat, sealed off from the squalid cruelty of the real world, and she, marooned on the other side, a seventeen-year-old hag with much to reflect on but little to look forward to.

She felt hardly any desire to keep them in her loop of life.

15.

On the vast northern plains the civil war rolled on, keeping the general populace of the country in a protracted state of confusion and jitters. Two streams of news were competing, fiercely, for the share of people's attention: the first, the media channels controlled by the ruling Nationalist government (public, legal, loud, and dominant); and the second, run by the contending Communists (illegal, suppressed, and underground, mainly in the form of secret radio broadcasts and stenciled bulletin sheets printed in basements). They were both equally active and vigorous, both declaring the same sweeping victories in the same battles, predicting the same optimistic outcome of the war, each to their own advantage.

Hushed speculation about the direction the war was headed filled the conversations in the change room, nursing station, and staff canteen. Chunyu listened in silence, with a cool, uncaring detachment. *Advancement, retreat, victory, defeat.* Those words, remote and hazy, meant little to her. Even the general unrest over the staggering inflation didn't quite agitate her the same way as it did others, since the hospital provided room and board. Besides, she didn't have a family to take care of.

No longer held in place by the force of gravity, drifting in an indolent, purposeless nonchalance, she watched herself helplessly slipping away from reality, further and further with every passing day.

Being a nurse's *aide* was never something she loved. The truth was that she didn't really care about her patients, the sick, filthy, groaning, paranoid, consumptive, death-fearing, and sometimes hypochondriacal people she was surrounded by day in and day out. The legend of the miracle saliva, still circulating around her, now carried a thorn of mockery to her ears. It was something one might do, perhaps, once in three lifetimes, out of raw compassion or guilt. She had been there, done that. She had no more saliva to give and no one worthy to give it to.

One day, a casual glance at the calendar seized her with a sudden paralyzing terror—it was her birthday. She'd just turned twenty.

What's the purpose of life if she was to waste all the wrangling and wrestling that had gone into the *outliving*, when she didn't even know what to do with the *living*? She came to a sober realization that she needed something substantial enough to weight her down and give her a new focus on life.

That *something* came, eventually, in the late spring of 1949. By then, she had worked in the hospital for nearly five years.

One morning, just as she had changed into her uniform, she heard her name announced unexpectedly through the PA system. "A long-distance call from *Shanghai*," the girl hollered, the thrill in her voice spilling all over. A long-distance call was such a rare occurrence, and *Shanghai*—God oh God—was another world.

It was Mei on the other end.

"Have you heard on the radio? We've taken Shanghai!" cried Mei, in a high-strung voice that could be heard across the nursing station. The familiarity in her tone reduced her five-year absence to almost nothing, as if they had just seen each other the night before. There was no *How have you been*, or *What a job tracking you down!*

"Guess where I am? At the Bund!" There appeared to be a large crowd around Mei waiting to use the phone, the noise of which nearly drowned out her voice. "Give us a little time to settle in, then you'll come to live with us."

During their short conversation, broken up by intermittent static and shouts, Mei did most of the talking, leaving Chunyu scarcely a moment to put in a complete sentence. From their brief exchange,

Chunyu was nonetheless able to extract, or rather infer, two facts: Mei had not yet contacted their father, and it was the Communist forces, not the Nationalists, that Mei had joined after her escape from the jailhouse.

Hanging up the phone, Chunyu suddenly realized that she didn't ask Mei what she had meant by *us*. Chunyu wasn't given the chance, anyway. But it was just a minor detail. Shanghai was a temptation too stupendous for anyone in their right mind to resist. She was going. Nothing could stop her.

Four months later, Chunyu packed her bag and left for Shanghai. After a series of transfers, from sampan to bus to bus, she finally boarded the train. First time on a train, traveling alone. She didn't look back. It was behind her now, that shabby hospital in a shabby county seat, the name of which she had no serious intention of remembering or repeating. She didn't know, at the time, that the years she had spent in the hospital, dull and vapid as they had seemed, would prove to be the most tranquil time in her entire adult life.

Chapter VI

Where Dreams Meet

1.

George Whyller woke up, stung by the glare of the bright electronic display on the desk clock. 07:16, 2011.12.31. The last day of the year, but he didn't know where he was.

In the dim daylight seeping through the edges of the blinds, there appeared abstract patterns: blurred green curves threading through dark cubes, reminding him vaguely of a strip of wallpaper. It finally dawned on him: he was in the Peace Hotel near the Bund in Shanghai.

He lay still, trying to gather the scattered crumbs of memory to reconstruct the route of his recent travels. Toronto to Vancouver; Vancouver to Shanghai; Shanghai to Wenzhou; Wenzhou to East Creek; East Creek to Water Ridge, the county that contained the village of Five-boys, now a town; Water Ridge to Wuli, the site of the field hospital, now no longer in existence; Wuli to Wenzhou; and Wenzhou back to Shanghai.

Write it down before you forget. A voice kept nudging him to get up, as he faded in and out of his re-created trip. He knew what it was, the lingering shadow of his last dream, reminding him of what came to him in the dream. The central heating had just woken up, plodding uphill, with yawning lethargy, to its full power. How could anyone resist the snug warmth of a bed with a memory-foam mattress on such a bone-chilling morning? *A little later,* he thought, dismissing the voice, now fading, and returned to the mental map of the trip he and Phoenix had just taken.

These were places that appeared in Phoenix's manuscript, some of which he had visited during their honeymoon almost seven years ago, but they struck him differently this time. How can any place look the same after it has been excavated in such a way? Story alters geography.

If he had had a globe with him to plot the trip on, he would have seen a mess of lines but not a circle—Rain (alias Chunyu) didn't quite finish a circle. It was the track of Rain's life that he and Phoenix had tried to trace, on a minuscule scale and in fast-forward mode.

Of course, there was another purpose (not yet accomplished) for this trip—to bring Rain home. Her ashes, rather.

Home. A word so common, yet so evasive.

When he was an audiology student, he minored in linguistics, which cultivated in him an idiosyncratic passion to dig into dictionaries (in a pre-internet age) for the definitions and etymologies of words and keep them with his then photographic memory. This passion, of little practical value, had nevertheless gained him moments of glory in his attempts to throw off some junior professors and impress certain female members of his class. A vain and childish attention-getter, pure and simple. It was a surprise to him that his memory, now fading, could still retain some of his youthful follies.

HOME: A house, apartment, et cetera where you live, especially with your family, or when it is considered as property that you can buy or sell; the social unit formed by a family living together; a place of origin . . .

These definitions were by no means mutually exclusive. If they were allowed to stand firm and alone against each other, then there emerged the real possibility that Rain's ashes were entitled to more than one home. After all, if one has lived during one's lifetime in several places that can be loosely termed *home*, why should death restrict one to a single and final resting place? It would be discrimination against the soul, as a liberal mind might argue.

It was along these lines that they had been planning the final destination, or destinations, of Rain's ashes. Rain had left nothing that vaguely resembled a will, her mind being too far gone. Phoenix was stuck in limbo trying to fill in the silent gap in Rain's final wishes. The general idea was to divide the ashes between Canada and China, both of which had served, at different points in Rain's life, as her *home*.

The Canada part had been relatively straightforward, with Scarborough jumping out as the natural choice, since Rain had lived in this section of Toronto for two decades.

They found a place near Bluffer's Park in Scarborough. It was a modest-size cemetery, hidden behind a tall and dense wall of junipers, with a narrow winding path flanked by silver birches with their watchful eyes on the trunks, vigilantly guarding the world of the dead. On a fine day, someone taking a walk along the path to the vantage point can actually see Lake Ontario glitter and shimmer all the way till it fades into the horizon.

It was not the closest spot to where they lived, but nevertheless conveniently located, only a bus ride away—if Phoenix chose to come by public transit, to spend half a day doing some reading or just to put herself into a better mood if she and George had a dragged-out row. There was a lot of guilt to be killed between them, and be buried.

Just before Phoenix left for Shanghai, they had interred a portion of Rain's ashes there. A small plot, a simple headstone, with the name, dates, and the word *mom*, in both English and Chinese.

The China part, however, turned out to be a little more complex than anticipated. The natural choice would be to inter Rain's ashes in Phoenix's father's burial plot in Wenzhou, but now they were no longer sure about the idea after Phoenix talked to a friend who worked in the city planning department.

Father had originally been buried outside the city's western end, on a strip of hilly ground deemed inarable. That was more than forty years ago. Over the past three decades, explosive economic development had pushed the city to three times its original size, and Father's burial ground had become, in the process, an invaluable pocket of land close to the new city center. Caught up in a frantic cycle of zoning and rezoning, his grave had been moved twice. A third relocation, which would be unthinkable, could not be ruled out, according to the friend.

The homecoming plan was now in limbo.

Phoenix was still asleep, having tossed and turned for the better part of the night, just settling down at daybreak. Gravity was hard at work in her sleep, weighing her down with Rain's secret. She still had plenty of time to sleep in, since they had nothing planned in the morning. In the afternoon, however, Phoenix would visit Auntie Mei while George went to an art show with an American couple he had met in the hotel. In the evening, Phoenix would bring Auntie Mei to the hotel to join George for a New Year's Eve dinner.

Phoenix had been working hard on the second draft of her manuscript whenever she could grab a moment of peace and quiet, even during their trip. *Before the impressions turn flat and stale,* she had explained to George.

Every conversation with Auntie Mei struck Phoenix with fresh and, sometimes, varied impressions. An event, when related on different occasions, would reveal a little discrepancy. A tiny change in where and when, a subtle switch of mood and tone. Of the myriads of rushed and sometimes conflicting information that pushed their way through her consciousness, Phoenix had to decide which piece to absorb and retain in her writing as *the* version of truth, which might change from day to day. A process so fluid and volatile, which seemed to lead, to George's growing dismay, further and further away from the final version of the narrative.

It was mind-boggling to watch Phoenix at work. Utterly cool, calm, placid, and disinterested from head to toe. Even the keyboard caught her phlegmatic air, spilling out a slow, flat string of monotony, airtight with no leak of emotion. *Tac, tac, tac.* A clinical detachment.

Where did the emotion go? he wondered. Could ice create fire?

Then, something esoteric happened. He started to infiltrate, in his dreams, her thoughts and emotions as they emerged in *her* dreams. It was all there in her dreams: the rage, the guilt, the sneer, and the blame. He couldn't quite explain what was happening in words that she, or he himself, could understand, without sounding absurdly metaphysical or, worse, superstitious.

It was as though his subconscious had hacked into hers, each drawn to the other, through a strange mode of communication that didn't require words. Silent, naked, deep, shameless, totally trusting and understanding.

This was the closest description he could come up with, a phenomenon completely unsupported by the chunks of knowledge he had acquired throughout his life from all branches of science, excluding, perhaps, theology. But is theology a part of science?

A title? Last night, in one of his entangled dreams, he heard a voice, silent but persistent, demanding an answer. A dream asking another dream.

Then the title came, in the wee hours of morning, presenting itself in the fuzzy space between the last round of the dream and first round of awakening. He held it tight for a while before giving in to another drift of drowsiness.

Finally, he was fully awake, and immediately seized by a fit of panic. Did he still have it, the miraculous dream title? He raked through his brain, finding it tucked away safe and intact. Thank God. Quickly he got out of bed, rushing, half-naked and barefoot, to the desk, searching for a pen and hotel letterhead.

Where Waters Meet. Yes, water*s.* He should not forget the plural. The *s* was crucial—he could almost hear the sibilant sound, of the finding, the clashing, the breaking, the merging and expanding. The pain. The joy. The *s* had turned an ordinary meeting into a cosmic event.

A sigh of relief. Now memory was pinned down, and held accountable, in black and white.

2.

Phoenix arrived at Auntie Mei's around 3:30 in the afternoon. Morning wasn't good for visiting, as it was Auntie's recreation time. Chorus practice, calligraphy classes, chess competitions, whatnot, all sponsored by the place she lived in. It was a care facility established for the special needs of retired senior officials. Glorified old-timers, one might say.

Despite a body and a mind that could make people much younger envy and fume, Auntie Mei decided to move to the care facility two years ago (she carefully avoided the term *nursing home*) because she hated grocery shopping and cooking—she had never been very domestic, even in her younger days. The idea of having a maid in close quarters repulsed her as much, if not more. Yes, a *maid*, not a *domestic assistant*, or *comrade*. Not anymore. Times had changed, bringing in words resurfaced from an older era, when a maid had been called a maid, and a spade a spade.

Another reason for her decision to move was loneliness, a reason she would never admit to herself. Uncle Chen had been dead for years, and she didn't mind trying out a little new company. But she soon found herself among company that was not exactly what she had desired. The empty-headed, senile coresidents, the frivolous young volunteers who only came for a good reference on their resume, the hastily thrown-together recreation programs totally lacking substance . . . Auntie Mei's list of complaints could circle the globe three times around, yet she never missed one group activity. She was the busiest lonely old lady.

This hour in the afternoon would usually find Auntie Mei at the peak of alertness powered by a long nap. At eighty-four, she shared few of the health problems that had haunted her sister Chunyu (Rain). The exhaustive annual physical (all paid for) had so far generated a miraculously clean bill of health for her age. Not even cataracts or hemorrhoids. Apart from her fading eyesight and an occasional bout of constipation, she found hardly any need for doctors.

But today, Phoenix noticed a difference as soon as she walked in. The air in the room was stuffy, stale, and overused.

Auntie Mei lifted herself halfway up from the reclining chair to greet her, a listless gesture of welcome—she was not her usual self. Today's nap hadn't quite done its duty, leaving her tired and leathery. Having been away for a week, Phoenix suddenly saw the wear and tear of age in her auntie.

Chunyu's passing seemed to have freed the locks and shackles on Auntie Mei, reducing the indelible shame of her past to a mere plotline in a multi-episode drama. Phoenix brought her mother to Auntie Mei in a metallic urn with an elegant floral design, and Auntie Mei returned to Phoenix a sister in a gory tale of survival. The mother version was familiar to Phoenix, but the sister version was the pearl in the oyster.

But truth had taken its toll on Auntie. The pearl was harvested, leaving behind a damaged oyster.

No more questions today, Phoenix decided, filled with remorse and contrition.

She retrieved the laptop from her backpack, placing it on a little tea table near Auntie's chair, and started to show her photos from the trip. Auntie had originally planned to travel with them but bailed at the last minute.

The street scenes in East Creek; the site of Grandfather's old residence, now a high-rise building; the high school the sisters had attended (unrecognizable due to recent expansions); the burial site of the grandparents; and the dinner gathering with the eldest aunt and the fifth one, the only two surviving siblings still living in East Creek.

Auntie Mei watched quietly, with occasional interjections of simple questions about a certain location or name. If there were emotions, they were certainly hidden well. Phoenix felt she was handing Auntie Mei a very old orange, with the parched skin of time peeled off, revealing wedges that resembled little their original shape and texture. A memory spoiled.

"The aunties wish to see you on the next Qing Ming Festival, to pay respects to Grandpa and Grandma's graves." Phoenix relayed the message gingerly.

There was a long pause before Auntie Mei responded, in a trailing voice. "Too late now."

Too late for what? Their invitation? Or her acceptance? Phoenix wondered but didn't press.

Then came a photo of a battered old bungalow with stone exterior and tiny windows that looked like holes knocked into the wall. It'd obviously been abandoned for years, bearing various scars of repair and disrepair. One could sniff out the mold and rust by merely looking at it.

Phoenix paused, unsure whether the image of the placard fixed on the wall had registered with Auntie Mei, as her eyes brushed past the photo.

PROVINCIAL HERITAGE SITE

OLD JAILHOUSE BUILT AROUND 1790

IN EMPEROR QIANLONG PERIOD, QING DYNASTY

Auntie Mei's eyelids fluttered, like the wings of a startled moth. Abruptly she jumped up from her chair, and with the agility of an eighteen-year-old, leaned over the laptop, slapping it shut.

"She doesn't need to see that!" she shrieked.

"Who?" Phoenix was flabbergasted.

Auntie Mei pointed, waveringly, towards a corner of the room, trying to work down a catch in her throat but was too exhausted by her sudden eruption.

Mother's urn in the closet, Phoenix suddenly understood.

3.

"Auntie, how did you find the Communist forces after your escape? We didn't quite get to that part, did we?"

Phoenix was surprised by her heartlessness as she decided, despite herself, to continue with her delving. Certain questions had to be asked. There would be plenty of dutiful naps Auntie Mei could take in the future for her to recover, but time was running out for Phoenix. Shortly after the New Year, she would fly back to Toronto with George. Long-distance telephone conversations could never be trusted.

"Not much to talk about." Auntie Mei spoke half sleepily, propping herself against a cushion on her reclining chair.

"I found a classmate who'd always talked about running away, her cousin was a gangster who knew every man and every dog around. He led us to a guerilla camp that had a connection with the New Fourth Army, a lot simpler than I thought. The biggest trouble was before that, when I tried to get your grannie's jewelry box back from the neighbor. The old bitch denied everything, lied through her teeth and kept a big fat straight face too. Never thought she'd be such a natural actor."

Auntie Mei seemed to have picked up some steam as the conversation rolled on.

"How did you get it back, in the end?"

"The rotten bitch had a half-decent pup, her son was ashamed." Auntie Mei snorted.

Phoenix couldn't help but be amused. Auntie Mei seemed to be going through a glorified process of regression, her tongue running a lot looser and her speech more juvenile as her body aged.

Regression.

That was the word. Did Mother go through it too? Yes, she did—now it all became clear in retrospect. All the weird, erratic, and childish behavior in the last years of Ma's life was just the small steps of her regressive crawl backwards to her youth, a dark alley of shame and fear.

The fear had always been there, now that Phoenix came to think of it, but it had been drowned out for a while by the perpetual distraction of raising a young family in a turbulent time, and then returned, in full force, when Ma grew old, her mind becoming less occupied.

A blessing; now the fear couldn't touch Mother anymore. Death had wiped clean all slates.

"Ma said you were always big on the Communist thing, all your friends in school caught in the frenzy," observed Phoenix.

"How much did she know about me?" Auntie Mei gave a little laugh, with a touch of scorn. "I just wanted to see the world. What chance did I have at home? Your grannie would never loosen her leash, not even an inch. The town bored me to tears. Besides, you have to be a fool once when you are young. Wising up is an old man's business."

Phoenix was taken aback. As best as she could remember, Ma had talked about Auntie Mei more than anybody else, perhaps, in the world. Mei's passion, Mei's belief, Mei's elation at the conquest of Shanghai, Mei's big ideas about changing the world . . . When did things start to change for Auntie Mei? Or was it a sham all along, and Ma just didn't have the nose to smell the rat?

"Tell me a little more about how you met Uncle Chen, will you?" Phoenix tiptoed towards the topic, as if approaching a land-mine zone. She had noticed, on her first visit, that there wasn't an inch of space in the room that held a memento of Uncle Chen. Not a picture, not a war medal, not a grain of dust carrying his smell. Uncle Chen didn't exist.

"He wasn't the only one who had a thing for me." Auntie Mei picked up the thread of conversation but didn't quite stay on track. All calm and cool, no danger of explosion. "His personal guard was really into me too. A real nice-looking young fella, quite a great show of muscles when he went swimming in the river, good heavens. You didn't often see a body like that in those days, everyone a sick bag of bones. He fell off a tree and broke a bone picking jujube for me, when I had a bad cold and lost my appetite."

A faint flush of girlish softness surged up, washing away the harshness of her cheekbones.

"But Chen was the biggest potato there. Your grannie might be old fashioned, but she was damn right about one thing—a gal needs a big umbrella for a rainy day, and there are plenty of them in life."

People marry for fear. Some things never change.

"What about my ma? Didn't Grannie tell her the same thing?" asked Phoenix with genuine curiosity.

Auntie Mei moved her body farther back, lying almost flat now, eyes half-closed, as if thinking hard for a proper answer.

"Sure your grannie did, but Chunyu's mind was never there. She'd always wanted children, the more the merrier. A hen, living just to lay eggs and hatch chicks, that's what she was; she didn't give a damn what coop she got into."

A pinprick of insult, more keenly felt now that Ma was gone. Phoenix's icy silence said it all.

Auntie Mei stretched out a knobby hand, giving Phoenix a pat on the lap, her half-hearted apology. "My big floppy mouth."

There is a child in all old people. The lock guarding the passage from mind to tongue, overused and rusty, now no longer holds. They speak their mind. Children are cruel, and old children, brutal.

"Old Chen once said something about me and your ma. A lot of stuff he said was plain old stupid shit, but this wasn't that far off. *You hold everything like it's a bomb, but Chunyu holds everything like it's a baby.* That's what he said, isn't it freaking funny?"

So vivid. So true.

"She got what she wanted. She had you," Auntie Mei said, a bleary smile trickling through the beautiful ruin of her face.

4.

During the late 1970s and early 1980s, when Phoenix, then called Yuan Feng, was attending college in Shanghai, she had been a frequent visitor to Auntie Mei's house, often for a nice hot nutritious supper that the school canteen couldn't provide (although she would never admit it).

When the Cultural Revolution ended in 1976, Uncle Chen had been promoted to the position of vice-chairman of a municipal political consultative body. A glorified rubber-stamp post, with a gilded business card and a car and driver at his disposal, awarded to him because of his seniority, and also because he hadn't quite joined in the frenzy or caused anybody any harm during the Cultural Revolution. The entire world, minus him, knew that his education (or the lack of it), age, and health status all went against him holding any substantive position, for which a long line of hungry young men was fighting tooth and nail.

In a new era, when the *in* topic for daily conversation was switched to making quick fortunes, war was still being fought but no longer with rifles and grenades, and his old valor found no proper battlefield. His elevated yet nominal position cut him off from the real world, hence conveniently nudging him towards the margin of power. A relic, that's what he had become, whose sole purpose of existence, it had seemed, was to prove the validity of the past.

The only consolation during the last years of his life was that his son in Shandong finally came to terms with his earlier abandonment, agreeing to resume contact. While the son could never learn to love the father, he was pleased, at least, with the inheritance his father left him. A quite sizable one. Uncle Chen had never been a big spender. From hindsight everything became clear—he had saved almost every penny, to the dismay of Auntie Mei, for a most powerful apology made posthumously.

Auntie and Uncle had, since the start of the revolution, been booted out of the French-style villa. A few more moves at different points in their careers finally settled them into a spacious and comfortable three-bedroom apartment in an elite neighborhood. Auntie Mei stayed there for years, first with Uncle, then alone as a widow, until she decided to move to the care facility.

Uncle Chen had struck Phoenix as a reticent and impassive man, older than his age (he was then in his sixties). There was a shimmer of anger buried somewhere in his expressionless face, deep and patient, not eager to find an exit. But when he broke his silence, he really broke it. He would shake the house with his fits of bone-shattering coughing, the early signs of a lung problem, undoubtedly the accumulative effect of cigarettes. *A chimney is cleaner than his lungs*, Auntie Mei would say, with a mixture of despair and disgust.

He became a heavier smoker as he grew older, without the slightest intention of cutting back, let alone quitting, even after the diagnosis of lung cancer several years later from which he eventually died.

Uncle Chen talked sporadically to Phoenix at the dinner table, asking about her school life, the dorm conditions, the food served in the canteen, the recreational activities, the sessions set aside for military training, et cetera. The same questions repeated, over and over, every time they met. Only after his death did Phoenix come to realize that he had racked his brain trying to strike up a conversation with her.

Once he attempted a topic that deviated, to some extent, from the usual boredom of her school life. "How're things back home?" he asked in a lowered voice, when Auntie Mei was in the bathroom.

Phoenix immediately understood what he was referring to. Her college fees and living expenses were covered by the state, thanks to her prior working years, which saved Mother from the dire situation of having to support her through school. Yet at the same time, Mother lost the salary from Phoenix's job, the only source of their household income.

"Pa's pension has been restored. We get by," replied Phoenix, in rather vague terms.

Get by, indeed. With her widow's pension, a mere twenty-five yuan a month, and the soaring inflation since the opening up of the economy, Mother could do little more than just *get by*. Phoenix had no idea how Mother managed to patch up the holes in her tattered finances. Matchboxes had given way to fancy lighters, and the envelopes were now all machine made, which rendered Mother's deft assembling skills obsolete and useless.

There was only one solution left, the old, reliable, never-dying business of blood trading. Phoenix shivered every time the word *blood* popped up in her mind. However, she would never tell Auntie Mei and Uncle Chen about Mother's plight. It had been ingrained in her, the beggar's pride, which Mother had held high all her life, like a torch, to the world, and especially to Mei and her husband.

"There're talks about setting up a new college in Wenzhou, I heard. They are dying to get new blood. She'll be real happy if you take a job back home after you finish school."

I heard. It was a day's journey, by sea, from Shanghai to Wenzhou. Uncle Chen had to have very long ears to hear such talk.

That was the only time, as far as Phoenix could recollect, that Uncle Chen talked to her, evasively, though, about her mother.

After her graduation, Phoenix did take a teaching position at the new college in Wenzhou to be with Mother.

"Before you got married, your ma called me all the way from Toronto. I was quite surprised. She didn't call me very often, a penny pincher, you know her. Her mind was clear that day. She was just upset." Auntie Mei's words jolted Phoenix out of her thoughts.

"About me marrying a white guy? Or about me getting married, leaving her behind?" asked Phoenix, taken aback somewhat by the sting of sarcasm in her tone.

"She worried about you. The Yuan women are cursed, she said, we run a bad thing in our blood, marrying for the wrong reason." Auntie Mei let out a breathy chuckle. "Your grannie, me, she herself, and maybe you too. She said you were rushed into it, because you were afraid to be left alone when she's gone. Her getting sick really scared the shit out of you."

A sudden tightening of the stomach. Phoenix hadn't realized that the bare truth could make one sick. The plaque of dementia didn't quite fog up Mother's eyes; she could still see her daughter.

"Was she wrong?" Auntie Mei queried, pursuing an answer.

Did she marry George for love? What a question to ask. Love, just like everything else in her youth, was rationed. She'd long used up the portion allotted to her. Kindness was rationed too, but not as stringently, so she still had a little to spare. A little kindness might go a long way.

"Why do you think I waited till I was an old hag to marry? He is the only guy who agreed to take Ma in," Phoenix blurted. Wrong answer, she knew, but she had nothing better to offer at the moment.

"Your ma had her chance, but she let it slip. They could've got married right then, but she wanted to wait till you finished high school and started working. *A real grown-up*, in her words. Then that stupid plan blew up in her face, what a damn fool—"

"What are you talking about?" cut in Phoenix, in utter confusion.

"Come on, don't tell me you know nothing about it. I mean she and that Meng Long fella. For two years after the disaster, he still kept bugging her, writing to her through a friend, asking her to join him. He had settled in Hong Kong, he said, now he had better connections to get around. But your ma couldn't make up her mind. You were then over eighteen, legally an adult, there'd be a record in your file if you failed again, but she couldn't possibly leave you behind."

Phoenix heard a loud screech as the world, like a gigantic Ferris wheel, ground to an abrupt halt. She could see Auntie Mei's lips open and close, and hear sounds drifting in the air, fading in and out, vague, deflated, devoid of meaning.

"Never seen her like that . . . like a little girl . . . the poems he wrote to her . . . every week . . ."

What a trip, the last two months in China. Surprises lying in ambush around every corner. And Auntie Mei certainly had kept the most brutal bombshell till the last.

Was this *the* last, though?

It was the stomach in the beginning, then the entire chest—a strange feeling like a deep cavity, accompanied, even more strangely, by a sensation of swelling. So empty, yet so full, she almost couldn't bear it.

Across the hazy temporal distance, it finally became obvious now what Meng Long had tried to tell her on that balmy spring night in 1970. It was about him and Mother. Meng Long would've killed her right then and there with the lethal news he was about to deliver, if the midterm exams hadn't stood in the way, mercifully thwarting the plan. Four decades later, his blade had become rusty and dull, and her skin, a suit of armor. Truth came as a seismic shock, but it was no longer fatal.

Phoenix got up and paced around the room, half-numb, trying to introduce the new reality, slowly and evenly, to all parts of her body. A reality reshaped, staggeringly, by a mother's death and an auntie's awful remembering. She held her silence for a long time, till every part of her was informed and reassured.

"He was quite a bit younger. I thought—I thought, she was almost a mother to him." Her jaw rattled audibly when she spoke, a stammer.

Auntie Mei cackled hoarsely, her features twitching and twisting in a weirdly gleeful, almost ecstatic, manner.

"Six years, seven? Eight at most, a bloody big deal! Chunyu was a born mother, men are crazy about the hen in her. You know what were the last words Old Chen said on his deathbed? He wanted his ashes to be returned to his village, to be with his *MOTHER*. After all these years, what am I to him? In the end, he wanted his dear old ma. He didn't even bother to write her a New Year's letter when he was still kicking! That's just men."

It quickly grew dim outside, with the eagerness of a winter's dusk. There are some days in life when one suddenly realizes that all the leaves are gone, and all the birds have left for places with a happier sun and greener trees. It's darn shameful that a year had to end on such a bleak note.

Hope springs eternal, says who?

"Good thing the government didn't listen to such nonsense," Auntie Mei continued. "With his rank and everything, he belongs nowhere else but the dedicated official cemetery, they said. No discussion, period. When it's my time to kick the bucket, I tell you now, I don't want to be near him, not a hundred miles. A life is long enough to be stuck with someone; after my death, heaven have mercy, I want my little freedom . . ."

Auntie Mei rattled on, but Phoenix had long ceased listening.

5.

The water does not have skin.

Phoenix heard her thoughts talking in her dream. Thought has a separate circulatory system, with its own heart, veins, and sensory organs. It breathes, sees, and talks, all on its own. Unlike a tree, an animal, or a human, water has no skin, and hence, no boundary. Water seeps through the narrowest crack, climbing up, with a little help, to a hilltop, dropping, effortlessly, to lowlands, evaporating, condensing, and falling again as rain or snow, back in its original state. The cycle repeats itself, no beginning, no end. It may assume different names when it travels to different parts of the world. It can be called the Nine Hills, or the Oujiang, or Mirs Bay, or Lake Ontario. Whatever the names, whatever the shape, deep down in the core, they are just water. They diverge, and then converge, always able to connect with each other, never truly dying, and always *free*.

Phoenix woke up, still thinking.

"Morning." George was already up, preparing the first pot of tea in 2012 with the tea maker in the room.

"Thank you, George," she muttered groggily.

"What for?" He turned towards her, baffled.

"For stitching me up."

He brought over a cup of tea, sitting himself down on the edge of the bed. "Are you all in one piece now? Care for a walk before breakfast?"

She yawned forth a half-hearted yes, slowly getting out of bed while listening to the strings of music leaking through the window. If the Bund was awake, nobody could sleep.

"Did you dream about a river, or something like that?" George asked.

Phoenix was startled, but not overly—she was slowly getting used to George's recent bursts of metaphysical insights.

"Hmm?" Her curiosity grew a little as she took a sip of tea from the cup in his hand.

"I saw ripples on your forehead."

She was quiet for a moment, to settle the tingling on her skin. When she next spoke, her voice was soft, dreamy, and lost in thought.

"I think I know where Ma wants her ashes to go."

ACKNOWLEDGMENTS

Writing a novel is like planting a tree—one needs to start with a seed. I want to thank Wenzhou, my hometown in southern China, the seed for this book, and for many others before. And perhaps, for many more to come, if I dare to hope.

When I was a little girl, Wenzhou was a small city, hardly more than a town. Airplanes and trains were what we read about in children's books, as our only connection to the outside world was through a waterway, the river called the Oujiang. I sat on the riverbank, my eyes following the current, wondering what kind of a world there was where the water and sky met. I didn't know, until later, that it was the dawn of my literary imagination.

Wenzhou fills me with memories, pleasant and unpleasant. Memories of a lonely and sickly child, holding, in a trembling hand, a crumpled note signed by my frail mother, asking for exemption from gym classes, or a school field trip to the countryside; memories of the carefulness, close to the point of stinginess, with which my mother planned the monthly budget; memories of the incessant social turmoil spilling over our doorstep; memories of a close-knit family that stuck together, through thick and thin; memories of the women around me, grandmother, mother, aunts, who bore the burden of life with a quiet resilience only matched by water. Year after year, I have drawn from the pool of such memories to quench my creative thirst, but it shows little sign of depleting. I don't quite understand the strange math of it.

In Wenzhou I have a handful of friends who always welcome my return. They take me everywhere, on a field trip, to a person with an intriguing story, to a private exhibition or a village ripe with history. Their help is sincere, timely, and unselfish.

I thank Wenzhou, the city of all cities, that I can claim as my own, regardless of how far I have traveled, and how long I have been away; the seed of all seeds, that gave life to my first tree, which, over the years, has multiplied into a small patch of trees.

I have worked diligently, over the last two decades, on numerous writing projects, but this book is special, as it's my first endeavor in English. I've been conscious, during the process of creation, of the distance between my overly active brain and partially paralyzed tongue, a plight typical of someone struggling in the slough of a second language. When my brain eventually finds my tongue, I discover a new world, different from the familiar, comfortable, old world built with my native language. I am grateful for the challenge, which, in the end, has turned into a reward.

I want to thank Barbara Ireland, who has tirelessly helped me through the process, patiently proofreading the different drafts, answering my questions, which often reached her at some ungodly hour, about a word, an expression, or a dubious subplot. Her speedy replies gave me not only knowledge and insight, but also comfort and confidence.

I want to thank Zoë Roy for her steadfast friendship and encouragement. Zoë, together with Mark D. Gaffey, Naomi Brown, and Kathy Frampton, was a part of the small circle of my first readers. Their frank and honest feedback has helped me to find a way to improve the structure of the story. The long conversations with Zoë and Mark, a son-in-law of Wenzhou, have offered me a third eye to view the manuscript.

I am also grateful for the assistance rendered by Jia Mei (Lulu) and Zu-Bei Chen in Japan. Through numerous overseas exchanges, they answered my questions about Japanese culture and the use of popular names during the 1940s.

I'd like to thank my editorial and production team at Amazon Crossing for their insight, enthusiasm, and patience. Their faith in my creative ability and their perceptive guidance in the long and at times intricate process of turning a manuscript into a book have greatly alleviated my self-doubt as a writer drifting between two languages and two worlds.

I also want to thank my agent, Kelly Falconer. Although we have never met in person, with COVID standing in our way, the numerous Zoom meetings have brought our thoughts and efforts together. Her patient labor and encouragement have been reassuring.

It would be remiss not to mention Aiping Chen-Gaffey and Xiaohua Yang. Our friendship dates all the way back to our youth in Wenzhou, when we shared a bold dream of venturing out into the big world (which we did). They are always there when I am in need, with arms warmly extended. Their support of my literary endeavors makes me feel that I, having little sense of belonging anywhere, nevertheless have roots.

I want to express my gratitude for the generous support of the Canada Council for the Arts and Ontario Arts Council, whose grants for this project meant a great deal to me while working on my first work in English.

Last, but not least, I want to thank my husband, Kun, who has labored so lovingly, over the years, to ease the burden of the daily household routine, granting me a space that's simple, safe, and undisturbed. His steadfast existence has given me the security and courage to be an adventurous writer.

So here it is, the final product, the joint labor of my brain and tongue, now walking into the world of books, quietly seeking an understanding audience.

ABOUT THE AUTHOR

Zhang Ling is the award-winning author of nine novels and numerous collections of novellas and short stories. Born in China, she moved to Canada in 1986. In the mid-1990s, she began to write and publish fiction in Chinese while working as a clinical audiologist. Since then she has won the Chinese Media Literature Award for Author of the Year, the Grand Prize of Overseas Chinese Literary Award, and Taiwan's Open Book Award. Among Zhang Ling's work are *A Single Swallow* (translated by Shelly Bryant), *Gold Mountain Blues* (translated by Nicky Harman) and *Aftershock*, adapted into China's first IMAX movie with unprecedented box-office success. *Where Waters Meet* is her first novel written in English.